PRETTY
RINGS
&
BROKEN
THINGS

KAT SINGLETON

For my girlies that are still waiting for a hot billionaire to call you "my wife" and spend a ridiculous amount of money on you. Your time is coming, I promise. Until then…enjoy Archer Moore.

PLAYLIST

End Game - Taylor Swift, Ed Sheeran, Future
Lose Control - Teddy Swims
Death of Me - WizTheMc
The Archer - Taylor Swift
The Best I Ever Had - Limi
Delicate - Taylor Swift
Say You Love Me - Jessie Ware
Love Story - Sarah Cothran
Close - Nick Jonas, Tove Lo
Daddy Issues - The Neighbourhood
Meddle About - Chase Atlantic
Fetish - Selena Gomez (feat. Gucci Mane)
Say Yes To Heaven - Lana Del Ray
Those Eyes - New West
Capital Letters - Hailee Steinfeld, BloodPop
Ever Since New York - Harry Styles
Stockholm Syndrome - One Direction

AUTHOR'S NOTE

Pretty Rings and Broken Things is a billionaire, arranged marriage, age gap romance. It is full of banter, sweet moments, and scenes that'll have you blushing. I hope that you love Winnie and Archer as much as I do. This is the second book in a series of interconnected stand-alones set in the Black Tie Billionaires Series.

Pretty Rings and Broken Things contains mature content that may not be suitable for all audiences. Please go to authorkatsingleton.com/content-warnings for a list of content warnings for the book.

1
Winnie

I HAVE A FEELING IT'S GOING TO BE A BAD DAY FROM HOW MY morning is already starting.

The first hint is when I reach across my bed and find the spot next to mine cold and bare. I continue to glide my hand across my silk sheets, hoping maybe I'll find the man I was expecting to be there within reach.

My eyes fly open when I'm still met with nothing, finding my room completely empty.

I push myself into an upright position, pulling the sheet around my body. A shiver runs through me when I look around my room, knowing what happened here the night before—and the meaning behind him leaving me alone after it.

Reaching out, I run my hand along the top of his pillow. It's cold, but his smell still wafts around me. I slip my hand underneath, thinking maybe I'll find something there. He always leaves a note if I'm still sleeping when he leaves.

But there's no note.

Even as I throw myself across the bed and look at the floor to see if maybe I missed it, I find nothing.

I had a nanny once who really believed in the power of the universe. She swore that it would always tell you if something was right—or if it was wrong. Before I even opened my eyes this morning, I had this gut feeling that things were off. It's only multiplied as I search my empty apartment and don't find any remnants of him.

His jacket isn't slung over the back of one of the dining chairs.

The old, black duffle bag he always kept here isn't sitting at the foot of my bed.

It's as if Blake was never here.

I check my phone, but I don't have anything from him. He's been a driver for my family for years now, and since the moment he first kissed me, he'd make sure to tell me when he'd be back when he went into work. It'd be a note, a text, or *something*. He always wanted me to know he was thinking about me.

Now, I have nothing. And it wouldn't bother me if we hadn't done what we did last night.

The feeling of dread settles deep into my bones when I try to call him and it immediately goes to voicemail. I try three more times before I give up. I'm just about to throw my phone on the bed and forget all about it when it rings.

My dad's caller ID shows up on the screen. And I get another gut feeling that something isn't right. That something's *terribly* wrong.

Hoping maybe Dad is just calling me to see if I'd want to have lunch with him, I ignore his call. My heart beats erratically against my chest as I wait to see if he calls again. It's been a while since we've seen one another. Maybe it's just that he wants to get a meal together. Or maybe there's an event I don't know about that he expects me to attend.

I know it's neither of those when he calls again. Dad never calls me more than once. He expects me to call him back as soon as I see his missed call.

I pace my bathroom, trying to decide what to do. Knowing there's no use in ignoring him, I place my phone on the cold marble counter and swipe to answer. I put it on speaker, my hands already shaking from the pit in my stomach to be able to hold it.

"Hi, Dad," I manage to get out, my throat feeling tight.

A loud sigh echoes through the speaker. It's one of disappointment. I've lived my entire life doing everything in my power to not hear those sighs from him. But this one seems bad. "Winifred," he clips. "Get to my office. *Now.*" He hangs up before I can ask any questions.

This is bad. So bad that I freeze, staring at my reflection in the mirror. I keep the sheet wrapped tightly around my body, suddenly ashamed of what I let happen last night.

For months, I'd found different ways to tell Blake I wasn't ready for us to sleep together. I knew I wasn't supposed to be doing anything with one of my family's employees, but I did it anyway. Because I knew what we were doing was wrong, I made sure we took things slow, but finally, last night, I didn't want to say no any longer.

It felt like he was falling for me, that we were falling for each other. And I was ready to take the next step, hoping the following step would be for us to tell my family.

Instead, I'm waking up alone after giving him what he'd been asking months for.

What does it mean?

I try to shove my fear and insecurity to the back of my mind. He'd planned a magical night for me. He'd surprised me by already being at my apartment after I got home from an event for my family's company. He'd made dinner and had candles lit in the bathroom.

I didn't do anything wrong by finally giving in to the tension between us. Except maybe sleeping with someone within the family business. But I knew Dad could forgive me for that if I told him Blake and I were in love.

But are we?

Taking a deep breath, I pick the hairbrush up from my vanity and run it through my long, red locks of hair. I get more resistance than normal, trying to work out the knots, probably because of the way Blake's fingers had tangled in it last night.

I don't have time to try and style it nicely, so instead, I opt to put it up in a slicked-back ponytail with a knotted headband. For makeup, I only apply mascara and a bit of blush to attempt to bring color to my face. My already pale skin is void of any color due to the nerves coursing through my body.

I know I'm already running behind. Dad left no room for interpretation on how soon he wanted me at his office. Taking time to quickly get ready will surely set him off more than he already is.

The sheet falls to the ground as I walk into my expansive closet. Even with the size of it, it's filled to the brim with clothes. It's been on my to-do list to have one of my best friends, Emma, come over to take anything she wants.

Hangers scrape against the rod as I look through all of my options. I have no idea what I'm about to walk into, so I'm not sure what I'm supposed to wear.

I finally opt for something nice because my job is to be a face of Bishop Hotels. I attend parties, show up to meetings, and overall, just do as I'm told.

I pull a Chanel two-piece set from my closet. It doesn't take me long to get on a bra and underwear and slide my legs into a pair of stockings. Then, I step into the lavender skirt and matching jacket.

I'd love to spend more time picking out a matching pair of heels and a handbag, but I know I'm already on borrowed time. I pick out a simple pair of nude heels and go with the purse I used yesterday since everything I need is already in there.

I'm not surprised when I find Rick waiting for me in the lobby. He stands next to Franklin, my favorite doorman. The tight-lipped smile Rick gives me tells me enough.

I'm in trouble.

With a deep breath, I follow him out to the waiting town car. He doesn't say anything to me. He normally comments on the weather or tells me a story about his newest grandchild. Today, he does neither, even though we're finally getting a glimpse of fall weather in Manhattan.

Eventually, the silence gets the best of me. "How bad is it, Rick?"

His eyes dart to mine through the rearview mirror. "He wouldn't tell anyone a thing. All I was told was to come get you and to hurry."

I sit back in the dark leather, a chill running down my body.

"Then *really* bad," I mutter under my breath, checking my phone once again and seeing nothing from Blake.

The feeling of dread never goes away. If anything, it gets worse in the short drive it takes to get to my family's office building.

2
Winnie

THE ELEVATOR RIDE UP TO MY DAD'S FLOOR SEEMS LIKE IT TAKES AN eternity. I thought Rick would come up with me, but he declined, saying he'd wait in the lobby. He *never* waits in the lobby. Things only get more ominous when Louise, my father's assistant and someone who's pretty much an aunt to me, won't even look up at me from her desktop computer.

"Good morning, Louise," I say sweetly, hoping to get her to glance at me. She doesn't.

"He's been waiting for you," she answers, still avoiding eye contact.

All I do is nod.

It's better to get this over with. It truly can't be that bad, *right*? The worst thing I've done is date someone hired by my family. Which isn't something I should do, but it isn't the end of the world.

I've always done as I'm told. This *one* thing can't be the reason my dad is this upset with me. The only problem is I haven't done anything else. It's the only thing that comes to mind when I think of what could be this urgent.

Maybe it has nothing to do with me at all. Maybe something is happening with the company.

My family has been in the luxury hotel business for genera-tions. I know Dad has been working on some big projects recently. He's needed me now more than ever to be in the public eye, for the public to see our family as approachable.

It's one reminder my father has been telling me for as long as I can remember. I've been told from a young age that we're *always* in the public eye. That our enemies are always watching —and my family has made plenty in this business—and because of that, we need to be ahead of the game.

His office doors feel heavier than normal as I push them open. I search his large office for him, taken aback by not finding him sitting at his desk. When my eyes do land on him, my stomach plummets.

He's in the far corner of the room, a glass tumbler in his hand. It's still morning. Even though he's known to drink far more than he should, it isn't normally this early.

"Dad?" His name comes out more like a question than anything. My mouth feels dry from nerves.

His back straightens as he looks out the office window. This building has one of the best views in the city; it just takes me by surprise that Dad is facing that direction, with his back to me and a drink in hand when most of the time he's seated at his desk.

"Take a seat, Winifred." His tone is dry and void of any emotion.

I try not to flinch at the use of my full name. It was my great-grandmother's name, and no one really calls me that. I'm just Winnie. But my dad reserves using it in times when I've disappointed him.

The large office chair on the other side of his desk makes a loud groaning noise as I pull it back slightly. I slide into it as quietly as possible, trying not to make any more noise than necessary.

"Everything okay?" I ask, hating how meek the question sounds coming from my lips.

I've always been naturally quiet. Maybe it is because my life has always been planned out for me. There's never been any point for me to speak up and give my opinion.

The most free I ever felt was in college when I first met Margo and Emma, my two best friends. Even then, I'd have to check in with my dad weekly to update him on my life. I still wonder if he's disappointed I didn't find someone rich and powerful to marry while there.

Something I've been reminded of at many family dinners because of how I could help the family by marrying someone that we could use to our advantage.

I try not to think about his regret if he ever found out about me and Blake. Blake has nothing to give to my family. He had a rough upbringing, one he wouldn't tell me about. He certainly doesn't bring anything to the table to help my father or Bishop Hotels.

Maybe that's why I liked him so much.

"Dad?" I push, my skin prickling with anxiety at the fact he's stayed silent.

His sigh is loud and full of regret. Finally, he turns to face me, and the moment our eyes connect, the pit in my stomach intensifies. The look on his face can only be described as immense disappointment.

He keeps eye contact with me the entire time he goes to take a seat. The chair groans underneath his weight. His knuckles turn white from the aggressive way he holds the sides.

"We have a problem. A *big* one," he tells me, his voice stern.

My foot taps anxiously against the ground. Luckily, it's completely out of view from him. He doesn't like weakness, and I don't want him to see how much his words rattle me.

My adrenaline spikes. "What kind of problem?"

"One that is because of some *terrible* choices you've made recently."

I swallow past the lump in my throat. He uses the silence as an opportunity to open the drawer to his desk and slap down a photo. My mouth falls open when I see who is in the picture—what's happening in it.

"What?" I gasp. A tremor runs through my entire body.

"There's plenty more where that came from," he spits. "A video, too," he adds at the last minute.

"I don't understand…" I blink repeatedly, trying to stop the burning in my eyes. *This can't be happening.*

"Blake dropped them off with my assistant first thing this morning. He's coming after our family, Winifred. How could you be so stupid?"

"He *what*?" My voice breaks at the end of the second word. I'm shocked I'm able to get any sound out at all with the feelings coursing through my body.

"He wants to take down our family as some sort of revenge. He's threatening to send this to every major publication."

"Revenge for what?"

Last night, I was questioning if I'd slowly fallen in love with this man. I thought I knew everything there was to know about what kind of man he was. Our secret romance had been going on for so long behind closed doors, and I thought last night was the first step in something new.

It turns out it was both the beginning and the end.

"We're still figuring out the details. He didn't give us a reason. He said he didn't have to, that he was the one with the power, not us."

I sit back in my chair, fearing my heart might beat right out of my chest from anxiety. "I thought he wa—"

"You clearly weren't thinking at all," he booms. I try not to jump at the venom laced within his words. "How could you be so stupid? How long has this been going on?"

My entire body trembles as I try to come up with how to respond. No excuse will be good enough for him. I don't know if I have a good one anyway. I was blinded by something I believed to be love.

Blake waited patiently for us to sleep together. Sure, I could tell he was frustrated when I always found excuses to tell him no. But still, he waited. He was tender and thoughtful, and I believed he might love me.

I believed *I* was falling for him.

"Last night was the first time we..." My words fall short. I don't know why I'm embarrassed to tell him we had sex. Obviously, he knows since Blake sent him photos—and a video—of the experience.

My dad opens his mouth to speak, but he gets cut off by his office phone ringing.

"Hello?" he clips out, his eyebrows furrowed so intensely that two deep ripples appear on the center of his forehead. "Send him in," he tells the other person on the line.

My stomach drops. Surely, he doesn't mean Blake...

I'm about to ask him who he's talking about, but I don't get the chance. His focus moves from the phone to over my shoulder.

His office door opens, and I can barely hear anything over the rush of blood pumping in my ears.

I wasn't expecting Blake to walk through the door. But I really wasn't expecting the man who steps through the door.

His intense focus pinned straight on me.

3
Archer

OUR GAZES COLLIDE THE MOMENT I WALK THROUGH THE DOOR. Winnie looks so afraid, sitting there in the large office chair perched in front of her father's desk with her shoulders drawn inward as if she's closing in on herself from shame.

"Good morning, Archer," Spencer, Winnie's father, says. Even though my focus is on her, I can see him stand up and come around his desk from the corner of my eye.

She stares at me, her full, pink lips parted in shock as she watches me closely. I force myself to rip my gaze from hers, knowing I have no business staring at her for longer than necessary.

My eyes meet the man I've been told was an enemy of my family my entire life. We've attended plenty of events together. We may run in the same circle, but the Moores and the Bishops avoid each other at all costs whenever possible.

Due to my great-grandfather being screwed over by Winnie's great-grandfather in what was supposed to be a partnership, there's been bad blood between the families. It's a battle that's still fought to this day, both Winnie's and my father ensuring to fuel the grudge between us.

I'd feel bad for what my relatives did in retaliation for the betrayal, but I can't quite bring myself to. It's the reason the hotel empire my family has built is more successful than the Bishops'.

"Thank you for agreeing to finish our meeting in person," Spencer continues, holding his hand out in front of him. I shake it, making sure to make it firm so he knows who holds all of the power in this situation. The slight frown to his lips tells me everything I need to know, regardless of the handshake. He knows who's in charge. It isn't him, and he hates it.

He'd called my father first thing this morning, needing help with the situation his family's in. The last thing I expected was for my father to call me into his office and give me the news that Spencer Bishop needed our help. We'd spent over an hour talking to him over the phone before my dad sent me here to finish the agreement.

"I've got to get to another meeting in an hour," I clip out, not wanting to beat around the bush.

"Take a seat," Spencer offers, pointing to the chair next to Winnie's.

Our gazes connect briefly before I sigh and pull out the chair next to hers. I make sure to pull it a little further away from where she sits so I'm not surrounded by her. Although I'm not sure how much distance it'd take for me not to smell the sweet, alluring scent of her perfume wafting around me.

It surrounds me as I unbutton my suit jacket and sit down.

"Winifred, as you know, this is Archer Moore. He's come to help us with your horrible mistake."

My teeth grind together at the tone he uses with his daughter. I wonder if he's even noticed the slight tremble to her body. Or the way her shoulders hunch over with anxiety from his words. It's as if she wants to curl into a ball to avoid his harsh tone and cold eyes.

"What do you mean?" she asks, her voice meek. My eyes bounce from her to her father. I don't want to know how he talks to her behind closed doors if he's so freely chastising her like this in front of someone new.

His face reddens with anger. "Our hands are tied because of

you and your reckless decision to get involved with an employee."

Winnie flinches at his words. "I never thought…"

"That's right. You *didn't* think. Fuck," he curses, pinching his large nose between his finger and thumb. "We'll talk more about your dumb decisions later. Right now, we need to focus on solving this problem."

I resist the sudden urge to reach across the space between us and lay my hand on her thigh to stop her leg from anxiously tapping. Instead, I keep my hands folded in my lap to keep myself in line.

There are so many places I'd rather be than sitting in the office of the CEO of Bishop Hotels. If it was anyone but my father who asked me to be here, I would've told them to fuck off. I wouldn't care what kind of help the Bishop family needed, they wouldn't get it from me.

But the intense need to make my father proud of me runs deep. It's in my blood, wanting to not disappoint him, wanting him to trust me enough to appoint me the CEO of the Moore hotel dynasty one day. And to get that, I *had* to come here today. I have to do whatever my dad and Spencer are asking of me, but it doesn't mean I have to be eager to do it.

Spencer must've said something while I rattled off the reasons in my head that keep me seated instead of rushing out of the office and forgetting all about what I'm supposed to do. Both Winnie and Spencer stare at me expectantly, clearly waiting for me to respond to whatever was said.

"Repeat that," I demand, trying to make it seem like I wasn't paying any attention.

Spencer refuses to look at his daughter, instead keeping his angry, beady eyes on me. "Would you like to tell her what the plan is?"

My fingers drum against my thigh. *Not really.* I'd rather not go through with the plan at all. The only reason I agreed to it is because Moore Hotels is getting a large stake in Bishop Hotels, one that will put me on the board as a decision-maker.

It'll shock the industry that a truce has been made, and it'll give my family even more power in the market. My father expected me to do this, so that's what I'm doing.

"Tell me what?" Winnie asks. Her voice is so soft the question comes out barely more than a whisper.

I let out a long, controlled sigh as I try to ease the tension in my shoulders. No one told me I was the one who had to break the news to her about our arrangement.

I expected to show up and meet with Spencer alone. We'd go back and forth until I felt like my family was getting the best deal possible. She wouldn't have even been involved until the agreement was done, the ink dry on the contracts. Instead, I get the fun luxury of undoubtedly ruining her life by telling her what her father expects of her.

I know very well how heavy the expectations of a father can sit on one's shoulders. If I cared more about anything, I might feel bad for feeding into what her father is forcing her to do. But I shouldn't care—so I don't.

There's a silence between the three of us as I try to think of how best to break it to the woman sitting next to me that she's about to bind her life to me. Sighing, I realize there's no gentle way to say it. I try not to think too hard into why I want to give her the news gently to begin with.

"We're getting married," I announce, my words slow so she can't misunderstand them.

4
Winnie

I'VE ALWAYS BEEN A NATURALLY QUIET PERSON. I'D MUCH RATHER listen to people's conversations than heavily engage in them. But no matter how quiet I typically am, I'm not usually so stunned I'm speechless.

Except right now.

I blink a few times, trying to figure out if all of this is some sort of nightmare. Maybe I'm still lying in bed dreaming, with Blake lying next to me. Not even realizing I'm doing it, I slide my hand to the side of my leg and pinch my thigh.

No. I'm *definitely* awake because that hurt.

I swallow slowly, trying to work out what's going on. My dad and Archer both stare at me expectantly, just waiting for whatever I have to say.

My mouth feels dry from nerves as I open it to speak. "What? I'm not getting married to anyone."

Archer has the nerve to smirk. He actually smirks. A smirk shouldn't be so cold and calculating, but his is. It sends shivers down my spine.

I pinch myself one more time to double-check if this is real.

"You won't be getting married to just *anyone*. You'll be marrying *me*. Tomorrow." He says the words so matter-of-factly, like it's common knowledge that we're supposed to exchange vows.

A choking sound comes from my throat, one that earns me a dissatisfied scowl from my dad. "Tomorrow?" I manage to get out, even though my throat feels like it's clogged and I'm beginning to feel dizzy.

What is even happening? My family *hates* the Moores. There's no way my father would let me marry Archer. He's been wanting me to marry strategically from the moment I started dating. This can't possibly be the match with his stamp of approval.

I wait for a few moments for one of them to elaborate on their own, but they don't. Instead, I suck in a deep, shaky breath, attempting to get myself together. My vision blurs, and my face feels hot, and all I can do is hope neither one of them catches on to the fact I feel like I might pass out. "I'm sorry, but I don't understand. I thought I was here to talk about Blake. What does me marrying Archer have to do with Blake?"

Archer's fingers twitch in his lap the moment I say his name. From the corner of my eye, I see his broad shoulders rise and fall with an annoyed sigh. "I was expecting you to tell her about the arrangement before I showed up," he rants. The look he gives my father across the desk is scathing.

My father doesn't look deterred by the fire in Archer's brown eyes. He manages to stay cool, keeping his face set in the same scowl that's been on it from the moment I walked in the door. "She was late, you were early. I didn't have the time." My dad's eyes bounce to me for a moment. He doesn't bother to hide the disappointment in them.

I never talk out of turn to my dad. I've known the rules from a young age. I do what he tells me to, and everything runs smoothly. Except right now, I'm so desperate to figure out what's happening that I can't help but question him. "Dad, what's going on? I'm not marrying him. I don't understand."

"You've given me no choice!" he snaps, his voice booming. I hope Archer doesn't see the way my body jolts at my father's raised voice. My father's chair falls backward as he quickly stands up, his body curling over the large desk so he can get closer to me.

Archer reaches out and places his hand on the armrest of my chair…almost protectively as my dad continues to get so upset with me a large vein pops up in the center of his forehead. "Because you were fucking stupid to get involved with one of my employees—someone you knew I'd never approve of—I'm now backed into a corner with no other options."

I hold my tongue, knowing it won't do me any good to talk back to him.

What I *want* to say is he puts every single employee through an extensive background check. While I knew it wasn't a great idea to date someone under the family's employment, I never could've imagined Blake doing something like *this*.

"Can you tell it's me?" I ask softly, not wanting to know the answer. "It was…dark," I finally get out. My mind goes to last night, even though now everything is tainted with what Blake did with our night together. "I didn't see any cameras. He didn't tell me. Isn't that illegal?"

Archer moves so stealthily I don't think my father even realizes that he's grabbed my chair and is slowly inching it closer to him. *Is he trying to protect me?* I stare at him in shock, trying to understand what is going on.

Our chairs are almost so close that I could reach out and loop my arm through his if I wanted. I *don't* want to, but I can't get over the soft gesture in the moment of my father's fury.

"Don't you think I've already thought of that?" my dad spits. He picks up the chair from the ground and falls into it with a thud, a look of defeat on his face. "Trust me. I've looked. My people have looked. He had a hidden camera—and you can tell it's you. If we take it to the police, the media will have a hold of it in an instant."

My eyes close in shame. I never gave Blake my permission to record us. My skin crawls with the knowledge this video even exists. That he recorded it without telling me. He took something that we'd waited months for, something that was supposed to be special, and made it into *this*.

Archer clears his throat before sitting forward. The new position puts him even closer to me. I try to move, but he just keeps his thigh pressed there. I wonder if he realizes that he's pinning it against mine. If it's his odd way of comforting me.

But why would he? He doesn't know me. We don't owe each other anything. Yet he's sitting next to me, his thigh pinned to mine, acting like maybe he's on my team in this.

"No one touches my family," Archer begins.

I can't bring myself to look him in the eyes. My cheeks are still heated from embarrassment. How many people have seen what was supposed to be a private moment between Blake and me? I don't think I want to know the number. All I know is I don't want that video to be seen by anyone else.

"That has nothing to do with me," I tell him, still staring at my lap—at where our legs are pushed against one another.

"Actually…it has *everything* to do with you. If you're my wife, Blake won't release that tape. He's clearly dumb. But he isn't *that* dumb. My family has connections with every single publication with any kind of audience. They know that we'd eviscerate them if they posted anything negative about *anyone* in the family—that includes my new wife."

I struggle to even find words to respond to this ridiculous plan. My chest feels heavy with anxiety as my life seems to fall apart around me, all because I trusted the wrong man. I shake my head softly. "We can't just get married tomorrow to fix this problem."

Archer quirks a dark eyebrow. "Of course, it fixes the problem. When you're my wife, no one will touch what's mine. I'd dare him—or anyone—to try." The light from my father's floor-to-ceiling office windows pours in, hitting his dark hair perfectly. The strands are dark, but not dark enough to look black. It's a mix between brown and black. Like the dark color of the wood of my favorite piano as a child.

My stomach lurches at his words. *When you're my wife.* I can't just be his wife. I haven't wanted to be *anyone's* wife. I've turned down plenty of men in this world because I wasn't interested in becoming somebody's trophy wife. I'm not going to start with him, even if he does have a point.

It's starting to make sense why my father would reach out to the *one* family he cannot stand. He knows the power they yield. No one dares to go against the Moores. They're too powerful. Too cutthroat. And right now, that might be the only thing to get me out of this mess with a shred of dignity.

I look to my father to gauge his reaction. I know he doesn't want our name to be ruined, but I also know enough about the people in this business to know the Moores had to have asked for a lot to come to this agreement. Archer is in the same position as me. He could marry for more power. I can't be his first choice. Quite frankly, I feel like I'm probably his last.

"What are you giving them in return?" I blurt, my hand coming to my mouth once I realize I asked the question out loud.

Archer catches my attention by letting out a low chuckle. I look over at him, finding him staring right at me with a hint of a smile on his lips. I didn't ask *him*; I asked *my dad* what he gets out of this. Even so, Archer is the one to answer. "A lot," he answers smugly, zero remorse in his tone. "The Moores will now be an active member on the Bishop Hotels board. We'll also now own thirty percent of everything."

A small gasp falls from my lips as my eyes dart to my father's. "You don't have to do this. I'll talk to Blake. I'll make him change his mind and give me the video."

"You'll do no such thing," my dad interrupts, his nostrils flaring angrily.

Archer pulls his legs together as he sits up higher in his chair. Our thighs no longer touch, and I try not to think too hard into why it feels cold from the loss of connection.

My eyes focus on my dad as I try to plead my case with him. "It *could* work. Maybe something happened, and if I just talk to him and see what that is, he'll change his mind..." My words don't come out as confident as I intend them to. I have no idea what Blake would do if I spoke to him. He isn't the man I thought he was. Not if he's doing this. But it doesn't hurt to try before having to resort to marrying a man I was raised to hate.

Archer gives one shake of his head. "No." He lets the word hang in the air between us for a moment. I'm sure he's used to people listening to him without any explanation. He's the only child of Timothy and Penelope Moore. He's the heir to the entire company. His entire life, he's probably been told how important he is. How much power he'll wield one day. It only makes sense that he knows how to command an entire room with just one single word.

But I'm not just anyone. I'm a hopeless romantic. One who always wanted to marry for love. To be loved intensely and fiercely. And because of that, I have to find another way to solve the problem I created that doesn't involve marrying Archer Moore.

5
Archer

I WASN'T EXPECTING HER TO ARGUE LIKE THIS. I GUESS I SHOULDN'T be surprised. After all, I don't know her that well. This was all supposed to be hashed out before I got here to begin with, if her father had done what he was supposed to.

"You *will* marry him," Spencer barks, looking appalled that she's even questioning it. "You will do it for your family. For everything we've worked toward, and I don't want to hear another question about it."

My jaw tightens because of the harsh tone he uses with her. It seems completely unnecessary. Did she make a mistake? Yes. But he's persecuting her for having sex. She's an adult. The man she slept with was an adult. It isn't her fault he was a total dick and used her for some absurd revenge plot.

I understand her unwillingness to want to marry me. It's the same feeling I had when my father told me what had to be done. I just always saw her as someone who does as she's told, but in this instance, she's doing anything she can to defy her father's wishes.

With a deep breath, I stand up. My palms press into the top of Spencer's desk as I lean in close to him. I'm already annoyed that there's a good chance I'll miss my next meeting, but this is more important. If I go to my father without finalizing the deal, he might disown me and find a new heir.

He's frothing at the mouth to have the contracts signed. For us to finally have a part of Bishop Hotels. Something we were supposed to have a partnership in years ago before Winnie's great-grandfather split Bishop-Moore Hotels into two and made sure to take as much as he could.

"Can Winnie and I have a moment?" I ask slowly, looking into Spencer's eyes.

I'm sure he isn't a bad man—or maybe he is. I know my family's hands aren't clean. But I don't like the way he's speaking to his daughter, no matter my disinterest in marrying her. She's a victim here, and it's really bothering me how much it angers me to hear him talk to her like this.

Spencer narrows his eyes on me. I admire the guy for trying to pretend that he's the one in control. He isn't. He knows it. I know it. I'm sure Winnie knows it, too. I hold all of the cards, and if I want to speak to his daughter—the woman who is supposed to be my wife come tomorrow—alone, then I will.

"Anything you need to say to her can be said to me," Spencer argues, casting a quick look to Winnie. She doesn't say anything. She sits there, her cheeks pink as she stares between the two of us, her face completely emotionless.

A cold laugh escapes from deep in my chest. Just because I can, I reach out and grab the expensive pen from its holder on Spencer's desk. I twirl it between my fingers, shaking my head back and forth. When I meet his eyes again, I make sure all humor is wiped from my features. "Let me rephrase this. I'm going to talk to my future wife—alone. You can leave your office or direct us to a more private location. The choice is yours."

He lets out a loud huff, not giving any indication that he's going to move. Always a man of my word, I roll my eyes and turn to Winnie.

"You're coming with me," I demand, wrapping my fingers around her wrist and pulling her from the chair. To my shock, she doesn't protest, at least at first. The moment I lead her into a small office and shut the door, she's opening her mouth to speak.

"I'm not marrying you, Archer," she states, ripping her hand from mine.

This office is only big enough to fit a small desk and an old filing cabinet. I take a moment to look around, wondering if this is actually someone's office or not. It seems empty. There isn't an empty office at our Manhattan headquarters. We're constantly expanding to keep up with demand.

"Did you hear me?" Winnie interrupts my thoughts. She's on the other side of the small room, her hips resting against the windowsill. Her hands are folded across her chest in a defensive position.

"I did," I answer, resting my shoulder against the wall. I mimic her position, folding my arms across my chest. There's a desk between us, but it still feels like we're chest to chest by the way we intensely stare at one another.

I hate the dull look in her eyes as they find mine. "So you understand, then? I won't marry you."

She surprises me. To the outside world, she seems like the perfect little doll for her father to use to his advantage, but behind closed doors, she seems to have more of an opinion than people would expect. I like that.

I guess I *should* remember that Winnie has a bit of a wild side. I've seen it before.

"You *will* marry me."

Her mouth pops open. I try not to focus on her perfect, pink lips. "No."

"Yes."

She lets out an aggravated sigh, twisting her fingers through the ends of her ponytail. "People don't do arranged marriages anymore, Archer," she comments, her hands settling on her hips.

I lift a shoulder. "Sure they do. It happens all the time in our world."

"If I wanted to marry for advantage, I would've married *any* other man but you. Plenty have asked."

I'm sure they have. She's more than ten years younger than

me, but the moment she graduated college and started attending more social events, all of the men began to talk about her. Everyone wanted her. She was beautiful and the only daughter of a powerful man. Men wanted to get in bed with her family. But she's right. As far as I'm aware, she hadn't given anyone the time of day.

At least, she wasn't giving anyone with social status attention. Turns out, her preference was an employee who is so worthless he shouldn't even exist in the same world as her.

"You don't have any other options." Lifting my wrist, I check the time on the watch my grandfather gave me at my college graduation. I'm already late for the next meeting, but I have no intention of leaving this office until she's understood that tomorrow she'll be meeting me at the altar whether she likes it or not.

Her eyes drop to the floor as she shuffles her feet. "I'll think of something else."

My head shakes. "You don't have the time. By tomorrow night, he'll have that video and all of the pictures out to every publication because he's sick and twisted." I scratch the back of my neck, wishing she'd just agree to this so I can leave this office and no longer be alone with her. "The only way to make it stop is for you and I to be married. I'll grant the media outlets interviews and photoshoots with us. Every single one of them will know not to run anything about you unless it's approved by me first."

She works her bottom lip between her teeth as she thinks through my words. I try not to be offended by the apprehensive look on her face. She isn't my first choice either—but no one would be. I didn't have any particular wish to get married until this opportunity fell into my lap. Now, I can't deny how much we gain by helping the Bishops, by having me marry her.

"How long?" she asks, catching me off guard.

"What?"

"How long do we have to be married? This isn't for love. I

want to marry someone I love. So how long am I expected to stay married to you? What will stop him from releasing it after we get a divorce? I wouldn't be under your family's protection anymore, after all."

I roll my lips together as I attempt to hide my smile from her. Damn. She's surprising me at every turn.

"There's no set time limit. We can discuss years down the road possibly if you wish. Then you'll be free of me and free to choose whomever you want to marry...for *love*," I finish sarcastically.

"I don't like that answer," she fires back immediately.

I move off the wall, rounding the desk so I stand right in front of her. She's cornered. There's nowhere for her to go. She's way too close again, her sweet scent overwhelming my senses.

Winnie tries to get away from me by fully pressing her body against the window. Her palms lie flat against the glass, her chest rising and falling with quick breaths. Against my better judgment, I crowd her space. Our chests barely press against one another.

If someone were to walk in, this position might look far less innocent than it actually is. I don't care how it looks. I want to get my point across and maybe even get under her skin in the process.

"You're in no place to negotiate," I tell her, my eyes roaming her face. The daylight from the window shines against her pale skin, showing the slightest splatter of freckles along her cheek. It doesn't look like she's had any kind of sun recently, so I'm wondering if these are permanently etched into her skin.

"We'll be married for one year," she negotiates. Her eyes briefly flash to my lips before her aquamarine eyes meet my gaze. "And we'll tell people it was an amicable split. That we support each other fully. Maybe people will even see us having lunch or something after like a couple of friends. That way, Blake doesn't try anything even after we're done."

I resist the urge to tell her that it won't be too long after we exchange vows that I'll be paying Blake a little visit. Give me a few days, and I'll make sure he never does anything to harm my wife or her reputation—even if she won't always be my wife.

"I don't see the point in negotiating with people when I already hold all of the power. Seems like a waste of breath to me."

My fingers twitch at my sides as I ache to reach out and run them through the locks of her red hair. It seems even brighter underneath the morning sunlight. Even though she has it neatly pulled back away from her face, bringing more attention to her sharp cheekbones and almond-shaped eyes.

"You're getting so much from my family. And I get it. You're doing us a huge favor. But can we agree to one year? *Please*." The last word is said so softly, so desperate, that it does something to my heart. I haven't felt bad for someone in a really long time. In fact, I can't recall the last time I felt remorse. But for the briefest of moments, I feel it with the pleading look in her eyes and the way her words get cut off with her plea.

She's right. My father went back and forth with Spencer so much that he ended up getting a far better deal in this agreement. If she only wants to be chained to me for a year to help prevent a scandal, it still works out fine for me and my family. We'll have a stake in the company far longer after our divorce papers are finalized.

"We'll *discuss* our arrangement again in one year," I answer, trying to ignore the way my chest feels heavy at the smile I've earned from her.

"Yeah?" She shifts slightly, making our bodies press against one another more for a fraction of a second.

"Don't get your hopes up. We might find this arrangement needs to last far more than a year. But I'm open to discussing it. No matter the length of this marriage, it has to seem real, and it has to seem real *immediately*. Are you ready for that?"

At first, she doesn't answer. She takes so long I wonder if she intends on answering at all. Maybe she doesn't care about her father's company. Maybe she doesn't care about her reputation and I've read her all wrong.

Or maybe she's just trying to pretend like she has some sense of control in a situation where everyone knows she doesn't have any at all.

She lowers her head and speaks to the ground. "Tell me what you want."

6
Winnie

I'M WAY TOO CLOSE TO ARCHER MOORE. HIS SMELL SURROUNDS ME, and he smells far better than any other man I've ever been around. It's rich but deep. One of those smells that'll stick with me even after he leaves my presence. All of the men who ask me to dance with them at parties or take me on dates all wear the same three colognes. It's as if they don't realize that they all smell exactly the same.

He doesn't.

It's absolutely intoxicating. I get so lost in trying to identify what it is that I miss whatever he says.

His lips pull into the slightest of smiles. It isn't much, but it seems like a lot coming from him. I've heard the stories about Archer Moore, one of the most powerful men in Manhattan. All of the women talk about him at every event. He's one of the most coveted men, and somehow, I've found myself with no choice but to marry him.

"Winnie?" Archer pushes. He reaches out like he's going to touch me but pulls his hand back at the last minute.

"Yes?"

"Are you listening? I'm not a fan of repeating myself. You'll learn that."

I nod, trying to push the thoughts of what I'm going to tell my best friends. They both know me too well. I'm a terrible liar.

And now I'm going to have to make them believe I've fallen in love and married a man behind their backs.

"Have we come to an agreement? We'll discuss the state of our marriage after the holidays next year."

I think through his words. It's a little over a year since it's only October, but his reasoning makes sense. "Fine," I answer with a bite to my tone. I still haven't fully processed that this is happening. Last night, I'd gone to bed thinking I'd fallen for a man. This morning, I found out that same man betrayed me, and now I'm forced to marry another.

"No arguments?" One of his dark eyebrows lifts like he was expecting more from me.

All I do is shake my head. I'm trying to pretend that I have some negotiating power in all of this, but I know I don't. This is all my fault, and I can't let the video get released. I can't let my father down more than I already have.

My brother will be the one who takes over the business when my father decides to step down, but I'm still as much a part of the family image as them. Anything that looks bad on me looks bad on everyone, and I don't want that to happen.

Tyson has worked hard to take things over from Dad, and I don't want to ruin it for him. And I don't want to disappoint my father more than I already have.

Archer's posture is rigid as his eyes roam my face. "I don't know if your silence should be answer enough or if I should be worried about whatever argument is brewing in your head."

His comment makes me smile. I wasn't expecting him to have so much personality. But then again, I don't know him at all. He only attends parties every now and then. And even when he does, he is a mystery to all. I expected him to be dry and boring. Maybe he is most of the time, but he at least has more personality than I first imagined.

I guess people could probably say the same thing about me, too.

"What I'd give to read your mind," he mutters.

My eyes find his immediately, finding his face pinned into a mask of indifference. The way he said it so quickly and quietly... I'm wondering if I was supposed to hear it at all.

"One year. We'll talk divorce after the holidays," I confirm, hating this is the position I've put myself in.

"No. We'll discuss our marriage after the holidays. Some people stay in arranged marriages their entire life, Winnie, so be grateful we'll have the discussion at all." His nostrils flare as he continues to look me up and down, making my skin heat under his intense stare. "One more thing. You'll move in with me... immediately," he insists.

I take in a sharp breath. "That wasn't part of the agreement."

"Yes, it was. Ask your father. You'll need protection after this. I'm going to further handle Blake, but you have no other option but to move into my house with me."

My nose scrunches. "I'm perfectly fine in my apartment."

His tongue pokes the inside of his cheek as he lets out a long breath. "Why did I think you'd do as you're told?"

I bite my lip. My father's probably asking himself the same thing. Joke's on me. The one time I don't do as I'm told, everything blows up in my face. "I don't even know you, Archer. I can't just move in with you."

"Tomorrow, we'll be husband and wife. It's silly for you to think you'd live anywhere *but* with me. To play the part, we'll have to live together."

He has a solid point, but I still hate it. I like having my own space. I don't want to give it up to move in with someone I hardly know.

"What if I don't like your apartment?" I ask. The question is childish, but I'm lashing out because all of my control has been ripped away from me.

My apartment in New York is the one thing I still have. I picked it out myself when I moved back from LA. I've made it my home. But it also houses so many memories with Blake. Ones

I'm not sure I want to relive. I'd much prefer to forget the man ever existed.

"You don't have to like my apartment. Because you won't be there."

"Didn't you *just* say we have to live together?"

"Yes. I have a penthouse apartment across from the Moore offices for nights I work too late. But I much prefer my brownstone in the Upper East Side. It's quieter out there."

"I've never lived with a man before."

A smirk slowly builds on his lips. He shifts, reminding me just how close our bodies are. "So are you going to give in and say yes to this, or are you going to keep wasting more of my time?" His words seem harsh, but his delivery of them isn't. They're all said with a slight twitch to his lips. As if he's fighting a smile. Maybe I'll make it my mission to make him smile more…

"I'm still thinking," I answer honestly.

His head tilts to the side. "About?"

"About why you're agreeing to this. It isn't a secret my great-grandfather really screwed your family over years and years ago. You don't owe my family a thing. If anything, maybe I should be worried that this is all your way of getting revenge."

He scoffs, his fingers reaching up to play with one of his cufflinks. The movement makes his knuckles brush slightly against my chest. "One could argue we've already got our revenge. We own more of the market than Bishop Hotels. We're expanding far quicker than your family. And we have a much higher customer and employee satisfaction rate. Although, I will not lie to your face and deny that we won't have far more of an advantage now that we'll own part of Bishop, too."

I allow my eyes to travel over his face as I let his words sink in. There has to be more to why he's doing this, but I just don't know what it is yet. People in our world marry for monetary reasons all the time. I guess if I were to think about it, most of the marriages I know of are simply business transactions, but the little I know of Archer Moore makes me wonder why he'd ever agree to an arranged marriage.

"No one knows me as a patient man, Winnie. And I'm really testing it with you right now, but I don't see the purpose in us going back and forth any further. Your family needs this. Quite honestly, *you* need this. Say yes. Become my wife tomorrow." He lets out a slow breath, like he's having to control himself. I swear his gaze flicks to my lips, but it must be in my head. "Let me protect you," he adds, his voice lowered to a deep rasp.

My heart beats wildly in my chest. It must be the emotions of the morning all crashing into me at once because it has no business picking up speed like this for a man I barely know. Deep down, I know all of this back-and-forth is pointless. If my dad tells me this is what I need to do, I'll do it because that's what's best for our family.

It just feels impactful to say yes, to agree to this, and I wish I knew why I had this feeling in my stomach that so much is about to change.

Because it is.

"Okay," I whisper, focusing on his shoulder instead of his deep, brown eyes. They're such a comforting color, but his dark, slanted eyebrows and the paleness to his skin make them seem intense.

"Okay?" he repeats.

"We both know I have no other option, Archer. I'll marry you tomorrow. But I want you to know one thing."

He leans in closer. "Tell me anything."

His words make me pause for a moment because they sound so...different. Pained isn't the correct word, but they seem forced. It dawns on me that so many women want his attention. I've listened to the girls I went to school with dream about having just one minute of his time.

Now, I'll have endless moments with him when I don't want them at all.

"Winnie..." he pushes, his voice rough.

"I'll marry you tomorrow, but I want you to know if I saw *any* other way out of it, I wouldn't be. I've made the mistake of trusting a man before. I'm not doing it again. You can call me your wife, but don't expect to have my trust."

Before he can say anything, I duck underneath his arm and rush out of the small office. As I pull open the door, I brave one more look in his direction. His eyes are hot on mine, two small creases appearing on his forehead from his scowl.

For a moment, I pause. I want to ask him why he looks upset by my words, but I think better of it. I slide through the opening of the doorway and leave him behind.

The next time I see him, it'll be our wedding day.

7
Archer

"Is it done?" my dad asks, staring at me from across the long boardroom table.

"What do you think?" I fire back. I'm insulted he thinks I'd show up here if I hadn't secured the arrangement. He raised me better than that. I know not to face him until I come with news that'll impress him. Or, at the very least, not disappoint him.

"Good," Dad answers, leaning back in his chair. He's just finished the meeting I was supposed to be in on before Winnie disrupted those plans. It was one with developers for a recent project on the West Coast. "Anything I should know about the deal, or can I trust it's solid?"

"It's solid. We got more than what we originally wanted. Spencer was desperate and agreed to everything I asked for."

He nods in approval. "Did you contact all of the publications already?"

I pause. He doesn't normally ask so many questions. "I did on the way here. They've all been made aware of the wedding. I've set up different media interviews and exclusives with them to ensure they're silent until we're ready to make the announcement."

"The announcement must be made soon. What are you thinking?"

"There's a gala this weekend. High press, a good cause, and

tons of people there. It'll be the perfect time to announce to the world about Winnie and me. On Thursday, we'll be giving an interview to Ruby Robinson about our love story. She's hungry for it. She'll run the complete story on Sunday."

"Good job, son." Dad swipes his hand over the yellow legal pad he always carries with him. It's filled with the messy notes he takes during every meeting. I've tried countless times to get him to at least organize his notes, but he never listens.

My back straightens with the praise from my father. I'm thirty-five years old, and I still find myself wanting to impress him. As I get older, the pressure to earn enough of his trust to completely take over Moore Hotels looms.

I was raised to become the CEO of the business, but being raised to take it over is only half of the job. For Dad to actually step down, he wants me to earn it. And I spend every day of my life trying to do that. Not necessarily because I want anything to do with the franchise, but because it'd be the ultimate stamp of his approval.

"I'm thinking we need to personally handle this Blake kid," I offer, pulling out one of the chairs and taking a seat. I haven't met the sorry-ass excuse of a man who is blackmailing Winnie, but I'm eager to just have a *few* minutes with him. To threaten him within an inch of his life so he knows not to even dare to talk—let alone think—about Winnie again.

"Why?" Dad questions, pinning me with a curious glare. The light hits the gray strands of his hair. He's trying to fight aging however he can, but he's getting older. It's not as easy for him as it used to be to work all day, to travel from hotel to hotel when needed.

I mull over his question for a moment. After seeing the fear and betrayal in Winnie's eyes after what this Blake guy did to her, I'm aching to teach him a little lesson.

My jaw tenses as I think through what answer I want to give him. It isn't the truth. Or at least *that* version of the truth. If I tell *that* to him, he'll question why I care. It's the same question I asked myself the moment I watched Winnie disappear from the tiny office at Bishop Hotels. I felt it in my chest that I cared about the comment she made.

I cared that she told me she wouldn't trust me. It never mattered to me if anyone but my father trusted me. If they did what I wanted, why would I need their trust? I trust no one. I don't expect anyone to trust me.

But her words hit hard, harder than I cared to admit because I wanted her to trust me, and I despised the man who took advantage of that trust. I feel this intense need to make him pay, and I keep telling myself this because this woman's about to be my wife.

Is that actually the reason? I don't care to think long enough on it to determine if it is.

"Archer," my dad barks, pulling me from my thoughts.

Before I can ask him to repeat his question, he beats me to it. "Why would I give a damn about talking to this kid? No one will run anything on him. He has no leverage. He's not stupid enough to go show that video to anyone else without getting paid for it."

I frown, despising the thought of him even having possession of the video at all. "I don't like loose ends."

I don't move underneath my father's intense stare. Whatever he's trying to figure out with his scrutiny, he won't get from me. "Whatever you do, make it discreet," he finally answers.

There's a reason my family always comes out on top. We know how to cheat the system, how to get what we want. And what I want is to know Blake will never come for Winnie again. He should pay for even daring to blackmail her.

With a nod, I stand up and walk to the door. "Always do," I tell him before walking out. There's no use for us to exchange any other words. I have work to do—and I have a man to take down.

The moment I step out of the doors, my assistant is running to me, his phone in his hands as he looks at me with expectant eyes. Luther has been with me for eight years now. When my previous assistant decided to stay home with her kids instead of working, it took me over a month—and countless interviews—to find someone I felt could keep up with me.

Luther's resume sucked, but he blew his interview out of the water. I'm lucky to have him. He knows my next move almost better than I do. So when I gesture for him to follow me, he's already got his notes app open ready to do whatever I ask of him.

"I want you to do research on a Blake Billings for me. He's a former employee of Bishop Hotels. I want to know *everything* about him. Where he lives, who he's worked for, his family history, all of it. And I want it on my desk before I leave tonight."

"Got it," Luther responds, his fingers furiously flying over his phone's keyboard. One thing I love about Luther is that he never asks questions. He does as I ask, and he does it well.

I let him take whatever notes he wants as we make it to my office. It's a large room, one with a fantastic view of the city. I've never lived anywhere but Manhattan. I hate crowds, but I love this crowded city. I walk to my desk, already not looking forward to the mountain of paperwork that's on it. At least Luther has it in neat piles with sticky notes that tell me the order of priority.

"Anything else?" Luther asks me as I take a seat at my desk.

"There's one more thing," I tell him, leaning back in the chair.

"What is it, Mr. Moore?"

"I need you to call St. Michael's church and set up a wedding for tomorrow afternoon."

"And who should I tell them is getting married? Should we send a gift?"

I put my hands behind my head. "No gift. The wedding is for me."

A choking sound comes from Luther's throat as he stares at me in shock. "Excuse me?"

"Tomorrow, I will be marrying Winifred Bishop. I want the

wedding to be at St. Michael's. Make it look nice. Spare no expense."

For once, I think I may have actually stunned Luther speechless. His fingers don't glide along his keyboard as he quickly takes notes. He just stares at me in shock, his mouth hanging open.

I arch an eyebrow, wondering if my requests really elicit this much of a reaction.

Before I can tell him to get it together, he does it himself. He shakes his head, wiping his face clean of all shock. But I can tell he's still slightly rattled by the way he slowly jots down my demands.

"And should I invite anyone?"

I shake my head. "It'll be intimate. No extra invitations needed."

He lets out a slow breath but doesn't question me any further.

"Will you come back in twenty? I'm going to need you to make a delivery for me."

"Should I do it now?"

I open up my desk drawer and pull out the expensive stationery with my name etched across the top. I shake my head. "No. I have to write the letter first."

At the moment, Luther is terrible at hiding his reactions. I don't blame him. I don't think I've ever asked him to hand deliver a note for me, but there's a first time for everything. "Back in twenty. Got it."

"One more thing."

"Yes?"

"Call every bridal store in Manhattan and set up an open account for me. My future wife needs to buy a dress."

"On it," he says, clearing his throat after it breaks at the end slightly.

He stands there, staring at me like he has no idea who I am.

"Luther?" I drag out his name slowly, running my hand along the blank piece of stationery in front of me.

"Yes?"

"That'll be all."

Luther nods and scrambles out of my office, leaving me to write a letter to my future wife.

8
Winnie

My hands shake as I stare down at the letter in my lap. I've read it word for word countless times since it was first dropped off at my apartment last night. I'd been lying on my couch, replaying everything that's happened to lead me to that moment, when there was a knock on my door.

WINNIE,

WE DON'T KNOW EACH OTHER WELL, BUT I WANT THIS WEDDING TO BE EVERYTHING YOU WANT IT TO BE GIVEN THE CIRCUMSTANCES. I HAVE STARTED AN ACCOUNT WITH EVERY BRIDAL STORE IN THE AREA. I'VE GIVEN THEM STRICT INSTRUCTIONS TO SPARE NOTHING WHEN IT COMES TO YOU CHOOSING THE PERFECT DRESS FOR TOMORROW. I'M EAGER TO DISCOVER WHAT DRESS YOU CHOOSE.

I HOPE IN TIME, I CAN CHANGE YOUR MIND ABOUT TRUSTING ME.

I'LL BE WAITING FOR YOU AT THE ALTAR.

YOURS,

ARCHER

. . .

I trace the word *yours* for what seems like the hundredth time. It was such an interesting word choice for him to use, and I've overanalyzed every reason why he'd do it. I guess in the eyes of the law—and those around us—he will be mine.

But I don't want to be his. And I don't really want him as mine. At least I think I don't, but I've read this letter one too many times for me to be fully confident that the sweetness of the letter isn't lost on me.

Taking a deep breath, I neatly fold the letter and tuck it into the clutch I've brought to the church. When I agreed to get married today, I thought I'd wear something from my closet that somewhat fit the bill for a wedding dress. I thought we'd get married in a courthouse, do something that didn't really feel like a wedding at all.

Archer had other plans.

I stare at my reflection in the mirror, admiring the dress I'd picked out for myself. When I first found out that he wanted me to choose an actual dress, I didn't want to listen. I've already been robbed of the wedding I dreamed of as a little girl. I, at least, wanted to save some things for when I get married for real one day.

One of those things was choosing a wedding dress.

The more I thought about it, the more I realized that I wanted to go look at dresses. There was nothing in my closet I wanted to wear, so I did what he'd asked.

And I chose a dress that hugged my body perfectly. It only had to be hemmed for length; everything else was perfect. When I tried it on at the first bridal shop, I cried. The bridal assistant thought it was because I found the one. She said we always know when it's the one—just like we know when we find the one to marry.

Her words made me cry harder because I hadn't found the one for me; I'd just made stupid decisions to get me into a marriage that wasn't for love in the slightest. The tears fell, and I didn't know if it was because I loved the dress, or if I was regretting the situation I'd found myself in. Either way, I didn't want to try on any others.

The details on it are exquisite. It has long sleeves with silk buttons from my elbow to my wrist. The neckline leaves a lot to the imagination. It cuts right under my collarbones in a straight line, but it fits so perfectly that the curves of my breasts is still visible through the ivory silk fabric.

It clings to my body all the way until it reaches my thighs, before spreading out in a trumpet style. The train is long and stunning, but I've opted to have it bustled for today. I wasn't going to wear a veil, but the assistant insisted. When she pinned it into my hair, tears welled in my eyes all over again.

I looked like a bride.

I just didn't *feel* like a bride.

Today should be the best day of my life, but as I stare back at my reflection, I don't see the happiness in my eyes that should be there. Instead, I have bags that no amount of concealer could hide. There isn't a lover's glow to my cheeks. If anything, my skin looks dull.

I know this is for the best, but I just wish things were different. I wish I was marrying a man I loved. A man who loved me.

At least I look the part.

I tenderly wipe underneath my eyes, trying not to ruin the makeup I'd carefully applied this morning. When I end up smearing some of my mascara, I grab a tissue from a small table inside the St. Michael's changing room. I dab underneath my eyes, taking deep breath after deep breath to calm my nerves.

A knock sounds at the door as I attempt to gather myself. My shoulders shake as the door opens. I expect it to be my dad or maybe even my mom.

It isn't either. Instead, I find Archer stepping through the door.

He looks more handsome than I could've imagined. It makes

my chest hurt a little to look at him. To know that I'm chaining my life to his in the saddest of ways.

"Archer?" I murmur, sliding my hands down the front of my dress. "You're not supposed to be here."

He moves to shut the door, not really looking at me until the door is fully closed. Mid-step, he pauses, his body freezing as his eyes finally meet mine.

For a short moment, we're both incredibly still as we stare at one another. So much is said between us at that moment, except I don't really know what any of it means.

All I know is I think Archer Moore—my future husband— just took my breath away.

"Hi," he gets out, clearing his throat. He appears to be fazed, like he wasn't expecting to find what he did.

"Hi," I whisper, suddenly nervous in his presence for reasons I don't understand.

He takes a few tentative steps forward, as if he doesn't know if he's allowed to stand close to me or not. For some reason, he seems so much bigger today as he comes to a stop in front of me.

Maybe it's not just the stature of his tall, toned body but the heaviness of knowing what we're about to do.

He wears a black tuxedo that has to be custom-made for his body. As he tucks his hands into the pockets of the pants, the fabric tightens around his thick biceps. He appears to play with something in his pocket as his eyes roam freely over my body.

"I wanted to check on you," he admits, his voice softer than it was yesterday.

"I haven't run if that's what you were checking on," I joke, trying to break through the tension between us.

He lets out a soft laugh, his eyes tracing my face. "I didn't think you would."

I'm quiet for a moment, not knowing what to say back to him. There's no playbook for what to do or say at this moment. Normal people with normal lives and normal families don't get married to try and save the reputation of not only a family but a business as well.

Yet here we are, two people who are about to promise themselves to each other for just that.

Today's the start of it, and with him standing right in front of me with a sort of tenderness to his eyes, I wonder if the marriage will really be as bad as I thought it'd be. Could it really be if he's capable of looking at me like this? Surely not.

"Have you ever heard of the rule that the groom isn't supposed to see the bride before the ceremony on their wedding day?" I ask, my voice lowered and unsure.

This makes him crack the smallest hint of a smile. "I think we've already broken so many rules by being here today. By doing this."

I lace my fingers together in front of me, not knowing what to do with my hands. It feels weird to not touch, considering we're about to be married, but I think it'd be even more odd for us *to* touch, given we know little to nothing about one another.

"You okay?" he asks, his voice gentle. His tone almost makes me believe he cares.

I brave looking him in the eyes, not expecting to see the softness in them. Everything else about him is tense. The hard set of his jaw, the thin line he's pressed his lips into. Everything but his eyes. They crinkle at the sides as he stares down at me. He watches me carefully, waiting for me to answer him.

I shrug. "As okay as one can be when they're marrying a stranger because someone they cared for took advantage of them."

I swear I can hear his teeth grind against one another as his jaw tenses. For a moment, the softness leaves his eyes, and it's replaced with anger. He lets out a long breath before taking a step back and holding his hands out in front of him.

"The dress is magnificent," he notes, all traces of anger gone from his features. "*You* look magnificent," he adds.

My cheeks flush from his words. "You didn't have to buy me

a dress." The bridal assistant wouldn't even tell me how much the dress was when I'd asked. She told me she was under strict orders to give me whatever I wanted despite the price. But I've been around luxury fashion my entire life. The dress is hand-sewn, every tiny button on it hand-stitched. I know it was probably incredibly expensive, but I do love the way it feels like it was made just for me.

Archer clears his throat before he takes me by surprise and reaches out to tip my chin to look him in the eyes. "If this marriage is going to work between us, there's one thing I want to make *very* clear."

It feels like my heart lurches from my chest in anticipation. The air feels electrified between us as I wait for him to finish his thought. "And that is?"

His fingers tighten on my jaw. The way he grabs me is possessive. Even if I wanted to, I wouldn't be able to turn my head away from him. He's making sure that with whatever he's going to say, I see him and *only* him.

"I'm not a man who does anything because he has to. I do whatever the hell I want. No one tells me what to do, Winnie. I thrive on being the one in control. So I'm well aware I didn't have to buy you a damn thing. I wanted to."

I wonder if he can feel my racing pulse underneath his fingertips. He doesn't loosen his grip in the slightest. If anything, his fingertips dig even deeper into my skin as he stares deeply into my eyes.

"Understood?" he gets out, his voice rough. The intensity of it makes my body shiver—or maybe the shiver is from how close he is. A primal reaction to the way he handles me—and how I don't hate it.

I don't answer him. I *can't* answer him. My body betrays me as I'm lost at being so close to him. The look in his eyes tells me that I don't have any other option but to give him an answer, so I attempt a nod, even with the intense grip he has on my chin.

He clicks his tongue. I don't know if it's in disappointment or approval until his next words. "Good girl," he mutters, letting go of me but not putting any distance between our bodies.

I feel a little dizzy as I try to compose myself. Luckily, he's quiet for a few moments, allowing me to get a grip on myself. *What's happening?* Two days ago, this man was my family's enemy number one. Now he has my heart racing and my mind spinning from whatever just happened.

Good girl. God, why did the way he say it sound *so* familiar?

As I get ahold of myself, he reaches into the pocket of his pants and pulls out an emerald-green velvet box. He averts his eyes from me—almost bashfully—as he holds the box between us.

"I know nothing about this is conventional. Even so, to the world, you're going to be my wife. You deserve one of the most expensive things money can buy on your finger." The box makes a clicking sound as he flips it open, showing off the biggest diamond ring I've ever seen nestled inside.

I gasp. "Archer…" I'm too stunned by the beautiful, elegant, round-cut diamond carefully tucked into the box. "No," I whisper. It's so big and expensive-looking, I'm too nervous to even touch it, let alone wear it every day.

"Yes," he corrects, his voice stern. He takes a step forward, putting us toe-to-toe as he delicately pulls the ring from the box. "We're minutes away from being husband and wife. And I'll be damned if I don't have the best ring money can buy on my wife's finger."

Before I can think better of it, I tuck my hands behind my back. It's not that I don't like the ring. It's just that it's too pretty —too expensive—for me to be expected to wear it. *What if I lose it?* I'd never forgive myself. I won't be his real wife—not really. I don't deserve a massive ring. Just a small band would work.

Archer lets out a sigh of disapproval. His eyes don't leave mine as he leans over me and wraps his cold fingers around my wrist. I try to lock my arm, but it's no use. He pulls it back to the front of my body and easily keeps my hand right where he wants it. Effortlessly, he slides the ring down my ring finger. It feels heavy on my hand. Can I even get used to feeling the weight every day?

"I can't wear this."

"You *will* wear this."

He begins to back away, what appears to be a satisfied smirk playing on his lips.

"Archer, no."

He shakes his head, standing in the doorway with a full smile now.

Why does he have to look so good when he smiles? No wonder every single woman I've met here in New York dreams of him. One pointed smile aimed at me and I'm almost melting at his feet. Or maybe it's the ring he just placed on my finger that I'm well aware had to have had a *hefty* price tag.

"My ring looks good on your finger, Winnie. I'll meet you at the altar."

He leaves, and it isn't until moments after he softly shuts the door that I realize I'm finally taking my first full breath since the moment he walked in.

9
Archer

I'VE NEVER BEEN A MAN THAT WORRIES ABOUT MUCH. I HAVEN'T ever needed to. One simple snap of my fingers—one command of my voice—and people do what I want. It's the weight my last name holds. Not only that but the persona I've built for myself from a very young age.

But as the aging woman at the organ begins to play the soft tune of the song Winnie will walk down the aisle to, for the first time in I don't know how long, I feel incredibly nervous.

I'll never admit to another soul how much she's been on my mind since the moment I left her family's headquarters yesterday. I haven't even admitted to myself how much she's plagued my thoughts since yesterday morning. If I pretend long enough, I can trick myself into thinking it's only because I know this woman is about to be my wife.

I've never had to share my life—my space—with anyone else. That's got to be the reason she's drifted into my mind more times than I could count.

Or maybe she has a pull on me that I don't want to face.

I knew it the moment I opted for the most expensive diamond I could find at the jewelers. Or the moment I arrived at the church and felt this intense pull to track her down, to make sure she didn't have any regrets about agreeing to this.

The doors to the church open, and it feels like my stomach

drops to my feet when I see her standing at the end of the aisle. She clutches her father's arm so tightly I wonder if he feels the bite of her nails even through the fabric of his sleeve. I don't pay close attention to their intertwined arms for long. I can't resist the urge to meet her eyes, to get lost in the reality of what we're about to do.

It hasn't been that long since we were alone in the dressing room of the church, but since then, she's applied a soft pink gloss to her lips and pinned a veil in the long red strands of her hair.

"She's beautiful," the priest whispers from my side.

I swallow, not wanting to openly admit that I wholeheartedly agree with him.

My mouth feels dry as I try to process the emotions crashing through me. I think she might be the most beautiful woman I've ever seen—and the tentative smile she gives me as they near us tells me she doesn't even know it.

I lay my palm against my chest. It feels heavy as I watch her and her father share an awkward embrace. The only people here at the wedding are our parents—although they've barely said a word to each other as they sit in opposite pews—plus Luther and the photographer and Ruby Robinson, the journalist running a story on our wedding.

The music stops as Winnie climbs the two stairs to the church altar. It's only when she comes to a stop in front of me that I realize I should've helped lead her to where we stand. I was too lost in her beauty, wondering why all the women I've met in the world have never made my heart beat the way it is at this moment.

I only saw her minutes ago, but this feels different. It feels...*real*.

Maybe it's because the priest begins the service, solidifying the fact that Winnie and I are actually getting married. It feels awkward for the two of us to stand facing one another and not touch. Reaching out, I grab her hands and loop my fingers around hers.

Her hands shake, and for some reason, it feels like a dagger to my chest. I don't want to make her nervous—even though that's exactly how I'm feeling right now because of her.

I'm lost, staring into her eyes through the mesh fabric of her veil, when she gives my hands a reassuring squeeze.

Maybe it wasn't her hands that were shaking after all. Maybe they were mine.

The intense sound of my pulse thrums through my eardrums as I wonder if I should call off the wedding before the vows are ever uttered. Maybe this is a terrible idea. I shouldn't be entering a fake marriage with a woman who is able to make my heart come alive in my chest like this from one single look.

The priest prays over us and our marriage while I'm too busy still contemplating if I should stop this wedding before it's solidified. I don't let anyone get under my skin. Not now, not ever. But the way my fingers tighten around hers, wanting to keep her close, I wonder if I give her long enough, Winnie will do exactly that.

I get swept up in reminding myself over and over again that she's only important to me because her family can give me something I want. That we have an arrangement, and that's all it'll ever be. But fuck, I didn't expect this wedding to feel so real. That has to be why I'm completely thrown off.

Before I know it, we've made it to the part of the ceremony where we exchange rings.

"If you're ready, I'll have the two of you hand me the bands. The ring has no beginning, no end…it represents the circle of life —the circle of love. May they be given and received to remind you of the vows you have made on this day."

I don't want to, but I let go of one of Winnie's hands long enough to slide my hand into the hidden pocket of my tuxedo. My fingers connect with the dainty wedding band I'd chosen for her while picking out her engagement ring.

I'm so lost in making sure I don't drop it that I miss that she's let go of my other hand and is slipping a simple gold band off her thumb. I'd been holding her hand and hadn't even noticed it there.

She doesn't look at me; she focuses on the priest as he blesses both of our wedding bands. I'd planned on picking one out for me that was just for show at some point, but I'd been more concerned about her rings than mine that I hadn't given the exchanging of rings today much thought.

All I wanted was to make sure she had a ring on her finger so the world knew she was under my protection. That she was my wife.

The priest hands me her wedding band carefully, gesturing for me to take her hand. I attempt to keep my hands steady as I take her hand in mine once again. I raise her small hand, her fingertips barely brushing over my chest with the movement.

"Repeat after me," he instructs as I line the band up with the tip of her finger. "In token and pledge of my constant faith and abiding love, with this ring, I thee wed."

I repeat after him, sliding the wedding band all the way down her finger. Before I can think better of it, I raise her hand a few inches and lay a kiss to the diamond on her finger. It's cold against my lips as I kiss the physical representation of the union we're agreeing to.

Her eyelids flutter shut for a moment, and I'd give anything to be able to take a look into her mind. Are regrets swarming through it? Or is she opening up to pretending together? I can't ask any of that, but I do let my lips linger on the ring I bought her for a few perfect, drawn-out seconds before I pull away and softly drop her hand.

The sound of a camera clicking almost breaks me from the moment, but I'm too caught up in watching her blush as she takes the simple gold wedding band she'd been wearing from the priest to look over at the shuttering camera.

Winnie repeats the same words I just did, her hand steady as she slides the band down my ring finger. It isn't the right moment for it, but I still fight the urge to ask her where she got it —ask why she got it.

The wedding mass seems to go by in a blur. All too soon, the priest is presenting us to the few witnesses we have. "I now pronounce you husband and wife. You may kiss the bride."

I'd lifted her veil earlier in the service, but it still frames her face perfectly. It seems like the entire church is silent as I lean in closer, anxious for all the attention on us. Our parents know that this kiss solidifies something that is for business only, but there are people here who have to believe that we've kissed a million times—and that this kiss will be the start of our forever.

A happily ever after between two families everyone thought were feuding.

Slowly, I take either side of Winnie's face. Her skin is incredibly soft against my fingertips. Without even thinking about it, my thumb traces her high cheekbones. It might be hopeful thinking, but I swear she slightly leans into my touch. My heart pounds at the thought of kissing her.

"Just do it," she whispers. Her voice is so low that I almost miss it, meaning there's no way anyone else heard it but me.

My eyes fall to her lips. They're slightly parted and perfectly pink, inviting me to press my own against them. I lean in, our breaths mingling as I place our lips inches apart. She angles her head slightly, allowing me the perfect position to press my lips against hers.

The moment they connect, she rises to her tiptoes, her hands finding my chest to help steady herself. Her lips are so soft it occurs to me I could get lost in them forever. She lets me lead as her hands tighten against my chest. She grips me so possessively that I can't help but pull her even harder into my body, despite the audience bearing witness to this.

It isn't the longest kiss, but even though brief, it makes more of an impact on me than I'd care to admit. The gloss coating her lips tastes like vanilla, and I'd give anything to slip my tongue between them and discover what her tongue tastes like, too. I know it isn't necessary, but I want to deepen the kiss despite the audience we have.

I don't, but I do go in for one more chaste peck against her lips after the first one ends.

"I'm delighted to introduce Mr. and Mrs. Archer Moore for the very first time," the priest says with glee, snapping his Bible shut.

For a typical wedding, this is where everyone stands and cheers with happiness for the new couple. They might throw rice or confetti or blow bubbles. None of that happens because this isn't a wedding celebrating love, and most of the people here to bear witness know that.

Yet, I still hold her hand in mine as if it were real. I still walk down the aisle and give the photographer a stiff smile like I'm a dashing groom dazed by finally getting to marry his blushing bride.

10
Winnie

THE WEDDING ALMOST FELT REAL—ALL THE WAY UP UNTIL THE moment Archer's driver shut the door to the town car and Archer and I were left alone in silence.

He sits on one side of the car, staring out the window with his knuckles pressed to his lips as he gets lost deep in thought. I, on the other hand, sit all the way on the other side, awkwardly shifting in my seat because I hadn't thought about removing the veil before getting in the car, and now it keeps getting caught.

My pulse hammers through my veins as I try to think if I should break the silence between us or let him take the lead. An hour ago, we were locked in a kiss that felt far more real than I was expecting. Worse, it almost felt familiar. Like we'd done it before, like my lips knew his.

I can't stop thinking about it, but by Archer's sudden cold demeanor, maybe he's already pretended like it never happened. Even as the photographer took wedding photos of us, he didn't act this way. He played the part of a loving husband—and he played it well.

"Where are we going?" I finally ask, hating to break the silence. Normally, I don't mind the quiet. It leaves me alone with my thoughts, but right now, the last place I want to be is lost in my own head.

"Home," he answers immediately, his gaze still focused out the window.

Why won't he look over at me? We just got married. I swear I saw a different side of him in that church—a softer side—but apparently, that's all it was...a glimpse. Because now, he's back to the Archer Moore that the world knows.

Quiet. Cold. Uninterested.

Those are all words I've heard people use to describe him. If you had asked me after speaking with him before the ceremony, I would've told anyone that he was different.

But is he different?

I feel naive all over again. All it took was for him to do one nice gesture and buy me one very expensive ring to question if I really knew him at all. If Blake taught me anything, it's that I trust too easily. I've already told Archer I won't let that happen again and I need to remember that.

He must not like my silence because he speaks up again. "Any arguments about that?"

I frown. Arguing is now exactly what I want to do. "I don't have anything to stay the night at your house."

"It's now your house, too." His words should sound sweet, but the delivery of them isn't. He spits them out as if he hates the fact that I'll be living with him.

"It doesn't have to be," I mutter under my breath, turning my body toward the window and away from him. I'm not typically an argumentative person, but he's being rude. I don't like the hot and cold. All I want is to establish a baseline with him and stick to it.

He lets out a long, exaggerated sigh. "It was part of the deal," he tells me through gritted teeth. "You signed it. You're living with me, no arguments."

"Then you can't just tell me without giving me the chance to get my things." I try to fully turn away from him, but my head gets yanked back. I yelp, wanting the veil out of my hair immediately.

Unfortunately, my dress is tight, and it's hard to lift my arms enough to reach the pins securing it in my hair. I let out a frustrated sigh, regretting being talked into the veil last minute.

Archer gives me a sigh of his own before he unbuckles his seat belt and slides across the leather seat.

"Let me help you," he insists, his tone harsh.

"I don't need your help," I snap, attempting to reach up and remove the veil myself but failing.

I'm pretty sure he rolls his eyes at me. "Clearly," he says sarcastically, not listening to me at all as he gently places his hand against my hair. His other hand works at softly pulling the pins from my hair. He's gentle, trying not to tug on the strands as he takes out each one until I finally feel the weight lifted as he removes the veil.

"Better?"

I nod. It feels *so* much better. I hadn't realized how heavy the fabric was and how much it was pulling on my scalp until it was gone. We stare at one another for a few moments with matching frowns.

I'm the one to break first. "I understand your reasons for demanding I live with you. But you can't expect me to go there without packing anything first. I don't have anything."

He presses his lips into a thin line. "Wrong."

"What?"

The sound of his palm running over his stubble fills the quiet of the back seat. "You're wrong. You have an entire room full of things waiting for you at my house."

"*How*?" I don't bother to hide the shock from my voice.

"It's called a store," he responds sarcastically.

I close my eyes for a moment to muster up the energy to deal with him. "So what? You bought me things and expected me not to need *anything* from my own apartment?"

The corners of his lips turn down slightly. Apparently, that's exactly what he thought by the look on his face.

I rub at my forehead, the dull throb of a headache popping up due to how insufferable he is. "Are you used to always getting what you want?"

"Yes," he answers immediately. He watches me closely, his eyes narrowed as he seems to bait me to argue more with him.

I can't help but give him a cold smile. How nice it must be to always get what you want. There are two kinds of people in this world: the ones who are pleased by people and the people pleasers. I've been raised to be the latter, while he was raised to be the former.

My head rocks back and forth. I sit up straighter, pushing my shoulders back so he knows that he won't always get his way with me. "Well, better get used to that not always happening. I need to go to my apartment."

"Why don't we just go to my house first and you can determine if the shopping my assistant did for you is satisfactory or not?" He pinches the bridge of his nose, his eyes shutting for a moment like he's fighting his own headache.

"I know it won't be."

"Why?"

I purse my lips. I don't want to tell him that there's one item lying on my bed that I never sleep without. I'm too embarrassed to admit it. But even though my cheeks heat with the idea of confessing to him that I sleep with a stuffed turtle every night, I feel even more anxious at the thought of not sleeping with the stuffed animal I've had since I was a child—Norbert. "Because I have things I need."

He plays with his collar, pulling the fabric away from his neck. "What *things*?"

"Just things. Why is it so important that we get to your house now? Just have the driver stop by my apartment, and I'll be quick."

"Because early tomorrow morning, we have an interview with Ruby Robinson, and she's going to ask us a *lot* of personal questions. Therefore, tonight, we're going to spend the night getting to know one another. It's our wedding night, after all."

The deep, husky way he says the last sentence makes my body heat. "I'll agree to that if you just let me stop by my apartment for two minutes."

"Maybe if you tell me what you need from there so badly, I will."

I let out an annoyed sigh. This man is really going to get on my nerves. He has an iron will, and for some reason, I want to defy him in any way I can.

"I need to get Norbert," I mumble, feeling incredibly embarrassed to even admit it at all.

"Excuse me?"

"I need Norbert," I repeat. My words are hurried and anxious, said against my hand as I try to cover the redness I feel pooling in my cheeks.

"Who the *fuck* is Norbert?" If he was anyone else, I might think that's jealousy in his tone. But this is Archer Moore we're talking about. I know enough about him to know he's probably never been jealous in his life.

"My stuffed animal. I can't sleep without him."

He stares at me with a blank expression. He gives no hint at what's going through his mind. His face is stone-cold. "Norbert is a stuffed animal?"

I nod. "A turtle." The specifics probably don't matter, and I feel embarrassed I'm even having to tell him about Norbert to begin with, but he left me no choice. I don't understand how he has the nerve to tell me to live in his house without even giving me the opportunity to pack up my belongings.

He works his jaw. Even from across the car, I can see the muscle of it clench and unclench as he thinks something through. "You're telling me we need to go by your apartment to get a stuffed...turtle?"

I angrily narrow my eyes on him. "Are you making fun of me?"

His lips twitch with humor, and his shoulders begin to shake. Suddenly, a loud laugh erupts from his chest.

"Archer!" I yell, covering my face in my hands and only peeking at him between my fingers. "Stop laughing at me."

He shakes his head, swiping his hand across his face to try and cover his laugh. "I'm not laughing at you. I thought Norbert was a person—or a dog. I just wasn't expecting it to be a stuffed turtle."

I cross my arms across my chest, angling my body so I can get a better look at him. He really doesn't seem to be trying to be malicious with his laughter. Maybe I just really took him by surprise with Norbert.

"Are you done now?" I ask once he's finally seemed to gather himself. His face is a little flushed from laughter, and it's a little jarring to see him so carefree. He seems younger and far less intimidating.

"Yes," he answers, letting out a long breath.

"Good. Now, are you going to tell the driver to go to my place, or should I?"

One of his dark eyebrows rises. "You're just going to show up at your apartment in your wedding dress?"

I look down at the dress, forgetting I'm wearing something that probably cost tens of thousands of dollars. I shrug. "Yep. People do long receptions in expensive dresses where drinks get spilled on them, and they parade around a dirty dance floor in it. Going to my apartment and changing shortly after seems pretty tame to me."

He runs his finger along his bottom lip as if he's deep in thought. All he does is stare at me, staying eerily quiet. Finally, the silence bothers me enough that I fill it. "What?" I ask nervously.

"Nothing."

"The look on your face says otherwise," I counter.

The corners of his lips rise slightly. "It's just *you*."

I swipe at my face, wondering if I have something on it. "What about me? Do I have something on my face?"

He reaches across the back seat once again. His fingers are timid as he wraps them around my wrist and guides my hand back down. "No. You're perfect." He pauses for a moment, as if those weren't the words he meant to say. He sighs, letting go of my wrist and letting my hand drop to my lap. "It's just you in general. I expected you to be different."

"You don't know me well enough to really have any opinions about me," I whisper, trying not to pay attention to the electricity in the air. He hasn't gone back to the other side of the car, and he's incredibly close to me—too close. His expensive cologne clings to the air, enveloping me in everything that's him.

"You have a point," he admits. He shifts but doesn't make a move to sit back.

"I get what you're saying, though. We haven't had much time, but you're already different from what I was expecting."

"What were you expecting?"

"A raging asshole."

He barks out a laugh. "Many people do call me that."

"I know."

His eyes narrow on me. It's quiet for a few beats. He breaks the silence by pressing a button on the ceiling. "Change of plans, Franklin. We're going to the Brentmore Apartments before going home."

"Yes, sir," a voice comes over the speaker above us.

Neither of us says a single thing until we arrive at my apartment building. I'm getting ready to open my door when he reaches across us and stops me. "Wait," he demands.

I stop, waiting to see what he needs.

"Just let me get the door for you? That's what a good husband does."

Before I can argue, he's throwing his door open and quickly rounding the car to open my door. He even holds out his hand for me, waiting for me to take it before I step out of the car.

All the way to my apartment, he holds the train of my dress for me, making sure I don't trip on the extra fabric at my feet. When I tell him in the empty elevator he doesn't have to do that, his only answer is a repeat of what he said in the car. "It's what a good husband does."

11
Archer

"ARE YOU JUST GOING TO STAND THERE?" I ASK WINNIE, TAKING A step closer to her so we're shoulder to shoulder. There's a slight chill to the air as it wraps around us, but she doesn't give any indication that she wants to step out of the cold and into the warmth.

"Yes," she answers immediately, her neck craned as she looks up at the building in front of us.

I sigh, setting down the heavy suitcase she brought from her apartment. "Can you at least tell me why we're standing here staring at my house?"

"Because it's your house."

"Okay..." My words pause for a moment as I try to figure out what she means. "So we're just going to stand in the cold, staring at my house?"

My comment awards me a dirty look from her. At least she looked away from staring at the home I purchased two years ago. She huffs as if my questions are annoying her. "You were raised in New York. There's no way you think it's cold right now."

She's got a point. "Can we at least judge my house from the inside? It's weird to stand out here staring at a house."

"When you told me you had a house, I just didn't expect this. This is...domesticated. You have pumpkins on your stairs."

"There's a little girl next door—Penny—and last year, she told me my front porch was sad because I didn't have any pumpkins."

"So you got them this year?"

I shrug. "I did." There's nothing more humbling than a five-year-old telling you that you need to make your front porch more appealing. I like the kid. She always waits for me to get back from morning runs and often has a glass of lemonade waiting for me in the summer heat. Her parents are both in the financial world and have become good friends of mine. If she wants pumpkins on my doorstep, then I'll hire someone to put pumpkins on my doorstep.

"I really don't know anything about you," she mutters, shifting on her feet.

An intense breeze blows through, lifting the long, curled, red strands of her hair. They dance around her face, almost hitting me in the face with the whipping wind. She laughs, trying to tuck the stray pieces behind her ear.

We'd been at her apartment for over an hour as she gathered everything she needed to move in with me. I told her I'd hire someone to move whatever she couldn't pack in a bag. Instead, she opted for two large suitcases, saying she couldn't narrow it down to a single bag.

"It's just pumpkins," I finally say, trying to not get distracted by the urge to push the hair from her face.

"It isn't, though," she says under her breath. "I guess let's go inside and see whatever new things I'm going to discover about Archer Moore."

"My full name isn't necessary. I'm just Archer."

She smiles. It's the prettiest smile I've ever seen because her entire face lights up with it. "Well, *just Archer*, show me our home."

I gesture for her to walk ahead of me, trying not to focus on the way she easily said *our home* like it was the most natural thing in the world.

"After you, *wife*," I tell her, lifting both her suitcases and following her up the stairs.

She laughs when she points at the absurd number of pumpkins that run up both sides of the cement stairs. "Are we going to carve them for Halloween?"

I frown, setting the luggage down long enough to unlock the front door. I've had my house staff busy all day trying to make this place seem less like a house and more like a home. The moment I open the door, I notice there are candles and actual decorations on the walls.

They did good.

Winnie stops in the entryway, her eyebrows raised high on her forehead as she looks around the space. "You're joking. This isn't your place."

I set her bags in the corner, content in watching her look around my space. My father thought it was strange for me to buy a house here instead of opting to live in the heart of the city. But I like things a little bit more quiet—as quiet as you can still get in this city.

Central Park is pretty much in my backyard, but it still feels different than being up high in a penthouse apartment. Sure, everyone around me moved here because they were raising families. I just moved here because it felt more private.

I like to be secluded, but with Winnie now in my life, I'm happy I get to bring her home to something like this.

"Archer." She says my name in shock, taking a few steps closer to where she inspects an entryway table filled with books I've never seen in my life. "You decorate?"

I fight a smile. "I hired someone to decorate. They were here all day."

Her head whips around to look at me. Her mouth hangs open as she looks at me in shock. "You did all of this…today?"

I nod, looking around the space to see what they added. There's now a giant vase with a floral arrangement next to the door. Candles are neatly placed along the dining table, and there are photos on the walls that hadn't been there this morning. The frames are filled with professional pictures taken of the city, but the thought pops into my mind how I'd like one day to fill them with personal ones.

"What made you want to decorate now? Were you afraid I'd judge you if you had a cold, empty, expensive house?"

I smile, shedding my tuxedo jacket and folding it over my arm. "There's plenty you could judge me on if you wanted to, Winnie. I didn't have to spruce up the space to prevent you from doing it."

She follows me as I step into the kitchen. I throw the jacket over the back of one of the barstools. I'm hungry and could use a glass of wine.

"What do you want for dinner?"

"Why did you do it, then?" she asks, completely ignoring my question.

I sigh, leaning back against the countertop. "Why did I do what?"

"Decorate. Change your space. You didn't have to do that for me."

This isn't the first time she's said something like this, and every time she does it, it bothers me even more. I don't know what else I can do to get through to her that no one makes me do anything I don't want to. That just isn't who I am.

"I did it because I wanted to. I know none of this is ideal, but the least I could do is make sure the house you're forced to live in for the next year doesn't feel cold and empty."

All she does is stare at me. No words leave her mouth for what feels like forever. I shift uncomfortably, trying not to break the silence on my own. I want to know whatever she's thinking about, and I don't want to interrupt her.

"That was…" Her words trail off, and I'm dying to know what she isn't saying. She doesn't make me wait for long. "That was really, really thoughtful of you," she finishes. She moves to tuck a piece of hair behind her ear, and the light catches the ring on her finger. I focus on it for a moment, loving the way it looks there.

Everything seems to fade away as we stare at one another, both lost in our own thoughts to say anything out loud for some time.

I clear my throat, pushing off the counter before I let the moment turn into anything more than it should be. "Tell me what sounds good for dinner. I'll order some food, and we'll get to work getting to know one another."

12
Winnie

"ARE YOU A DOG OR A CAT PERSON?" I ASK, POPPING A PIECE OF pita bread into my mouth.

Archer leans forward, tearing a chunk of bread for himself and dipping it into the hummus. "I'd love to know which you think I am," he counters, his eyes trained on me.

I think for a moment. I don't know if I see him really being a dog or cat person. He seems to like order; it's hard to imagine any kind of pet wandering around this house. "Cat," I guess, trying to imagine him with a cat curled up in his lap. I think cats are known for being a cleaner animal so I went with them instead of a dog.

Archer shakes his head, sitting back in the dining room chair with a smile on his face. "Nope. If I had to choose, I'd pick a dog. But my life is too hectic to be responsible for any kind of living being."

I let out a low whistle, shaking my head. "I really had you pegged for a cat guy."

He laughs. "No, you didn't. You had no idea."

I throw my straw wrapper at him, but at the last second, it curves to the right and floats down to the tabletop. "I almost said neither," I argue, mad at myself for not going with my gut.

"What about you? Cat or dog?"

I shrug, taking a drink of my iced tea. It has way too much sugar in it and is overly sweet, but I need the caffeine if we're going to spend most of the night getting to know one another. "I've never had a pet, so I don't know. I guess I'd probably say the same thing as you and go with dog."

He stares at me incredulously. "You never once had a pet?"

A nervous laugh bubbles from my throat. He looks so stunned that my family never had pets. "No. Unless you count Norbert as one."

"A stuffed animal does *not* count," he argues, shaking his head.

"Are you telling me you had pets as a kid?" I ask, unable to imagine his family with dogs or cats running around their expensive house.

"Yes. I had a dog named Skip as a child and a cat named Butters."

My mouth falls open. "No, you didn't."

"I'm sure my mom has photos of them somewhere. You'll have to ask her. They both slept with me every night. I'd throw them birthday parties every year, and I'd refuse to go to school unless I'd taken Skip for a walk."

"That's actually adorable."

He rolls his eyes like he hates the idea of anyone calling him adorable. "*Anyway*. Let's talk about what we're going to tell the journalist tomorrow when she asks how we met."

I push my plate away from me, completely stuffed. I'd told Archer to choose what he wanted for dinner. I'd been starving, but nothing really sounded good. We proceeded to argue for five minutes when he consistently demanded that I choose until I finally agreed to it.

He'd laid out at least twenty takeout menus along his granite countertops, insisting I choose one. I'm learning very quickly just how stubborn he is, but it doesn't bother me. At least this didn't. I thought it was kind of sweet that he was so insistent on me choosing.

We've been sitting at the table for almost an hour now, going over random facts about each other so it can be more believable that we've fallen in love. There's so much I didn't know about him. I didn't know he was quarterback on the football team in both high school and college. He wouldn't really tell me how good he was, but just by the nonchalant way he talked about the awards he'd been given and the championships he'd won, he must've been good. Not that it really mattered; his career path was always going to end in him taking over Moore Hotels. It is kind of annoying that he was so good at a sport when it was never his intention to do anything with it.

"You must *really* be thinking about what our love story is," Archer says, breaking me from my thoughts.

I sit up in my chair, trying to not think about him hot and sweaty on a football field. The mental picture is too easy after he elaborated on everything he had to do to stay in good enough shape to play.

"Well," I hurriedly get out, trying to pretend I really was intensely thinking about what we'd tell people. "Everyone already knows that our families have known each other for ages. We don't have to tell people how we met because we've just always kind of known one another."

"That part is obvious," he clips out. His eyes darken, but I don't know why. Maybe he's thinking about what tore our families apart.

"I don't see you offering an epic love story for the two of us."

"Epic, huh?"

I smile, leaning forward on the table to rest my chin between my palms. "Yes, epic. The luxury of being fake married is you get to tell whatever story you want. Let's see...what should we tell them?" I think for a moment, trying to remember all of my favorite rom-com plots to see if I can pull ideas from any of them.

"Oh!" I smile, my top teeth digging into my bottom lip with

excitement. "We're definitely going to tell them that you chased me. That it took forever for me to agree to a date with you."

His forehead wrinkles with a frown. "We're not telling people that you denied me."

I nod, my smile getting wider. "Oh yes, we are. Our families are enemies, remember? They'll never believe I said yes to you immediately."

He lets out a resigned sigh. "So what exactly will you tell her?"

My finger taps against my chin as I think about his question. "I'll say we struck up some small talk at an event. That for once, we had a civil conversation. It was nice—friendly even."

Archer reaches back and scratches his neck. "I'm not sure anyone would ever call me friendly."

"For me, you were," I counter. Because of him, my heart beats erratically in my chest. I didn't think I'd have so much fun coming up with a pretend love story for the two of us, yet here I am having the time of my life doing it. There are so many things we could tell people, so many different versions of a story I can imagine.

"Or we tell people that you chased me. I've never chased a woman. People might not believe us if we said I changed for you." He leans forward, resting his sharp jawline in his large palm. His eyes stay focused on me. I try not to squirm under his intense stare.

"Love changes a person," I tease. I probably could think of a story that seems a little more realistic other than he chased me, but it's fun to imagine. A man like Archer Moore putting his sights on you and only you is any woman's dream.

"So what's the rest of the story?" he asks, his eyes intent on mine. He has this ability to capture your attention with just the way he looks at you. It's intense, like he's focusing on no one else but you.

"We talked that night. You decided I wasn't as bad as you

thought. I enjoyed talking to you, but I never imagined you enjoyed it too…"

He continues to give me his undivided attention. He barely even moves as he waits for me to complete the story.

"We didn't talk for a bit, but of course, we'd end up at the same events as one another. One night, we bumped into each other, and you asked to grab dinner sometime. I denied you at first, thinking you were wanting to talk business."

"But eventually, I convinced you that it wasn't about business for me," he interrupts, his deep voice confident and sure.

"Perfect," I whisper, my face heating with the way he just said that sentence. It was deep and raspy, and I feel like he could get any woman off just by the sound of his voice.

I blink. *Did I just have a dirty thought about Archer Moore?*

Technically, it was just about his voice, but now that I'm thinking about it even more, I'm wondering what he's like in the bedroom. Is he this commanding in bed? What does his voice sound like when he's about to come…

"What are we telling them for our first date?" Archer's voice breaks me from my thoughts. I bolt up in my chair, worried somehow he became a mind reader and knows exactly what was just running through my head.

He raises an eyebrow, clearly noticing my sudden change in demeanor. "Does talk of our fake first date get you excited, Winnie?"

"No," I squeak. Why does my name coming from his lips sound so sexual? Maybe I just need him to not talk at all. I'm tired, and it's been a weird day. That's the *only* reason I'm reacting to him this way.

The slight smirk on his lips tells me he doesn't believe me, but he doesn't push it either. Instead, he seems to really think of a good story to tell the world about our first date. His fingers fumble with the fancy watch on his wrist. "For our first date, I did something private but over-the-top. Only the best for you."

My heart flutters inside my chest, even though I know none

of this is real. It doesn't matter. I can't help but feel giddy to plan this with him. To imagine him planning some big, elaborate first date for me. "Tell me more," I insist, my voice just above a whisper.

"I flew in a private chef from Italy to make your favorite meal."

"And what's my favorite?" I ask, knowing he won't have any idea of what my favorite dish is. I'm curious to find out what his guess is, though.

"Cacio e pepe," he answers without any kind of afterthought.

My mouth pops open in surprise—because he's right. That's by far my favorite dish, but how did he know it? I rack my mind trying to figure out if we talked about our favorite dishes and I just completely forgot about it. We did talk about our favorite type of food—his was also Italian, same as mine. But I really don't remember either of us specifying what dish we each preferred.

"The chef made cacio e pepe that was to die for. You couldn't stop raving about it. He even made a caprese salad that was so good you joked with me that you'd fallen in love with him."

I'm quiet because I love caprese salad—but that guess is easier. Everyone loves it. There's a reason it's served at almost every event we attend.

"We had homemade bread and dipped it in olive oil he brought over from Tuscany and paired it with a bottle of wine that was the best you ever had."

"Maybe I don't like wine," I counter, my voice soft. He's surprised me so much that I can't put much emotion into my argument.

"That's a lie," he states matter-of-factly.

All I can do is watch him carefully, wondering how he seems to know so much about me when I know little to nothing about him at all. Sure, he's told me all about how he could've gone professional if he wanted to with football and how he has a weird obsession with sour candies. He also told me his favorite color is black and that his favorite season is fall—although winter is a close second. He loves to snowboard and wants to try out a new mountain this winter in Colorado.

I know all these small tidbits of information he shared with me tonight, but I don't know things he hasn't divulged.

And yet...he seems to know little details about me that I never told him. I shake it off, telling myself he's just got to be incredibly good at guessing. For his job, he has to be good at reading people. Maybe I'm simply an open book, and he reads me easily.

"What else did we do for our date?" My voice comes out far breathier than I intend it to. I hadn't even realized that I'd sat up in my chair and my body is angled toward his. He has my full, undivided attention. I'm ready to hang on to his every word as I wait to hear more about the beginning of us falling in love.

"After we ate, we said our goodbyes to the chef and had a quiet night in. You were excited to get to know one another out of the public eye. We both knew that us spending time together would catch the attention of the people around us, and at least for the start, we wanted something that was between just the two of us. I opened up a second bottle of wine—Pavillon Blanc, your favorite. And we just talked. We talked about everything we could, enjoying being able to get to know one another without anyone else knowing. It was so good that as you left, you asked about a second date."

I lean in. "*I* asked about the second date?"

He takes a drink of his wine. He'd offered me a glass, but I'd declined. I was already nervous about going over all of the details for the interview tomorrow. I wanted a clear head. "Yes, you did. And I agreed immediately. It was a phenomenal first date."

"And then I left?"

This makes him smile. "Then you left."

"What about a first kiss?" I blurt.

"Kissing on the first date?" he teases, showing off his perfect teeth with a wide smile. "Scandalous."

I roll my eyes. "I have an ex-boyfriend—not even a boyfriend, really—threatening to release a video of us having sex. A kiss on the first date wouldn't be the most scandalous thing I've ever done."

His eyes darken as he roughly sets his glass of wine on top of the table. He looks angry, the muscles of his jaw flexing as he clenches it. "He took a private moment of the two of you and did something really fucking shitty. What you did wasn't scandalous —and I don't want you to think it is." His voice is furious, sending shivers down my spine. I wasn't expecting that tone from him so it takes me by complete surprise.

He's letting little glimpses of him being protective show... and I like it. A lot.

"Understand?" he asks, his voice still gruff.

All I do is nod because no words come to mind.

Archer leans in, spreading his legs wide so that his knee bumps against mine. I don't move away from the slight press of our bodies, instead too focused on waiting for what he's about to say. His eyes flick to my lips for a moment before they meet mine. "For the record, we kissed on the second date. And it was the best kiss you've ever had."

"It was the best kiss *you* ever had," I correct, trying to tease him to ease the tension in the air around us.

"Yes, it was," he responds, a cocky smirk on his lips.

For the rest of the night, I find myself laughing far more than I ever thought I would. I'm not quite ready to admit it to myself yet, but I think I really enjoy Archer's company. It was an easy night with him and far different than I was expecting.

I don't love how he goes from hot to cold so easily. Hot at the church, cold in the car, and then to this teasing—maybe even flirty—man he was tonight. But it doesn't bother me enough for me to not have enjoyed the night together.

I climb into the large bed in the guest room he'd pointed me to, reveling in how comfortable the mattress is. Everything about the bed is far more comfortable than I was expecting. As I drift off to sleep, I'm fairly confident that this won't be as bad as I thought it'd be.

In fact, I could find myself really enjoying pretending to be in love with Archer Moore—and that's a dangerous realization.

13
Archer

"STOP MOVING," I TELL WINNIE, TIGHTENING MY ARM AROUND HER waist to try and keep her still.

She doesn't listen; if anything, she squirms even more despite my requests. "I'm not doing anything," she whispers, the smile on her face not faltering in the slightest.

I groan, trying to hold her up by the hips so I don't feel her grind against me again. I try to focus on the sound of the camera clicking. The photographer seems to be taking her sweet time with this position she has Winnie and me in, which is tragic for me, considering Winnie keeps grinding against my cock like we're at a high school prom.

"Winnie," I grit through clenched teeth. Her name comes out quiet enough for just the two of us to hear, but I have no doubt she clearly hears the pleading tone of my voice.

"I'm not doing anything," she repeats, doing exactly what she says she isn't doing by shifting her hips. If she didn't look so innocent and unaware of the effect she's having on me, I'd think she was maybe doing all of this on purpose.

I can't even close my eyes or have any kind of reaction to feeling her ass against my cock because there's a camera catching every single one of our movements.

I've really got to get a hold of myself. Maybe once the photos and the interview are over, I'll go for a run and hit the gym if needed. I need to do something to work off all the tension in my body—and all of it is because of my completely unaware, doe-eyed wife in my lap.

Last night had been far more tolerable than I was expecting it to be. At first, it pissed me off how I was enjoying her company, but then I realized it wasn't fair to take my anger out on her. It isn't her fault that the wedding didn't feel as for show as it should've been—that taking photos after together felt natural.

Even after we sat at the table for hours, getting to know one another, I found myself enjoying our time together. I've spent years building walls taller than the towers here in New York so no one would be able to get under my skin. Yet, we've spent one night as husband and wife, and I'm already fearing the worst— no matter how much I fight it, I know I'll let this woman in.

If she gives me enough soft smiles and timid laughs, I know all efforts to keep her at arm's length will be futile. It's hard to not let someone as kindhearted as her through the barriers.

"Just hold this pose for a few more seconds." The photographer's enthusiastic voice breaks me from my thoughts.

My grip tightens around Winnie's waist. I can feel the heat of her body through the thin fabric of the ivory dress she's wearing. Being this close to her means I can also feel her breath hitch when I bring her body slightly closer to me. I don't even realize I've done it until her back is pressed fully to my front. I must've shocked not only myself but also her with the movement because finally, she stops wiggling against me.

"We're almost done," I tell her, wondering if I said it to reassure myself that this is all almost over. I've spent the last hour pressed up against her in one way or another, and it's testing my restraint.

At least the photo part of the interview is almost through, but we still have to do the sit-down interview portion of it. I'm not as worried about the questions because we'll both be in our own space for it. "These are perfect," the photographer compliments, looking at the tiny screen on her camera with a wide smile on her face. "You guys can go ahead and get seated for the interview."

My hands drop from her waist like she's on fire. I'm half tempted to shove her off me, but I don't. Lucky for me, she slides off without any help from me. I try not to stare as she adjusts the skirt of her dress, her palms sliding down the fabric to smooth out any wrinkles that had formed during the shoot.

It's hard to not look at the line where the ivory fabric dances along her pale thighs. Some of the positions the photographer had us in today made the fabric drift even higher up her freckled thighs, making it hard to focus at times.

Why does the sight of her bare skin do something to me?

I clear my throat, realizing Winnie's already crossed the room and taken a seat in one of the lavish armchairs the team had styled for the interview. While they won't be taping the interview, they will be taking candid photos to possibly include in the feature. They wanted us seated right next to one another with the fireplace and decorated mantle behind us.

"Need a minute?" our interviewer, Ruby, asks, her eyebrows raised.

I shake my head, not wanting to think deeply into the satisfied smirk that's playing on her lips. "Nope. Let's get this started," I state, bounding over to the empty seat next to Winnie. I sit down next to her, tugging slightly at the collar of the sweater my stylist, Sara, had picked out for me this morning.

Both Sara and Winnie had asked for my input on the clothes we wore today. If it were my decision, I'd choose a variant of the same thing I wear to work every day. A button-up and a custom-made suit. Sara wouldn't hear anything of it. She'd insisted I wear something that coordinated with Winnie.

The two of them developed a fast friendship when they went to Winnie's room to pick something out. Quick on her feet, Winnie had explained that she didn't like sharing closet space, and that was the reason we weren't sharing one. Sara didn't seem to question it.

Those little details are things I hadn't really thought through when hastily agreeing to this marriage. I have staff in and out of my house almost every day. Luckily, they've all signed ironclad NDAs that they'd be stupid to ever break. It still reminded me that even when at home, Winnie and I will need to be careful playing the part of a newly married couple.

To keep up with the charade, I look over at my wife with a forced smile on my face. Hopefully, Ruby doesn't realize it doesn't reach my eyes. It's hard to smile through the tenseness of my body. I haven't had time to fully recover from having Winnie grinding against my cock for what felt like an hour but probably was only five minutes.

Winnie returns my smile, except hers does actually meet her eyes as she stares at me in a way that makes my heart come to life. She's too beautiful for her own good. So stunning, that for a moment, I'm lost in her wide, blue gaze. I pull my eyes from hers, instead letting my gaze travel down her body for a moment because I can't help myself.

I don't know if it was her or Sara who decided on her outfit for the day, but whoever it was did absolutely amazing. The dress fits her body perfectly but still leaves a lot to the imagination. Too much to the imagination, apparently, because I'm imagining too much of what she hides underneath the smooth fabric.

She's paired the dress with a blazer that cuts along her torso. It's a soft camel color, matching perfectly with the sweater Sara laid out for me to wear. For some reason, the little pearl buttons on the blazer catch my attention. I can't help but wonder what it'd be like to carefully undo every single one of them so I could see what she hides underneath.

There's a headband in her hair that matches her blazer. It's thin but brings a pop of something else to her red hair.

"Good to go?" Ruby asks, breaking me from my thoughts and pulling me back to the present.

Clearing my throat, I sit up in my chair and focus on Ruby

instead. She's still watching me with a knowing smile I'd love to ask more about.

"Yes," I answer, my voice tight. "Sorry," I add awkwardly, even though that's not something I typically do. "Got lost in thought for a minute." I end the sentence there, not wanting to admit what—or who—had me lost in thought. Not that she'd find it odd in the slightest; to her, Winnie and I are blissful newlyweds.

"You both just look so in love," Ruby, our interviewer, admires, a wide smile on her lips. "It's really refreshing to see."

"Wow," Winnie marvels, her gaze hot on my cheek. When I meet her eyes once again, I find it hard not to get lost in her aquamarine irises. "That's so nice, thank you," she finishes, not looking away from me.

Wanting to feed into the moment and play the part, I reach between us and take her hand in mine. My hand dwarfs hers, but somehow, it still seems like the perfect fit as my fingers interweave with hers. Her hand is cold in mine, so I squeeze hers, trying to make her skin as warm as possible.

Ruby stares at our joined hands for a few beats before she sits up straighter and plasters a smile on her face. "I really want this interview to feel like a conversation between friends. I know we don't know each other well, but I'm hoping we can really get to know one another through this process. And that you guys will be open about your love story. About what brought us here today."

She lets her words hang in the air for a bit. The other pairs of eyes trained on us, as well as the studio lighting aimed directly at us, make this seem like the furthest thing from a private conversation between friends. I don't voice my opinion, instead choosing to keep my jaw shut. I'm going to give her exactly what she wants—an epic love story.

If we really sell it today, it'll solidify Winnie's and my whirlwind romance to the rest of the world. If after today everyone believes Winnie and I are epically in love, then it'll keep her safe.

At least for now, and it buys me time to make damn sure Blake never does anything with that video.

"Where would you like us to start?" Winnie asks, surprising me by taking the lead.

She isn't who I thought she was, and it annoys me. Her father has allowed her to seem like this dutiful daughter with not a lot of personality outside of who he tells her to be. I guess Winnie has allowed that narrative as well.

But since our wedding yesterday, I've learned there's more bite to her than people would expect. She knows who she is—at least who she wants to be—but she seems at war with who she's supposed to be.

I give her hand a reassuring squeeze, wanting to communicate to her that I appreciate when she takes control. I swear she squeezes my hand back, but I half wonder if it's something I made up in my head.

Either way, she seems to get more comfortable by leaning back in the chair, all while keeping a hold of my hand.

"You could say it wasn't exactly love at first sight..." she begins.

14
Winnie

"So tell me, what was your first impression of Winnie?" Ruby asks, her tone excited, like she's about to get the hottest new gossip.

Maybe she *is* about to get the newest gossip. My stomach does a weird flip from nerves about what story we're about to give this reporter. I thought we'd ironed out the details enough last night, but now with her staring eagerly at us, I'm worried we didn't prepare enough.

Archer lets out a low chuckle that sends shivers down my spine. Or maybe it's his thumb absentmindedly tracing circles on the center of my palm that makes my skin break out in goosebumps.

"I'm not sure I could tell you my first impression." He looks over at me, something unreadable in his eyes. I so badly want to ask him what the pause in his words means—why he's looking at me like whatever is running through his mind is both happy and sad. "I've known about Winnie for as long as I can remember. It's no secret that our families have...history."

Ruby laughs. It doesn't have the same effect on me that Archer's did. "You could say that."

"So I don't think my very first impression of her is important here. I can tell you the impression I gathered from my grandfather and father, but that doesn't matter. The question you should be asking is what was my first *impactful* impression of her."

Ruby's eyebrows rise, seemingly unbothered by Archer telling her what questions she should be asking.

"Tell me about the first impression that mattered, then," Ruby requests, a smile still on her face.

I watch Archer carefully, wondering what he's going to say. My heart races in my chest because we hadn't talked about this question. We'd discussed that we'd tell her about the first time we hit it off, what our first date looked like, but we didn't prepare for first impressions.

But I guess our first impressions could go hand in hand with the night things supposedly cooled off between us. Or I guess you could say heated up, depending on how you look at it.

Archer leans back slightly, like he's completely at home with the cameras on him. "It was a charity function for breast cancer research. A year ago almost to the day. It was a cheesy masquerade theme. Everyone wore elaborate masks and evening gowns."

"Masks?" Ruby pipes up, crossing her legs and watching Archer with eager anticipation. "Was Winnie wearing one?"

He nods confidently. "One that matched her dress perfectly. The dress was a deep navy color, so dark it looked black unless you looked at it underneath the light. The mask was the same color."

"And you knew it was her?"

My eyes drift to Archer, watching him closely because I have no idea what he's about to say. "Yeah," he finally answers, his voice deep and raspy. "She's hard to miss."

I can't look away from him as I hang on to his every word. I remember the event vividly...but I don't remember him. I didn't even know he was there. Yet...he seems to talk about it as if he was and I just somehow missed him.

He runs a hand over his mouth. "My first thought when I

saw her was that she was absolutely breathtaking, so breathtaking that it was a haunting, chilling feeling."

Ruby leans forward, just as enthralled with what Archer is saying as I am. "Why's that?"

"Because my second thought was that, given our family history, I knew she was the last person who should've caught my attention."

I wonder if either one of them hear me sucking in air at his words. He talks about that night so clearly, but I truly don't remember him being there. And I've replayed that night in my head over and over again countless times.

It was a night I could never forget because of what happened.

Was I so preoccupied with what was happening with me that I never noticed he was there?

Even though I think he'd prefer it to not be that way, it's hard to ever miss Archer. He takes up so much space, his sheer presence so dominating that I don't know how I could've forgotten he was there altogether.

"Did you have that same impression that night?" Ruby asks, breaking me free from my memories.

I don't answer at first, too busy staring at Archer, wondering where he was at that party to immediately give a response. "Uh," I begin, awkwardly shifting in my chair. My fingers loosen around his for a moment, but he doesn't take the hint to drop my hand. If anything, his fingers wrap even tighter around mine. "That night is a bit of a blur to me," I confess.

It isn't too far from the truth. I'd had a few more cocktails that night than I typically do after getting in an argument with my dad. But I still wasn't drunk. I remember the night; I just couldn't give you any details about the man sitting next to me— about my husband.

Archer saves me by speaking up, the nonchalant tone to his voice getting rid of any of the awkward tension in the air. "While that was my first real and raw impression of her, it took a few more events for me to finally get the nerve to talk to her."

"You don't strike me as a man who gets nervous," Ruby fires at him.

This makes him smile, a slow smile that takes a few heartbeats to build. "No one ever made me nervous until Winnie." He looks over at me, and if he wasn't so wealthy, I'd tell him to look into acting because there's so much adoration in his eyes I almost believe him, even though I know none of it is real. "Do you blame me? Look at her."

I'm just left staring in awe because there are so many feelings hitting me at once while hearing him talk about our fake beginning like this. To hear him talk about me like this, it's too much all at once, yet somehow still not enough.

My blush creeps up my chest and spills into my cheeks.

It's all pretend, I remind myself. *Pretend, pretend, pretend*. He doesn't mean it.

My stupid, naive heart leaps in my chest, not getting the hint that none of the loving words he's saying about me are true.

Ruby's eyes are wide with delight as she looks from Archer to me and back. "So, what? You waited patiently until you finally spoke with her at another event, and you guys hit it off?"

Both Archer and I laugh at the same time. He's probably remembering the same thing as me. Us sitting at his dining table last night arguing over who was going to be more interested in our made-up love story.

"I waited. I'm not sure you could call me patient about the entire situation." Archer laughs. He wipes his free hand down his face, trying to remove what I think is a genuine smile and not one for performance's sake.

Ruby focuses on me. "Did you make him work for it?" Everyone in the room seems to be leaning forward, as if how we started dating is really that interesting. We're just two people—I don't get the allure, but they're all waiting for me to answer, staring at me expectantly.

So I give them an answer, pretending that everything out of Archer's and my mouths isn't fake. "I had no desire to seek him out. There are so many people to speak with at those events; how was I to know that the heir to my family's rival wanted to speak with me?"

Archer shrugs, that charming smile still on his lips. He doesn't look fazed at all by me telling everyone in the room I didn't want to talk to him. "Eventually, I made my move. We had a normal, boring conversation. One thing led to another, and she finally agreed to a first date with me."

I shake my head, pretending to laugh at his joke. "*Finally* being the key word."

The entire room laughs with us, obviously amused by the thought of *the* Archer Moore having to really work for a first date with me. He had a point last night when he said it'd seem out of character for him to chase a woman.

If the wide eyes and bright smiles of those in the room with us give any indication of how they feel about him changing, they all love it. They're eating out of the palms of our hands, and I think Archer can see it, too, because he effortlessly feeds into the narrative, even if it paints him as a different person from how the rest of the world envisions him to be.

"Was the first date a good one?" Ruby pushes, her question hurried like she hadn't even really thought about it before voicing it.

I keep my one hand locked in Archer's, but the other reaches across and traces his sharp jaw. He jumps at my touch but then leans into it when he realizes we aren't alone and I'm doing it for a reason. At least, I think I'm doing it for everyone watching.

Or did I just need to feel more of his skin against mine?

"I married him, didn't I?" I tease, not looking at Ruby with my answer. Archer and I are too busy staring at one another, seemingly trapped in some kind of moment I don't want to think too deeply about.

"Everything about your courtship seems dreamy. How does it feel to lock down Archer Moore?" Ruby asks. She laughs nervously, as if she knows it's kind of an outlandish question but she wanted to ask it anyway.

"Sometimes it doesn't feel real," I answer honestly.

"Sometimes I look at her and lose my breath at the wonderful, life-changing realization that I was the man to steal the attention of Winnie Bishop," Archer responds, the husky timber of his voice and the intense way he looks at me sending shivers all over my body.

15
Archer

"Do you feel like it went well?" Winnie wonders, stretching her legs out in front of her on the couch. I sit on the opposite side of the room from her on an entirely different couch because after being near her all day, I had to put some space between our bodies for my own self-preservation.

The interview ended a few hours ago, but the moment all of the extra bodies were out of the house, Winnie and I went our separate ways. I practically ran to my room to strip out of my dress clothes and into something I could work out in. I didn't have anything scheduled with my trainer, but I needed some sort of release after spending all day with her pressed against me.

I shouldn't be thinking about all the skin the dress and blazer hid from me. I have no business replaying the way her stomach muscles tightened underneath my touch when I pulled her body flush to mine. To the world, she's my wife, but in private, I don't have any right to have dirty, filthy thoughts about her.

So I rid myself of every one until my body was on the brink of exhaustion at the gym. I did the rowing machines, lifted, and even cooled down by going for a three-mile run because my body needed to do something to get rid of all the pent-up tension.

And yet, the moment she walked downstairs, her hair wet

from a shower as she searched for something to eat, I knew it still wasn't enough.

The problem is, I'm fairly confident I'm desperate to fuck my fake wife. And while we haven't set it as a boundary, I know it isn't a good idea for anything physical to happen between us. It'd only complicate things, and marrying someone to save their reputation—and get a foothold in your rival's company—is complicated enough.

"Was it *that* bad?" Winnie groans, sitting up on the couch and looking at me with curious eyes from across the room.

I sigh, trying not to think about the way she's propped herself on her elbows and how it makes the fabric of her silk camisole tighten around her peaked nipples. I don't think she even realizes the matching robe she'd thrown on has fallen down her shoulder, giving me a view that's far too distracting.

"I think they bought every word we said." I pin my eyes to the ceiling as I reassure her. She's across the room from me, and I can still smell the sweet scent of her body wash—or maybe it's her shampoo. I don't know what it is she uses that smells so fucking intoxicating, but whatever it is, it permeates my senses and causes way too much inner turmoil.

All I can smell is vanilla and oranges, and the combination is lethal, considering I already can't get her out of my head.

"Did I do okay?" Her voice is so soft, so hesitant that it breaks my heart a little. How many times has she been scolded for not doing things correctly during interviews or out in public that it makes her so unsure of herself?

I pinch the bridge of my nose, wondering why I thought it was a good idea to come downstairs at all. I should've locked myself in my room—or my office—and not retreated until the morning. It would've been easy for me to ask Luther to stop by with a food delivery. He'd even bring it to me in my office if I'd asked, and then I wouldn't have had to see Winnie at all.

But instead, I'm stupid—or a masochist—probably both—

and came downstairs when I knew she'd eventually come down because of her own hunger.

What I hadn't expected was to be so disarmed by the sight of her in a damn pair of pajamas.

"You did great, Winnie," I tell her, trying to lace my tone with conviction, even though I'm exhausted. "You were perfect. You're perfect," I add, the words escaping my mouth before I can think better of them.

If she notices my slipup, she doesn't say anything. Instead, she brings her legs to her chest and wraps her arms around them. Her chin rests on her knees as she stares at me. I don't know what she's looking for in my eyes or if she finds it. "I just want to do this right," she admits, her voice low and vulnerable. "I don't want to mess anything up."

"We're the authors of our own narrative through all of this. There's nothing to mess up."

"There's more to mess up because of it. What if I don't play the part good enough and they find out it's fake? Then not only could I have a video of me having sex released, but the world would know I agreed to marry someone to protect myself. What does that make me then?"

I take a deep breath, fighting the urge to tell her I'd burn the whole fucking world down before I ever let any bad press be released about her. The thought pops into my head that I'd allow a thousand negative articles to run about me before I'd ever let one run about her.

I push it from my mind as quickly as it came. I barely know her. She's still the daughter of our direct competitor's CEO, and no matter how much we now own of that business, there's no reason for me to ever put her reputation over mine. I need to remember that.

"I know you said you don't trust me, Winnie, but I need you to trust my words when I say this, there's nothing I wouldn't do to make sure that video never gets released. I'd never fucking allow it, even if it cost me my reputation to protect you, I would do it at all costs." I want to tell her to trust not just my words but also trust me. Her words from the other day are still replaying in my head. She doesn't want to give me her trust, and that upsets me. I sigh, trying to come up with more ways I can assure her that nothing negative will ever be said about her on my watch. "We played the part beautifully. And we'll continue to play it so well that anyone who knows us—and those that don't—will believe us to be in the happiest, realest marriage one could imagine."

She's quiet for so long I wonder if it's the end of our conversation. I don't know which I'd rather. For her to go upstairs and finally be rid of her presence or for her to stay right here and let me inside her mind a little. We finished dinner an hour ago. There isn't any real reason for us to both be sitting here other than wanting each other's company.

"I wanted to tell you I'm sorry," Winnie finally says. Her tone is so hushed that I almost don't hear her at all.

Her words have me sitting up and pinning her with a look of uncertainty. "I said you did perfect. There's nothing to apologize for."

She shakes her head. "No. Not for that. I'm sorry for dragging you into this with me. If I hadn't been stupid and—"

I'm across the room and practically heaving my body against hers in an instant. My fingers press to her mouth, stopping her from saying anything else. "Don't even think about finishing that fucking sentence," I hiss, furious she'd even think she had to apologize for this. "You have nothing to be sorry for. Both of our families get something from this deal, Winnie. Don't make me out to be this white knight who saved you out of the goodness of my heart. That isn't who I am. I'm not a good man and I came into this deal with *very* selfish intentions."

She blinks, her chest rising and falling in rapid succession. I don't know if it's because of our close proximity or because of my deep, angry tone, but something makes her breaths get heavy.

"Don't make me out to be a good man. I'll only disappoint you," I finish, letting my gaze drop to where my fingers press to her lips. With every single one of her exhales, her chest brushes against my arm and it makes me not want to move at all. I want to stay locked in this position with her, but I know better.

I pull away, sliding down the couch to put distance between us. But I don't change couches, even though I know I should. "And don't you ever apologize to me again. You were put in a terrible situation—one that wasn't your fault. You have nothing to be sorry for, and you'll just piss me off if you apologize again. *Okay?*" My voice breaks a little with the last word, and I hate every second of it.

I hate that she gets real, raw emotions out of me. I hate that we've barely spent any time together and she's making me feel things. Albeit, right now, it's red-hot anger. It's still something. And I don't like to feel anything. I much prefer leaving emotions out of everything if possible.

She bolts upstairs without any further explanation as to why she's leaving, and I'm all too aware of the rush of disappointment I feel because of it.

I despise that the moment I'm left alone downstairs—a place I've been alone countless times before—that I miss sharing the same air as her.

16
Winnie

EMMA

Can I just say how grateful I am to have rich friends? I can't wait to party tomorrow night with all of New York's finest men!

MARGO

I remember our NYU frat parties still being very fun.

EMMA

Gasp! Don't let Beck read that text. He can't know you ever had fun before him.

MARGO

Shut up. You know he knows everything. I've even let him look at some of our old, drunk college videos.

EMMA

If you showed him the one from Halloween sophomore year I will end our friendship right now.

MARGO

Beck says you made such a great naughty nurse!

EMMA

MARGO MORETTI I AM SO MAD AT YOU
RIGHT NOW.

My fingers hover over my keyboard as I think about what to
say back to Margo and Emma, but I can't think of anything. It
feels weird to talk about our drunk college days when I'm
keeping such a big secret from them.

I got married. And neither one of them was there. I know
whenever they find out about the marriage—which they will,
and soon—it'll crush them both to know I didn't include them.

The guilt eats me alive as I ignore their texts, even though I
miss them terribly. Emma's already onto me. She's called three
times this morning, and I've ignored every single one of them.
Emma's persistent. It wouldn't shock me if soon she showed up
on my apartment's doorstep to figure out why I'm ignoring her.

Except she won't find me there. Because I'm married and
playing house with a man I barely know.

But a man I want to know...

A man I want to know everything there is to know about. I
tell myself it's because if I figure out Archer Moore, maybe it
could help my dad in some way. Sure, I'm the one who backed
us into this corner to begin with. But maybe if I knew more
about Archer, I could help us become better than the Moore
dynasty.

Or maybe, just maybe, I want to get to know Archer for
reasons that have nothing to do with our last names and everything to do with the fact that he intrigues me. He's hot and cold,
mysterious but blunt, and long after we parted ways last night—
or me running for the hills from him—I lay awake wondering
who exactly my husband was.

MARGO

Camden is coming into town with his new girlfriend. They're both attending the gala tomorrow with us.

EMMA

OH MY GOD! CAMDEN HAS A GIRLFRIEND?

I'm so excited to get to know her! Although, I feel a little bad for her.

Camden's kind of a grumpy asshole.

MARGO

I thought we could have some dresses waiting at Camden's apartment tonight for us to try on. Her name is Pippa and I thought it might be fun for her to pick something out to wear. The guys can cook while we play dress up.

EMMA

I get to try on dresses that cost more than my paycheck AND have Beck and Camden cook for me?

This sounds like the best night of my life.

MARGO

No. The best night of your life would involve a rich, single man buying you a dress and making you dinner.

EMMA

The dream. When will it be my turn?

MARGO

I'll tell Beck and Camden that we're in. Now we just need to hear from Winnie.

EMMA

Winnie, where are you? I know you're incapable of sleeping in. Look at your phone, bitch.

A sad smile creeps onto my face as I stare down at my phone. The light pours through my large bedroom windows. Orange light dances along my comforter. Part of me wants to pull on some of my running gear and get outside and go for a run. Or even a walk. I miss the fresh air, and I think getting out is exactly what I need to clear my head.

Just as I begin to climb out of bed, my phone vibrates again.

MARGO

> She's probably just busy. Winnie, just let me know if you'll be there tonight so I can plan accordingly! It'll be a fun girls night catered by the guys.

I sigh, deciding I'll use the fresh air to help me think through a way to tell the two people who matter most to me in this world that I got married without telling them. Margo and I haven't talked as much as we normally do lately. She's busy being a world-renowned artist and a newlywed. But Emma, she knew minor details about Blake. I know she's going to have a ton of questions when it comes out that I got married, and it wasn't to the man I last told her about.

I've always been good at avoiding things when I really want to, and this is one of those situations. Without a second thought, I turn my phone off and slide it underneath my pillow. I don't need it to go for a walk, and if either of my friends tries to call me, it'll go straight to voicemail, and they'll assume my phone probably died. I have always been known for forgetting to charge it anyway.

It doesn't take me long to pick out an outfit for the morning. Later today, I'll put on makeup and get ready for whatever Archer has planned for us, but for the morning, I want to have a fresh face. I want to feel the sun on my skin immediately and don't want to take any time to paint on makeup that I'll just wash off in the shower.

I slide my legs into a pair of black workout leggings and adjust the band, making sure it lies flat and comfortably around my waist. Next, I pull on a sports bra and the matching long-sleeve workout top. I didn't bring too many of my exercise jackets from my apartment. I hadn't really thought about packing much outside of outfits for brunches and events and fancy things. But I did bring one of my favorites. I pull it on, leaving it unzipped until I get outside.

I rush through pulling my hair into a tight ponytail, slicking back any of the red flyaway strands before I grab my tennis shoes and head downstairs.

It's quiet in the house. So quiet I wonder if Archer is even home. I'd rushed away from him so fast last night we didn't even talk about the plans for the day. Typically, I receive a text from my father's assistant with my plans for the day. There's always some luncheon, some ribbon cutting, or something for me to attend.

I haven't received any news of today, and I'm wondering if my marriage to Archer gets me out of some of the obligations typically given to me.

Or maybe he's still so angry with me that he doesn't even want to see me.

And maybe I'm just going to have to live with that.

It feels weird to have a day wide open—at least for now. It's possible Archer will show up and tell me all the things I have to do, but for now, as I creep down the stairs and look for any trace of anyone else being home, I don't have a single obligation.

It feels almost…liberating.

It's eerily quiet in this big house all alone. Everything seems so neat and perfect. It was this time yesterday the living room was filled with people and cameras, all eager to know how Archer and I fell in love.

Today, it just feels empty and lonely. I open the fridge to grab a water bottle, wondering if it always felt like this for Archer, too. He made it seem like he didn't always stay here. It wouldn't shock me if he was married to his work and not here much at all.

Unscrewing the cap from the lid, I take a drink of the water as my eyes trace over his living space. The decorators did a great job, although there are a few things I would've done differently if it was me who was doing the interior design. No matter if my vision would've been different or not, I feel a tinge of sadness in my chest of how empty it must've been before he hired them.

For a minute, I wonder if I should go upstairs and grab my phone so I can listen to music, but I decide against it. Today, it'll just be me, my thoughts, and the sounds of the city. Which sounds perfect. My eyes dance around the clean kitchen as I wonder if I should leave Archer some sort of note on where I am, but I decide although he's my husband, he isn't my keeper. I'm allowed to come and go as I please without having to tell him.

I head to the front door, caught up in the excitement of getting lost in the business of New York when I collide with a hot, chiseled body.

"Fuck," Archer snaps, his large hands grabbing my shoulders as if to make sure he doesn't take me down in the collision.

"Sorry," I mutter, steadying myself by pressing my hands to his hard, sweaty chest.

My eyes go wide, realizing exactly what I'm doing. I quickly pull my hands free, tucking them into the pockets of my jacket as I try not to think about how hard and defined his abs were under my touch.

"Where do you think you're going?" Archer demands, pulling headphones from his ears. His eyebrows bunch together on his forehead in a scowl.

No wonder he didn't hear me before running right into me; he was listening to music at full blast.

My lips twitch with the start of a smile. "Are you listening to Taylor Swift?"

"Are you leaving without telling me where you're going?" he

fires back, completely ignoring my question. He twists the wire of his headphones around his finger, watching me closely with his face pinched together in annoyance.

I won't let him off that easily. "I didn't pin you for a secret Swiftie," I tease.

He frowns. I try not to focus on the sweat running down his neck. It's October and chilly outside. Why is he so hot and sweaty? And why can't I look away?

"She makes great music," he continues, using the back of his hand to wipe sweat from his brow. "Now, tell me where you think you're going." His voice is rough and demanding, and if any other person talked to me like that, it might rub me the wrong way. I've been bossed around my entire life; I don't need someone else to answer to. But I swear there's almost an undertone of worry in his question, and it makes my body break out in shivers.

"I'm going for a walk. Or maybe a run. I haven't decided. Either way, I didn't know I had to tell you every single one of my movements."

He takes a step closer. The music gets louder with his proximity. I think he might be listening to a Taylor Swift playlist because a new song has begun, one from a completely different album than the one that was playing when he first walked in. "Two days ago, your ex-boyfriend was threatening to sabotage your image out of pure hatred for your family. He had so much hate for them that no amount of money would have him handing that video over. You can't just walk through the city alone."

I roll my eyes. "It's Blake. He's obviously an asshole, but he isn't going to physically hurt me, Archer."

"You don't know that." His voice cracks slightly at the end. There it is again, a little glimpse that makes me wonder if he is, in fact, worried about me.

"Okay," I say, drawing out the word dramatically. "I'm going for a walk. I don't think my crazy ex-situationship is going to find me all the way out here. He always hated Central Park."

Archer's abs tighten as he pulls a deep breath in. "I'm coming with you."

A weird sound comes from my throat. Something between a gasp and a yelp. My eyes roam over his body. It's very obvious that he's already worked out. *Too obvious.* God, he's really hiding a lot of sharp lines and defined muscles underneath those fancy suits. I can't look away. "It looks like you've already, uh…"

"Already what?" he asks, his tone annoyed that I can't come up with words.

Got all perfectly sweaty. Thank god what actually leaves my mouth is, "Worked out. I can go alone. I'll be fine."

He rolls his eyes at me. Like actually rolls his eyes as he wipes sweat from his forehead. I fight the urge to ask him if there's a secret workout room in this house I should know about. Surely, he wasn't walking around New York in a pair of workout shorts that hug his thick thighs perfectly and no shirt.

"I'm going to go get a hoodie. Do not leave without me." His voice is so commanding that my feet stay planted even as he disappears upstairs.

If I rushed out the door right now, I'd be able to ditch him. I could disappear into the groups of people walking around Central Park. But then I'd miss out on getting some alone time with him, and for some reason, I really like the idea of casually walking around Central Park with him.

It seems almost normal, and I want it more than I should.

Maybe he thought I'd run, too. Because when he rushes back downstairs while still pulling his sweatshirt on like he didn't want to waste a second of leaving me alone, he looks shocked to see me standing in the same place.

"I don't need a bodyguard to go for a walk," I argue, trying to fill the awkward silence as he comes to a stop in front of me. My fingers ball in my pockets with the vivid memory of what his muscles felt like underneath my fingertips. At least now the sweatshirt hides his perfectly sculpted body.

"And I don't care. I'm going to go for a walk with my wife because she wants to. Let's go."

He stares at me for a few seconds, his face serious. I want to know why he clenches his jaw, to ask him why he seems so angry to be doing this with me when he's the one who insisted on it. But I don't say anything. Instead, I follow him out the door.

We're waiting at the crosswalk when I finally look up at him, noticing some of the tension from his face has disappeared.

"Good morning, by the way," I say, not bothering to hide the sass in my tone.

This makes him smile. He looks way too handsome when he smiles. It's jarring, earning something so real from him when I've learned he doesn't offer genuine smiles very often. "Good morning, Winnie."

17
Archer

By the twentieth time Winnie looks over at me out of the corner of her eye, I finally say something.

"Why do you keep looking at me like that?" I blurt, keeping my eyes trained on the path in front of us instead of looking at her.

She sighs, but her steps don't falter as we continue to navigate the busy Central Park path. "How am I looking at you?"

"Like there's something wrong with me," I answer her, fighting the urge to grab her elbow and pull her close to me as she almost walks right into a jogger running with their dog because she was too busy staring at me.

"I just don't understand why you insisted on coming for a walk if you're going to scowl and stay silent the entire time."

"I don't scowl."

This makes her laugh. It's loud and free and one of the best sounds I've ever heard. I want to make her do it again. Which is unfortunate for me because I've never been known to be a man with a great sense of humor.

But I'd do just about anything to hear that sound again.

Winnie stops, leaving me no other option but to follow suit so we stay together. With a loud sigh, I turn around to face her—fully aware that the look I'm giving her right now is indeed a scowl.

Her mind must be in the same place as mine because she shakes her head. She takes a step closer to me and reaches out to place her fingertip at the corner of my mouth. "You're scowling right now, Archer."

Archer. The way she says my name rattles something deep inside my chest. So many people over the years have said it, and it did nothing for me. When she does, I want to hear her say it again and again.

She keeps her fingertips pressed to the corner of my mouth while I fight an inner battle with myself. Part of me wants to pull her closer; the other part of me wants to push her away and not see her until I have to again because this pull I feel toward her can't be good.

Her eyes go to my lips for a fraction of a second before she meets my eyes. Her fingers push my lip up as she attempts to wipe away my permanent scowl. "You should try smiling more," she insists, her voice soft and sweet. "You look handsome doing it."

Everything about her is soft and sweet. Nothing about me is soft or sweet. The two of us have a marriage that is on paper and for appearances only. With her this close, I worry how I'll continue to resist her.

With her this close, I'm also realizing that she's not wearing any makeup. I've always seen her at parties and events with a full face of makeup. She's stunning no matter what, but this might be my favorite way I've ever seen her.

It's like I'm getting to see the real Winnie. Not the person her father told her to be, but just her. And while I can pretend the only reason I demanded to go on a walk with her this morning was to keep her safe, I have to admit to myself that part of me also wanted to have more stolen moments with her that weren't for show.

I wanted to continue to get to know who she is when her mask isn't on.

Because one thing I'm quickly learning is Winnie isn't the

person everyone thinks. She's so much...*more*. That realization makes me want to know everything there is to know about her. Maybe it's because I know who I show the world and who I am inside are two different people, and I've found solace in knowing maybe she and I are one and the same.

She pulls her hand away from my face and tucks it back into her pocket. The wind hits my cheek, and suddenly, everything feels more cold without her touch. "Your silence tells me you have no plans on trying to smile more anytime soon."

I smirk. "At least we're on the same page."

She narrows her eyes at me, her nose crinkling with the motion. "You know, telling me you never smile only makes me want to get you to do it more."

I find myself smiling more with you already. I swallow, knowing I will not be admitting that out loud. "You can try. It's not going to work."

She nods, a playful smile on her lips. Something tells me she doesn't believe me at all. "Noted. You can scowl all you want on our walk, but you could at least have a conversation with me."

People walk by us, probably annoyed that we're standing in the middle of the pathway, seemingly unaware that there's anyone around us. It's rude, and I can't seem to care. I don't want to look away from her. I *can't* look away. She's captured my attention, and until she stops looking at me like she believes I'm a decent man who deserves to spend a lazy morning with her, I'm not going to break the moment.

"I wasn't aware you wanted to talk," I confess, dipping my chin low to look at my shuffling feet. "You were going for a walk alone. I thought you wouldn't want to talk to me."

"What if I always want to talk to you?" Her eyes go wide the moment the words spill from her lips. She regains composure as quickly as it happened, but it doesn't matter. I still saw her reaction. It's as if she didn't mean to ask that question out loud.

But she *did* say it out loud. I heard it, and I know it's

dangerous and reckless, but I weave my arm through hers and guide her down the path. "Then, let's talk."

She follows my lead easily, our steps falling in sync as we take in the beautiful October morning. The leaves have turned from green to brilliant hues of orange, yellow, and red. Fall is always one of my favorite times of the year. There's just something about how beautiful Manhattan looks as it prepares for another cold winter that captivates me. Fallen leaves crunch under our feet as the breeze wraps around our cheeks in a way that isn't too cold but actually refreshing.

"What do you propose we talk about?" she asks, returning a smile from a woman pushing a stroller.

I mull her words over for a moment, relishing in the way her fingertips press against my bicep. "On our way over here, you seemed quiet."

"I'm always quiet."

"This was a different kind of quiet. It's like your mind was somewhere else."

I feel her arm tense in mine. Something is definitely bothering her, and I want to know what it is. "It's nothing. It doesn't matter."

"It matters to me." My jaw clenches in irritation. I wish she'd open up to me so I can fix whatever is clearly bothering her.

She takes far too long to answer for my liking. "Why?" she asks, her voice lowered and full of curiosity.

Because despite knowing better, I think you matter to me. "Because it's obviously something that's bothering you," I answer, knowing that answer is safer.

"My friends want me to hang out with them tonight."

"And you don't want to?"

"I *do* want to. I want to see them. I miss both of them so much. But I also don't know how to tell them about us."

I nod, trying to think of what to tell her. The truth is, I don't really have people in my life who question my decisions. Sure, I have friends. But none of them will bat an eye when I say I'm married. We just don't care about each other's lives like that. I understand that for someone like her, someone who has best friends she tells everything to, this will be hard to navigate.

"Tell them we were keeping our life private."

She glares at me. It doesn't look as menacing as she probably thinks it does. She's far too sweet and beautiful to look scary, even when she's attempting to give me a dirty look. "Emma doesn't know the word 'private.' Margo, maybe. She kept a lot of things from us when she married Beck, but Emma will hound me with questions. She knows me well. I'm scared she won't believe me."

I'd forgotten one of her best friends married Beckham Sinclair. He was a year above me in school. He was a nice guy—or as nice as guys come at a prep school full of rich assholes who were all born with a silver spoon and a promise of being someone important in the world.

"We'll just have to make her believe us. Friends keep secrets from friends all the time."

She gives my words some thought for a moment. The silence between us is comfortable. I don't feel the need to prod her with more questions to get her to answer the one I asked moments ago. I know she'll answer me; she's just coming up with what she wants to say. "I want to go tonight, but I don't think I will. They'll be at the event tomorrow. It'll probably be easier to make them believe we're married if we're together."

"We'll figure it out. We had people almost weeping during our interview yesterday when we were telling them our love story. Tomorrow will be easy."

A sarcastic laugh comes from her lips. "You obviously haven't met my friends. Nothing with Emma is ever easy."

"I'm excited to meet them. It'll all work out."

"You sound so sure."

I pull her against me for a moment. It's quick, something a friend would do to a friend in an encouraging way, but any time we touch doesn't feel as friendly as it should. "I am sure. Look at me. Anyone would fall in love with me. They'll believe it easily."

She shakes her head, but the worry on her face seems to melt away. "It probably is easier to believe we fell in love as opposed to the real story." She plays with the end of her ponytail as she aims a playful smile in my direction. "My friends would never believe me if I looked at them and said a guy I was dating decided to try and blackmail me with a sex tape. But there's a kicker—he's not doing it to get money because that'd be too easy. He's doing it because, for some odd reason, he hates me and my family and wants revenge. So I was forced to do the next logical thing to fix it...marry into a family people are afraid of."

I can't help but frown at her reminder of this Blake guy. I've already had my assistant look into him. Sure, no publication will listen to him, but he's still a loose end, and I don't like loose ends. I plan to pay him a visit, and by the time our conversation is over, I'll be sure that all traces of that video and the photos are gone.

He'll know that he's as good as dead if he ever tries to mess with Winnie again.

"See? I told you it's really not as complicated as you think. People love love stories. Our grand announcement to the world tomorrow will go smoothly."

She lets out a burst of air, her cheeks puffing out with the movement. "Let's hope."

18
Archer

THE APARTMENT BUILDING IS DISGUSTING. I TRY NOT TO GAG AS I walk past an open garbage bag, trash spilling out into the hallway. It looks like something ripped open the bag and rifled through the contents, and it is so molded and decayed I can't even make out what they originally were. It smells, and I'm already ready to be out of this shithole.

I refuse to leave until I talk to this Blake kid. As I look for the apartment number Luther swore was his, I try to imagine Winnie ever coming to this place. I fucking hope he never invited her here. It's not a safe area, and I cannot envision her having to step over trash just to get to the apartment of the boy she liked. I'd call him a man, but his actions don't deserve that in the slightest.

My feet come to a halt in front of apartment thirty-six. The six has turned upside down on the screw, looking more like a nine but I know better. Wanting to get out of this place and never step foot anywhere near it again, I bring my knuckles to the rotting wood door and knock.

There's movement on the other side of the door but no talking. As far as I'm aware, he lives alone. I was disappointed to not find out as much about him as I wanted to, but I still found out enough.

It was stupid for Spencer to hire him in the first place. If he'd done the research he was supposed to, he'd know there was more to Blake Billings than anyone knew. I've taken it upon myself to silence him once and for all.

I know he's on the other side of the door from his loud movements. When he doesn't answer, I knock again. This time, much harder. He isn't going to avoid me.

"Blake!" I bark, letting my palm slap against the wood. "I know you're in there. Open the door."

Footsteps approach and then come to a stop. He's got to be standing on the other side of it, probably trying to figure out who I am and why I'm here. He must realize that I'm not going anywhere because he eventually opens the door.

Fuck. He looks rough is the first thing that goes through my mind. The second is what the hell did Winnie see in this guy?

Maybe if I looked past the overgrown beard and the dark circles under his eyes, I could see the potential, but I'm still not sure of it.

"Who are you?" he asks, barely holding the door open enough for us to talk.

"Your worst fucking nightmare," I respond, kicking his door open and strolling into an apartment even messier than the hallway.

"What the hell!" he yells, barreling right at me.

I hold my hands up, knowing this boy couldn't fucking touch me if he wanted to fight. "You might want to think twice about laying a hand on me."

"Then get out of my apartment," he spits. The more I look at him, the more I want to ask Winnie what she possibly could've seen in this pathetic excuse of a man.

My eyes roam his dirty apartment. His entire makeshift dining room has been turned into an office. There are two plastic tables against the wall with four monitors spanning them. Empty beer cans and cigarette butts litter the table and floor. "Trust me," I sneer, absolutely judging him for the filth he's living in, "I want to get out of this disgusting shithole as quickly as possible. But first, I'm here to have a little chat with you, Blake."

His face turns white. "I don't want to talk."

I smile, loving the rush of adrenaline that pumps through my veins. This will be fun.

"I don't remember asking what you wanted to do." My eyes cut to his dirty couch. There's a large stain on the tan fabric—but the longer I look at it, the more I wonder if the couch is supposed to be that color or if it started out much lighter. I wince, my skin crawling from being here. "Sit," I demand, knowing there's no way in hell I'm going to sit anywhere.

He takes a seat, jamming his hands into his armpits as his eyes watch me carefully. "Who are you, and why are you here?"

I look down my nose, scoffing at him. "Archer Moore. There's really no use in trying to act like you have the upper hand here by being the one asking the questions, though. I'm in control."

"Still don't know why you'd be here," he responds.

"I'm here because you've disrespected my wife." I don't even bother to hide the venom laced in my words.

This catches his attention. His eyebrows draw in on his forehead as a pronounced wrinkle appears between them. "Your *wife*?" He laughs, as if he's relieved that was my comment. "Was she at the club last night? Fuck, sorry, dude, I didn't think any of them were married."

I see red. My vision goes blurry for a second, and I have to stuff my hands into my pockets just to fight the urge to stop my knuckles from connecting with his face.

"No," I growl, taking a step toward him. He must see the anger radiating through my body because his eyes go wide in fear. "Winifred Bishop. My wife."

His shoulders tense. Surely Spencer told him about our marriage. Or maybe he didn't. Maybe he was lazy and knew that even though this guy could take the video to any publication he wanted, none of them would actually run it.

Now it isn't only Blake's face I want to connect with my knuckles. I want to do the same with Spencer for being so careless. Did he really just expect us to clean up everything now that he's married his daughter off to me?

Apparently.

"Winnie would never marry you," he hisses, his voice desperate, as if he's trying to figure out for himself if she would or not. "She loved me a week ago. There's no way she got married."

I laugh, loving the sound of shock—and maybe even hurt—in his voice. The fucker apparently cared about her. Just not enough to stop whatever revenge plot he has. "Oh, she got married—to me. And I don't like people messing with what's mine."

He flinches. "She isn't yours."

I cock my head to the side, wondering how the hell this guy can think he cares for her when he's trying to ruin her life. "Oh, but she is. She's my wife. *Mine.* And I'm very, very upset that you had the goddamn nerve to come after her."

He spits at my feet. I take one step to the side. His spit isn't the grossest thing on this cesspool of an apartment's floor, so it doesn't bother me. "I don't believe you, asshole." He seethes, my words clearly affecting him more than he wants to let on. "I know an obsessed chick when I see one. Last week, she was pretty much begging on her knees for me. She was so desperate for attention. Begging isn't the only time she got on her kne—"

Before he finishes the sentence, there's a loud cracking sound throughout his living room as my knuckles connect with his eye.

He shrieks like a goddamn child.

I push myself away from him before I punch him again. The desire is there, but I have to be at a charity gala soon, and I don't have time to deal with such a pathetic excuse of a human. It's been years since I've thrown a punch, but I couldn't hold back after hearing him say such vile things about Winnie. "You don't get to talk about my wife like that." I seethe, anger coursing through my veins.

The punch split his brow, blood beginning to seep from the wound. I knew I'd only throw one. I wanted to make it count. By the blossoming redness under his eye, it's clear I did just that. He runs his fingertip through the blood, glaring at me with his remaining good eye. "She's not your fucking wife."

Bored, I pick at a pretend piece of lint from my sleeve. "I can't wait for Monday when all the press on our wedding runs. It was a beautiful, private ceremony. We even gave an interview after to let people in on our love story that's been blossoming over the last year."

His nostrils flare with rage. "It's a fucking lie. Why? Because I gave the media the video of us fucking? Whether she's married or not, that video is going out on Monday."

My fingers twitch at my sides. Maybe just one more punch. It wouldn't take that long, and it'd feel so fucking good to do it again.

I click my tongue. "The only thing going out on Monday is our wedding announcement and interviews. No one will touch your video. They're not stupid enough to go against my family."

He squirms, poking at the skin around his eye that's now puffy and discolored. "So that's why you got married. To cover it up." He nods as if he's had some life-altering epiphany. "Then I'll just release it on my own."

"No, you won't."

"You can't stop me."

My family has done some questionable things over the years. I could *easily* make this man disappear. It's what he deserves after what he's done to Winnie—what he's still trying to do to her. But I know she wouldn't want that, so I take a calming breath before I lose my shit on this man.

The angry tone to my voice cuts the air around us. "My family is very, very powerful. At a snap of my fingers, you could be gone. And from what I know about you, no one would even miss you. So I'd be very careful how you speak to me—and how you speak about my wife."

His head rears back. "You know nothing about me."

"Your father worked for Spencer many years ago. He worked in accounting. It was a good job. It paid well, and it was enough to give the two of you a good life. Your mom abandoned you, left you with your father, and your father didn't have anyone in his life. The job with Bishop Hotels would've been perfect if your father wouldn't have been stupid and greedy."

He jerkily shakes his head back and forth. "Don't talk about him like that."

It's clear I've touched a nerve. *Good.* I want to strike one. I want to find the wound and dig my fingers into it until he gives up the control he foolishly thinks he has. By the time I leave here, I want him to feel powerless. Just like how he made Winnie feel when he betrayed her by threatening to make something public that was very much supposed to be private.

I give him a satisfied smile, loving the rush of adrenaline that courses through me that this is going exactly to plan. "Oh, but he was both greedy and stupid. He had a great job. Good hours. Good management. But instead, he wanted what everyone always wants—more. So money started disappearing. And Spencer saw to it to fire your dad himself. It put the Bishops in hot water at first. How could they not have a finger in what their employees are doing when it comes to missing money?"

If Spencer had hired someone to do background checks and not left it up to software, he would've discovered that Blake Billings is not actually Blake Billings. He'd put down a different name when he applied to be a driver for the family. He used the name of someone who existed, so he got away with it. This revenge plan never would've worked if Spencer was more competent. I'll make sure to tell him that—now that we have a stake in Bishop Hotels.

Lifting my hand, I pick at my nails. "Things got rough for the two of you. Your father was blacklisted. Spencer made sure that no one would hire him. Long days and long nights working really took a toll on him. I'm sorry to hear about the heart attack he had a few years back. What a shame."

It isn't a shame. Blake's father—or should I say Colin—wasn't a good guy. He had a few arrests on his record for theft and battery after getting fired. The apple didn't seem to fall far from the tree because it's clear the man sitting in front of me isn't any better.

His face turns red with anger. Sweat beads above his brow as he glares at me with pure hatred. "Now you know why money won't do anything to change my mind. I have nothing left. My dad is gone. He would've been healthy if Spencer didn't ruin his life."

My head cocks to the side. "You see, to me, it seems like it's your father who ruined his own life. I've never been particularly fond of Spencer Bishop, but he did what any competent businessman would do."

Blake's body shakes with rage. I love it. He's reacting exactly how I want him to. I hope he feels angry and hurt and every other fucking raw feeling imaginable. It just makes me even more excited for when he realizes that he'll have no choice but to agree to my terms.

"You say money won't sway you. And it's admirable...kind of, that you think you don't have a price. But we both know you will once you realize you cannot release that video or those photos. It'd be fucking stupid. The media won't touch it, and if you release it yourself, you can join your father in the grave. You say you don't care, but you do. You aren't ready to disappear, *Colin*," I emphasize his real name so he understands how serious I am, "are you?"

His jaw clenches. He stares at me as his chest heaves up and down with heavy breaths. Eventually, he does one small shake of his head.

I let out a sigh of approval. "Now that we have an understanding—" I reach into my jacket and pull out an envelope filled with cash. I don't like paying the guy, but it's nothing, considering what he has on Winnie. "You will take this money. You will leave New York—better yet, leave this country—and you will never, ever contact Winnie again. You aren't allowed to breathe in the same fucking state as her again."

"And what if I leave and decide to release the tape anyway? I could hide somewhere you'd never find me."

I laugh. It's cold and bitter. "There's not a place on this planet you could hide from me. Be sure to remember that because as I've mentioned, I don't take well to others threatening what's mine. Do anything that could hurt my wife or her reputation, and I will hunt you down myself."

He opens the envelope, his eyes going wide at the amount of money in there. While he looks at the bills, I go to his computer setup. He's dumb and doesn't have any kind of password protection, so it's easy to sort through the files on his desktop.

"What are you doing?" he demands, rushing over to me.

I hold up my hand. "Don't even think about coming any closer." It isn't hard to find the file where he has the video of Winnie, along with pictures that make me sick to my stomach. I hate that he violated her this way. For a split second, I think about making him disappear right now. I'd get my money back, and I'd be doing the world a service.

"How do you know I don't have multiple copies of the video? I sent it out. I can get them from there."

I don't answer him at first. I focus on clearing his computer of everything. His accounts, his files, all of it gone. He tries to come up to me again but at the last minute realizes it's a dumb idea.

At least he has some sense of a brain.

My eyes scan his desk, finding a hard drive and a USB tucked underneath a stack of papers. I put both in my pocket, making sure he doesn't have possession of those either. When my eyes finally connect with his again, I find him staring at me in horror.

It's about to get worse because as I stand up, I shove the PC's tower to the ground. It lands with a *thud*.

"Fuck, dude!" he yells, going to look at his computer. I walk to it, kicking the tower until it crashes against his wall.

Satisfied that there's no trace of that video or photos left in this house, I focus on him for the last time. "Just know if I find out that video is anywhere else, I will personally make you regret it. And trust me, Colin, you don't want to ever see me again. You're getting out of this relatively unharmed because I've got a party with my wife to attend in two hours."

He lifts his hands, resting his fingers against his temples as he looks at the broken pieces in disbelief. "You just broke my computer!"

I nod to the envelope still wrapped in his grimy hands. "You've got enough money to buy a new one. Might want to think about a laptop. Heard they travel better, considering you're going abroad."

Rage washes over his face, but he luckily keeps his mouth shut.

I walk to his door, ready to be done with all of this. I stop in the open doorway, looking back at him. "I want to make one thing clear, Colin. I'm not a man to mess with. I've given you mercy today because I know that's what Winnie would want. I won't do it again."

He narrows his eyes on me as if he's trying to figure out if I'm bluffing or not. I stare right back, daring him to call me out. He'll learn quickly I'm a man of my word.

"I'll go," he finally concedes.

I smile. "Good. If you ever touch my wife—better yet, if you even breathe the same air as her—know it will be the end of you."

I storm out the door. The fear in his eyes tells me enough. I won't be seeing him again.

I race down the stairs, finding my driver waiting for me. The moment he sees me, he rushes to open the back passenger door of the town car for me. Sliding in, I look at the time with a wince. I'm running late—by a lot. We were supposed to be leaving for the event any minute now, and I'm not even home. I try calling Winnie, but it goes straight to voicemail.

Fuck. I feel bad, and I never feel bad about anything.

"We need to hurry," I tell Ryan, sitting back in the seat as I come up with an excuse to tell Winnie where I've been.

19
Winnie

HE'S LATE.

And no matter how hard I try not to be disappointed at him not being here when he said he would, I can't help it.

There are so many reasons I shouldn't be excited about tonight. I'll have to face my friends and tell them I got married in secret. I'll have to answer their numerous questions. I'll have to speak to so many people and relay the pretend love story of Archer and me over and over again. But despite all of that, a small part of me was excited to go to an event with him. To spend more time with him since he disappeared after our long walk yesterday morning.

I've tried not to wonder if he was avoiding me. He's a busy man, and just because we're in a fake marriage doesn't mean he has to give me any of his time, but still, I was looking forward to tonight so I could see him again.

But he isn't here.

I sigh, looking at the clock on the oven. The event has already started. Even if we left right now, we'd miss the red carpet beforehand. I'm never one that loves to talk to the press. I was always at the very end of the galleries they uploaded because I wasn't as important as the celebrities that'd attend these things, but Archer and I were supposed to give some coy interviews tonight on the carpet for our newlywed debut.

I sit still, watching each minute tick by on the clock for another ten minutes until I realize how desperate and pathetic I seem. If he doesn't want to attend the event, then we won't go. I'll have to call Emma later and come up with an excuse for why I didn't meet them there, but I can handle it.

I'd honestly rather deal with her questions right now than have to face Archer and ask him why he decided not to attend the event without any kind of explanation.

Tossing my clutch on the kitchen counter, I slide out of the barstool and head upstairs to my room. The moment I cross the threshold to my space, I kick off my heels and jump onto my bed. I should've brought my clutch up so I could charge my phone, but now I'm too comfortable to do anything about it. Or maybe I'm just letting the disappointment get the best of me when I know I shouldn't.

I'm busy staring at the ceiling, dreading having to get up to pull the pins from my hair and wash my face, when two knocks on my doorframe have me pushing off my comforter.

"Winnie," Archer says, his voice breaking a little, like he was slightly out of breath.

I stare at him for a moment, wondering if I'm actually seeing him. He looks disheveled. Pieces of his hair fall into his face as his hands run awkwardly down his wrinkled clothes.

"Archer?" I ask in shock, noticing that his knuckles are bleeding. Before I can get up and cross the room to ask him where he's been, he's coming to a stop at the end of the bed.

He gives me a pained expression. "I'm sorry I'm late. I just need five minutes, and I'll be ready."

I'd stand up, but he's standing so close to the edge of the bed that if I did, it'd put us chest to chest. Instead, I stay seated, my legs awkwardly parted to make room for him. If the dress didn't have a slit that went all the way to the top of my thigh, I wouldn't be able to adjust to the position at all.

"Where were you?" My eyes track over his body. I figured he was working late, but nothing about his appearance makes it seem like he was working. "What happened?" I press, needing an explanation. I don't even care about the party anymore. I just want to know where he's been and why he has blood on him.

He lets out a heavy sigh. "It doesn't matter. I'm here now, and I want to go tonight." His eyes travel over my face, but I can't tell what's going through his mind as his cold gaze sweeps over me. "Can you give me five minutes?"

I want to ask him again where he's been, but if he wanted to tell me, he would have already. I still fight the urge to ask him a thousand more questions, but he seems insistent we still go tonight, and I can't argue because I still want to go despite him being late and showing up like this.

Archer must not like my silence because he looks back at my heels that lie by the door. He steps from between my legs, walking across the room to grab them and return to me.

"We don't have to go if you don't want to anymore. I know I'm late, and you're probably mad at me. But I'd love to attend"—he holds up the heels with the most sheepish smile I've ever seen on him—"and introduce you as my wife tonight."

Before I can answer him, he drops to his knees. He carefully sets one of the heels on the rug, holding the other one next to my foot. His eyes hold what seems like a million different questions as he looks up at me. Without any words, I know what he's asking. I nod, letting him know that I'll still go with him despite everything.

His sigh of relief is loud, so loud there's no way I could miss it. I hate that inside, my heart seems to come to life from that one simple breath. I can't help it.

Archer Moore—the cold, calculated man I've been told to avoid my entire life—is on his knees for me. And it might be my favorite thing I've ever seen.

His fingers are cold as they wrap around my ankle. I shiver, telling myself it's from the temperature of his fingers and not because it feels so intimate to have his fingertips press against the inside of my ankle. He's gentle as he slides the heel onto my foot. I'm pretty sure his fingers linger a second longer than they need to after the shoe is on securely.

When he goes to slide the next one on, he looks up at me. It feels like something is happening, but I don't know what exactly it is. The air just feels heavy between us, and I feel like part of it is because of where he just came from.

He keeps his fingers wrapped around my ankle as he sits back on his heels. "Five minutes," he says again, running his hand over his mouth. The movement brings attention back to his bloody knuckles.

The sight makes me realize there's so much I don't know about him. Does this happen often? Is he always late, or did something happen tonight that isn't part of his typical routine? I have so many questions but ask none of them because even though to the world I'm his wife, I don't feel entitled to his answers.

"Five minutes," I repeat, knowing I'd give him as long as he wanted. Maybe I should argue with him and get mad at him for making me feel like a fool for waiting for him, but that isn't me. I don't feel like a fool. One look at his appearance tonight and I know I'd do anything he asked. Because wherever he was, whatever he was doing, I know he never intended to leave me hanging.

He leaves before saying anything else. I use the time he gets ready to freshen up my appearance. Lying down on the bed has slightly wrinkled the delicate fabric of my dress. I glide my hands over the smooth, black fabric, trying to get rid of any wrinkles I can.

Archer's stylist, Sara, had dropped it off earlier, saying it's been in her client closet waiting for the perfect person to wear it. I took it with a smile, knowing the dress is brand-new and has definitely not been sitting in her closet.

I saw it in a catalog last month as a new dress to market. One of my favorite things to do is look at the fashion trends to find out what's coming next. I love to do it for both fashion and interior design trends. But I didn't tell Sara that. It was sweet of her to think of me and bring it over, even though I'd had other options to wear tonight.

I do love how she brought a pair of silk gloves to go with the dress. I'm not one who normally wears gloves to formal events, but I understand her vision. With the black fabric running up my pale skin, it's hard to miss the giant diamond on my finger. It sticks out against the dark fabric, the diamond glistening anytime any kind of light hits it.

If I were bold, I'd ask Archer what he thinks of the dress. It fits me perfectly. The sweetheart neckline does a lot for the average amount of cleavage I have. The dress isn't flashy at all. There are no crystals or embellishments on it. Even the fabric itself is just plain black. It leaves all the attention on the ring he put on my finger. One that still takes my breath away every time I slide it onto my finger due to how large and stunning it is.

I'm swiping red lipstick along my bottom lip when Archer steps into view. I meet his eyes through the bathroom mirror.

It couldn't have been more than ten minutes ago that his business clothes were wrinkled and disheveled, but you'd never know by looking at him now.

He's far too handsome. He knows it, I know it, the world knows it.

Archer Moore was meant to be a man of power. It's in the way his broad shoulders are always pushed back, like he knows he's the most important person in the room. He carries himself confidently, which is impressive because he doesn't even have to speak to command a room. His dark hair is perfectly styled once again. It's shorter on the sides, and he's slicked back the longer strands at the top.

I want to look at his knuckles to see if I'd made it up that only minutes ago they were bruised and bloody, but he's got them tucked into his pockets. His chestnut eyes watch me closely. I feel every inch that they move over me as he lets them trail down my body. I try not to squirm underneath his gaze, knowing he's doing the same thing I was just doing by looking him over.

Archer clears his throat. "Are you ready?"

I nod, grabbing the lipstick so I can put it in my clutch downstairs.

His hand reaches out, waiting for me to take it. I do without any kind of second thought. Neither of us says a word as he leads me downstairs and into the waiting car.

"Nervous?" he asks as the car pulls away from the curb.

"No," I lie, suddenly incredibly nervous because our situation is about to feel far too real as we play the part to a room full of people I've known my entire life. People who know the history of our families and will be sure to ask tons of questions.

"It's okay if you are," he encourages. He reaches across the seat, acting as if he was going to touch me. At the last second, his hand drops between us, but he leaves it there.

I stare at it for a moment, wondering what he was reaching for. My hand? My cheek? My leg that I'm just now realizing is bouncing up and down with nerves?

"I'm not," I lie again. For some reason, I don't want to tell him how nervous I am.

"Then let's go tell the world about our love."

20
Archer

I KNOW DOING THE RED CARPET TOGETHER WOULD'VE BEEN WISE from a press standpoint, but I love that we're able to quickly get into the event without having to answer a ton of questions. It allows for us to make more of a grand entrance. The moment we step through the doors, the dim lighting of the party does nothing to hide the eyes that all shift and stay focused on us.

I stop before I can lead Winnie down the large ballroom staircase a few feet ahead of us. She's been completely stiff since the moment we walked through the doors, and before we keep going, I need to know she's doing okay.

"They're already staring at us," Winnie whispers.

I lay my hand over hers to try and calm her nerves. "It's because you look absolutely breathtaking tonight." I wince, wishing I would've told her that sooner.

She hadn't noticed me when I first got home tonight. There were a few seconds where I just stood in her doorway, feeling incredibly guilty for being the reason for the disappointed look on her face. But even with seeing the sadness in her eyes, all I could think about was how beautiful she was.

The thought hasn't left my mind since.

Her hand tightens against my bicep. I don't know if it's from my words or from the sheer number of people looking in our direction. "You don't have to say that to distract me." She takes a hesitant step forward.

I follow her lead, knowing that we'll only garner more attention the moment we start going down the stairs. "It wasn't a distraction."

Her head whips to me for a second. Her eyes roam over my face as she gives me a questioning glance. There's no time for us to continue the conversation because I've led her to the top of the stairs, in view of everyone in the waiting ballroom below us.

Gently, I grab her chin and force her to focus on me for a moment. I want her to block out everything else and really listen to my next words. "Don't think about any of them," I plead, knowing it's easier said than done.

There's a reason I avoid these events anytime I can. I don't care for attention all that much. But getting it tonight is inevitable. I know no one could've expected Winnie and me to show up together, and it's written all over the faces of the people who watch us.

"Is this more people than normal?" Her words come out frantic and rushed as we take the first step down. I hold her tightly, making sure she doesn't stumble from the nerves. You wouldn't know she was nervous from the soft, polite smile on her face. Although she hides it well, I can tell by the way her fingers clutch the sleeve of my jacket so tightly she might be stretching out the fabric.

"I actually think this is less than normal," I answer, refusing to hold anyone's eye contact. It feels like the entire room has gone quiet as we make it down.

"There's no way," she whispers as we step off the final stair. Her steps falter for a fraction of a second. I follow her eyeline to find her group of friends all staring at us with shock written all over their faces.

"Should we speak with them first? We can get it over with." I know it's been eating her alive to tell her friends about our marriage, so maybe if we do it sooner rather than later, she might be able to enjoy the rest of the evening. Or maybe it'll make things worse, but I know there's no way we can talk to anyone else in this room until we talk to them. "Are you good with that?" I ask, wanting to make sure she's okay with my plan.

All she does is nod. Her hand shakes against mine, making me feel a tinge of guilt. For some reason, I feel like I'm the one who put us in this situation, even though I know it wasn't all me.

"If you want, I'll do all the talking," I assure her, trying to do whatever I can to ease her nerves as we get closer to her friends.

"I don't know what I want," she whispers back, almost in earshot of the group. Her breathing picks up pace the closer we get to her friends, and it pains me to know telling them is causing her this much anxiety.

I can't hear what her friends are saying, but they whisper to one another, clearly just as confused as everyone else. I recognize Beckham Sinclair and his new wife, as well as Camden Hunter. There are two women I don't recognize, but by the pure shock on one of the unnamed faces, I guess that's Emma, someone Winnie has mentioned quite a few times.

Winnie has a death grip on me as we come to a stop. They've created a circle with a gap for us to step into. I look over at Winnie for a minute, making sure she hasn't gone pale from nerves. She's doing okay at hiding her unease, but she stares right at me and nobody else. I look to the two people I know from the group. "Sinclair. Hunter. Good to see you two."

I hold out my hand, shaking hands with both of them. They're both cool guys. I liked them enough in school—as well as I would like anyone, for someone who prefers to do most things alone. I've gotten to know them a little bit more over the years, and they've both done a lot career-wise that's impressive.

I respect when a man carves out even more of a name for himself, despite the family they were born into.

Beckham and Camden were both born with a lot being

handed to them—just like I was. But they also made sure to do things on their own.

Realizing Winnie isn't going to say anything to ease the awkward silence, I try to come up with something to create small talk. I'm opening my mouth to comment on the number of people here when Beck speaks up.

"I thought events like this were never your thing," he comments, his tone questioning. He smiles, but it doesn't reach his eyes. His wife gives him a look like she's a little shocked by his question. Maybe he typically isn't one to pry.

"I had to come to celebrate," I answer, putting on a smile of my own. I look over at Winnie again, finding her still focused solely on me.

Her fingernails bite through the fabric of my suit jacket, but I don't let anyone know of it. Her nerves are clearly getting to her, but she's doing her best to hide it. She looks at me like she's absolutely enthralled with every word that comes from my mouth.

The only thing that gets me to look away from Winnie is her friend who I think is Emma. She tries to get Winnie's attention, but Winnie is apparently pretending like she doesn't notice.

"Celebrate what, exactly?" Beck asks, looking over at Camden as if he'd have any answers.

There's no use in me dragging this out, so with a smile on my face I lift Winnie's hand. I make sure to angle it perfectly, wanting the light from the chandelier above us to catch the light of the ring I bought her. A collective gasp ricochets through the group as they all stare with their mouths hanging open at the diamond on her finger.

"What?" I think Emma yells, ripping Winnie's hand from mine before I can stop it. She and Beck's wife both lean in close, looking at the ring like they've never seen an engagement ring before.

Annoyed that Winnie's friend ripped her hand from mine without asking, I pull it from her and welcome the warmth of it once again. I know they're all probably shocked by what we're telling them, so to really sell the point, I plant a kiss on the diamond. "We couldn't pass up the opportunity for our first event as husband and wife."

"I think I might pass out," comes from a wide-eyed Emma.

"What is he talking about?" Beck's wife asks, taking a step closer to us.

Finally, Winnie looks away from me and looks to her friends. She gives them a timid smile. "We've got some things to catch up on."

Beck's wife loops her arm through the arm of someone I don't recognize. Whoever it is must be someone new to New York because she doesn't seem to have any idea what's going on. "I need to go to the ladies' room," Beck's wife interjects. Without any questions, she grabs Winnie and yanks her away from me. "You're coming, too, Win."

I wait for Winnie to respond, but she stays quiet. All she does is toss a nervous look over her shoulder as her friends pull her away from me and across the ballroom. I miss her presence the moment she's gone, a realization that doesn't sit well with me as I turn to face Camden and Beck again.

"It appears congratulations are in order," Camden comments, lifting his drink in a half attempt to cheers.

My eyes scan the room for Winnie, but she's been pulled out of view. I tuck my hands into my pockets, straightening my spine. "Thanks, Hunter."

"Did we miss the invite?" Beck muses. There's a hint of humor to his voice, like he finds Winnie and me showing up together tonight amusing.

"She wanted something small." I swallow, trying to hide the lie. She didn't want any kind of wedding at all, but they don't need to know that.

Camden's eyes seem to catch on something across the room because before anyone else can say anything, he's stepping away from me. "I'll be back," he announces, already walking away with his eyes pinned on someone blocked from my view.

"I'm not going to lie, I thought you'd stay single forever. I sure as hell didn't expect you to show up married to *Winnie*. Don't your families hate one another?" Beck takes a drink of his champagne, his eyes watching me closely. He seems genuinely curious about how Winnie and I ended up together. I guess it makes sense if his wife is one of her best friends. I don't like that there's a good chance he knows more about Winnie than I do because of the closeness of his wife and mine.

My eyes scan the room for a waiter. A drink would be fucking great right about now. Unfortunately, I don't see anyone. With a sigh, I look back to Beck. "Didn't your wife used to date your brother? Or am I making that up?"

Beck scowls, his blond eyebrows pulling in on his face. "A long time ago, yeah. Prefer to not talk about him, though. I'm not his biggest fan." Beck adds the last sentence with a harsh tone before taking a long sip of his drink.

It's quiet between us before he speaks up again. "So are you and Winnie really married? She never struck me as the type of person to be so…spontaneous."

My nostrils flare. I'm tired of people having so many opinions of her when they really don't know her at all. "It's been building up for a year, so I wouldn't exactly call it spontaneous."

He nods. "Got it." He drags out the two words, the tone of his voice indicating he still has so many questions but he isn't going to ask them. "Well, it seems like we might be spending more time together, then. Margo keeps telling me how we should get our friends together for a big, elaborate dinner party soon."

"Can't wait," I lie, not interested in the slightest of attending any more parties than I need to. No matter my opinion on events, I can see Winnie being interested in being able to spend time with her friends, so I fake interest. There are worse guys in our life to spend time with than Beck.

"Great," Beck responds, his eyes searching the room. "Let's find you a drink so we can celebrate your marriage. I need something stronger than this champagne."

Maybe I'll end up liking him more than I thought. "That sounds like the perfect idea," I agree, following him to one of the bars.

21
Winnie

MARGO DOESN'T EVEN HAVE THE DOOR ALL THE WAY SHUT BEFORE Emma is turning to me with an expectant look on her face. "Talk. Now." Her voice is demanding and a bit higher than I'm used to hearing from her. It's obvious she's trying to keep it together after Archer just casually told her we were married.

"Uhhh…" I begin, wondering where to even start. How do you tell your best friends that you not only had a relationship you hid from them, but you also had an engagement and wedding without telling them any of it? "What do you want to know?"

Margo laughs, looking over at a girl I recognize from Margo's wedding. Wasn't she the one Camden kept yelling at? The baker? If they weren't giving me the third degree, I'd ask if she's now Camden's girlfriend. I keep my questions to myself, knowing that as soon as Emma forgives me for keeping my wedding from her, she'll give me all the details on what's happening there.

A shocked, strangled sound comes from Emma's throat. "I don't know, Winnie, how about you start with when the hell did you get married? What happened to that Blake guy? Doesn't your family *hate* the Moores?"

I'm thinking about which one of Emma's questions I'm going to answer first when Margo chimes in. "Who is Blake?"

Emma crosses her arms over her chest. "The last time we talked, he *was* Winnie's boyfriend."

"He was *never* my boyfriend." My body shudders at the thought. Blake and I had been casually flirting for well over a year. But the relationship was never defined—apparently because he wasn't in it the way I thought he was.

I try not to let my face show a reaction. I'm not hurt to lose him; he wasn't who I thought he was. What stings is that I didn't see any of the red flags and that I blindly went into having feelings for him because I liked the attention.

Emma rolls her eyes and lets out an annoyed sigh. "Winnie Bishop, he was at your apartment all the time. Whatever you want to call it, you never once mentioned Archer. How long have you two been together?"

I can't tell her it's only been two days. I also can't tell her the same story we've told everyone else. She can typically read me like an open book; I don't know if she'll believe me.

My lips rub together as I try to think of an answer. "It's complicated." Camden's date backs away from the circle slowly, heading to the bathroom door. I want to tell her goodbye—or at least properly introduce myself—but she's gone before I can say anything. Plus, Margo and Emma are staring at me with such lost looks that I can't focus on anything other than the story I'm going to give them.

Margo lets out a little laugh, tucking her dark hair behind her ear as she reaches for my hand. "If *anyone* knows complicated, it's me. I married my ex-boyfriend's brother—who was also my boss at one point. I get complicated, Win. Just tell us the story."

"I guess you could say things have been on and off between us for about a year," I lie. Technically, you could say things have been off between us from the moment we both were born, thanks to our families. But I know that isn't the answer Margo and Emma are looking for.

"So you were talking to both Blake and Archer?" Emma asks, confused.

I'd confided in her about Blake after she once saw a text from him on my phone. It started as an innocent conversation; we'd been going over details about when and where he'd pick me up. But he'd followed up his text asking me when I was going to say yes to a date with him. Emma saw it, and I couldn't keep it a secret any longer. I had wanted to tell her that I had a crush on someone, even though I knew it was a man who was off-limits.

I shrug, knowing I have to give her an answer. "Sort of. You know the history between Archer's family and mine. Even when I realized there was a spark between us, I didn't think anything would happen."

"And your family is just okay with all of this?" Margo asks, leaning in closer to me. She still holds my hand, giving it a tight squeeze like she's reminding me that she's here no matter what.

"They are." This might be the first true answer I've given. My dad had to give up a lot to convince Archer to do this, but at the end of the day, he still gave his stamp of approval. The marriage is what he wanted, given the circumstances.

"When was the wedding?" Emma asks, sadness creeping into her voice. Emma has always been the strong one in our trio. She's the one who'd wipe the tears away for Margo and me. She'd threaten anyone that hurt us, but there were times when her act cracked, and you could tell it took a toll on her to be the strong one.

Right now is another one of those moments. She doesn't want to act like me doing this without them hurts her, but I know it does, and I hate myself for doing it.

"Two days ago," I answer truthfully. Pictures from our wedding day will be plastered all over the internet on Monday. It'll say the date—there's no point in me hiding that detail.

Emma and Margo share a look. "Why didn't you invite us?" Emma presses.

"We would've loved to be there, Win," Margo continues. "You were in my wedding. I always dreamed about being in yours, too."

I had, too, but I don't say that out loud. I'd always dreamed of a big, elaborate wedding with all of the people I love most. There'd be flowers everywhere, an orchestra for the ceremony, and a live band for the reception. I would've designed my own dress—or a few different ones because why choose just one—and even had a part in designing a custom dress for each one of my bridesmaids. I'd dreamed of doing all these things for when I finally said "I do," but none of that happened.

I swallow, looking down for a moment as guilt weighs heavy on my chest. "We wanted to be married before things went public. You know how the media is. We wanted something that was just ours. To only address our relationship once and then just enjoy being together. So we got married in a very small and intimate ceremony. The only reason we invited any media at all was because we didn't want to have to answer many questions after the fact. If we let them in, gave an interview about our love story, they'd leave us alone."

Margo lets out a sarcastic laugh. "They never really leave you alone. I've been asked if I'm pregnant all night tonight."

My eyes go wide, flicking to her abdomen and back up to her. Before I can ask if she is, she holds her hands up. "I'm not, but it hasn't stopped them from asking. Trust me, you guys would be the first to know if I was."

I smile, looking forward to the day. Margo has always talked about wanting to be a mom. She's already planned how she'd paint their portrait for every birthday and how she'd paint a mural in the nursery. It makes me a little sad to think about because, just like her, being a mom is something I want to be. And I don't know when that will happen since, for the time being, I'm locked into a fake marriage.

Emma rolls her shoulders, pushing them back as a smile blooms on her face. "Winnie, I just can't believe you're *married*. I probably shouldn't say this, but I do feel like you upgraded. Archer is hot—way hotter than Blake."

I smile because it's a total Emma thing to say. She isn't

wrong, though. Sometimes I look at Archer and catch my breath. He's so strikingly handsome it takes me off guard.

Emma's eyebrows lift. "If you were to look up tall, dark, and handsome in the dictionary, it'd show you a picture of Archer Moore. Like holy hell, Winnie, his muscles seem to have muscles —and I've only seen him in a suit."

Margo and I both laugh at Emma. She has absolutely zero filter, and it's something we love her for.

"I'm glad you find my husband hot," I tease. Her words don't bother me at all. For one, he really isn't mine to claim— even though I don't want to think too deeply into that fact. And for two, it's obvious how good-looking he is. I don't need my friend to lie and tell me he's ugly in an attempt to not make things weird.

"I will forgive you for not telling me that you got married if you promise to not keep us out of the loop anymore," Emma begins, knocking her shoulder against mine. "We want all of the details—even some of the dirty ones. And you have to promise to spend time with us now and get out of your love-filled bubble and leave your husband occasionally."

"Or Archer can come, too," Margo offers. "Beck would love it. We can do double dates!" Her voice is so excited that I don't want to tell her I'm not sure if Archer is the kind of guy to do double dates. I guess I wouldn't have really expected Beck to be either, but these days, it seems like he'd do anything for her. I can't tell Margo that Archer's and my relationship isn't really like that.

"Let's do it," I say through a forced smile. It might take some convincing to get Archer to do it, but I'm going to try. It'd be fun to do dinner or maybe even catch a show with them.

Emma's lip juts out in a pout. "When will it be my turn?" she whines, her eyes bouncing between me and Margo. "All I want is for a rich man to lay eyes on me and fall madly in love with me. Surely that isn't too much to ask for."

"I thought you wanted a cowboy?" I fire back, wrapping my

arm around Emma's neck. The awkward tension has dissipated, giving me my best friends back.

Emma rolls her eyes. "Honestly, right now, I'll settle for a man that actually knows how to give me an orgasm. Bonus points if he takes me out to dinner first. I went on a date the other night with a guy who is in finance, and he bought me one drink before he was asking if we could go back to my place because his mom was staying at his."

Margo laughs. "Is that code for he's still living with his mom?"

Emma's hands shoot up in the air, a sad laugh bubbling from her chest. "Yes! His screensaver was even a photo of just the two of them." She shakes her head, ducking out from underneath my arm and walking to the large mirror of the bathroom. "There were a *lot* of red flags with him."

"Is it safe to assume there won't be a second date?" I ask, walking up next to her. I blot around my red lipstick, making sure none of it has smeared as I talked.

Emma meets my eyes through the mirror. The look she's giving me tells me she isn't amused by my question. "I left halfway through the first one. I didn't even give the guy a chance to give me an orgasm. Fred did a great job at it when I got home."

Margo walks up to Emma's other side. "Your new dildo's name is *Fred*?" She doesn't bother to hide the amusement in her face.

I smile, trying not to let my laugh escape my throat. "God, Emma. Why do you give your sex toys the worst names?"

Emma rolls her eyes at the both of us, pulling a tube of lip gloss from her purse. She swipes it across her lips, completely unbothered by Margo's and my teasing. "Fred is a strong name. Plus, I'm limited on names for my toys. My vibrators and dildos can't have the same names as guys I've dated. You know what I haven't dated? A Fred."

I can't hold back my laugh any longer. It echoes off the stone walls of the extravagant bathroom. "I've really missed you, Emma," I say with affection. It feels good to be back with both of them. To be laughing and teasing and poking fun at Emma's lack of a filter.

She turns, tapping the end of her tube of lip gloss against my nose. "You didn't have to miss me, bitch. I've been here trying to get your attention, and you were ignoring me—for a man!" She gasps as if that's the worst thing I could do.

"I'm sorry," I say, really meaning it. A lot has been going on, and in that, I've lost touch with the two people who matter most to me in this world. I won't let it happen again.

She shrugs, pulling me in for a hug. "I forgive you—only because I might forget about you, too, if a hot billionaire was sweeping me off my feet."

Margo joins in on the group hug, and we remain in the embrace for a while. My arms wrap around them tightly. I hadn't realized how much I missed them until now.

"You have our full permission to go silent when you find yourself a man, Emma," Margo says against my hair.

Emma pulls away. "A nice, *rich* man, Margo. Who doesn't have his mother as his lock screen. Don't forget all the details."

Margo laughs. "Yes. A rich man."

"Maybe older, too. An age-gap love affair seems to have worked out better for the two of you."

Margo and I share a conspiring look. Although nothing about Archer's and my marriage is conventional, I still very much see the appeal of being with someone who is older—even if it isn't real.

"Should we go back out there?" I ask, knowing Archer and I probably need to mingle with everyone together.

Margo nods as Emma grabs her purse from the counter. "We probably should," Margo answers, reaching to pull the bathroom door open. "We need to look for Pippa. You need to get to know her better, Winnie. You'll love her. She and Emma together are hilarious."

"Sounds dangerous," I tease, following them out the door.

We've almost made it back to the guys when Emma immediately turns around and stops in front of me. She holds up a finger, a serious look on her face. "Don't think you got out of telling us all of the details about how you ended up married. Me and Margo are your best friends, and I'll be pissed if you told a gossip column more about your life than you told me. So later, be prepared to tell us every last detail."

I nod. "I'll tell you everything," I lie, knowing I won't tell them anything near the truth. But I will tell them what we've told everyone else and even give her made-up details I haven't given anyone else.

"I just know you have some good stories about how Archer is in bed."

I laugh, trying to hide the blush that creeps on my cheeks.

Now, that's something I wish I knew.

22
Archer

I'D KEPT UP POLITE CONVERSATION WITH BECK AND OTHERS WHO had stopped by for small talk, but I hadn't realized how tight my body had gone with Winnie's absence until she returned with her friends. The moment I saw her—and noticed how happy and carefree she looked—I took my first deep breath since the moment she left.

When her friends had dragged her away from us, she'd looked nervous and almost scared. Now, there's a slight flush to her cheeks, almost as if she's been laughing. Maybe she has been. She has a smile on her face, one I know isn't fake at all.

I stare a little too long, waiting for her eyes to meet mine. The moment she looks at me, I can't help but let the corners of my mouth turn up in relief and maybe a little bit of awe that she's mine.

"We've returned your wife to you in one piece," the friend who I now know as Emma jokes. She holds her hand out, waiting for me to take it. "My name's Emma, but I'm sure you know that already."

I hold my hand out and take hers. "Archer."

"Oh, I know," she responds with a sly smile on her face. With her hand still wrapped in mine—and a beaming smile on her face—she squeezes a little tighter before talking. "I want you to know that if you hurt my best friend, you better watch your back."

My eyes go wide as I repeat what she said in my head to make sure I didn't misunderstand her. The people in the circle all laugh, letting me know it wasn't a figment of my imagination.

"Emma!" Winnie shouts, shaking her head at her friend. "You can't just say that."

Both of our hands drop, the handshake being done with. Emma shrugs, not looking sorry in the slightest for her threat. "Well, I already did, sooo…"

"Don't worry. She threatened my life—and my dick—when Margo and I got engaged," Beck adds, smiling at Emma.

Emma points to me. "I'll threaten yours, too. I'm telling you, don't hurt my girl."

I look over at Winnie, feeling the need to touch her but not knowing if I should or not. Instead, I just stay locked in her gaze. "I don't plan on it," I answer truthfully.

We're still getting to know one another, but I know she's got to be one of the kindest people I've ever met. You don't have to know her long to know that her heart is genuine—that *everything* about her is genuine.

My words award me a wide smile from her that's aimed just at me. She only holds my gaze for a moment before she looks to the floor, not used to all of the attention being on her.

"You guys are so cute I could throw up," Emma interjects, pulling me from the moment.

Good. At least our show is working.

"We need to make a toast!" Margo says eagerly, her eyes already searching the room for a waiter. I wouldn't mind another drink; Beck and I had both almost finished our drinks in the time it took for the girls to return.

"That really isn't necessary," Winnie argues.

Margo rolls her eyes, waving down a waiter with a tray full of champagne flutes. "We're going to toast to the new, happy couple. You're married, Winnie! We have to celebrate that."

Winnie laughs nervously. Almost like it's out of habit, I wrap my arm around her and bring her body flush to mine. I let my fingers trace over her bare shoulder, trying to ease the nerves that have clearly crept back up. I want to see the carefree flush to her cheeks she'd had when she got back from talking to her friends.

Margo and Emma pass champagne flutes out to us. Camden still hasn't returned with his date, so it's just Beck, Margo, Emma, Winnie, and me. I don't mind the group. Beck and I got to catch up a little, and I enjoyed talking business with him. I want to talk to my dad about using Beck's company, Sintech, for some cybersecurity needs that have come up for us recently.

"Emma, you're better with words than I am," Margo muses, holding her champagne flute in the air. "You give the toast."

Emma gives her a dirty look. "I just want to point out that it was *your* idea."

"You guys really don't have to say anything," Winnie adds to the conversation, shifting on her feet.

Both Emma's and Margo's heads whip toward Winnie. They roll their eyes in almost perfect unison.

"Emma loves hearing herself talk," Margo teases. "She's dying to give a toast. We both know it."

Emma raises her glass at Margo's words. "Guilty." She laughs. Her eyes focus on Winnie, her features softening when looking at her best friend.

"To one of my very best friends. I'm so happy you finally found the forever kind of love that you deserve." Her eyes move from Winnie to me. "And to the man who swore to protect my best friend's heart." She focuses back on Winnie. It's fascinating to watch how much love is shared between these three best friends. I don't have anyone I'm that close to in my life. Friendships were never a top priority of mine when I was being raised to run an empire of hotels. "Congrats on being fucking married! To a lifetime of happiness—and hopefully *really* great sex," she teases, making everyone laugh. "Cheers!"

All of our glasses clink against one another before we all take a drink. If the toast made Winnie uncomfortable, she doesn't show it. I feel bad, knowing *she's* probably feeling bad for lying to her friends like this. I could tell Emma's toast was heartfelt, and it can't be easy for Winnie to listen to it, knowing why we got married in the first place.

"Now, lock in the toast with a kiss," Margo demands, a mischievous smile playing on her lips.

"That isn't a rule," Winnie protests.

"It is now!" Emma adds, leaning closer to us. She waves her hands in the air, trying to direct us to kiss. "C'mon, we want to celebrate you guys. Let us have this, and kiss already!"

I look down at Winnie, trying to figure out if this is something she wants.

We'd kissed at our wedding. I'd be lying to myself if I said I hadn't thought about it a lot since it happened. It was the way her body went almost lax against me the moment her lips pressed to mine. Like she fully trusted me with the kiss.

It was a chaste kiss, done in the middle of a church for very few witnesses, but it still did something to me. It left some kind of mark I didn't really want to delve into. But if I kiss her again right now, I'm scared I might not want to stop.

Winnie looks back at me, a timid smile on her lips. Her eyes move from mine to my lips, as if maybe she's thinking about my mouth the same way I'm thinking about hers.

"Oh my god, just kiss already!" Emma demands, getting impatient.

Winnie's tongue peeks out to wet her lips, and it captivates my attention. Her lips are a deep red. The color should make me want to avoid her lips, knowing it's bound to transfer to my mouth. But I almost want to taste the shade she carefully applied —to wear the proof that she's mine.

My fingers circle her shoulder again once before I let my hand travel down her back. I wish I wasn't still holding my champagne so I could pull her against me with both hands.

Feeling her bare skin against mine sends a rush of adrenaline through my body. My hand keeps drifting lower until it stops on her lower back.

With it now at the small of her back, I pull her against me even more. She steadies herself by placing her free hand against my stomach.

Leaning down, I tip her chin up towards me using my index finger, the rest of my fingers still holding on to the stem of the champagne flute. With her being this close, I can see the sparkles on her eyelids and can see that some of them have even fallen to her cheeks. She watches me carefully, clearly waiting for me to be the one to seal our lips together.

I hope that with her hand placement, she can't feel how much my heart races at the thought of kissing her again. My mind screams at me, knowing it's dangerous for me to want to kiss her this bad, but I don't care. She's my wife, after all. If people ask us to kiss as newlyweds, I can't tell them no. Can I?

I don't care that we could brush it off. I want to kiss her. Right here. And I can admit to myself that I want to kiss her later, too. And maybe even tomorrow.

Her breath hits my chin as our faces get closer and closer. I'm ready to taste her again.

I forget that people are watching us. All there is in the world is Winnie and me as our lips finally brush against one another. She sighs when her lips press to mine. The little noise drives me more mad. I go in again, this time with not as chaste of a kiss as before.

She tastes like champagne. I've never been a fan of it, but fuck, I could learn to like it if I got to taste it from her tongue. Speaking of tongues, when I cautiously let mine slip against hers, she lets me. Her mouth opens, her tongue meeting mine.

I'm only reminded that her friends are all staring at us when I hear Emma speak up. "Jesus. Get a room, you two!" She whistles, and I hate that there are so many eyes on us.

I hate that I want to deepen the kiss but can't. I want to drop the champagne and let it spill at our feet so I can grab her face between my hands and angle her head just the way I want it. I want to kiss her long and hard, but none of that can happen because I'm sure countless eyes are aimed our way. For once, I don't care if they look. I *want* them to look.

I want them to know she's mine.

Finally, our kiss breaks. Winnie laughs, pressing her forehead to my chest as both Margo and Emma make obnoxious sounds after seeing us kiss. I keep my arm wrapped around her, meeting the eyes of her friends with a coy smile.

"That was hot," Emma notes, taking another drink of her champagne.

Beck points to my face. "You took a little of her lipstick with you, Moore."

I shrug, looking back down at Winnie, who has now untucked herself from my chest. Her cheeks are flushed, and I hope it isn't from embarrassment but instead from the intensity of that kiss.

"I hope you know everyone is staring at you two," Margo adds, her eyes sweeping around the room. I follow her lead, noticing so many eyes aimed at us.

I take a deep breath. "Yeah, I figured. As much as I'd rather spend time with this group all night, I think it's time my wife and I at least mingle for a little bit."

"Get ready for a flood of questions," Beck warns.

Winnie reaches up, swiping her thumb underneath my lips. "You do have a lot of my lipstick on you."

"Good," I tell her before taking her hand in mine. I smile, not dreading the rest of the night at all. In fact, I might just be looking forward to feeding into our narrative tonight. "Let's get this over with."

23
Winnie

IT'S BEEN ALMOST A MONTH SINCE ARCHER AND I GOT MARRIED, and it's been the most chaotic month of my life. People were mildly interested in me when I attended events for my family. I was a socialite; if there weren't a lot of famous people there, then the press would ask me questions.

Everything changed the moment Archer and I announced we were married.

Suddenly, everyone cared about me—about us. Our pictures were everywhere, our interview was being shown all over TV. They've called us the modern-day version of Romeo and Juliet, making the past month a whirlwind.

Luckily, Archer doesn't seem too eager to go to every event we're invited to. We've attended some to keep up appearances as husband and wife, but it's our quiet mornings that I look forward to the most.

Archer is already my husband, but through the fake kisses and the small, private conversations, he's started to become a friend—a companion. And I don't know how I'm supposed to feel about it.

Maybe that's why I find myself pacing in front of the front door of our house this morning, knowing any minute, Archer will come downstairs to go and work out. He is the most punctual person I know. I've memorized his schedule in the weeks we've been living together.

First thing in the morning, I can hear his footsteps in the hallway as he goes downstairs to make a smoothie. I'm pretty sure he makes the same exact one every morning.

One scoop of vanilla protein powder, one frozen banana, a tablespoon of peanut butter, a scoop of Greek yogurt, and a handful of spinach. Some mornings, I've sat at the counter and watched him make it, barely awake to have a conversation.

I tell myself I wake up early in the mornings because I want to change my schedule, but I know part of me does it because the mornings and the occasional evenings are the only time we get together.

If I'm going to be married to him for the foreseeable future, it only makes sense for me to get to know him better. After he chugs his smoothie, he takes more vitamins than I've ever seen someone take. Then, he makes a cup of coffee and drinks it black as he answers work calls and emails.

After that, he changes into workout clothes and goes to the gym to work out. Recently, he's started the habit of coming back and going on a walk with me before he leaves for work. We've established a routine. On the walk, we talk about the small, insignificant things about each other that have added up to mean a lot to me.

He's beginning to mean something to me.

I'm mid-pace when he comes down the stairs, his dark eyebrows scrunching on his forehead the moment he spots me at the front door.

"Going somewhere?" he asks, his voice low. I'd been busy getting ready when he came down for his smoothie and coffee earlier, so this is the first time we're seeing each other this morning. I don't know if it's the fitted long-sleeve exercise shirt he wears or the joggers that fit just a little snug around his muscular thighs. Maybe it's just him in general that makes it so I can't look away.

"Maybe," I answer, my voice quiet because I'm too distracted by his appearance.

Archer Moore is dangerously handsome—and he knows it.

He uses it to his advantage. I watch him do it when he talks with others. I can tell he'd rather not have to give interviews or make small talk with people he doesn't care about, but he still does it well. He's great at eye contact and giving whoever is speaking all of his attention. He knows how to smile just enough to make them want to earn it but still so little that he gives off this mysterious vibe.

I've started looking forward to the times we go out in public because it's the only time his touch lingers against my skin. I love playing the part with him because it's fun to pretend his jokes about our first date and the little quirks of mine he tells people made him fall in love with me are all true.

Deep down, I know he's made up every single thing he tells people and that his touch doesn't mean a thing, but it doesn't change the rush of anticipation I feel anytime we're in public.

"We still have two hours until our walk," Archer points out, taking a seat on one of the bottom stairs to pull on a pair of tennis shoes. It still takes me by surprise to see him in such normal clothing. He shouldn't be allowed to look so good dressed up in a suit but look even better when he's getting ready to go work out.

"I was thinking..." I begin, wondering if maybe I shouldn't ask him this, "that I could go to the gym with you today."

He stops right in the middle of tying his laces. Slowly, he looks up at me. "You want to come work out with me?"

I nod. Maybe it's a silly request, but I'm over being in the house all of the time. My dad still hasn't asked me to make an appearance alone at events. He knows that no one wants to see just me right now; they want to see Archer and me together. The stock in both hotels has gone up because people are excited our families are no longer feuding.

"Are you not going for a walk?" he asks, pushing off the stairs and standing up once again.

I try not to be obvious about taking a deep inhale of his cologne when he gets closer. "I'd still be good with a walk, but I want to do more." I let out a nervous laugh. "To be honest, I'm a little bored, and maybe I'm having a quarter-life crisis and want to get into working out more." I shrug, too deep into asking him to take me with him to give up. "There's worse hobbies I could take up, right?"

He stays silent, his eyes pinned on me. He's quiet for so long that I lift my hands and wave at the air dismissively. "You know what? I don't actually want to work out." I look down at my matching leggings and sports bra, knowing that the outfit I chose this morning is exactly for working out. "And if I do, I'm going to ask for the trainer all of my school friends use. I hear he's young and great and I'm sure will know how to get me in shape," I ramble, already backing up to the stairs.

I'm turning to race up the stairs and prepare to not see Archer for the rest of the day when his fingers latch onto my wrist. He pulls, turning me to face him.

His eyes are darker than normal. Maybe it's because it's early and he isn't fully awake. Or maybe he'd rather just go alone since he's never asked me to join him before.

"You don't need a trainer." If I'm not mistaken, there's a bit of an angry tone to his sentence.

Oh man. Maybe I really made him mad by trying to crash his plans.

"You're right." I let out a nervous laugh, trying to pull my hand from his grip, but it's too strong. "Going for a walk is all I need."

He sighs, his eyes focusing on the ceiling for a moment before his chestnut gaze is back on me. "You don't need a fucking trainer because I'll work with you."

I shake my head. "Oh no, you don't have to do that. I know that you probably have a trainer and that you've got a system there. I don't want to barge in on it. I just want to go there with you, that's all. You can pretend I'm not there," I offer with a smile, hoping maybe I will be able to get out of the house with him.

His nostrils flare as his gaze rakes down my body. I try not to show him that I feel the warmth from his heated stare. "That's impossible."

"Me going with you?"

His fingers tighten around my wrist. "No. Me pretending you're not there. Not when you're wearing this. Not ever." He drops my hand like I'm on fire. Before I've even processed what he said, he's out the door and rushing down his front porch steps to his waiting driver.

"If you're not in the car in the next minute, you're getting left behind!" he yells, not bothering to even look over his shoulder.

I yelp, chasing after him. I've barely slid into the back seat before he's barking at his driver to get going.

24
Archer

"YOU REALLY DON'T HAVE TO HELP ME," WINNIE INSISTS AS SHE stands next to a weight rack like she's never seen one in her life.

I grunt, trying not to look at her now that she's shed her jacket and stands in just a bra and a pair of leggings that do nothing to hide every curve of her body. "I'll start and show you how to use each piece of equipment, and then you can follow my lead. Does that sound good?"

She watches me with a hesitant stare. I'm not sure I blame her —I'm as charming as a fucking bear right now, but it's only because I come to the gym to work off the tension I feel after being around her constantly.

I know with every part of me I shouldn't want her, that I shouldn't think about her unless we're out in public. The problem is, I *do* want her, and with each day, she seems to take up even more and more space in my mind.

The gym is the *one* place I can get her out of my head. It's the two hours where my trainer pushes me to the brink of exhaustion and I don't have any other brainpower to think about how much I want my fake wife.

Because of her, the gym isn't a safe place right now. I'm even more angry because it's never occurred to me to rent out the entire place so I can work out in private. I pay a lot of money for a private trainer, but there's enough equipment here that I've never needed anything all to myself.

Until today.

Because part of my terrible mood is from all the eyes on Winnie. Every person here should know that she's my wife, but they're still staring, and it's driving me insane.

I know my trainer, Alec, has been happily married for over ten years now. He always talks about his kids in between reps and how he thinks his wife hung the damn moon, but I even canceled the private session with him today because I didn't want him anywhere near Winnie.

It's a fucking problem.

"I don't want to take up your time. It's fine, really," Winnie comments, thinking that my gruffness with her is because I'm annoyed she wants to work out and not because I can't control how badly I want her. And that I can't control how mad it drives me to see another man's gaze even focus on her for a second longer than necessary.

She reaches her arms above her head to stretch, showing off a strip of skin between the band of the bra and the top of the leggings. The movement makes my resolve finally snap. Without an explanation, I'm pulling her through all of the exercise equipment.

"Archer!" she yells, attempting to keep up with me. I don't even look back at her—I'm too busy looking for somewhere to take her that doesn't have countless men checking her out when she's just trying to work out.

Finally, I find one of the recovery rooms. Shoving the door open, I pull Winnie into it with me and let it slam shut behind us.

She watches me carefully through wide eyes, like she doesn't know what's gotten into me. I don't blame her. I know I'm acting childish, but I don't give a shit. It was driving me crazy to have her in there with me, and we hadn't even started working out. I pay almost a grand a month to work out at this private gym, and I'm tempted to never come back—at least with her in tow.

"What are you doing?" Winnie asks. Her chest heaves up and down, and every time she takes a deep breath in, the spandex material of her bra tightens around her chest, giving me a glimpse of her peaked nipples.

I sigh, turning around to face the wall because I need a break from looking at her. I need a break from *wanting* her, but I don't think that'll happen anytime soon.

Somehow, I've let Winnie in—*deep*. Deep enough that she's stealing too much of my attention.

"Archer…" Winnie prods. Her voice is still far away, allowing me the distance I need to get my head on straight.

"What?" I ask, my voice tight and angry.

"Was it something I did out there? Something I did wrong?"

Her question breaks any sort of resolve I have left. Without thinking of all the reasons I shouldn't be doing this, I turn around and hastily close the distance between us. I take her by surprise, backing her up against the black door and pressing her into it.

She gasps, her hands finding my chest because I've left nowhere else for her to put them.

"You haven't done anything wrong," I hiss, pissed at myself for making her feel this way. The only thing she's done wrong is get mixed up with a man like me.

A man who can't control his impulses, even though he knows better.

Her lips part as she sucks in one heavy breath after another. "Then what is it?"

"It's…" I want to reach out and touch her, to run my fingers along the sides of her cheeks. All I can think about is tracing her bottom lip with the pad of my thumb so I can memorize the feel of her lips on my skin. Knowing I shouldn't, I press my palms to the wood above her head.

I don't know if this position is any better. Now I fully cage her in. If I took one step closer, our bodies would be fully pressed against one another. If I leaned down, I could trap her lips with mine. It wouldn't be the first time we kissed, but fuck, it might end up being my favorite.

"It's what?" Her eyes search my face. She doesn't shy away from my touch at all. In fact, she seems to be fighting the urge to pull me in by the way her fingers clutch the fabric of my shirt.

"It's you," I confess, knowing I don't have the willpower to fight this any longer. Marrying her was supposed to be a simple business transaction—an opportunity for us to finally get a foothold in our fiercest competitor's decisions. It's turning into something more than that. Something far more terrifying because I'm a man who loves control, and I find myself losing it more and more with her.

"Me?" Her voice cracks.

My hands slide down the door slightly, now lining up on either side of her face. "Yes, *you*, Winnie." My fingers brush her temple. "You're in my head, and I hate it."

Her eyes go wide. "I am?"

I nod, keeping my fingers pressed to her skin, even though I know I shouldn't. My thumb skirts over her cheek. She leans into my touch, making my heartbeat intensify.

"I don't think I've ever been jealous in my life. Why would I need to be? I get anything and everything I want." My fingers drift to her neck. Watching her react to my touch does nothing to stop me from doing something I know I shouldn't. "But today... fuck, Winnie, I was jealous when any of the men here simply glanced at you."

With my fingers wrapped around the back of her neck, I use my other hand to grip her chin so I can tip her head up to look at me. "It's been almost a month of pure torture being married to you. Each day has become more and more unbearable because all I want to do is..." I let my words fall between us because I don't know if I should say them out loud. Once they're said, they can't be taken back. And if she knows how much I want her, what will she do with that information?

I can feel her pulse pick up pace underneath my fingertips. She swallows, letting her eyes drift to my lips for a moment. "All you want to do is?"

"This," I answer, slamming my lips to hers. She doesn't hesitate for a second, but then again, she never does. Every time we kiss for the cameras, she's ready. I always thought it was her playing the part, but with the eagerness she meets my lips and no one around to witness it, I wonder if maybe this isn't all in my head.

Our lips crash against one another in a tidal wave. There's tongue and teeth, and it's so much more than the ones we've shared for the sake of appearances. It's wild and untamed—and it's the best kiss of my life.

Even with my tongue against hers, I still don't feel close enough to her. Needing to feel her everywhere, I lift her by the narrow of her waist and wrap her legs around my middle. It gives her more height, allowing my tongue even deeper into her mouth.

Her hands wrap around my neck as she pulls her body closer to mine. I back her up, pressing her body up against the door so my hands can explore more of her. She moans, and I love that I get to taste it. I slide my hand until I cup her ass, reveling in the way she arches her back.

"Fuck," I growl, ripping my mouth from hers only to kiss along her neck. All I've thought about every time we've had to give each other a chaste kiss for the cameras was how badly I wanted to taste her skin. I want to nip at her neck, to feel her racing pulse against my lips.

"Archer," Winnie moans, and if I hadn't already given in, that would've done the trick. I'm obsessed with the way she says my name. I want to make her say it again and again—just like that. Sultry and a little raspy as she gives in to the temptation between us.

"You're too fucking tempting," I tell her, my tongue caressing a red mark left by my teeth. She stretches her neck, allowing me more access to her skin. She gives me so much room to explore, and I don't know what I want to do first.

"We shouldn't be doing this," I tell her, knowing I have no intention of stopping right now.

"Why?"

I laugh, my breath tickling her throat as I kiss along her collarbone. "We may be married, but it's supposed to be business between us. And this…" I bite down on her throat, hoping to leave another mark. Her moan only makes me want to do it more, to leave a necklace of hickeys along her neck to claim her as mine. "This doesn't feel like business."

"This can be business," she pants, rocking her hips against me.

I didn't choose an outfit based on hiding my cock today, so I know the thin pants I wear do nothing to stop her from feeling how hard I am for her. If she's going to play this game, I'll play better. When she rocks again, I let her slide down my body only enough to line her up perfectly with my straining cock.

Her moan undoes me. It takes everything in me to not throw her onto the physical therapy table and have her naked in an instant. I surprise myself by not doing anything except kissing back up her neck until our lips are almost touching once again.

"I don't mix business with pleasure," I state, watching her closely for her reaction.

She smiles, her eyes traveling to my lips. "What a shame. I really wanted you to make *my* pleasure *your* business." *Fuck.* She knows exactly what she's doing when she rocks up against me again. I've always thought of her as this quiet, reserved woman who was a puppet for her father. But she surprises me at every turn.

My grip on her falters slightly, but it's enough that she unwraps her legs from me and drops to the ground. Even with her feet back on the floor, she doesn't stop touching me. In fact, she grabs on to my forearms and smiles at me with the biggest grin. "Let me know if you ever change your mind about that." I don't even realize she's reached behind her and grabbed the handle of the door until she's pulling it open and sliding through the opening. "Since we won't be working out in here, I think it's time for me to do it out there."

She disappears, and I'm left standing there watching her, completely speechless. She's so fucking different than what I thought, and it's horrible.

Because this version of her? The real one...I think I might be obsessed with it.

25
Winnie

"WHAT ARE YOU SMILING AT?" ARCHER ASKS ME AS WE SIT ACROSS from one another at dinner. His chef had prepared chicken with vegetables that smell amazing. We'd gone all day without talking after the kiss at the gym that hasn't left my mind since the moment it happened, but somehow, things haven't felt weird. They just feel…electrified.

"I'm not smiling," I answer, rubbing my lips together to try and hide that I definitely am smiling.

His sigh is loud as he sets down his fork. He's barely even taken two bites, but his food seems forgotten as he looks at me from across the long table. "Winnie, you're a horrible liar. You wear your emotions all over your face."

My lips twitch, only fueling him further. He holds his hands up, a small laugh coming from his chest. "See! Right there. You're smiling."

I shake my head, trying to stab a piece of chicken but I'm not in the least bit interested with my food. "I was thinking about you at the gym today. How you almost bit the head off the poor guy who offered to help me after the closet incident."

He chokes on the sip of water he'd just taken. "*Incident?*"

This time, I don't hide my smile from him. "Yeah. Incident."

He grinds his teeth. "I'm sorry, I wasn't aware tasting your moans as you pretty much begged for me to keep kissing you was an incident."

I swallow, feeling my smile falter. He's right. I would've begged and begged if it meant he'd keep kissing me. No one had ever kissed me with so much passion—so much possession. It's like he became an entirely new person from the other times we've kissed while keeping up appearances.

And it'd rocked my world.

I'd thought about it all day and wondered if it'd ever happen again. In the heat of the moment, I'd been bold to tell him I wanted to mix business and pleasure. But now that his hands aren't traveling over my body and his lips aren't on me, I wonder if he has a point.

We signed a business contract to be married, but we never even broached the subject of what would happen behind closed doors. Why should we have? We're two people who were taught to hate each other. Now, I'm wondering if I'm still supposed to hate him or if maybe it isn't so wrong for me to want to kiss him more like that.

He taps the table with his knuckles, catching my attention. When I focus on him again, I find his gaze pinned on me. His eyes are dark, his posture rigid as he stares at me. "Is that what you call an *incident*?" He pretty much hisses the last word, like he hates the sound of it coming from his mouth.

I shrug. "Yep," I answer casually, finally taking a bite of the food. It's absolutely delicious, but everything Archer's chef makes is phenomenal.

"I'm about to kiss you just to prove to you that there's nothing about our mouths meeting that's an incident."

I stop mid-chew, thrown off by his words. I swallow, even though the bite isn't fully chewed. He stares at me expectantly, his eyebrows slightly raised as if he's already amused by whatever my response will be.

"What if that was your one chance?" I respond, my voice not coming out as confident as I want it to.

"Was it?" he immediately fires back, his voice rough.

I sit back. "I don't know."

"I don't believe in only having one chance. If you work hard for it, second chances aren't out of reach."

I mull over his words, not sure how to respond. The easy answer is that I want to kiss him again—and not just because we'll undoubtedly have to at an event or for a photo op. But I want to kiss him because it feels good to kiss him.

It surprisingly feels right. But that isn't really an easy answer because I shouldn't want to kiss him. I really shouldn't want anything to do with him outside of the obligations we have for public appearances.

"I think we need more rules," I finally get out.

"Rules?" He drags the word out slowly.

"Yes. Rules."

His smirk is so devilishly handsome that I almost want to tell him that rules aren't really needed. Are there really any rules when it comes to marrying someone to help keep your name clean? "Why do you think we need rules?" It's a simple question, but the way he asks it makes it seem so seductive.

I shift in my seat. He stares at me so intently that it makes me squirm. Why is his eye contact *so* sexy?

"Because there's no playbook for kissing your fake husband."

"Technically, I'm your *real* husband. We kiss for people all the time. Why can't we kiss for ourselves?"

I adjust my position in the chair. "That seems complicated."

He shrugs. "Life is complicated."

I stare at him, wondering where this is coming from. I was the one who was pretty much begging for him to make things complicated at the gym today. If he wanted more of me at that moment, he could've had me. But he didn't. I don't know what's changed since then, but he's being far more direct than I was expecting.

"Can I ask you something, Winnie?" Archer asks, his voice

calm and collected. It occurs to me that I'd love to see him in a boardroom. I have no doubt he commands it easily.

I hold eye contact. "You can ask me anything. It'll depend if I answer it or not."

He nods, his dark eyes roaming my face as if he's looking for answers. "You told me you were never going to trust me. Did you mean it?"

His question surprises me. I thought he'd ask if I wanted to kiss him again or maybe even mention the rules I'd requested. But instead, I'm stunned for a moment because I didn't have an answer prepared for the question he ended up asking. "I want to mean it," I answer truthfully. I don't want to put my trust in another man again. And while Archer is different than I was expecting, there's history between our families. I don't want to blindly trust him because he's a great kisser.

"I make it a point to never trust people," he admits. He sits up in his chair, trailing his thumb along his bottom lip as he thinks deeply about something.

"That makes sense."

His finger taps against his lips as he stares at me through heavy eyelids. "But it seems like it'd be easy to let myself trust you."

I give him a sad smile because I want that. Between our early morning walks and our late-night dinner conversations, I've started to care for him. Of course, I want him to trust me. But we were both raised by powerful men who make it a point to not trust a soul. It's safe to say we both may have trust issues. "We both know better than to ever really trust each other," I answer.

He frowns. "I'd like to think I'll earn your trust."

"Why?" Archer doesn't strike me as the kind of man to care if somebody trusts him, so I don't know why it matters to him whether I trust him or not.

"Because I'd really like to kiss you again. In private where I can take my time with you." His eyes rake down my body, and I find myself squirming in my chair all over again. I want to toss the food aside and crawl across the table and tell him to do just that.

"Then what's stopping you?" I feel like I pretty much panted that question, but I can't even be embarrassed by it because I'm so turned on by the thought of kissing him again...by doing more.

"You said you wanted rules, so that's what I'm giving you. One rule. We'll finish what we started when you trust me."

My mouth snaps shut in shock. He's constantly surprising me, showing me that he's not who I thought he was. "That wasn't what I meant by making rules."

"What rules were you thinking of, then?"

I shrug because I can't remember what rules I wanted to make in the first place. Maybe that we shouldn't kiss—or that if we do, we're clear that things can't get weird. We're still at the beginning of our marriage; we have to somewhat get along. And if we're blurring the lines behind closed doors, will that complicate things further?

"So it's settled. Once you trust me..." His face breaks out into a wolfish smile—one that's full of promise—that makes my stomach fill with butterflies. "Once you trust me, we'll have a lot of fun."

"Are you saying you trust me, then?" I ask, trying to pretend that he isn't looking at me like he's picturing me completely naked. God, how does he have the ability to undress me with nothing but his eyes?

"Is there a reason I shouldn't trust you?"

"I'm the daughter of your biggest competitor. What if my father arranged the marriage so I could get a foothold into your family and Moore Hotels?"

This makes him laugh, like the thought of me ever doing that is so outlandish the only thing he can do is laugh. "If anyone got a foothold in anyone's company here, it's me getting one in your father's."

He has a point. My father has barely talked with me since

Archer and I got married, let alone asked me to get any inside information. He probably knows that Archer isn't dumb enough to tell me anything I could use against his family. "Still. We're not supposed to trust each other."

"You could use the same argument for us being married. We were probably the least likely to end up wed, yet..." His eyes roam my face slowly. "Here we are."

"You're something else," I respond because I don't know what else to say.

He sits up, taking a drink of his wine. "So it's settled. The rule is we'll be able to enjoy being married even more once you admit that you trust me."

I blink. Who is this man, and what am I going to do about him?

His eyes move from my face to the full plate of food in front of me. "Now, eat your food," he demands, spearing a piece of chicken and popping it into his mouth.

26
Archer

"DO YOU HAVE ANY PLANS THIS WEEKEND?" WINNIE ASKS ME during our typical morning walk.

It's Friday, and I surprisingly didn't have any meetings I had to rush to, so we've been leisurely strolling Central Park, even stopping to grab coffees to stay warm in the late November cold.

I look over at her, trying not to focus on how adorable she looks in a pair of puffy earmuffs. Never did I think that thought would cross my mind about anybody, but it's something that's crossed it multiple times this morning since she met me downstairs for our walk.

"You mean, do *we* have any plans this weekend?" I respond, knowing it'd be better for me to put distance between us, considering she's done nothing to show me that she's wanting to talk about the little rule I've put in place for us. Meanwhile, all I've thought about in the last week was kissing her again, tasting her little moans as my hands explored her body.

"There's kind of a lull since we already had Thanksgiving, but all of the Christmas events haven't started up yet. So I was thinking we could go to the Hamptons with Beck and Margo..." she answers, holding the coffee close to her mouth to keep warm.

For the first time in a long time, I actually enjoyed Thanksgiving. We stayed inside, neither one of our families particularly demanding that we attend it at their houses. The night before, we stopped by my family's annual Thanksgiving dinner because it was the first time our families were to be seen together, but we were there all of an hour before we got to sneak out because they took all the photos needed.

It worked. Both Moore and Bishop Hotels are prospering at the union of our families. Honestly, marrying Winnie was the last thing I ever thought I'd do, but it's turned out to be a smart business move. On the actual holiday, Winnie and I played board games before she forced me to watch cheesy Christmas movies I'd never seen and don't intend to watch again.

"But if you have plans, don't worry about it," Winnie interrupts my thoughts when I don't answer. She tries to mask the disappointment in her voice, but I still heard it.

"What makes you think I don't want to spend the weekend with you?" I come to a stop, putting my body in front of hers so we can have this conversation face-to-face. Her cheeks are pink from the cold, making me fight the urge to tell her to pull her scarf up higher to get warmer.

"We've spent a lot of time together lately. And when Margo asked if we wanted to visit the Hamptons with them this weekend, I at first said I'd join but that you were busy. She said she really wanted it to be all of us so we could spend time together, so I told her I'd ask you. But really, I can go alone, and you can have your house to yourself for once, and it'll be—"

"Winnie," I interrupt, completely cutting her off before she continues to ramble.

"Yeah?" God, the way she shows every single one of her emotions on her face might just undo me. I've never met someone who is okay with showing their vulnerabilities so much, but she wears them like a badge of honor. She watches me, her body tense like she's bracing herself for me to let her down.

"If you want to head to the Hamptons this weekend with your friends, then we'll go."

"Really?"

My head cocks to the side. "Did you really expect me to say no?"

She shrugs, holding the coffee to her lips in an attempt to hide her shy smile. "I didn't know if it's something you'd want to do."

"Go to the Hamptons?"

"Spend more time with me than necessary. I could easily tell everyone that you have to work this weekend."

I've waited every single day for her to tell me that she trusts me. That she knows I don't want to hurt her and that I won't let her down like she has been before. Our family history—and her terrible taste in men—give her every reason to not trust me.

But I want to go against that. I want to give her all the reasons *to* trust me. Even if I feel things for her I shouldn't, even if I want her when I shouldn't. I just don't know if that'll happen.

I reach to touch her, letting my fingers drift down the soft skin of her cheek. "I force my assistant to constantly shift my calendar because I refuse to miss our mornings together, Winnie."

"You do?" she whispers as my thumb traces over her cheekbone.

"I do. So if you have any questions about whether or not I want to spend time with you, that should give you all the answers you need."

She smiles so wide, so freely, that I ache to lean down and taste it. I want to feel those lips curve around mine, to feel her sighs against my skin. I ultimately just want to kiss her again, but I'm a man of my word. I want her to give in, to admit that our time could be put to much better use if we were to finish what we started in that room at the gym.

"Okay," she finally manages to say. Her voice is breathy, like she's coming to terms with what I said.

"You seem shocked," I tease.

"Because I am shocked. You're always taking me by surprise, Archer Moore."

The smile I give her is genuine. "You know I've thought the same thing about you, Winnie Moore."

Her nose scrunches. "My last name isn't Moore."

"It could be."

She rolls her eyes, not knowing I'm dead serious. I know there are so many reasons why it shouldn't bother me that her last name is Bishop—but it does. I won't ask her to change her last name for something that isn't supposed to be anything more than a contract, but I can't fight the urge to want her to have *my* last name. "No one expects me to change my last name for you, Archer. Anyway..." She bites back a smile. "You'll really come with us?"

I nod. I know it'd be much smarter for me to stay home. I'm busier than ever, and I shouldn't be spending any extra time than necessary with Winnie, considering she's already taking up too much space in my mind.

"Where are we staying?" I ask, starting to walk forward before I lean down and kiss her.

"Beck and Margo apparently have a house there." She turns to me. "Where do you own houses?"

I laugh. "I own a lot of properties. It'd take a while for me to list them all."

She bites her lip as we keep walking. We're nearing the house. Normally, this is the part of the walk where I feel sad because I know that our time together is over, but I don't feel that today at all. Instead, I feel excited at the prospect of spending all weekend together.

"Why?" I push, wanting to know why it matters to her where I own houses. "Is there somewhere you'd like to have a place? Tell me where, and I'll buy it."

She laughs. "If you don't already own one there."

"True." I wait for her to tell me where she envisions herself visiting, but she never answers. I try not to think too hard about how serious I was when I told her I'd buy a place anywhere she wanted if that's what she was looking for.

When we get back to the house, we stop in front of the stairs. She doesn't make a move to climb them, so I don't either, wanting to stay locked in this moment a little longer.

"I think they have a jet leaving later this afternoon," Winnie begins. She sighs, her hot breath mixing with the cold in a cloud of air. "We can always go later if we need to. Or I can go with them, and you can meet us there later. I don't know what your schedule looks like, but—"

I press my fingers to her lips. They're warm against my cold fingertips. "I'll call Sinclair and see what the plan is. If you want to fly there with them, then that's what we'll do."

She stares at me in disbelief. She's quiet for so long that I shift from one foot to the other. "What?" I ask.

"I was just expecting some kind of argument from you, is all."

I bite my tongue, not wanting to admit that with anyone else there would be. With her, everything is different. I still don't know if that's a good or a bad thing.

"I'm sure I'll find something to have an opinion on later," I tease, trying not to get lost in her eyes.

She smiles. "I'm sure you will."

And then she turns to climb the stairs, leaving me to wonder if I should really go on this Hamptons trip with them or if I should back out now while I can.

27
Winnie

"I'm convinced you guys don't even know what a house is," Emma states as we stand in the driveway of the Hamptons house Beck and Margo purchased not too long ago. When Margo asked us to come stay with them for the weekend, I wasn't sure if Archer would agree to it. But it was only this morning when he shocked me by saying yes and completely clearing his schedule to come.

Margo walks up between Emma and me, wrapping her arms around our necks as we stare at the huge, beautiful two-story in front of us. "Emma, what are you talking about?"

"You told me you guys bought a *house*. This isn't a house, Margo. This is a *mansion*." Her wide eyes slowly track the house, as if she can't quite believe what she's seeing.

Margo laughs. "It is a house. We wanted a lot of space so we could have people come visit us."

"How many rooms does it have?" Emma wonders, mouth parted in awe.

"Seven...I think."

"Seven?" Emma shrieks. She rolls her eyes. "God, I can't imagine just casually buying a house with seven bedrooms."

I laugh. "It just means we get to reap the benefits of our best friend marrying rich."

Both Emma and Margo look at me with narrowed eyes.

Emma's the one to actually speak up. "Okay, don't pretend you're modest. I'm sure your family has a house here somewhere with fifteen bedrooms. You were born with money and married rich. Way to go, Winnie Boo Boo."

I roll my eyes at the terrible nickname that was drunkenly given to me. I'm busy cringing at Emma still using it to this day when Archer comes to a stop in front of us.

"Winnie Boo Boo?" he says with a smirk.

Emma looks at me with a satisfied smile. "Isn't it cute?" She taps my nose as if I'm a child. "It's something we called her in college, and it's just stuck."

"It's terrible," I argue, trying to take my bag from Archer, but he doesn't let go.

"I agree," Archer begins. "It's *very* cute, Winnie Boo Boo."

I elbow him in the stomach, glaring at Emma for even telling him about the nickname. "It's so cute we should never mention it again. Sound good?"

Margo laughs, sliding out from our grasp to follow Beck toward the house. "Okay, everyone. It's time to see the house!" She claps as if she can hardly contain her excitement.

We follow her in. It's hard not to marvel at how gorgeous the house is. The Hamptons is actually somewhere I haven't visited much. My dad didn't enjoy it, so I only came as a teenager and adult when there were parties here. I forgot how much I liked it here. It's classy and quiet and has this sophisticated feel to it.

"Holy shit, Margo," Emma exclaims, stopping in front of me once we walk through the front doors, almost making me walk right into her. "This place is huge!"

"It's stunning," I agree, my eyes looking around the first floor. It feels cozier than you'd expect for a house that has seven bedrooms. But it's decorated beautifully. It's got a coastal theme mixed with some modern accents that really make the place feel homey despite the size.

All of us stand in the entryway, our eyes taking in the place. I'm the first one to break the silence when I spot a giant painting above the mantel. "Oh my god, is this yours?" I ask Margo, crossing the space to get closer to the giant canvas. "It's breathtaking."

"Isn't it magnificent?" Beck asks. I look at him, finding him staring at his wife with so much love and adoration.

Margo comes to a stop next to him, wrapping her arms around his waist and burying her cheek against his chest. "Stop feeding me compliments. It'll go to my head."

Emma plops down on the couch, giving herself a perfect view of the painting we're talking about. "Damn, Mar. That might be my favorite of yours yet. Is that the view outside?"

We all focus on the swirling colors of blues and tans. It's got to be the house mixed in with the view of the ocean, but it's done in a way where you don't know which side to focus on. One side of it looks like the rich colors of the beach in summer, the other in the dead of winter.

"Yeah. I painted it after we first looked at the house. We didn't know if we wanted to be here or not," Margo explains.

"She'd barely started this piece before I already had an offer on this house. It felt like fate," Beck adds.

Margo rolls her eyes. "Nothing is fate with you, Beck. You just go after what you want without asking any questions."

He pulls her closer to him. "Worked with you, didn't it?"

I smile at how cute they are, looking away to find Archer's eyes trained on me. There's a look on his face I can't quite read, but it's one that I can't get out of my head, even as Margo continues to show us the rest of the house.

Emma's already picked out her room on the other side of the house when Margo leads us down a narrow hallway. It's off the main side of the house but isn't too far from the large living area. I thought this would house the primary bedroom, but that has almost an entire wing to itself on the opposite side of the house.

"I hope you like this one," Margo tells us with a bashful smile. She opens a door with a brass doorknob, escorting us into a room much larger than I was expecting. "For some reason, this room reminded me of you, Win," Margo explains, looking around the room that has a very vintage vibe. The comforter on the bed reminds me of one I had as a child with its horses and scalloped edges.

I laugh, marveling at how pretty the room is. "This looks perfect," I assure her.

She giddily claps her hands together, pointing to a desk at the far side of the room. It's pushed up against a large floor-to-ceiling window that looks over the water. "I wanted you to have a desk and a view in case, you know, inspiration strikes. There's still so much of this place I need to decorate..." She winks at me, which makes me blush as I feel Archer's eyes hot against my skin.

"You've done a great job," I tell her, looking at how beautifully decorated the room is. It seems like she's done different themes for the different rooms, and I like that. It brings character to each unique space. "I don't know if you need my help."

She rolls her eyes, running her hand along a folded quilt at the end of the bed. "I'd still love your opinion on things. The room Camden and Pippa will be staying in seems boring to me. And don't even get me started on the pool house once the renovations are over."

I nod, laughing at her. We used to go to flea markets together while in college to give us something to do on the weekends. She always told me one day I'd have to help her decorate a house. Turns out, she has multiple houses to decorate, but I still don't think she needs my help. "Shopping trip soon?" I ask her, already looking forward to it. Margo and I haven't spent much time together since she got married, but I'd love a day with her soon. We'll ask Emma, but she always tells us no and uses her typical excuse that after having to grow up with hand-me-down clothes and used furniture, she doesn't enjoy buying other people's unwanted items now.

Margo nods, her eyes lighting up with excitement. She looks at Archer for a moment, as if she forgot he was even here to begin with. I'd have forgotten, too, if I hadn't felt his eyes trained on me during our entire conversation. Margo tucks her dark hair behind her ear as she begins to shuffle to the bedroom door. "Well, I'll let you guys get settled in here. There should be towels and everything you need in the bathroom. Emma's already told me she was going to take a nap, so feel free to take your time in here. We don't have any plans until dinner tonight at the club. Sound good?"

All I can do is nod because it's only just now occurring to me that everyone here thinks we're married. They wouldn't think twice about us sharing a room, but I definitely hadn't thought about it once.

I don't say a word to Margo as she leaves, too lost in wondering how we're going to navigate this. We can't request another room—it'd be weird. My eyes scan the room, disappointed to find not even a couch in this bedroom. How does she furnish a room this large and not even put a chaise lounge at the end of the bed?

Finally, my eyes land on Archer's, finding him already looking at me.

His eyes are dark and lit with something I can't put my finger on.

"What's going through your head, *wife*?" I try not to react to the way he says wife. I could swear it's with affection, but I don't want to let it get to my head.

I look at him, then to the bed and back at him. "There's only one bed."

He nods, his eyes flicking to the king bed in the middle of the room. "You say that like it's a bad thing."

"It *is* a bad thing," I argue. "Archer, we can't share a bed."

He reaches behind him and shuts the door. He doesn't do it gently, the smack of the door hitting the doorframe ringing through the room. "And why can't we share a bed? Afraid you won't be able to keep your hands off me?" he teases.

My eyes go wide because why does he seem almost excited at

the prospect of sharing a bed? Doesn't he remember what happened the last time our bodies were in close proximity to each other? We hadn't been in that room alone together for a minute before we were making out.

"*Archer.*" His name comes out like a plea. I've already come close to begging him to forget about his rule and ask him to kiss me many times. The most recent time was when he got back from the gym completely shirtless, stunning me speechless at the ripple of his perfectly sculpted muscles.

Despite the dirty thoughts I've had of him, I've been holding strong. I won't tell him I trust him and give him that power, even if I do think about kissing him again way more than I should.

"What?" he asks, grinning ear to ear. God, he looks so much more boyish this way, and I love it. I think I love it so much because I know he doesn't act like this around other people. I've seen him at many events now, and they barely get a tight-lipped smile from him. The way he smiles right now is one of mischief and humor—and it's incredibly sexy on him.

"I'll sleep on the floor," I announce. The old hardwoods look terrible to sleep on, but I can tell they've been recently polished. There doesn't seem to be a speck of dust in this room, which means I'm sure they're clean. Plus, Margo left us numerous blankets and quilts. I could maybe make a decently comfortable bed on the floor.

Archer lets out a low chuckle, one that sends tingles down my spine.

"What's so funny?" I ask, wondering if it was a bad idea for me to invite him this weekend. I clearly hadn't thought things through.

"You," he answers immediately, taking a step closer to me.

"Nothing I said was funny."

"Actually, the idea that you think I'd ever let you sleep on the floor is hilarious." He grabs my chin. I try not to meet his eyes despite the position he's put my head in, but he leans down to put his face in my view. I lose the battle at avoiding his gaze, unable to look away from his deep, rich chestnut eyes.

"Why?" I ask, my curiosity getting the best of me.

The only place he touches me is where his fingertips dig into the tender skin of my jaw, but it feels like he's touching me everywhere. Maybe it's because of the intense way he looks at me, like he's just dying to lean in and take a taste.

I think if he made the move, I'd let him. I forgot I even asked a question until he clears his throat before talking. "Because I care about you too much to let you sleep on the hard ground."

All I hear is the beginning of his sentence. *Because I care about you…*

I don't know what he sees on my face, but whatever it is makes him let out a low chuckle. His fingers dance along the curve of my neck before he drops his hand.

"You're sleeping in the bed. I'm sleeping in the bed. The only thing in question for tonight is if you're going to give in and let me do to you the dirty, filthy things I have running through my head."

He turns around, opens the door, and leaves as if his words didn't just completely take me by surprise. My entire body is flushed from them.

I don't know how long I stand there staring at the open door, but it's long enough for my feet to begin to ache in my heels.

Finally, I take a seat, running my hand over the soft, fluffy comforter. My cheeks heat all over again when I look at the bed, wondering if maybe both Archer and I will break the rule we created for each other.

And the more I think about feeling his lips against mine again, his hands on my body, I wonder if I really care about the rules at all.

28
Winnie

I'M SITTING IN THE LIVING ROOM WITH MARGO, BOTH OF US drinking an afternoon coffee and looking at design magazines, when Archer gets back from his workout. I know his run along the beach wasn't necessary; he'd gone to the gym early this morning before our walk. If I had to guess, I would think he may have wanted some space from me. Or maybe the short flight from Manhattan to here really made him feel like he had to let off some steam.

Or maybe he's as worked up as I am at the thought of having to share a bed together.

"Good workout?" Margo asks Archer as he opens the refrigerator.

He sets an empty glass on the counter before taking the pitcher of filtered water out and pouring himself a glass. He nods before sucking down the water in just a few gulps.

Why does he have to look hot while doing something as simple as taking a drink of water?

He closes the door of the fridge, bracing his hands on the lip of the counter. "It was great, actually," he tells Margo, his eyes flicking to me. "I had to let off some steam."

My eyes go wide as I squirm in my chair at the undertone of his words. There's no way I'm going to be able to resist him tonight, and there's no way I'm going to tell him I trust him tonight. I've found myself in a bit of a predicament.

"I'm so happy to hear that. Beck had to jump on a call, but I know next ti—"

"Hey, Margo, before I forget to ask. Do you have any spare pillows anywhere?" I blurt, not caring that she was mid-sentence.

Both Margo and Archer look at me with a confused stare. Margo's the one to speak up.

"Um, yeah, we have extras in the linen closet in the hallway next to your room. Are there not enough? I swore I gave you six…"

I nod, knowing I'll need as many pillows as possible to create a barrier between Archer and me tonight. That'll fix our little problem for the weekend. If I create a wall of pillows between us, maybe I'll be able to forget about the six-foot-four man lying next to me who has abs of steel and also happens to be my husband.

Yeah, pillows between us will definitely make me forget about how much I want to roll around in the sheets with him.

"I just like a lot of pillows," I lie. It's terrible for your posture to sleep with any more than one, but I don't mention that.

Margo stares at me with a blank expression while Archer watches me with his eyes narrowed. He knows exactly what I'm doing, but I'm in too deep to stop it.

"Okay," Margo finally gets out, shutting the magazine we were looking at. "I can show you where they are," she offers.

I shake my head, watching Archer back away from the two of us and disappearing into the hallway without a goodbye. "Oh, I'll find them when I get back to the room. I just wanted to check with you." I look away from the empty hallway, wondering if Archer is mad or if he was just done with the conversation.

Luckily, Margo changes the subject and takes me from my own thoughts for a moment. "Thank you again for looking these over with me. I feel like I at least have an idea of what I'll want for the pool house."

"I love that you're making it into such an entertainment area but keeping the same classy, old-school vibe you've established with the main house," I tell her.

We sit together for another five minutes, going over her vision after the renovations are done until I can't sit still any longer. I want to find Archer to see why he left so abruptly.

"I might go lie down for a little bit before getting ready for tonight," Margo says, getting me out of having to come up with an excuse to leave her alone to find Archer.

I let out a sigh of relief, giving her a soft smile. "Same," I lie. I'm not tired at all, but she doesn't need to know that.

Margo wraps her arms around me, pulling me in for a long hug. "I'm just so happy you're here this weekend. I can't wait to spend time with you and Emma and have Pippa with us, too." She pulls away, a wide smile on her face. "This is going to be the *best* weekend!"

I give her a tight-lipped smile. The jury's still out on how this weekend will turn out, but no matter how much tension there is between Archer and me, I'm excited to spend the weekend with the girls. Tomorrow, the guys are going to go to some kind of fancy whiskey tasting at the Pembroke Hills Country Club, leaving us girls to enjoy a morning at the spa, followed by a tasting at a local vineyard.

"I'll see you in a bit for dinner," I say as she begins to walk to the other side of the house. Quickly, I spin on my heel and rush down the hallway toward the room I'm sharing with Archer. I make a quick stop to grab the pillows Margo mentioned. There are only four in there, and they're not as fluffy as the ones on our bed, but I take them anyway. They'll do the trick. Anything will work as long as it creates a barrier between us.

The door to our room is shut, but I open it anyway. He might be taking a work call or finishing up changing from his workout gear, but he didn't lock it, so I slowly push it open. I step inside, finding his phone on one of the cream wood nightstands. Quietly, I set the pillows on the bed, wondering where he could be.

I'm about to go looking for him in the rest of the house when I notice the sound of the shower coming from the en suite bathroom. I stop at the opening. I know I should leave and give him privacy. He probably wasn't expecting me to come back to the room so quickly. I'm about to sneak back into the hallway when the sound of his voice stops me in my tracks.

I freeze, leaning closer to the bathroom to see if I heard him correctly. I swore I heard my name, but maybe it's my mind playing tricks on me. It's quiet except for the sound of the water hitting the tile.

My back presses to the wall as I decide what to do. I should leave and pretend I never came in here in the first place, but I can't get the idea out of my head that I swear I heard him say my name.

"Winnie," Archer groans.

My eyes widen. There's no mistaking it this time. He *definitely* said my name.

I slowly lean into the bathroom. Due to the layout of the room, I can't see into the shower. There's a wall that blocks him from my view, but it doesn't block the sound. He grunts, and it makes my heart speed up.

Not knowing what's come over me, I take one step into the bathroom. My heart slams against my chest in anticipation. I know I shouldn't be doing this, but I just want one little peek. What is he doing? Why is he saying my name?

I take another step in, making sure I tiptoe as softly as I can. Leaning forward, I look in the mirror to see if I can see him at all.

My entire body flushes because I can see him perfectly. I can see all of him.

I catch my breath as I find his back to me, his body turned at a slight angle, giving me a view of every muscular inch of him. He braces his body up with one hand against the shower wall. My eyes travel down his muscular back, marveling at the way his muscles bunch together on his upper back every time the hand not against the wall moves.

This invades his privacy in so many different ways, but I can't move. I can't do anything but let my gaze travel down his perfect, naked body. All I can think about as I look at his back is how I wonder what it'd be like to feel those muscles move underneath my touch as he slid into me. Would he let my fingernails scrape along his spine? Would he ease himself in slowly or push himself inside me hurriedly at the same pace his hand is moving now?

He groans, and that's when my eyes finally focus on his other hand—on what he's doing. His large hand wraps around his cock, pumping up and down in a quick rhythm. I can't look away. He's huge, way bigger than anyone I've ever seen.

"Fuck." He lets out a loud growl as his hand slows a little, and he takes extra time pumping just the thick head of his cock before he goes down to the base again.

"*Winnie...*" He moans at the same moment I realize that not only is he getting himself off...but he's getting himself off to *me*. Or at least to thoughts of me as he groans my name again in what can only be described as an intense want.

I clamp my thighs together. It's all kinds of wrong, but I'm turned on by the sight of him stroking himself with my name on his lips.

His head rolls back, and the muscles on his back tighten. Is he close?

God, my clit throbs. My fingers twitch at my sides as I fight the urge to slip them into the waistband of my skirt. If I could just relieve the building pressure for a second, I'd come to my senses and leave him to finish alone.

But I don't want him to finish alone. I want to watch him fall apart. Will he moan my name again? My curiosity is getting the best of me. Slowly, I let one hand drift up my leg. It'd be easy to lift my skirt and glide my hand against my clit. My fingers slowly drift up my thigh as my eyelids feel heavy with desire.

"If you're going to get off on watching me stroke my cock, at least come closer so I can watch."

My body jolts, my hand slapping against my thigh as I try to act like I wasn't just doing exactly what I was doing.

My cheeks feel hot as I find Archer watching me closely. He's turned around, giving me an even better view of what he's doing.

His hand doesn't stop.

He continues to pump up and down his girth as he stares right at me.

I wet my lips, wondering what it'd be like to fit him in my mouth. I'm not that close to him, but even from here, I know he's massive. I know I'd have to stretch my lips and cheeks to even fit my mouth around him.

"Winnie," Archer growls. His tone makes me jump, my eyes moving from his cock to his eyes. The moment our eyes meet, he smiles.

And it's the sexiest thing he's ever done. He's so confident, and normally, I'd hate the arrogance written all over his face, but right now, it's the hottest thing I've ever seen.

"Come here," he demands. There's not a hint of question in his words. It's like he already knows that I'd do anything he asked right now.

I take a step forward, my body moving of its own accord. He keeps his eyes pinned on me, but his hand never stops.

I come to a stop in front of the shower. He's so much bigger up close. I swallow, wondering what I'm doing right now. I just went to great lengths to gather pillows to put as a barrier between us while we sleep, yet here I am, watching him stroke his cock like it's the best thing I've ever seen.

"Closer," he instructs.

My mouth pops open because I can't come any closer unless I physically get in the shower with him.

"Winnie." My name comes out as a warning. I love the way it sounds coming from his mouth.

"What?" I whisper.

"Get in here and touch yourself."

29
Archer

My cock throbs in my grip as I wait for Winnie to make a decision. She's constantly surprising me, so I truly don't know if she'll step in the shower with me or if she'll run.

I don't know which I'd rather see her do. I want to watch her touch herself as much as I want my next breath, but I'm a man with only so much restraint. If I see her fingers play with her clit, will I be able to watch without touching? Is it best not to play with fire and for her to leave me to finish alone?

I stroke up and down, lost in the way she hungrily stares at my cock. She stares at it like she's starved and the only thing that will cure her hunger is getting a taste of me. My eyes shut for a moment with the vision of her on her knees for me, her mouth opening wide as I push my cock between her lips.

"I'm waiting," I growl, my patience wearing thin.

I want to open the door and pull her in, but if I get to feel the smallest part of her skin, I know I won't stop. Before I finally touch her and have my way with her, I want to break down her defenses until she admits she trusts me.

The world has given us every reason not to trust each other, yet I'm all too aware that she has my trust. I trust her far more than I trust any other person, and that fact alone is very, very dangerous.

At the moment, I don't care. All I want is for her to step into the stream of water with me, to give in to the burning tension between the two of us.

"I can't," she says. I barely hear her over the water.

My hand doesn't stop on my cock. If anything, it speeds up. I'm turned on by the way she stares at my cock so greedily. I know she wants to step in here. I know she even wants to touch it—maybe even suck it. But she's still trying to do the sensible thing and leave before we continue down a path we shouldn't travel.

"I know you want to touch yourself," I begin, my eyes flicking to where she grips the fabric of her skirt as if her life depends on it. She's clutching it so tight that her fingers have turned white.

She takes another step closer. "We shouldn't..."

"We don't have to touch each other." I say the words as a formality. Even if we don't touch, this interaction is still dangerous. I just simply don't give a fuck. How could I when she's staring at my dick like it's the best thing she's ever seen?

"Okay..." she finally whispers. Her tongue pops out to lick her lips, and it shreds the last bit of resolve I have. I toss open the shower door and pull her in here with me.

She yelps, stumbling into the stream of water fully clothed. "Archer!" She tries to step out of the running water, but the setup of the shower doesn't really give her any chance to stay dry. Water pours from one head at the top and two on the sides.

I drop her hand, telling myself I'll keep good on my promise to not touch her now that she's in here with me.

I'm having to force myself to have some self-control. She's *so* close. Close enough that if she reached out, her little hand could easily grip my cock.

I take a step back, putting a little bit of distance between us but also giving myself a better view of her. The corner of my lip lifts. "You're not even naked yet, and I'm hard as a fucking rock."

She looks down as if she needs to see the proof of my words herself. "You were already hard," she states.

"Because I was thinking of you. I had to go for a run after our conversation earlier." I stroke up and down, circling my head as she watches my movements like she's trying to memorize everything I do to get myself off. "I was so tense after thinking of sharing a bed with you. Even the run didn't help. I thought I'd ease it alone in here, but…" I smile when she rubs her thighs together, as if my words alone are turning her on. "Then you showed up."

"I was coming to apologize."

"You can apologize by fingering yourself, baby."

Her shirt is soaking wet, making it cling to her body so perfectly it shows off all of her. The light pink fabric does nothing to hide the outline of her champagne-colored bra underneath.

And then there's her perfect, peaked nipples. They fight against the fabric of her bra and shirt, just begging to be nipped and sucked on by me. Fuck, I want to run my tongue along them and find out what sounds she'll make if I let my teeth graze the underside of her breast.

The only reason I keep my feet planted where they are is because she bends at the waist, pulling the fabric of her skirt down her thighs. My cock pulses in my hand at the sight of her in a thong that matches her bra and a pair of stockings. She goes to pull the stockings down, but I shake my head.

"No. Keep those on."

She looks up, a slight smile on her lips. I love that she keeps eye contact the entire time as she unbuttons her blouse. It falls to the ground at her feet. She kicks the skirt and blouse out of her way, shoving them in the corner.

"Do you want me to keep this on, too?" she teases, pulling the straps of her bra down.

I shake my head. "No. That comes off."

In one fluid movement, she reaches behind her back and

undoes the clasp of her bra. It falls to the ground and becomes something else she kicks to the side.

Fuck. She's absolutely breathtaking. She stands in nothing but a pair of stockings and a thong, her eyes watching me closely as if she's waiting for more direction on what to do.

I think she likes being told what to do, and fuck do I love telling her exactly what I want from her.

I click my tongue, pulling my gaze from her perky, full tits to the scrap of lace that still hides her pussy from me. "You're still too covered for my liking," I muse, eager to get rid of the sheer fabric that hides all of her from me.

She tucks the wet strands of her hair behind her ear in a move that makes me wonder if she's feeling bashful about baring herself to me like this. She shouldn't be at all. She's fucking perfect in every way. I've never been more turned on in my life, and she hasn't even touched me.

"Step out of your panties," I demand.

At first, she acts as if she doesn't hear me. Her fingers reach up to play with her nipples. She rolls the peaked buds between her finger and her thumb. It's so fucking sexy, watching her palm her tits, knowing it's exactly what I want to do with them.

"Winnie..." I warn, my voice hoarse. My hand hasn't stopped stroking up and down on my cock, and I'm worried that when she finally does give me a view of her pussy, I won't be able to hold out for much longer. I won't let it happen. I won't come until she's made herself come once—maybe even twice.

"I've never..." she begins, her fingers looping through the fabric on her hips. She keeps them there, as if she's nervous to show me all of her.

"You've never what, baby?" I ask, desperate to know what she's about to admit.

"I haven't ever touched myself with someone else watching."

I smile, reveling in the fact that I get some kind of first from her. "That's what I like to hear," I praise, gripping my cock a little tighter.

My eyes stay focused on her as she pulls the thong off. Her thighs stay pressed together, so even though she's completely naked except for the stockings, I can't see the part of her I'm dying to see the most.

She stares at the floor for a minute before her eyes meet mine again. Her hair sticks to her face from the water, and there's a slight flush to her cheeks. I don't know if it's from the hot steam billowing around us or from what we're doing.

I'd like to think it's from the latter. That her blush is because of me.

Having her naked and within reach is the ultimate test of my restraint, but if I can't touch her, I at least want to see all of her.

"Sit," I command, pointing to the long bench seat in the shower.

"Why?"

"So you can spread your legs open wide for me. I want to see your fingers push in and out of your pussy, to see you play with your clit."

She swallows slowly, taking a cautious step toward the bench. "What if I don't do it right?"

I fight the urge to close the distance between us, to wrap my arms around her and pull her into me. I hate the unsure look on her face.

"Just make yourself feel good, baby," I croak. "Something tells me that you can be a dirty girl. You know how to finger yourself, so show me how you do it."

She takes a seat, opening her thighs slightly and giving me the smallest glimpse of her.

"Pull your legs up so your feet are on the edge." I have to stop pumping up and down my cock for a moment because I'm far too turned on.

She shivers as she presses her back to the cold stone wall, but she does as she's told. Her thighs spread open with the new position, and fucking finally, I see all of her.

"Your pussy is so pretty," I marvel, wanting to get on my

knees and taste her. Water rushes over us, making it hard for me to see what's wet from her arousal and what's just from the shower.

She closes her eyes the moment the words leave my mouth. I love that I can see her reactions to just my words alone. It makes me even more excited to see how she'd fall apart if she let me touch her and talk dirty to her.

For a moment, I just appreciate the view in front of me. Winnie was raised to be so prim and proper it makes me hard as a rock to see her on the verge of coming undone. Her mascara runs down her face as pieces of red hair stick to her flushed skin. Her lips are red from where she's bitten them, and all she wears is a pair of black stockings.

"You're so pretty like this, Winnie," I tell her, licking my lips. "With your tits begging for my touch and your pussy eager for attention. Are you going to be a good girl and touch yourself for me now?"

30
Winnie

MY FINGERS SLOWLY DRIFT ALONG MY INNER THIGH AS I GET THE nerve to do what Archer tells me to. I want to—I'm already so turned on just by the possessive way he watches me. But anytime I've ever got myself off, it's been alone in my room with the sheet pulled over me—and more often than not, with some kind of toy. I don't ever just use my fingers. I'm not used to it, and I'm certainly not used to the idea of someone watching me.

But god...what other reactions can I get from him if my fingers slipped between my legs? If he watched me slide a finger inside myself. I want to watch him come and it be because of me. Because of this, I inch my hand higher and higher until it barely skirts along my clit.

"That's it," he rasps. His voice is deep and rough, sounding way too hot for me to keep control of myself.

I hold my hand right at the edge, not touching myself quite yet. I know in teasing him, I'm also teasing myself, but I love it. The hand not between my legs reaches up and palms my breast. He'd stared so hungrily at my breasts earlier I'm wondering if watching me play with them will drive him even more mad.

"What about this?" I ask, pinching my nipple.

A crease appears on his forehead as he frowns. I wonder if it's taking everything in him to stay on the other side of the shower. His body seems tense, his muscles taut as he continues to stroke up and down his length.

"Is that what you like?" he asks, watching me closely. "Do you like having your nipples played with while being fucked?"

"Last time I checked, I'm not getting fucked right now." I don't bother to hide the disappointed tone in my voice. He could easily come across the shower and be inside me in an instant. I'd let him, but I'm not the one who made a rule that I had to trust him for us to be able to have sex.

I'd been ready the moment his lips met mine at the gym, and I've thought about it many times since.

"You're going to fuck that pretty pussy with your fingers. That's still getting fucked, baby."

My eyelids flutter closed because his words send a rush of need throughout my entire body. I love how filthy he is. He's being so vocal about what's going through his head, and it's only fueling my desire. He's always so businesslike, keeping his cards close to his chest. Right now, it feels like he's letting me into his mind, and I think being in his mind might be one of the sexiest things ever.

When I open my eyes again, Archer's watching me, looking between my thighs like if he stared long enough, he could hold my hand for me to do as he demands. Lucky for him—and me— I don't tease any longer.

I circle my clit, my hips slightly bucking off the tile because it feels far better than I was expecting. I know it's only because of the way he watches me with pure need. That mixed with watching him stroke himself is one of the hottest moments of my life.

"It's sexy as hell to watch you play with your clit, but I want more. Fill yourself, Winnie. Use two fingers and imagine it as my cock."

"You're a lot thicker than two of my fingers." I do as I'm told, slowly coaxing two fingers inside me. My body shakes with how good it feels when I begin to rock against them, allowing them deep enough to hit the right spot.

My words make him smirk. "Obviously. But you need to prepare yourself to take me."

"Are you saying you're going to fuck me?"

"One day, you'll give in and tell me you trust me. Or fuck, maybe I'll give in." Goose bumps break out over my skin because his words come out like a threat and a promise, and I love it.

"Says you," I tease, knowing I'm already looking forward to the day I'll feel all of him. I want to feel him move in and out of me. I don't know if anything would ever make me feel more powerful—more sexy—than feeling him come undone inside me.

My body trembles as my fingers begin to pick up their pace. I keep a steady rhythm, feeling the orgasm already beginning to build.

"Fuck, this is so hot, baby," Archer growls. His jaw clenches as he also picks up pace.

"I'm getting closer." I moan, imagining it's his fingers moving in and out of me.

"Yes." The muscles of his forearms ripple as he continues to move up and down. He's been working himself so hard, the veins of his forearms are even more pronounced.

"Are you imagining that it's me making you feel this way right now?" he continues, his voice strained.

All I can do is nod. That's *exactly* what I'm doing. I'd give anything to feel him hook his fingers inside me as his mouth moved against mine. Would he tease me and move slowly in and out, or would he move them fast and possessively?

"I'm watching everything you do to make yourself feel good so when you finally let me have my way with you, I'll make it perfect."

My head rolls back. I don't tell him he could do anything and it'd be perfect with him. My toes curl as the orgasm builds even harder. "Archer," I moan, drawing his name out because it all feels too good.

"Yes, baby?"

"I'm going to come." I brush my thumb along my clit. Everything is so sensitive it almost pushes me over the edge.

"Good girl," he growls. "Now, open your eyes and come with me. Watch what you do to me. Let me hear what I do to you."

I force my eyes open, even though it's so hard to keep them that way with the pressure building throughout my body. I don't know if I've ever had one build for so long. I'm so close. I spread my fingers inside me slightly, stretching myself as my thumb still brushes over my clit.

"God, you're so fucking sexy. I'm going to come now, and I'm going to be pissed if you don't come with me."

He doesn't have to worry about that because a loud moan comes from deep in my throat and echoes throughout the shower. The orgasm that tears through my body is the most euphoric pleasure I've ever felt. My moans are loud and untamed, and I don't even care that someone could hear me because it feels too good.

Archer's eyes stay locked on mine. His jaw is so tight it has to hurt, but he doesn't falter. His bicep bulges as he pumps up and down quickly.

"Fuck, baby," he groans. *God*. Does he always make sounds like that? Would he moan as he pounded into me? I'd love to hear it right against my ear.

I bite my lip, and seconds later, thick ropes of cum spill from him. I watch in fascination, loving the way he comes apart. He continues to stroke up and down, milking himself completely before his hand slows.

"Careful how you look at me," he warns, stepping closer to me.

"How am I looking at you?"

"Like that one orgasm wasn't enough."

I smile. If he touched me, I know he could pull another

orgasm from me easily. "I was actually thinking about how I'd love to swallow one day...if you'd let me."

His eyes go wide. And I don't know why because he just watched me give myself an orgasm and he held on to his self-control, but something in him snaps. He closes the distance between us and pulls me off the shower bench with one easy tug, my body now flush against his.

He places his hands on either side of my face as he gently swipes strands of hair from it. "You'll swallow every last drop of me someday, baby. I can't fucking wait. But first, you're going to admit you trust me."

I smile, trying not to show him how much his words have an effect on me. "Or you're just going to drop the need to have me trust you before fucking me."

"Not a chance." Little wrinkles appear on the sides of his eyes with his smile.

I shrug, all too aware of how close our bodies are. He just came, and his dick is still hard as it brushes against my hip every time he shifts on his feet.

I want to touch him, to feel his stubble against my palm. I reach up to do that but remember my hand is still covered in my arousal. Before I can put it directly under the stream of water, Archer grabs my wrist, keeping my fingers away from the water.

"I need to wash myself off me," I tell him, my cheeks heating.

He quirks an eyebrow. "I'll help with that." And then he pulls my hand to his mouth and wraps it around my finger. A whimper falls from his lips as he tastes me for the first time. His thick eyelashes stick together from the water as he watches me closely.

My mouth pops open in pleasure as he circles my fingers with his tongue. Why is this so hot? Why is everything with him so freaking hot?

He licks my fingers completely clean before he pulls his mouth from my skin. "You're fucking addicting. I know soon I'll need another taste." With the lightest touch, he moves his fingers down my skin until his fingertips barely brush against my clit.

I gasp, unable to help it. It was featherlight, but I felt it everywhere.

"Soon, I'll have to taste it straight from here," he continues.

I swallow, wishing that he would do it right now.

He chuckles, taking a step back. I miss his warmth and the feel of his body against mine the moment we break contact. A rush of cold air hits me from the loss of connection, and the realization of what we just did hits me in the face. Not knowing how to proceed, I reach for the shower door.

Archer steps in front of it, blocking me from being able to push it open. "And what do you think you're doing?"

"Letting you finish your shower."

He stares at me for a moment with a frown. "Finish it with me," he finally gets out.

"You want that?" I hate how hesitant my voice sounds. There's no playbook for what to do after you let your fake husband watch you make yourself come. Are we supposed to hug after? Kiss? Or do I just slide out of the shower and pretend this never happened?

Archer doesn't seem to want to give me an option because he softly nudges me deeper into the shower. He stays quiet, reaching for a bottle of shampoo and pumping it into his hand.

"Can I?"

"Can you what?"

"Wash your hair," he answers, as if his question was obvious. "Clean you up after getting you messy."

"Technically speaking, *I* got myself messy." I turn around, my back facing him. He walks us directly under the stream of water that comes from the top of the shower. The water beats down on us, getting my hair evenly wet before he begins to lather it against my scalp.

My eyelids flutter shut as his strong fingers massage my

scalp. He lathers the shampoo into the long strands of my hair far longer than necessary.

It feels so good that a low moan escapes my lips. His chest brushes against my back as he chuckles. "Give me the chance and I can find far more fun ways to make you moan," he comments, humor in his tone.

I smile, stretching my neck back and forth to move his fingers where I want them. "I'd like that," I confess, imagining what it'd be like to feel all of him.

"I'd like that, too." He angles my head under the water to wash the shampoo from my hair, but I don't miss how he cups over my forehead to make sure none of the soapy water gets in my eyes.

"Then let's do it." Feeling bold, I back up just a little. The closeness has his length brushing up against my back.

Even through the pouring water, I hear his deep inhale.

He drops my hair, his suds-covered hands finding the small of my waist. He pushes my hips away from him but still keeps a firm grip on my body. "I'd love to," he tells me, his lips moving against my ear. "Except I'm desperately trying to stick to my word. Trust me, and I'm yours to use how you want, Winnie."

Turning around, I wrap my arms around his neck. Any other time, I might not be brave enough to put us in this position. I'm used to affection with him in public but not in private. But what we did with each other watching seems to have broken some kind of barrier between us. It doesn't all feel like pretend, but I don't allow myself to let it feel perfectly real either. I choose to live in the between—just the now.

"We need to get out soon and get ready for dinner," I say, changing the subject.

His eyes narrow playfully on me. Leaning down, he places a chaste kiss against my lips. Before he fully pulls away, he nips at my bottom lip slightly. "You're really going to be the death of me aren't you, Winnie Bishop?"

I smile. "Not if you're the death of me first."

31
Archer

"So I think I may have missed the explanation, but how did you two go from yelling at each other covered in icing to dating?" Winnie asks, looking at Pippa and Camden with a soft smile playing on her lips. She leans back, fully snuggling into me to keep warm.

After an extravagant dinner at the Pembroke Hills Country Club, we returned back to the house to sit around the fireplace and talk. I'm not one to typically sit and mingle with friends. Drinks and talking about business? Sure. A poker game with someone interested in investing in Moore Hotels? Easy. But to sit around and chat with friends is out of character for me.

As I sit here with this group of people, I realize that I could easily find myself calling them actual friends and not just people who can be assets to me. Although, my wife is friends with women with very powerful partners. Camden Hunter dominates the art world, and Beckham Sinclair is the future of cybersecurity.

I get so lost in my thoughts I miss the first part of the conversation between Camden and his girlfriend, Pippa, but I tune in to hear enough.

"So basically we fell in love because of a bet. One that Camden lost big-time," Pippa teases, looking back at him.

Even though he was a year older than me, everyone knew the reputation Camden had as a ladies' man. Hell, Beck had it, too. It's new to see them both so deeply in love with their partners. They seem to be thriving in both their careers and personal lives, and it's something I find fascinating.

I've always been under the impression that to have one flourish, the other has to suffer. These two men are proof that isn't necessarily the case.

"I wouldn't say I completely lost the bet," Camden argues.

"You just bought half the town, man," Beck counters, running his hand through his blond hair. "I feel like you absolutely lost the bet."

Leaning down, I whisper in Winnie's ear. I try not to focus on the way her body shivers with the movement. She's so reactive to me that I want to find out in what other ways her body reacts. "What was the bet?" I ask, wondering if I missed that part of the story.

Emma, who sits right next to Winnie and me, raises her hand. I didn't think I spoke that loud, but apparently, she has supersonic hearing because she answers. "Oh, I know the answer to that. The bet was that Pippa told Camden he was going to fall in love with Sutten Mountain. You have to visit sometime, by the way," Emma adds, looking at Winnie and me. "It's the cutest little town in Colorado."

"It really is the best town," Pippa adds.

"Did I fall in love with the town or the girl?" Camden counters, wrapping his arms around Pippa's middle. He whispers something in her ear, something that makes her cheeks turn pink. She elbows him in the stomach before pushing him off and speaking to the group.

"Don't let him fool you guys. He fell in love with both." She looks at Beck. "And he didn't buy half the town; he bought a block. And he let everyone buy themselves out."

Beck throws his hands up defensively. "It's okay to admit he's whipped. I'm right there with you, Hunter."

"I didn't buy an entire company just to get someone to talk to me," Camden teases, raising his eyebrows at his friend.

"No, but you spent ten million on a block of business lots in a small town as a fuck-you to Jason because you didn't like how he treated the woman you loved," Beck argues.

Camden smiles and gives a shrug.

"Are you talking about Jason Vincent?" I ask, recognizing the name. "I've always hated that guy."

"Yes," both Camden and Beck answer in unison.

Camden's the one who continues. "He deserved it." He laughs, shaking his head. "He pissed me off enough that I had the pleasure of exposing just how in debt he was."

I join in on the laughter between Beck and Camden because if there's one thing the three of us can agree on, it's that Jason Vincent is fucking terrible. I like Camden even more now, knowing he was the reason that Jason moved away to the Cayman Islands and disappeared.

"Can we go back to Sutten for ski season?" Emma pipes up. She reaches across the couch cushion and grabs Winnie's hand. "Winnie will teach me to ski. Won't you, Win?"

Winnie laughs. "I can definitely try. I swore you've said before that skiing is more about drinking in the lodge afterward, though. Or am I mistaken?" she teases.

Emma rolls her eyes. "It's mostly about getting a cute outfit. I want hot pink everything. The coat, the pants, the hat. Everything has to be pink."

"That doesn't shock me in the slightest," Margo says from her spot next to Beck. "Emma, I feel like you and I will need a day or two of private lessons before even attempting to do it on our own."

"That's why we have Winnie."

"We do have some amazing instructors in Sutten," Pippa adds. "I went to school with some of them. You guys will do amazing! I can help, too."

Winnie turns around to look at me. "Would you want to do that sometime? Do you even ski?"

I try not to roll my eyes at her question. Of course, I know how to ski. "I actually go between skiing and snowboarding. I tend to prefer to board. And I've heard a lot about Sutten Mountain recently, thanks to Hunter bringing more attention to the town, so I'd love to."

The smile she gives me is so radiant it makes me want to pick her up and carry her back to our room so we can be alone. It does something to me—to my heart, and I hate that I can't act on the feelings coursing through me because we have an audience. "So it's settled. We'll all go back to Sutten this winter," Winnie says, watching me closely. It's as if she's waiting for me to change my mind, but I won't. If she wants to do that, then I'll be there, too. Plus, I feel like there are far worse groups of people I could spend time with.

This marriage with Winnie is teaching me a lot of things, but maybe the biggest one is that it's okay to take a break every now and then.

"It's kind of late at this point to plan it, but next year, you guys should come over for Christmas. Sutten is beautiful during that time of year. There are lights everywhere. All of the main street has lights and ribbons, and there's always snow on Christmas. It's so magical."

"That sounds amazing!" Winnie says eagerly, looking back to me for confirmation.

I nod. It's hard to admit, but I can easily picture the holidays with her over the years. Our fake marriage wasn't exactly meant to stand the test of time, but I kind of hope it will. I'm already excited about this Christmas with her. We've talked about all the things we'll do—just the two of us. And it doesn't sound too bad to spend next year with this group of people around us.

Emma lets out a loud yawn next to us, breaking me from my daydreams about Christmas mornings with Winnie and trips with her friends and what things might look like for us later in the future and not just right now. "Friends, this has been a blast. But those three glasses of wine made me sleepy." She drags out the last word dramatically. "I think I'm going to bed."

"I'm exhausted, too," Margo adds, standing up.

I try to look disappointed that everyone else in the group agrees that it's time for us all to head back to our rooms. I'm actually fucking ecstatic at the thought of getting Winnie alone. I've been thinking about our little shower encounter all night, and I want to take her back to our room and strip her of her fancy outfit and see her beautiful naked body again.

There's just one little problem—I don't want to concede. For some reason, I need to know she trusts me. I want to know she trusts me because she told me it's the one thing I'll never get from her. It's bothered me from the moment she said it. It bothers me even more now because I know without a shadow of a doubt that I trust her, when I know I shouldn't.

I don't want to be the only one in this. I don't know where her head is, and it feels like if she at least told me she trusts me, we'd be on a more level playing field.

But I don't know if that'll happen.

I'm lost in wondering what I can do to gain her trust when she places her palm on my cheek. My eyes meet hers.

"Ready to head back to our room?" she asks, nodding her head toward the hallway.

I sigh, standing up and taking her hand without any kind of forethought.

It's quiet as we walk hand in hand to our room. The air changes the moment we walk in there and I shut the door behind us.

The two of us stare at the one bed with countless pillows piled on top.

Winnie sighs next to me, her eyes trained on the same spot as me. "It's going to be really hard to sleep tonight after…" Her words drift off.

I smirk, my arms crossing over my chest. "After you touched

yourself thinking it was my cock?" I finish, not bothering to hide the smug look on my face.

She nods as her eyes get even wider. "Yeah. After that."

32
Winnie

MY WALL OF PILLOWS WAS A STUPID IDEA. I DON'T KNOW WHY I thought that big heaps of feathers could do anything to break the tension between Archer and me. Then again, when I first grabbed the pillows, I hadn't caught him in the shower with his hand around his dick, moaning my name.

But I *did* catch him. And I did watch him get himself off as he watched me do the same, and it's changed things in a big way.

"Are you going to keep moving?" Archer asks from the other side of the pillows. He'd argued for a while as I set them up between us, but eventually, he relented and let me build the barrier. We'd watched reruns of some sort of house-hunting show on the TV before he finally turned it off, and we both attempted to get some sleep.

No matter how hard we try, sleep hasn't found either one of us. There were times I thought he was asleep, but I'd sneak a glance over the barrier between us and would find him staring up at the ceiling.

"I know you're not asleep," Archer continues. I can't see him over the mound of pillows between us, but I still feel him all the same.

"I'll try to stop moving," I answer, knowing it'll be near impossible for sleep to take me. I'm way too aware of the man next to me, of the tension between us.

I lie perfectly still for a few minutes before I can't do it any longer. With a loud sigh, I push off the bed and lean over the pillows between us. "I can't do this, Archer."

The sheets have slipped down to his hips, showing me too much of his shirtless torso. It's obvious how much work he puts into his body, how hard he works to maintain the beautiful cut of his muscles.

"Do you think if we maybe just slept together once, we could get it out of our systems?" I mutter, paying close attention to his reaction.

His muscles stiffen, as if I delivered a blow to him with the question. "It's cute you *actually* believe once will ever be enough," he counters, tucking his hands behind his head. The position brings way too much attention to his defined biceps. I want to grab on to them, to let my nails dig into the skin as he pushes into me. Part of me wonders if he pinned his hands behind his head to make sure he keeps his hands off me.

"Once seems better than nothing," I whisper. Slowly, I pull pillow after pillow and toss them to the ground until there's no barrier between us at all.

I've had enough of lying here next to him and not doing anything. He's my husband. I'm attracted to him in a desperate way that I've never felt with anyone else. I'm tired of pretending otherwise, of fighting it when all I want is to know *all* of him.

"What are you doing?" Archer questions, his voice tight. I want to wipe my fingers across his forehead and get rid of the wrinkle that's appeared because of how tense he is.

My eyes travel over his body. It was beautiful to watch him come in the shower earlier. I felt powerful in knowing that his reactions were because of me. But it also left me wanting so much more. Even if Archer wasn't my husband, I'd want him like this. Now that I know him, now that I've heard his moans and groans—heard my name fall from his lips in pleasure—I want more.

And I don't think I can stop until I get it.

"I'm thinking I want you, Archer Moore." I keep eye contact with him, letting the strap of my nightie fall down my shoulder. Without the help of one of my straps keeping the fabric on my body, the swells of my breasts come into view. It's got to be the middle of the night at this point, but the moonlight shines through the bedroom windows enough to illuminate the room.

"The problem isn't that we want each other," he snaps. He lies so still, his eyes focused right on me. He doesn't move, even as I inch closer and closer to him in bed.

"Then I don't see a problem at all." I adjust my position until I'm on my knees. One of my knees presses into his thigh. I push my thighs open as I pull the fabric of my nightie up so he can get a good view of me. He keeps his eyes trained on mine, but I can tell how hard he's trying not to look between my legs. His jaw is so tense that the muscle along his jawline ticks away angrily.

He squeezes his eyes shut like it's taking every inch of his willpower to not give in. I know it's wrong of me, but I want to push him to his breaking point. It's my sick way of knowing that I'm not the only one developing feelings I shouldn't be. I can't identify what kind of feelings have blossomed between Archer and me, but I know I now look at him and don't just see a man who plays the part of my husband.

I let my hand slowly fall to his stomach. His muscles immediately tighten underneath my touch. I keep my hand there to see what he does. Will he push it away or allow it to happen?

When I pull my gaze from where my hand rests on his abs, I find his eyes open and pinned right on me. "Winnie…" My name falls from his lips like a plea.

"It's in our contract that we can't see other people during our marriage. And I have no interest in anyone but you anyway. Why can't we indulge ourselves?" I ask, letting my hand drift a little lower.

"We can. I just want to know you trust me."

"Why?" My fingertips drift underneath the waistband of his boxer briefs.

"Don't ask me that." His voice comes out pained as my hand goes lower. The hair of his happy trail brushes against my fingers as I travel lower and lower. The moment my fingertips come in contact with the soft skin of his dick, he's pushing off the bed and grabbing my hand before I can do anything else.

In one quick movement, he pins me to the bed as he positions himself above me, his hips fitting right between my thighs.

"Why can't I ask you that?" I push, my breath heavy with our new position. I wiggle my hips a little, relishing in the way his jaw tightens when his dick brushes right against my center.

"Because I might just answer you." I get lost in the intensity with which he looks at me. If only I could know what was going through his head right now. Why is he so insistent that I trust him?

"I want you to answer me." A moan falls from my lips when he allows himself to brush over me again. There's a layer of fabric between us from his briefs, but it still does the trick. I'm wet and ready for him. He could easily slide in. I have no panties on, but he'd first have to finally break and let this happen between us.

"I want you to trust me," he throws back at me. "And I want you to admit that if this happens, you're aware that it'll happen again and again. One time with you would never be enough for me, baby. And fuck, I kind of want to punish you for thinking it would be."

I try to reach between us so I can push his briefs down his hips, but he grabs my arms and pins them above my head in one easy movement. He's got me totally at his mercy, panting with need for him, and he hasn't even really touched me yet.

"I trust you with my body," I tell him, knowing it's the truth. After things with Blake, I didn't know when I'd be ready to sleep with someone else. But I've never questioned it with Archer. The moment I started wanting him, I knew I trusted him like this.

His grip around my wrist tightens. His free hand drifts up the side of my face and cups my cheek. "What if I want your head and your heart to trust me, too?" His fingertip taps my forehead and then drags across my neck and chest until he places it right in the center over my heart.

I swallow, not knowing what to say back to him. I never imagined him asking me to trust him with either of those.

"Don't hold back on my account," he muses, letting his cock brush against me again. "Tell me what's going through your mind."

"I just wasn't expecting you to say that, is all," I whisper. My eyelids flutter when he softly brushes hair from my face. "Or even want that," I continue, confessing the real reason why his request threw me off.

"You'd be shocked by all the things I want from you."

"Like what?"

He smirks, pulling his body from mine. I don't have time to get disappointed because he still stays between my legs. "I can't tell you about them yet. I can't be *too* much of an open book for you, Winnie. Not when you're still holding back from me."

My entire body heats when he pushes the fabric of my nightie up. Cold air hits between my thighs, but I barely feel it because I am too warm underneath his hot, needy stare.

"Fuck, you're tempting," he mutters. His eyes stay trained between my legs. Feeling shy, I try to push my thighs back together, but he stops me before I can. He clicks his tongue. "No, you've started this, baby. Don't hide from me now."

His fingertips press into the tender skin of my inner thighs. He's so close to where I want him, but it still isn't close enough. As if he can read me like an open book, he lets his hands drift even higher on my legs until he rests them right between the apex of my thighs.

"God, baby…" he marvels, still staring between my legs.

"What?" I ask, my voice breathy because he shouldn't look this hot staring at me. He'd be so much hotter if he'd actually touch me.

"You're already so wet that your cum leaks out of you." His

tongue peeks out to wet his lips, and I fight the urge to moan at the sight. Everything this man does is so sexy it'll be my undoing. "You're soaked, and I haven't even touched you yet. How wet will you be when I fuck you?" he adds, his tone thoughtful. He gets this faraway look in his eyes, like he's imagining fucking me.

"Why don't you find out?" I counter, my tone more insistent than I was intending it to be. Or maybe that's exactly what I was trying to do.

"I want to," he offers. His lips press into a thin line. He takes me by surprise when his finger lightly brushes over my clit.

I moan, my hips bucking off the bed because that one small touch lit my body on fire.

"I'm about to break every one of my fucking rules for you, Winnie," Archer fumes. "I want—need—your trust, but I also need to taste this pretty pussy."

"Do it," I plead, arching my back to get him to touch me again. It works. He runs his fingers through my wetness again.

"Just tell me you trust me," he argues, his voice trembling slightly.

I shake my head. I don't want to trust him.

We both were raised the same way. It was preached to me from the very beginning to never trust a Moore, but I don't want to be the naive girl anymore. I'll trust him with my body, knowing he'd never do anything to betray me this way. But outside of this room, I have to fight trusting him with anything else because our families tried to put their faith in each other once before, and it ended terribly.

"You want me to get on my knees and beg for your trust, baby? Because I will. Just say the word." He slides off the bed, and I miss him the moment I no longer feel his touch.

I push myself off the bed by my elbows, trying to figure out what he's doing. The way he keeps calling me baby, the way he said beg...I'm too turned on for him to just stop. I'm seconds away from opening my mouth to argue when his fingers wrap around my ankle and pull me across the bed. I yelp, my head falling to the mattress from the sudden movement. He pulls me to the end of the bed, all the way until my hips almost hang off the edge.

"Look at me," he demands.

I listen, finding him staring up at me from between my thighs. He places my heels on his shoulders, spreading me open wide when I still have no idea if he has any intention of touching me.

"Here I am," he announces, holding my stare. "On my knees. Is this what you wanted? What you need?"

I moan because his fingers circle my clit again. God, if only he'd apply more pressure, give me just a little bit more. He's teasing me, and it's driving me crazy.

"I'll get what I want from you," he continues, his voice matter-of-fact, like there's not a doubt in his mind about his words. "But right now, you're a *very* lucky girl, Winnie. I want to eat this beautiful, soaking wet pussy of yours and give you exactly what you need. And since I'm in the business of giving you exactly what you need, your perfect cunt needs some attention from me."

33
Archer

I SHOULD'VE KNOWN FROM THE MOMENT WE LANDED IN THE Hamptons that this would happen. I'm normally a man with incredible restraint—except when it comes to Winnie. With her, I'm weak. I can't seem to deny her a single thing. Her pathetic attempt to put a barrier between us did nothing to alleviate the sexual tension.

My fingertip runs through her wetness. I allow just the very tip to push inside her, wanting to see her reaction. She moans loudly and freely, making me want to slip another finger inside her and push as far inside as she'll take me. My mind drifts to a night that feels like a lifetime ago, one where I heard her moan for the first time.

I wait. If I'm going to be the one that loses this battle and gives in to her, I'm at least going to tease—and maybe even punish her—a little for making me give in.

"Archer," Winnie moans, her hips circling as she tries to get more friction.

"Yes, baby?"

"Please," she pleads.

I smirk, because at least I'm not the only one begging for more when it comes to us.

"Is this what you want?" My thumb pushes against her clit as my finger inches deeper inside her. Her pussy greedily clenches around me. My cock strains against the fabric of my briefs as I imagine what it would feel like to push inside her with my cock instead of my finger.

"Yes," she pants, arching her back to allow me even deeper. "And more," she adds. Her hands roam her body like she doesn't know where to put them.

I stare at her hard nipples, which fight against the fabric of her nightgown. The moment she walked out of the bathroom wearing it, I knew I was fucked. It's too short and too thin, making my mind race with imagining the skin it hides.

"Play with your tits, baby," I demand, easing my finger out of her.

She lets out a moan of displeasure that sounds more like a whine. "Don't stop," she begs, her eyes opening to meet mine.

Fuck, she's so sexy. The moonlight pours into the room, illuminating her perfectly. Her cheeks are flushed with pleasure, and her lips are parted in desperate need.

"I'll start again when you do as you're told," I respond, watching her carefully.

Her chest stills for a moment, her breath catching at my demand. It's only a small reaction, but I pay attention to every single one of them to find out what she likes. Judging by the way her breath hitches before picking up, I think my wife might like being bossed around in the bedroom. Which only turns me on more.

All I want to do is pull my cock out and push inside her, but I'm going to be patient and take my time with her.

One of her hands snakes up her body. She pulls the fabric of her nightgown down and frees one of her full, perfect tits. God, I want to get off my knees and cover my body with hers and take her hard nipple into my mouth. Instead, I stay put. It's hot as fuck to watch the way she rolls the bud between her fingers before pinching it.

"Good girl," I praise, pushing two fingers into her this time around.

She moans at the same time her pussy tightens around my fingers. She's already so fucking tight around them I can't imagine what she'll feel like around my cock. I can't fucking wait to find out in due time.

"Earlier, when you were playing with yourself, I watched you closely," I tell her, copying her movements from the shower. I was the perfect student, paying attention to everything she did so when it was my turn to touch her, I'd make it perfect. My thumb brushes along her clit as I spread my fingers to stretch her. "You like your clit played with while you're being fucked, baby?"

Her head rocks back and forth as a loud moan escapes her throat.

I smile, leaning closer to get a better view of my fingers fucking her. She's so fucking wet that there's a small wet spot on the bed below her hips from her arousal. It's the hottest fucking thing I've ever seen.

"I wonder if you'd like it even more if my mouth played with your clit while my fingers kept stretching you to get you ready for me..." I muse, talking right against her inner thigh so my breath teases her. I'm so close but still not where she wants me.

"Yes," she answers immediately.

I look up at her from between her thighs, loving that she's still doing exactly as I told her to and playing with her tits. Her bottom lip is red and slightly swollen from biting it with pleasure.

"I'm looking at your mouth and your pussy, and I don't know which one I want to kiss more right now. Both look in desperate need of my attention."

"Archer." My name falls from her lips as she lets out another moan.

"I've been dreaming about kissing you again since that day at the gym. Fuck, Winnie, sometimes it was all I could fucking think about." I break eye contact to watch my fingers push in and out of her. "But this pussy—getting to taste it for myself— has also taken up so much space in my mind…"

I lean closer and blow hot air right against her slit. Her hips buck with the teasing. "So many options," I muse, continuing to tease her. "Which one do I choose?"

"My p…" She doesn't finish her answer.

"Your what?" I press. "I want to hear you say it, and I'll do exactly what you want."

"My pussy," she moans. "And then my mouth."

This makes me smile as I adjust my position slightly to line my mouth up perfectly with her. "My wife is a dirty fucking girl wanting me to kiss her cunt before I kiss her mouth."

My tongue runs through her wetness. I've been dying to taste her pussy, and I can't waste another second without knowing exactly what she tastes like. Both of us moan with the second swipe of my tongue against her clit.

She's fucking perfect. And tastes exactly like *mine*. My fingers push inside her as my tongue circles her clit over and over.

One of her hands finds my hair, her fingers twisting in it. Her grip isn't gentle, but I don't want it to be. It's fucking sexy the way she yanks and tugs as my tongue works her clit.

Tasting her is everything I want, but it still doesn't feel like enough. I slide my fingers out of her and pull her body even more to the edge of the bed, forcing me to support more of her weight but also bringing her pussy even closer to me.

My arms wrap around her thighs, my fingertips pressing into the soft skin of her inner thighs. I pull them open so she's spread even wider for me. "This is the most beautiful sight in the world," I marvel, taking a moment to take her in. "You with your cheeks flushed, your legs spread open wide as your cunt drips with desperation for me."

"Archer," Winnie moans, her fingernails brushing against my scalp.

"Now I'm going to eat this pussy like it's my last fucking

meal, baby. And I won't be done until I feel you come around my tongue at least twice. You got that?"

She nods her head up and down, giving me all the permission I need. I lean in and do exactly as I say I'm going to do.

34
Winnie

ARCHER'S MOUTH ON ME IS PURE HEAVEN. I'VE NEVER FELT anything like it. His tongue is relentless, never letting up as he works hard to pull an orgasm from me. His fingertips dig into my legs as the orgasm builds and builds. I'm so fucking close, and I'm worried that the orgasm building inside me might just rip my body in two from pleasure.

"I'm so close," I whisper, barely able to form words from the way my entire body is on fire with anticipation.

My words egg him on. He pulls his hand from one of my thighs and presses two fingers on either side of my clit. I feel him spread me even more open for him seconds before his tongue is even deeper inside me.

"Oh god, oh god, oh god," I moan, my eyes squeezing shut from the looming orgasm. I've never had one take so long to build before exploding, and it's almost too much for me to handle.

His teeth brush against my clit slightly. Not enough to hurt, but enough to finally send me off the edge. A scream comes from my body, and I've never been more thankful that Margo gave us an entire wing for ourselves because there's no way I'd ever be able to be quiet with the pleasure coursing through my body.

My thighs squeeze the sides of Archer's face in pleasure as I ride out the orgasm. He never stops, even though I know it must be hard for him to breathe with his face buried between my thighs. If he wanted to, he could push them open to give himself more air to breathe, but instead, he keeps his grip tight on me.

Maybe he likes the feeling of breathing in nothing but me, and that realization has me moaning all over again as the remnants of the orgasm course through my body.

I lift my hips, trying to back away from him because even though the orgasm is gone, his tongue doesn't stop. It almost tickles, but his tongue working against my clit feels even better than I'd imagined. It's almost like one orgasm finished and started to lead right into another.

"Archer," I plead—or maybe it's more like a moan. "I came," I tell him, wiggling my hips, but his mouth just follows.

He pulls away but doesn't stop for long. His fingers replace where his mouth was as he looks up at me. My head lifts off the bed so I can get a better look at him. I don't want to miss the way he watches me carefully.

Archer Moore has always been the most handsome man I've ever laid eyes on, but the way he stares at me right now has got to be my favorite view of him ever. Him on his knees, his mouth wet with my arousal, and his eyes hungrily pinned on me like he'll never get enough of what just happened between us.

"I know you came," he answers smugly as he slides three fingers inside me this time. It's too much. Every single part of my body is more sensitive from the orgasm I just had, and the way his fingers stretch me hurts in the most euphoric of ways. "Trust me, baby, I know. I tasted your cum and felt that pussy spasm against my tongue. I told you I wanted two orgasms from you, and I meant it. I want this perfect cunt of yours to be nice and ready to take my cock, and you need to be relaxed for that to happen. Trust me on this?" He watches me closely. It's so intense, and I can't look away, even as his fingers continue to stretch me and get me ready for him in both pain and pleasure.

I nod, not knowing what else to say. I've never had a man want to make me come multiple times before we even get to the sex, but I should've known Archer would be different. He's always asking for more, and I won't deny him.

I didn't know it was possible to keep going after having an orgasm, but his fingers work my body so perfectly I know he'll easily have me screaming his name all over again.

My head hits the bed when his tongue gets back to work. He's everywhere. His fingers, his mouth, the way he moans against me with every lap and lick of his tongue. My senses are on overdrive, and the only thing I can focus on is the way my body heats with the start of another orgasm.

It's like he can read my body like an open book because he hooks his fingers inside me and picks up the pace with his tongue. It doesn't take long before my back arches off the bed as his name falls from my lips like a plea as he makes me see stars.

I chant his name over and over again as the orgasm overtakes my body. I've never felt one so powerful, and Archer makes sure to milk it for everything it's worth. He doesn't stop until my thighs squeeze his face and my hands press to his forehead to push him away because the feeling is too much.

He leans back on his knees, watching me with a very content smile. My cum is all over his lips, and you can tell exactly where I yanked at his hair in perfect pleasure.

"I'd ask you how they were, but I don't have to." His smile is boyish and charming and makes a shiver run through my body because I've never seen it on him before.

"Why is that?" I ask, still a little breathless from the intensity of the orgasms.

He gently slides my legs off his shoulders and places them on the ground. His hands find either side of my hips as he pushes himself off the ground and brings his face close to mine. I think he's going to kiss me, but instead, he playfully nips at my bottom lip.

"Because the way you screamed my name over and over again. Fuck, Winnie, it was the hottest thing I've ever heard. I can't wait to hear you again as I fuck you until you can't walk tomorrow."

"I have a girls' day. I need to be able to walk."

He smirks, going for my bottom lip once again and trapping it between his teeth and holding it for a moment. He lets go as his eyes roam my face. "Then I'm going to fuck you senseless and make damn sure that you're reminded of me all damn day tomorrow."

My cheeks warm with the thought. I want that...a lot. It's what I've wanted for a while. I look down at where his dick strains against the fabric of his boxer briefs, but first... "I want to taste you the way you tasted me," I whisper, suddenly feeling embarrassed, even though the man I'm telling it to is covered in my own arousal.

He grabs my chin, directing my eyes to his. "You're so fucking sexy. You know that?"

My eyes narrow because his comment wasn't what I was expecting. I smile, giving him a bashful shrug.

His eyes rake over my body. Technically, I still have on a nightie, but the straps have been pushed down, one of them so far that my nipple hangs out. "You're so exquisite that you take my breath away."

I lose my own breath for a moment because that's just another comment I wasn't expecting. He goes from saying the filthiest things to the sweetest things in a heartbeat, and it makes me want him even more.

"Does that mean I get to..." I reach between us, running my hand along his length through his briefs.

Air hisses through his teeth with his deep inhale. I repeat the motion, this time letting my fingers wrap around him a little to see the effect it has on him.

"I've pictured you gagging on my cock far too many times to count. But I'm so fucking turned on right now I don't know how gentle I'll be with you if I feel those lips wrap around me."

"I don't want gentle." I slip my hand into his waistband and finally fully wrap my fingers around him with nothing in between us.

It's easy to tell the moment his resolve snaps. One pump up and down his length and he's pushing my body into the mattress, his body coming down on top of mine.

I try to get out from underneath him so I can roll our bodies and come out on top to finally wrap my mouth around him, but he doesn't let me move. He keeps me pinned to the sheets.

"You say you don't want gentle, but I'm not so sure," he warns, his voice low. His breath tickles my cheeks with the proximity. I glance at his lips, feeling the intense need to kiss him.

"You don't get to tell me what I want," I argue, still focusing on his lips. Because I'm paying such close attention to his mouth, I watch as both corners of his perfect, full lips slowly turn up in a smile. This smile isn't the same charming, boyish one from earlier. This one is almost predatory, like I've challenged him to a dare he refuses to lose.

"Fuck, I love when you surprise me with that smart mouth of yours. I wish you'd use it around others more often." He begins to kiss along my neck, making me groan because all I want to do is make him feel good the way he did for me, and instead, he's drawing it out.

"If the first time I feel you wrap around my cock," Archer begins, kissing right under my jaw, "is with it in your mouth, will you be able to handle it? It'll be rough."

I moan, arching into his lips as he kisses along the hollow of my throat. Since he's already made me come twice, my entire body feels electrified. Every small touch or featherlight kiss lights my skin on fire. All I can feel and think about is him; I'm completely consumed. And I want to make him feel the same way. "I want that," I tell him, my voice hoarse with the pure need to make him lose control.

His face lines up with mine once again. He watches me closely for a moment, as if he's giving me a chance to change my mind. I don't falter. I want him, desperately.

He presses the softest kiss against my lips as a tease. "If you want to be a good girl and suck my cock, then who am I to deny you?"

I smile, my fingernails digging into his back in excitement. My body heats with just the thought of finally being able to do this.

"But first..." he begins, tenderly brushing hair from my forehead. "You're going to taste your cum on my lips."

35
Archer

THE WAY SHE KISSES ME AS IF SHE'S DEPENDENT ON MY MOUTH FOR her last breath will be my downfall. She will ruin me, and I'll thank her for it. My tongue greedily pushes into her mouth. She opens even wider for me, her tongue meeting mine eagerly.

We taste each other's moans, getting lost in the tangle of our limbs and tongues. Her nails scratch down my back, and my fingers pull at her hair. The kiss is fucking hot, but then again, every time I kiss her, I'm left with that same thought.

She's the one to pull away first. Her little hands press against my chest as she gives me a timid smile. "I tasted myself on you. Now it's time for me to taste you."

My cock stirs at her words. Somehow, she's so shy but also says exactly what she wants. It's hot as fuck, and I'm scared I'll never get enough.

I nod, kissing her one more time before sliding off her body. I miss her warmth immediately, but I'm too fucking turned on to not let her do what she wants.

"Tell me where you want me," I say, wanting to watch her take charge.

This makes her smile. She pushes her body off the mattress and slides off the bed.

"Sit," she commands, pointing to the edge of the bed.

I raise an eyebrow. She's putting me exactly where I just had her. I do as she says, taking a seat at the edge.

"Without those," she says, pointing to my boxer briefs.

I smirk, standing up and shoving the fabric down my thighs. She stares at my cock hungrily, the same way she did earlier in the shower. Fuck, it's hot. I never imagined I'd be able to get off just by the way someone looked at my cock, but with her, I could.

"I think it's time you strip down, too, baby," I croak, my voice rough with the desperation I feel for her.

"Why does it matter what I'm wearing when I give you a blow job?" she asks, her fingers messing with the straps of her nightgown.

"Because I still want a view of those perfect tits and that pretty pussy while you gag on my cock."

Winnie rubs her lips together, trying to hide the smile that blooms on her face. "Good answer," she whispers, slipping her arms through both straps and letting the fabric fall to the ground.

My breath hitches for a moment as I take in her naked body in the moonlight. She's too fucking perfect, so fucking sexy, that I lose all sense of myself for a moment. I'm overwhelmed with my desire for her.

I don't realize my hand has wrapped around my cock and started to rub up and down until she looks away from my eyes and pays close attention to my movements.

She takes one step toward me and then another until she steps between my open legs.

Slowly, she gets to her knees and places her hands on the tops of my thighs. Her mouth is so close but yet so far from where I want her. My hand doesn't stop going up and down my shaft as I wonder how the hell I'm not going to come the moment her mouth wraps around me.

"You sure about this?" I ask, my voice gravelly.

Her tongue peeks out to wet her lips as she nods her head.

"I've never been more sure." She looks away from my cock to meet my eyes. "I want this. I want *you*," she adds, and I have to close my eyes for a moment to remind myself she only means in this moment. My stupid fucking heart gets too excited at her words—too hopeful—and I have to push them from my mind before I overthink and overanalyze what she just said.

She pushes her hair off her shoulders so it's out of her way. The long, red strands fall down her back, swaying along her skin as she reaches for my cock. Her fingers wrap around me, right above mine.

Her eyelashes tickle her eyebrows as she looks up at me with a determined smile. "My turn," she states, moving her hand down in an attempt to move mine.

I let her, trying to keep my breaths calm as she begins to pump up and down. Her grip tightens as she repeats the motion, creating a circling movement that feels too fucking good.

"Fuck, baby," I groan, my hands falling to the mattress to keep myself up. "This already feels too fucking good."

She laughs, her hot breath hitting the head of my cock. "I haven't even started yet."

I'm about to tell her that I don't know if I can handle another second without her mouth on me, but she doesn't make me wait. Her tongue circles the head of my cock, making me jolt.

Holy shit.

She doesn't waste any time. Before I can say anything, she's opening her mouth wide and inching my cock deeper and deeper down her throat. She only gets about halfway before she comes back up and repeats the motion.

"Deeper," I demand, wondering how long I'll be able to last without taking control. All I want to do is drive my hips upward and force my cock so far into her mouth she won't have any option but to gag on me.

"I'm trying," she responds, pulling her mouth from me for a moment. "But you're so big. It's hard to fit it all in."

I tuck a stray piece of hair behind her ear before letting my fingers tangle in it to allow myself some control. I don't apply any pressure, at least for right now, but I leave the grip in place just in case. "Spit on it."

Her eyes go wide at my words. The moonlight reflects in her aquamarine eyes, making them even more striking than normal. "What?" she breathes.

"Spit on it. It'll make it easier for you to take every fucking inch of my cock."

"I've never…"

"I don't care what you've done before," I croak, needing her hand to start moving on my cock again. "All that matters is right now. And I'm telling you to spit on my cock. *Now*, baby."

Winnie swallows, her eyes trained on me. I wish I knew what was running through that pretty head of hers. Just when I think I might've gone too far with my request, she does as she's told and spits. She moves the saliva around with her tongue, making sure to coat the skin her mouth hasn't reached yet. My jaw clenches as I watch her, completely in awe. Her tongue circles my head again, and I know we both hear the air hiss through my teeth as I suck in a large gulp of air.

"Fuck," I groan. My fingers tighten against her scalp when she licks from the base all the way up my length. She does it again, and I can feel my muscles shake with all the tension in my body from how turned on I am.

"Like that?" she asks sweetly, her thumb spreading precum around my head.

"Just like that," I praise.

Her tongue presses flat against my shaft as she coaxes me further into her mouth. The spit worked; she's able to get a little further this time before she gags, but it still isn't enough.

I need more from her, and as fun as it's been letting her take control, I can't do it anymore.

"More," I demand, my body shuddering with need. I press against her head, easing her even further down my cock this time.

Her loud moan tells me all I need to know. She meant it when she said she wanted me to lose control with her. I thread my fingers tighter in her hair, no doubt causing knots, but I don't care right now. My fingertips press into her scalp as I guide her head. Each time, I bring her further and further down my cock, relishing in the way she moans, even when her throat involuntarily gags.

"You're so fucking sexy with your mouth full of my cock, baby," I praise, my abs tightening with the building of an orgasm I'm not ready for. I attempt to take a calming breath to try and fight it off.

I will come in her mouth one day, but tonight isn't the time. Tonight, I'll come in her pussy as I feel her come around me. I just have to get a better grip on the primal desire I feel for her and my body's inability to fight how much she drives me wild.

Tears begin to stream down her face from the impact of my cock hitting the back of her throat over and over again. I try to ease up a little to give her a break, but she doesn't let me. She continues to push herself to her limit in an attempt to take all of me, and fuck, I love her for it.

She keeps her hand wrapped around the part her mouth can't reach, no matter how hard she tries, and it feels so fucking good. Too fucking good. I only make it a few moments longer before my hands fall from her hair and I'm pulling my cock free from her mouth.

Her bottom lip juts out in a pout. "I wasn't done," she insists, trying to lean forward and start all over again.

I click my tongue. "I love how greedy you are for my cock, baby." My voice trembles with the desire to finally fuck her. "But I need to be inside you. Now." I pull her into me, both my hands coming to rest on either side of her cheeks. "Is that okay with you?"

She nods, her teeth digging into her bottom lip as she smiles. "Yes."

That one word is all I need. My hands find her hips as I pull her onto the bed with me. Once again, I spin our bodies in the sheets until she's under me. My hand presses into the bed right next to her head as my cock pushes against her hip.

"Have you thought about this as much as I have?" I ask, taking a moment just to soak it in. I've wanted this for longer than I should, and even though all I can do is think about pushing inside her and finally feeling her cunt mold to me, I don't want to rush things either.

I want to do this every day from now until forever, but I have no idea if that's what she wants. I want to savor the moment, to remember every single detail of the way our bodies mold together for the first time.

"I need you to answer me," I plead, kissing along her neck. Her skin tastes like vanilla. I could spend all night kissing up and down her body and memorizing the feel of every slope and plane against my lips. "Tell me you've thought about us finally doing this as much as I have."

Her hands run down my spine as I continue to trail my lips along her neck. "I've thought about it a lot. All those mornings you came back from working out…it was hard not to."

I laugh against her throat, loving the way her back arches when my breath hits her skin. "Good." The one word says more than enough.

I want her to think about me as much as I think about her. I want her to know the intense pull I feel to be near her, to be as close to her as possible, isn't just one-sided.

"Are you going to fuck me now?" she asks, her tone begging.

"Yes," I answer immediately, needing to be inside her.

I push off the mattress so I can reach between our bodies and line my cock up with her. She jerks when my head runs through her wetness, driving me even more wild.

"Please tell me you're on the pill. I think I have a condom somewhere if we need it, but fuck, I don't want there to be anything between us."

"I am," she whispers, moving her hips to get friction. "I don't want anything between us. I want to feel you. All of you."

"I'm so fucking ready for that," I tell her, leaning down and kissing her to prolong the inevitable. I know the moment I push inside her, I will further ruin myself for anyone but her.

36
Winnie

ARCHER RUNS HIS COCK THROUGH MY WETNESS, PREPARING HIMSELF to finally fuck me. It feels like forever since I first realized how badly I wanted him in that small room at the gym. I didn't know if he'd ever actually give in to this tension between us, so the longer he teases me before actually sliding in, the more desperate I get for him.

"Archer, please," I beg, lifting my hips to try and force him in myself.

He laughs, the sound coming from deep in his throat. If I wasn't so turned on, I'd be annoyed with the laugh and the smirk on his lips. Instead, they just further fuel how attracted I am to him and how much I need him.

"Is my wife ready to take me?" he asks, his voice coming out smooth like velvet.

I nod, unable to form words.

His deep brown eyes find mine, and I try not to read too much into the way he's looking at me right now. "If it's ever too much, you just say the word. You got it?"

I nod again, knowing there's no way anything would ever be too much with him. If anything, it'd never be enough because I don't know if I could ever get my fill of him. But I nod to tell him I understand anyway to make him feel better.

He circles my clit with the head of his cock once before he

finally gives me what I want. He slides in slightly, allowing me time to stretch around him.

"Oh god." I moan, knowing there's still so much of him left.

"I'd much prefer you call me Archer," he responds, a teasing tone to his voice as he leans down and places a kiss to my lips.

"Archer," I say, his name breaking on my lips as he continues to fit himself inside me. He's too big. I'm scared it won't work, but he continues to slowly push in and allow my body to acclimate to him.

"That's better, baby," he responds, his voice tight. I wonder if it's taking all of him to not speed things up. I appreciate him giving me time to adjust to him, but I'm also ready for him to pick up the pace.

Finally, he gets all the way in, and we both let out a rush of air.

"Fuck." Archer's the one to speak first. "My cock fits perfectly. Like it was made for you and you were made for me."

I moan, his words driving me crazy. *More.* I need more of him. My back arches off the bed, and the new position allows him to go even deeper.

He rolls his hips back, pulling out and pushing in. He repeats the motion over and over, picking up the pace each time until his hips are slapping against the backs of my thighs in a quick rhythm.

His pace is punishing in the most euphoric of ways. I've never been more thankful to be on the opposite side of the house than everyone else. Neither one of us is quiet as he continues to drill into me.

"Goddamn, you're so tight." The moan that falls from Archer's lips is the sexiest sound I've ever heard. I didn't know a man could moan like that, and it's the hottest thing in the world. I love that our sounds of pleasure and our skin slapping against each other fill the room.

My nails dig into his back as I try to keep him as close to me as possible. He can't possibly get any deeper, but I want—need

—more from him. I keep one hand on his back and let the other slide up his body until my fingers find the back of his neck. I pull on him, bringing his head down so he can kiss me.

He takes the hint immediately, his tongue possessively sliding into my mouth. The swipe of it falls in line with the rhythm of his hips. He stretches me every time he pushes inside, and it almost feels like it's too much.

I think even having him inside me all night won't satisfy my need for him.

I moan. He moans. Sweat drips down my spine from the exertion of our bodies.

"I think I'm going to come," I pant, unable to fight it any longer. I don't want this to end, but everything he's doing feels too good for me not to.

He rips his mouth from mine for a moment. "Do it. I'm ready to feel you come all over my cock."

"I don't want this to end yet," I admit. My words come out rushed as the orgasm builds and builds.

Archer's lips close around my nipple for a moment. He swirls his tongue around it, making my body tingle all the way down to my toes. "Oh, I'm not done with you, baby. You'll come now…and you'll come again. You'll be reminded all day of me tomorrow, remember?" He switches to my other nipple, this time biting the fuller part of my breast first before kissing it and easing the sting.

The pain with the pleasure is what finally sends me over the edge. I gasp at the sensation of the orgasm taking over my body as he continues to fuck me at a quick pace. His mouth continues to work my sensitive nipples as his hips set a punishing rhythm to milk the orgasm for everything that it is. My legs shake with how powerful it is, but I don't want him to stop.

"Fuckkkk…you feel so good," Archer says against my skin, his hips beginning to slow but not stopping fully.

My chest rises and falls in quick breaths from the intensity of the feelings overtaking my body.

"You ready for more?" Archer asks, his eyes looking into mine.

I nod. I don't know if I'll be able to come again, but it still feels so good that I want more of him. I don't want to miss what it feels like for him to come inside me.

Will he moan the same way he has been? Will that filthy mouth of his continue to whisper dirty things to me, or will he be too lost in the feeling of the orgasm that he says nothing at all? These are the questions I need answers to, and I won't let him stop until I know.

He doesn't wait for me to say anything else. He pulls out of me and flips my body around. I yelp, not expecting him to put me face down on the bed. Quickly, he lines his cock up with me once again, but this time in a totally new position.

His hand pushes me into the bed, forcing my back to arch even more as he inches inside.

"You're doing so good, letting me in even deeper now," he says, his voice coming out restrained. I open my eyes, looking behind me to find his jaw tense. The view gives me the perfect glimpse of his rippling muscles as he pumps into me.

I moan, my fingers gripping the sheets to give myself something to hold on to. His hand possessively runs along the curve of my ass as he continues to push in and out.

"One of these days, I'm going to fuck you while there's a perfect handprint from me right here." He continues to run his hand along the skin.

Another moan breaks free at the thought of it. I roll my head until my forehead presses against the sheets. I don't know what he's doing to me, but every single thing he's saying and doing is driving me crazy.

"Not tonight, though," he continues, his fingers tracing along my ass cheek. I jerk because never has anyone touched me there. "You're being such a good girl and taking me so well, tonight, you won't get punished."

My response is to arch my back even more to feel more of

him—to feel more of us joining together. I already want to cancel all plans for tomorrow so I can spend the day just like this with him.

With every moan that leaves his body and every filthy thought that leaves his mouth, I feel more and more empowered. I'm addicted to making him lose control like this, and I'm well aware that I'm just as addicted as he is—maybe even more.

It's incredibly dangerous, but when it feels this good—this perfect—I can't seem to care.

"I love this position because I get to watch myself push in and out of you. I get to see the way you greedily take me, even though I know your body is spent from orgasms already."

"Archer," I moan in response.

"Fuck, my name sounds perfect coming from your lips," he notes. As if it's a reward, he wraps his arm around my hips and begins to rub my clit in slow circles, the pace of his hips never relenting.

His palm runs along my spine as he moves from my ass to my neck. Once again, his fingers thread through my hair. This time, he yanks on it, pulling my body from the mattress and bringing my back to his front.

Our bodies touch in so many places, our skin sticking together from the sheen of sweat on both of us. Archer continues to play with my clit while his fingers move from my hair and begin to play with my nipple.

It's as if he's trying to make sure I feel him everywhere. His lips possessively kiss along my shoulder, his fingers play with my clit as he continues to roughly fuck me, and his other hand pinches my nipple.

"It's time for you to come again, baby," he says next to my ear. His voice is deep and rough, and I wonder if it's because he's close to coming.

"Are you close?" I ask, my voice coming out weak because my senses are on overdrive in this new position and with the ways that he touches me. I don't want to come again until he's right there with me, needing to feel him ride the wave with me.

"Yes," he responds immediately, his lips pressing a kiss to my throat. "I'm so fucking close to filling you full of my cum, but I need you there, too."

"I'm there," I pant. My head falls backward, letting him hold my weight as he goes even faster.

"One more," he moans, his voice strained. I don't respond because the pace of his hips and the circles of his fingers on my clit have a scream ripping from my body. The orgasm came on so fast I wasn't expecting it yet.

He beats in and out a few more times before a low groan comes from his chest. His hands still for a moment, wrapping tighter around me as he finishes. I wish I could see his face as he finds his own release, but I know it must feel good by the sounds he makes and the way he clutches my body.

His hips begin to slow, and then they still altogether as we both recover from what just happened. He doesn't pull out of me; instead, he leaves himself inside me as he leans forward and begins to kiss tenderly across my shoulder blades.

"We've got a problem," he rasps, his fingers gentle as he moves my hair from his trail of kisses.

"What is that?" I ask, looking over my shoulder at him.

"I think I'm fucking addicted to that—to you—now. And I don't think I'll ever have enough."

I smile, letting him press his lips to the side of my forehead this time. I let out a long breath, wondering if I should admit this or not. It only takes a few seconds for me to question my answer before I tell it to him anyway.

"Same," I whisper, wondering if I'll come to regret admitting it one day.

37
Archer

"KNOCK KNOCK!" A VOICE CALLS FROM THE OTHER SIDE OF OUR bedroom door.

I groan, pulling Winnie's body into mine and completely ignoring whoever is on the other side of the door. It seems like Winnie and I had just fallen back asleep from getting lost in each other's bodies when the person started rudely knocking.

"Winnie," another voice calls, this time in a singsong voice. "Oh, Winnie Boo Boo, it's time for our spa day!"

Winnie begins to stir, but I keep her body pressed to mine.

"Ignore them," I plead, not wanting to leave this bed. I haven't had enough of her, and the last thing I want to do is be away from her all day.

She laughs, intertwining her fingers with mine and snuggling deeper against my chest. "They won't go away no matter how much I want them to."

Another groan falls from my chest. "I *just* got you. It's too soon for you to be gone all day."

Winnie turns, her beautiful aquamarine eyes finding mine. "It's just a day. We'll see each other tonight for dinner at the club with everyone."

"That's too far away," I grumble, pressing my lips into a thin line.

She leans in and presses her lips to my cheek. "You'll survive it, I promise."

"Winnie Boo Boo, I'm going to open this door, and if I find you and your husband naked, I'll be scarred for life. Don't put me through that!"

Winnie laughs as she rolls her eyes. I miss her warmth the moment she begins to slide out of bed. "Emma really has always been the dramatic one," she explains. She grabs a cream-colored robe hanging on the back of the bathroom door and pulls it on.

I scowl, already missing the view of her perfect, naked body.

"Make sure you pull the covers over you," Winnie instructs as she walks up to the door.

"You're not opening it now," I argue from the bed. I'm completely naked—and my cock is half-strained at the sight of her bare skin.

She tosses a smile over her shoulder, her cheeks turning pink with amusement. "I'm definitely opening it. Pull the covers up now, Archer."

I let out an aggravated growl and pull the comforter all the way up, even covering my head as I hear Winnie pull the door open.

"Good morning," Winnie says, her voice far too nice when her friends just rudely interrupted our sleep. Technically, we overslept, and she's supposed to spend the day with them. I'm just grouchy that I won't be able to bury myself in her all day.

"Have fun last night?" one of the voices asks, this one I recognize as Emma. She's the fiery one, where Margo is a little more reserved. And then Camden's girlfriend, Pippa, is funnier than I expected. She had me laughing last night.

"I slept great," Winnie responds, her voice breaking a little.

The group of girls breaks out in a fit of laughter.

"Pippa found the best little coffee shop here that we already visited this morning while you were, uh…preoccupied," Margo finishes, another giggle falling from her lips. I lift the corner of the comforter, taking in the sight at the door.

Winnie stands in front of Emma, Margo, and Pippa. Margo holds a coffee in her hands, pushing it into Winnie's chest and waiting for her to take it.

"Hi, Archie," Emma calls, popping her head around Winnie to give me a knowing smile. "Did you break in the Sinclairs' new house last night?"

I've never been one to blush, but I feel my cheeks heat because of the four women all smiling at me with wide grins.

"My name is Archer," I clip, sitting up in bed but keeping the covers pulled tight around me.

"Archie has a better ring to it." Emma shrugs. "Winnie and Archie sounds adorable, you can't deny that."

"Emma," Winnie whines, shaking her head at her friend.

"Emma *does* kind of have a point. Maybe we'll have to start calling you Archie," Pippa pipes up. Damn, I thought she might've been my favorite friend of Winnie's, but maybe I'll have to reconsider. Margo is the only one halfway minding her own business right now.

"Call me Archie again and Winnie and I are on the first flight back to Manhattan today," I warn. My arms cross against my chest defensively as I stare at my wife's beautiful smile.

Winnie takes a drink of the coffee Margo gave her. "He doesn't mean that. We're here to stay. But I *do* need to get ready, so if the three of you would give me ten minutes of privacy, that would be amazing."

"Thirty," I argue, my lips twitching with a budding smile.

Margo's eyes go wide, Emma snickers, and Pippa's eyebrows rise to her hairline with my comment.

"Should I arrange for our housekeepers today to replace your sheets?" Margo asks, trying her hardest not to laugh.

Pippa loses the battle behind her, a cough escaping from her chest as she tries but fails to fight a fit of laughter.

She's far away, and I can only see her from the side, but I notice that even Winnie's chest goes pink from embarrassment. I love watching her flush—it only makes me want to make her friends disappear even more so I can get her alone and get back to memorizing every inch of her body.

"Probably for the best," I say, answering Margo with a smirk on my lips.

Winnie shoots a look my way before outstretching her arms and attempting to shuffle her friends from the doorway. "Give me ten minutes and I'll be ready to go."

"Thirty," I repeat under my breath but still loud enough for everyone to hear.

"If we get done early enough, we thought about hitting some of the shops in town," Margo offers.

Winnie nods. "I'd love that! We can look for some pieces to decorate here."

Margo's entire face lights up. "I was hoping you'd say that."

"Before any of that, you guys have to let me get dressed and make myself presentable. *Leave!*" Winnie teases, beginning to shut the door to force them out.

"We'll be back if you're not done in ten minutes!" Pippa yells, throwing her arm over Emma right before Winnie completely slams the door.

Winnie turns and looks at me with a shy smile. She presses her back to the door, watching me closely.

I reach across the bed and pat the spot she vacated. "Come back to bed."

"I've got to get ready to leave. And so do you."

"No, we're not leaving the room today," I protest, even though I already know her well enough that she won't agree to it.

Winnie rolls her eyes before pushing off the door and heading to the bathroom. "We're leaving the room. I'm going to spend some time with my friends for the first time in forever, and you're going to get to spend some time with the guys. We'll have a great time, and then tonight, we'll see each other again and…"

"And then we'll fuck all night?" I offer, placing my hands in my lap. I probably should get up, too, but I'm having too much fun watching her bring different outfit options to the mirror to decide what she wants to wear.

She glares at me through the mirror, holding up a cashmere sweater to her body.

"I like that one," I tell her. "The pink reminds me of the same color your cheeks turn when you blush."

"Sometimes you say really sweet things."

I smile, climbing out of bed and closing the distance between us. My arms wrap around her middle as my chin comes to rest on her shoulder. "I can say even sweeter things with my face buried between your thighs."

"Archer!" She playfully elbows me but still leans deeper into the embrace. For a moment, we stay locked in it, the two of us watching each other through the mirror. It feels so… normal. Like something a typical married couple who are in love would do in the morning. I close my eyes for a moment, savoring it, knowing that things between us are far more complicated.

"Just pointing out the truth." I kiss her cheek. "I definitely vote yes on the sweater. Although, I already want to rip it off you."

Winnie swallows slowly, keeping her eyes pinned on mine through the mirror. "I haven't even put it on yet."

I shrug, backing up to allow her to finish getting ready even though I don't want to. "My point still stands."

"Then, I'll wear it…just for you."

I give her a smile of approval. Fuck, what is she doing to me? I don't think I've smiled this much in my life, and yet I can't stop myself from doing it around her.

She strips out of the robe and lets it fall to the ground. It doesn't take her long to get dressed in the sweater and a pair of jeans.

Finally, I realize I should probably stop watching her get ready and get myself ready. Although I'd much prefer staying locked in this room with her all day, I do think I'll enjoy myself with the guys. There are worse things I could be doing.

Speaking of worse things, my phone vibrates on the night-stand. Winnie works on pulling her hair into a ponytail on the top of her head as I walk to grab my phone.

I sigh, seeing my dad's caller ID on the screen. The last thing I want to do is talk to him right now. I'd actually like to forget all about work for once, but I answer it anyway because I know that's what's expected of me.

"Hi," I clip out, wanting to cut to the point.

"Archer. There's been a new development. I need you back in the office as soon as possible."

I look at Winnie, who curiously watches me through the mirror as she ties a ribbon around her ponytail. "I'll be back in on Monday."

"*Monday*?" My dad doesn't bother to hide the shock in his voice. Typically, if he asks me to jump, I ask how high. Any other time he'd tell me he needed me in the office, I'd show up there. Not this time. I promised Winnie we'd have this weekend with her friends, and I don't want to go back on my promise.

"Yes, Monday. I'll get to it first thing."

My dad sighs. "This isn't like you, Archer. Is it the Bishop girl?"

I turn my back to her. I know there's no way she can hear my dad through the phone, but I do it just in case. "I'll get to it on Monday."

He hangs up, and for a moment, I stand in place with the phone still pressed to my ear, wondering how much I'll regret that come Monday morning. When I turn to see Winnie, I know that I won't regret it too much because this weekend has already been worth whatever wrath I'll get from my dad.

"Everything okay?" she asks, her voice worried.

I watch her for a moment, not answering. Sometimes it's hard for me to forget who she is—who her family is. I was raised to believe anyone with the last name Bishop is enemy number one.

It was basically a family mantra to never trust a Bishop. My father and grandfather would be so disappointed to know that I do trust her, even with the knowledge of knowing exactly who she is.

"I'll find out on Monday," I tell her, crossing the room and grabbing clothes from my suitcase.

For a moment, I wonder if I should let the guys go to the club without me and I can stay back and help handle whatever my dad needs, but I also don't want to go back on what I told him. If I call back now and try to fix this, I'll be doing the same thing I've always done.

For once, I want to set at least a small boundary with my dad. He ran a company without me for years; whatever it is, he can handle it on his own, or it can truly wait until Monday.

At least, that's what I hope.

38
Winnie

"I still can't believe this is what you guys call a country club," Pippa says from her lounger at Pembroke Hills' spa. She looks like she belongs in an ad for the spa with the cucumbers on her eyes and the drink with orange and cucumbers floating around in the glass she's holding.

"There's a beautiful country club with a stunning golf course in Sutten," Margo argues, lifting one of the cucumbers off her eyes to look at Pippa. "I know this because my husband wants to golf there all the time."

Pippa laughs. "Good to know for this summer. Should I expect Camden to always be joining him?"

Margo nods. "Oh yeah, we'll lose them to golf and business talk. The things the men do." She laughs before stretching out her legs on the plush lounger.

"Well, they can golf all they want. You can find me at the spa. Although the Sutten Country Club is very nice, it doesn't even compare to this."

I discard both of the cucumbers from my eyes on the small table between Emma and me. Mine keep slipping off, and I'm over adjusting them.

"To be fair, this is the top country club in the US. It's *prestigious*." Emma drags out the last word dramatically. Her eyebrows wag underneath her cucumbers. Somehow, hers stay on way better than mine do.

"Emma, how do you even know that?" I ask.

"I did my research. *Duh.* You guys can't invite me somewhere fancy and expect me to not find out every single detail about it. Do you even want to know how much a guest pass is to be here today?"

"Probably not," Pippa chimes in, shaking her head.

"It's a lot. The fact that Beck could get so many is actually very impressive."

Margo laughs. "He can be *very* persuasive. It's hard for anyone to tell him no."

Emma's nose wrinkles. "Gross. I don't want to know any of that information."

The door opens, and one of the spa assistants walks in with a tray of mimosas with cut strawberries lining the rim.

"Are we beginning to feel relaxed here, ladies?" she asks, passing out the mimosas.

Everyone sits up, peeling their cucumbers from their face and discarding them.

"I feel very Zen," Emma responds, eagerly taking the mimosa.

The woman smiles. "I'm so happy to hear that." She keeps her voice low to keep that same "Zen" Emma talks about.

As soon as everyone has a mimosa and she tells us we're welcome to hang out as long as we'd like before leaving the spa, she leaves just as quietly as she came in.

"Let's do a toast," Pippa offers, getting off her lounger to come sit next to me. Margo follows her lead, sitting on Emma's lounger so we all sit in a makeshift circle.

"A toast is perfect," I agree, raising my glass in the air.

"To being young and hot!" Emma cheers, sticking her tongue out.

"To being young and hot," both Pippa and I repeat, clinking our glasses together.

Margo just sits there for a moment, staring at the mimosa in her hand.

My eyebrows scrunch on my forehead. "Mar?" I prod, leaning forward to tap her knee.

Her eyes meet mine. "I think I'm pregnant," she blurts, her eyes wide.

"*What?*" Emma shrieks, almost tackling Margo.

"Oh my god!" Pippa gasps.

"Margo," I whisper, happiness overtaking me as I squeeze her leg.

She hands me her drink and pulls the twisted towel from her hair. "I don't know if I am or not. You know Beck and I have been trying, and it really hasn't been in the cards for us yet. We kind of stopped talking about it and decided it would happen when it was meant to be. But I woke up this morning feeling nauseous, and my boobs hurt *so* bad."

Pippa looks like a lightbulb went off in her head. "Oh my god, is that why you were so insistent on finding somewhere with a chocolate croissant?"

Margo laughs. "It's the only thing that sounded good. I thought that maybe it was just from traveling yesterday, but all morning while we've been here, I can't get rid of this feeling that I'm pregnant."

Emma jumps off the lounger and begins to race toward the women's locker room door.

"Emma, where are you going?" I call.

"We've got to get dressed!" she yells as if the answer is completely obvious. "We have to get out of here so we can buy a test."

"Oh my god, I don't want to ruin everyone's day by having you take a test with me. I can take it by myself. I don't want to tell Beck and get his hopes up if it's negative." I hate the sad tone of Margo's voice. This should be exciting.

"There's nothing more I'd love than to be there when you take a test," I tell her. "As long as you're okay with that."

"We're here to support you whether it's positive or negative," Pippa adds, getting off my lounger and wrapping Margo into a hug.

"I'd love to have you guys there with me if you really don't mind," Margo says over Pippa's shoulder. She laughs when Emma rushes through the door and starts throwing clothes at all of us.

"Emma! We're coming," I say, getting up and pulling the towel from my hair. We were supposed to get ready here before going to a vineyard, but we've got way better plans now.

"Then hurry up," Emma demands, forcing her feet into the legs of her jeans.

"It really isn't a rush." Margo laughs, she and Pippa breaking the hug so the both of them can get dressed. "It'll probably be negative anyway," she adds.

I shake my head. "No. We aren't putting that into the universe. It'll be positive. Let's go find out if our bestie is knocked up!" I tease.

All of us giddily get ready as quickly as possible before we talk about where the nearest store is.

—

"Emma, you really don't have to watch me pee on the stick," Margo says from the toilet inside the tiny corner store. The store only has one bathroom, so we've all piled inside as Margo sits on the toilet with her pants down, her eyes glaring at Emma, who apparently forgot what personal space is.

I laugh, looping my arm through Emma's and pulling her back.

Emma looks over at me with a glare. "What? I'm just making sure she doesn't miss!"

"I'm peeing on a stick—I can't miss. I've done this before, you know," Margo says, her eyes meeting all of ours.

"What if we turn around?" I offer, waving both Pippa and Emma to spin so at least Margo can pee in peace.

"Yes, maybe that'll help," Margo agrees, smiling at us before a loud snort comes from her chest. "I can't believe I'm about to find out if I'm pregnant in a random gas station bathroom with all of you guys staring at me intensely."

We laugh with her, the three of us facing away and looking to the wall.

"Just make sure you hold it in your stream for the full five seconds!" Emma demands.

I giggle.

Emma glares at me once again. "What?" she asks.

"You're just being really bossy," I tease.

"I'm being helpful," she corrects with a grin. "I'm sorry for being excited about having my first niece or nephew."

"How's it going?" Pippa asks, still staring at the wall.

"I can't get anything out!" Margo admits, humor in her voice. "It's hard to force anything with you guys in here. Or maybe I'm just nervous."

"Think of running water," Emma offers.

"Oh, look, you cured me of being pee shy," Margo counters sarcastically.

"What if we turn on the fan?" I ask, flipping the switch up. It roars to life, definitely filling the quiet of the bathroom.

"Oh, that's perfect," Margo says from behind us.

We all wait as we hear her flush. The moment the water turns on as she starts to wash her hands, we turn around and close the distance to the small pedestal sink.

One single pregnancy test sits on the counter. She's put it facedown, so we can't see the results yet.

"How do we want to do this?" Pippa asks.

"Yeah, do you want to look first and then tell us?" Emma adds on to Pippa's question. "One of us looks and tells you? Or do we all just look at the same time?"

Emma shifts on her feet nervously. I hit her thigh, not wanting to make Margo even more uneasy.

"I think I want us all to look at the same time," Margo answers, anxiously pulling on the neck of her turtleneck. "Just don't be disappointed if it's negative, okay? There's always next month."

"We're just excited to be here with you for this. No matter what," I assure her.

Both Pippa and Emma nod their heads in agreement. We all take a step forward, our shoulders hitting one another as we stare down at the turned-over pregnancy test.

"Okay, I think we can flip it over now," Margo whispers, worry evident in her voice.

"You want to do the honors?" Emma asks Margo.

Margo shakes her head. "I'm too nervous. One of you do it." She holds up her hand, showing us how shaky it is.

I take it, and before long, all of our hands are piled on top of Margo's as we reassure her that we're with her on this.

"Okay, Emma, turn it over," Margo demands, her voice full of anxiety.

"One...two..." we begin to count as Emma wraps her hand around the stick. On three, she flips it over, and we all lean in with our breaths held.

"Two lines means pregnant, right?" Emma asks, grabbing the box from the sink to confirm.

"Oh my god," Margo cries, her hand covering her mouth as she stares at the test.

"*You're pregnant!*" Emma yells, wrapping her arms around Margo's middle.

"Holy shit," Pippa says excitedly, joining the hug.

I'm the last to join, completely speechless as tears begin to well in my eyes.

My best friend is pregnant.

"Mar," I sob, crying right along with Margo as we all hug one another. "You're going to have a baby."

Margo's shoulders shake as she looks at us. "That's positive, right? I'm not making it up?"

Pippa laughs. "That's absolutely positive. Those lines are dark."

"I'm going to have a baby," Margo whispers, her eyes wide with disbelief. "I can't wait to tell Beck."

My heart swells with love for my best friend and her husband. It's surreal, knowing that they've wanted to start a family for a long time now and it's finally happening for them. All we ever used to talk about in college was how we wanted to be moms. We'd talked about our list of baby names we loved, and now her dreams are coming true.

"You're going to have a baby," Emma repeats, tears running down her face. Emma never cries, so in return, I cry even harder at the sight of her doing it.

"I'm just so happy for you," I sob, wiping under my eyes in an attempt to stop blubbering like a baby.

"Okay, now we need to think of a cute way for you to tell Beck. Are you going to do it today?"

Margo nods. "I suck at secrets. I'll have to tell him almost immediately after seeing him, or I'll just blurt it out instead of doing something cute."

"No, we've got to do cute," Emma argues, throwing the pregnancy test box away. "Looks like we're going shopping after all. But now for baby clothes and a way to tell Mr. Sinclair he knocked up his wife!"

We spend the rest of the afternoon picking out outfits, even though Margo argues with us to wait. We're too excited, and by the end, she is, too. We didn't end up going to the winery, but instead, we got to celebrate our friend being pregnant and coming up with a way for her to tell Beck they're expecting.

39
Archer

"Okay, Moore, are you going to spill how you actually ended up married to the only daughter of your family's rival, or are we just going to pretend that didn't happen?" Beck questions, being far more nosy than I expected him to be.

I laugh, twirling the bourbon around in the crystal glass. "Should I ask you the details on how you two found your relationships?" I lift an eyebrow, my focus on Beck. "Funny how you ended up engaged right after this big article came out about how much of a playboy you were. Let me guess, your board of directors really didn't love seeing the face of their company being talked about so negatively?"

Beck smirks, trying to play coy as he takes a drink from his own glass. "It was the investors that were the real worry."

I nod my head. "Convenient how you got engaged *right* after. To your brother's ex-girlfriend, no less."

"When two people are meant to be, there's no reason to wait," he responds. "It seems you understand that."

"Indeed." I take another drink, my eyes roaming around the dark, private room of the club. It cost a fortune just to spend the afternoon here, but I've been enjoying myself. Although they're some of the most powerful men in their industries and in New York in general, they're actually cool.

I've been around pretentious men my entire life. Men who

want to show off the number of zeroes in their bank account and talk about all the women they're fucking behind their wife's backs. Camden and Beck aren't like that.

There's easy conversation with them. If we weren't sitting in a private club that costs thousands each month to be a member and dressed in suits that custom fit our bodies, you'd never know how much any of us made.

Except maybe their conversation back and forth about Camden looking to build a new house in Pippa's hometown and all he wants to do with it.

"Well, Pippa and I are not engaged—yet—so there's nothing you can give me shit for, Moore," Camden says smugly, taking a large puff of his cigar.

"I'll think of something," I joke, leaning back in the leather seat. My phone has gone off a few times since we arrived at the club, but both Beck and Camden have stayed off of theirs, so I've done the same. It's refreshing as hell. I don't know anything but working, but this weekend has taught me how burnt out I truly was and how much of a break I needed.

"So your family approves of the marriage? It's no secret how much Winnie's family fucked over yours. I just don't see your father welcoming Winnie into the family with open arms," Beck prods.

I don't mind all of his questions. I'd be curious, too. Everyone in the circle of New York's elite is more than aware that the Bishops and the Moores hate one another. A marriage between two of the children is their own version of Romeo and Juliet— except this one has a far less dramatic ending.

"Do you know my dad well?" I ask, giving me more time on what answer I want to give these two. I actually like them both. I might even view both of them as friends, so I don't really want to lie to them if I don't have to.

Beck laughs, but Camden's the one to answer. "Yeah, kind of. He's a bit of an ass, though, not going to hold back." He sets his cigar down and takes a drink of his bourbon. "And I can say that because mine's even worse."

A low chuckle comes from my chest. "He doesn't give warm, fuzzy feelings, that's for sure."

"Scale from one to ten, how much did your father fuck you up?" Camden asks, his voice teasing even though the topic is dark.

"Zero," Beck answers, holding his hands up defensively. At least one of us had a father that knew how to show love.

"I'd say about an eight." I laugh. "Can't be a ten when he grooms you to be the heir to his billion-dollar company, can it?"

"To me, that makes it an eleven. When I have kids, my only goal is to make them know they're loved and that I have no say in the path they choose for their life," Camden responds.

"Damn, Hunter. When did we get sentimental?" Beck leans forward, his fingers smoothing back his hair.

"Pippa makes me talk about my feelings. Put in a good word for me and tell her I'm getting better at it," he jokes, lifting his eyebrows.

We all laugh, the conversation drifting into silence for a moment as we all get lost in our own thoughts. I think about Camden's words and what they mean. I never saw myself as a father figure, but it isn't because I don't want kids.

I think I would like to have them one day; I just never envisioned doing anything other than work. I barely saw my father as a child because he never stopped working. The moment he felt that I was old enough to learn from him, he pulled me into working right alongside him.

We never played catch or watched a game of football together. The only thing we've ever bonded over is Moore Hotels, and it's kind of sad when I really think about it.

I sigh and shake my head. Pippa might be encouraging Camden to talk about his feelings, but I'd much rather pretend that I'm not coming to the conclusion that my life was eerily pathetic before Winnie.

To avoid thinking about this, I look around the small room. There's another group of men on the other side of the space, but other than that, it's pretty empty at Pembroke Hills. It's probably because it's the off-season. I'm sure during the summer, this room is filled to the brim with men who are pretending to talk business but are actually gossiping.

I'd like to come back this summer, which is something I never thought I'd say because the last thing I want to do is say I'm going on vacation only to spend it with the people I try to avoid in Manhattan at all costs.

"Well, Sinclair," I begin, finishing off my drink. "I think you may have convinced me."

Beck's eyebrows pull in on his forehead. "Convinced you to tell me why a Moore married a Bishop?"

I laugh, shaking my head. "The only answer to that is love, Sinclair. Love can ease even the harshest of grudges. There's no other explanation." My lips turn down slightly as I think about my words and what from them are real.

"Then what did I convince you of other than to start reciting poetry?" Beck prods, a smug smile on his face.

"I'm thinking about buying a property here to visit during the summer. I'll get a membership to the club, and I don't know, I feel like it'd be a nice getaway for Winnie and me sometimes."

"I think the girls would love it, too, if we came up more this summer. We could golf, they could shop. Sounds like the perfect plan," Camden offers. He pulls his phone from his pocket for a moment, ignoring a phone call before tucking it back into his pants.

I nod, surprisingly liking the idea of that plan. I've been wanting to add a few more real estate properties to the ones I already own, and this seems like the perfect place. Buying a house here means you'll never lose out on your money; houses fly off the market down here. People are always trying to prove they are wealthy by buying a vacation home in the Hamptons.

I don't need to prove anything. I just want an easy getaway location for Winnie and me to get out of the city if we choose to.

"I'll start looking at places next week," I confirm, twirling my glass between my fingers even though it's empty.

"I love that you guys keep following my lead on buying properties," Beck muses. "Camden buying a property in Sutten, Archer buying a place in the Hamptons. Who knew I had so much influence?"

Camden and I both shake our heads.

"I bought a place in Sutten because I own a gallery there and the woman I love lives there. It has nothing to do with you," Camden jabs.

Beck still snickers, clearly not believing a word Camden says. "*Sure*," he responds. "I didn't see you looking at business properties in Sutten until I chose to get married there. Just saying."

Camden rolls his eyes.

I shrug. "I just like the thought of having somewhere close for Winnie and me to visit. If I've learned anything about my wife, it's that she loves spending time with your significant others. So it really isn't you, Beck. It's the fact I know it'll make Winnie happy to spend more time with her friends this summer."

Beck's features soften slightly. It's weird, and the longer he stares at me, the more uncomfortable I get.

Finally, I can't handle his deep inspection any longer. "What?" I snap, wanting to know why he's looking at me like that.

Beck breaks eye contact, looking over at Camden with a conspiring smirk. The two of them share a knowing smile that makes me even more annoyed.

Beck looks back at me. "It's just good to see Camden and I aren't the only ones completely and obsessively in love with our girls."

40
Winnie

"DID YOU HAVE FUN THIS WEEKEND?" ARCHER ASKS, HIS LIPS brushing against my temple.

I nod, snuggling into his body further. "I did. Even though you cut it short a little earlier than we'd planned."

His chest vibrates against my cheek with his laugh. "I wanted to have you all to myself for part of today. I'm not used to lazy Sundays, but today, I want that with you."

The private jet's engine hums around us as we coast through the sky on our way back to Manhattan. We'd had an early morning, all of us waking up and drinking coffee around the table as we celebrated Margo and Beck having a baby.

Emma wanted to go back to Sutten Mountain with Camden and Pippa to help out with a new project at Pippa's bakery, so it seemed like an easy decision for Archer and me to head back to Manhattan just the two of us. The plan allowed for Margo and Beck to have some alone time together after finding out they're going to be parents.

"A lazy day does sound nice." I yawn, exhaustion catching up with me. The past two nights, Archer and I have been up very late—and early—getting tangled in the bedsheets together. It's been perfect, but the further and further we get away from the Hamptons, the more reality begins to sink in.

Did this weekend change everything, or did it change

nothing at all? Will we go back to skirting around the attraction back at the house we share? Will we still go to separate rooms at night? Or did things actually change between us?

If I'm being honest with myself, I'm not sure which I prefer. It's hard to differentiate what's real and what's pretend when Archer's lips are on mine with no one but us around.

"I was wondering if next weekend you'd want to go on a date with me?" Archer asks, tracing his fingertips over our intertwined hands. His voice sounds a little hesitant, like he might even be nervous to ask me that.

I push off his chest so I can look into his eyes. Our two flight attendants are in the back, leaving us alone in the cabin. I don't want to admit that I like how intimate he's being even with no one around. It makes it feel like maybe this isn't all a charade.

My eyes narrow on him for a moment as I try to figure out what he means by his question. "Is there an event we need to be seen at?" I ask slowly.

He stares right back at me, seemingly unbothered by my question. "There isn't."

"We don't typically do dates unless it's for a reason."

"There is a reason," he answers, as if it's the most obvious thing in the world.

"And what is that?" I breathe in, waiting for his answer. His smell surrounds me, the mix of the bergamot and clove completely wrapping me in him as I wait for his answer.

"Because I want to take my wife on a date."

Blood rushes to my cheeks as my heart rate intensifies. It's the possessive way he says 'my wife' that completely unnerves me. This man, he's unlike any other, and it's incredibly dangerous for my heart.

He reaches up, brushing his thumb along my cheekbone and cupping my cheek. "Have I ever told you how much I love it when you blush? You do it more and more lately, and it still drives me crazy every time I see it."

I fight a smile, not knowing what to say back. Surely things can't all be for show between us when he says things like that. The doubt in the back of my mind tells me that he's always been charming, and maybe this is just him being just that—charming.

"I hate how much I blush. My skin is pale and gives me away when any extra blood rushes to my cheeks."

"How could you hate something so beautiful?" he marvels, running his thumb along the heated skin of my cheek.

"Stop saying things like that," I whisper. At this point, my heart beats so erratically and my pulse thumps so strongly that he must be aware of the effect his words have on me.

"Saying things like the truth? I know you don't want me to lie to you, Win."

My heart flutters at his use of my nickname. My whole life, the only people to ever call me that are my two best friends. It's special to me, and for reasons I don't want to delve into, I love the sound of it coming from his mouth.

"Please don't ever lie to me."

He presses his lips together while his eyes roam my face. I could get lost looking into his deep brown eyes. They're so much more than just brown. There are flecks of gold in there that captivate me.

"Then I'm going to be honest when I tell you the things you do that drive me mad."

I lean in closer, wanting to feel the press of his lips on mine. "I drive you mad?"

"Absolutely insane," he immediately responds.

I can't help but smile as our lips move closer together. I want to grab the sides of his face and slide into his lap and make out like a couple of teenagers, but I fight the urge. A crew member could walk into the cabin at any moment, and I'd be incredibly embarrassed if they found me in Archer's lap, pretty much begging him to touch me.

"That smile," Archer breathes, closing the distance between our lips. I let out a content sigh as we lazily kiss, pretending like we can do this for the rest of our lives and never run out of time.

He eventually pulls away, pressing his forehead to mine. "You just love knowing you completely unravel me, don't you?"

I shrug. "I don't hate it."

Archer shakes his head, his hand moving from my cheek to the back of my head. "So is that a yes for a date?"

"Of course," I whisper.

He smiles the most handsome of smiles. "Good. Because I've already got it all planned. The only thing I needed was for you to say yes."

My head rears back as I narrow my eyes at him. "And what if I'd said no?"

Even with me moving, he keeps the contact between our bodies. His hand slides down my spine until it rests on the small of my back. "Then I would've kept begging until you finally said yes." He pulls me to his body once again, but instead of lining his lips up with my mouth, he lines them up with my ear. "And I can be *very* persuasive when I'm on my knees begging, but you know that already."

This time, my entire body flushes remembering him at Beck and Margo's home. He certainly knows how to beg, so much that I ended up seeing stars.

"What's the date?" I ask, trying to change the subject to distract myself from how much I want him right here and right now.

He must feel the same because his hand tucks into the waistband of my leggings. His palm is warm against the underside of my ass as he cups it. "It'll be a surprise for you. I'll make sure you have everything you need for it."

"I don't want to wait to find out." His hand lowers, making my body shudder when his fingers run along the seam of my ass cheeks. Oh god, I'm getting wet for him right now, and he's barely touched me.

I risk looking over his shoulder, making sure we're alone. We're tucked into a loveseat at the front of the plane. The blanket I asked for at the beginning of the flight helps cover where his hand is traveling—now down the front of my leggings—but it still doesn't change the fact that we're thirty thousand feet in the air and at any moment could be caught.

"Ever joined the mile-high club, baby?" Archer asks, his teeth raking against my ear.

I shake my head as his finger brushes against my clit. "No. And we can't." My answer isn't very firm, however, because when he begins to inch a finger inside me, I moan instead of telling him to stop.

"Then this will be a first for both of us," he rasps, trailing kisses along my neck.

"What if someone finds us?"

"They won't. We'll go into the den at the back of the plane. No one will have to know I'm making my wife come on my cock as I fuck her thirty thousand feet in the air."

I moan again, this one louder. All he does is laugh. He doesn't seem to care if we were to be caught or not, but I do.

"Room," I pant the moment he slides two fingers in. "Right now."

Archer wastes no time. He slides his hand from my leggings and pulls me from the seat. I laugh, taken aback by how hastily he was out of the chair and throwing me over his shoulder. The blanket comes with us, dragging along the ground as he hurriedly goes to the back of the plane.

"Archer," I whisper-shout, trying not to laugh at how he carries me over his shoulder like a caveman. "I didn't mean right now so literally," I chide, trying not to yelp when he throws me on the tiny bed in the small back room of the plane.

"Well, I, for one, take my wife's needs very seriously," he answers, his tone lowered as he shuts the door. "You said right now, and your wish is my command."

I shake my head at him, watching him closely as he begins to unbutton his dress shirt. I pop each one of my shoes off and let them fall to the ground.

"If we were out there any longer, you may have moaned loud

enough for everyone on this plane to hear. At least back here, they might hear you...but they won't walk in."

I wet my lips at the sight of his bare torso. I don't know if I will ever get used to seeing the defined muscles of his body. He works hard to keep them like that, and it shows. Even on our small weekend getaway, he worked out—even if we technically worked out in the privacy of our bedroom as well.

Apparently not willing to wait another second without touching again, Archer crawls across the bed with nothing but his pants on. "I'm dying to fuck you, baby," he begins, wrapping his fingers in the waistband of my leggings and tugging. He easily pulls them down my thighs and takes them off of me completely. "But first, I'm going to eat this pussy—my pussy—the way it deserves. You just have to be quiet for me, okay?"

I nod, my head falling onto the bed when he spreads my thighs open and begins to do exactly what he promised.

And then Archer introduces me to the mile-high club...twice. Except the second time, his thrusts are slow, and it feels like so much more than just the two of us using each other's bodies for a release.

41
Archer

THE WEEKEND WENT BY FAR TOO FAST, AND FOR THE FIRST TIME IN my life, I'm dreading walking into the office.

Leaving Winnie alone at the house today sucked. I wanted to spend all day with her doing the most mundane things, and the moment I walked out the front door and felt like I left my heart back at the house, I knew without a shadow of a doubt that I've fallen in love with my wife.

I've never been in love. It was never a desire of mine to fall in love, but it didn't stop it from happening. I've fallen deeply and insanely in love with Winnie, without even realizing it was happening. Leaving the house this morning knowing I'd have to go all day without seeing her felt like I was plucking my heart from my own chest and placing it somewhere else, hoping nothing would happen to it in my absence.

And the realization is completely terrifying.

"You okay?" a stranger asks in the lobby of our headquarters. I'm stopped just in front of the security line, undoubtedly holding up the line of people trying to start their Monday morning at work.

I nod, rubbing over my chest where it feels like there's pain when nothing's even happened. "I'm fine," I grunt, not wanting to talk to anyone at the moment.

My head spins as I wonder how the hell I got here and what

I'm going to do about it. I've done everything—even begged—to get Winnie to trust me, and she still hasn't told me she does. It feels like slowly, she's let her guard down for me, but I still don't know how she truly feels.

If she doesn't trust me, I can't ever expect her to reciprocate my feelings. It's a hard fact to come to terms with, but I also know that no matter how she feels about me, I'm too far gone.

I'm in love with her. My dad would be furious if he knew. The first thing I was ever taught was to never trust a Bishop. The way my great-grandfather was fucked over by hers will forever haunt my family. It was casual dinner talk about how one day the Moores would get their revenge. And now I've gone and fallen in love with the one woman in the world I shouldn't have.

But there was no stopping it. It was hard not to. The early morning walks, the easy dinner conversation, I was left with no choice but to fall head over heels for the amazing, caring, beautiful woman she is.

Now, I just have to make sure I hide it from my father. It'll be the first thing I truly hide from him, but if he knew this business transaction had turned into more, I fear what he'd do.

I take a large inhale, getting my shit together before walking through the security line. My head needs to be in the game and not muddled with thoughts of Winnie. My dad's already going to be pissed at me for not returning his calls this weekend or coming into work, so I need to be prepared with whatever version of him I'll get when I walk into his office.

The elevator ride up to the top floor seems like it takes an eternity. I tuck myself into the back of the crowded space, my hands in my pockets as it climbs higher and higher. I should be looking through my emails to see if there's any hint of what I could expect from my dad, but instead, I pull my phone out to text with my real estate agent. There's something I want to show Winnie tonight when I get home, and I've got to get things in order for it.

Finally, the doors open on the top floor. With a sigh, I tuck my phone back into my pocket and step out. My assistant, Luther, waits for me, his eyes looking suspiciously nervous this morning.

"Good morning, Luther," I say, giving him a tight smile.

Luther looks at me with a lost look, his mouth slightly hanging open.

"What?" I ask, confused as to why he hasn't begun to tell me what I've missed since I left for the Hamptons on Friday.

Luther clears his throat, attempting to gather himself, but he's already piqued my interest. He must realize I won't relent with the way I intensely keep my gaze on him, my eyebrows raised expectantly as I wait for him to answer my question.

He scratches his neck. "It's just that...you're smiling this morning. It took me a bit by surprise, that's all."

The smile is wiped from my face, instead turning into a frown. Apparently, even Luther can tell that I'm in a better mood than normal after the weekend I had with Winnie.

"Tell me the situation with my dad. Is it bad?" I ask, completely changing the subject. I've always respected Luther. He does his job well, but I don't need to tell him that the reason I can't stop smiling is because of a certain woman with the last name Bishop.

Luther tilts his head back and forth, his jaw clenching as he thinks about an answer. "I'm not sure about that," he answers honestly.

I nod, not knowing if his words comfort me or make me uneasy.

"Is he in his office?" I ask, looking at the piece of paper he hands me to find out what my schedule is for the day. My entire morning is blocked off, something only me and my dad have the power of doing. Since I'm not the one who blacked out everything this morning, it had to have been him. My gut says I should definitely be feeling uneasy from that.

"No. He's in conference room four," Luther answers, his voice tight. He shifts on his feet, clearly uncomfortable.

I rip my eyes from the paper and look at him. "Four?" I question. That room is only used for private meetings. Ones where no one can look in because it's behind cinder block walls instead of the glass like our other conference rooms.

"Yes," he confirms, giving me a forced smile. I don't return it.

I swallow, handing the piece of paper back to him and beginning to walk toward conference room four. With every step closer, I wonder if I maybe should've taken my dad more seriously over the weekend. Maybe things are worse than I was expecting. Surely if they were terribly bad, he wouldn't have relented in getting me to come in.

Finally, we make it to the closed door of the conference room. I look back at Luther. "Take care of anything that comes through while I'm in the meeting. Unless it's an emergency, I don't want to be bothered."

"I understand," he responds, already backing away. I don't blame him. I don't necessarily want to be anywhere near whatever's happening in here either, but I'm left with no choice.

My hand rests on the doorknob as I smooth my features into a face of indifference. Even if I feel uneasy about what I will find on the other side of the door, I don't want my dad to know it.

Pushing the door open, I prepare myself for whatever I'm about to find.

Just as I expected, I find my dad at the very end of the long conference table in his normal seat at the head of it. He's got his hands folded in front of him like he always does, a pen in his hand, even though the piece of paper laid out in front of him is completely blank.

What I don't expect is the three other men sitting in the room with him. I recognize them immediately as being members of the Bishop Hotels board. It wouldn't be as odd to see them if it wasn't for the lack of Winnie's dad in the room.

My dad meeting with board members of Bishop Hotels without a Bishop present is concerning, but I don't let that show on my face.

"Morning," I drawl, pretending like it's totally normal to find them here at Moore Hotels headquarters.

"Archer," my dad responds, his voice thundering through the room. "Come in, son. Take a seat."

I watch him carefully, wondering where this is headed. There's no hint of the annoyance that was present on the phone on Saturday. Instead, he seems happy to see me. Like we're your everyday, loving father-son duo. We aren't, but I don't give that away because I want to know what's happening here first.

"Good to see you again," I tell the men sitting on the opposite side of the table from me. They all give me forced smiles, no one in this room giving any indication of what the meeting is for. Last time I saw them, we were all seated around a table almost exactly like the one we're at now, but it was at Bishop Hotels—where any meetings with each other should take place.

"We're thrilled for you to join us this morning," Dad goes on, clapping his hands together excitedly. "We've got some big moves we wanted to discuss with you."

Big moves?

My stomach sinks. I already don't like where this is going. "I'm looking forward to hearing them," I lie. At this very moment, I'm thankful for the years of pretending that my dad and I don't have a strained relationship outside of work. It makes it easy to give these men a relaxed smile despite the alarm bells ringing in my mind.

I lean back in the office chair, making sure I'm the picture-perfect vision of indifference. They want me here, it's clear. Even my dad is showing more of his cards than he thinks. Whatever scheme he's creating, he needs me for it. And even though I don't know the details yet, I'm comforted by the fact it seems like I hold the power currently, and I'll use it to my full advantage.

My eyes track over the men in the room, including my dad. I meet each pair of eyes, waiting for someone to break. Finally, my dad does. And I never could've prepared myself for the words that leave his mouth.

"Son, today we're going to be talking about how we're going to take the Bishops' hotels right out from under them. And how you're going to be the one to do it."

42
Winnie

"MY DOCTOR'S APPOINTMENT IS SCHEDULED FOR FRIDAY," MARGO tells me on the other end of the line. It's halfway through Monday, and I'm busy putting together a vision board for some of the rooms in her Hamptons house that still need to be decorated.

"I can't wait to hear all about it," I respond, shaking my head and deciding against one of the paint colors I initially liked for one of the guest rooms.

"I'm so nervous but also so excited. I didn't know I could be both, but overall, I'm just ready to have a professional confirm it for me and not a stick I peed on."

I laugh. "It's going to be great. You know how I always get feelings about things, and this time, I feel excitement and joy. I'm so excited for a baby to love on."

My bed is littered with different ideas I found online for Margo's decor. I love that she asked me to help decorate for her because it's given me something to do. After my morning walk and workout with Archer, I got ready and went right to the store to get poster board and fabrics so I could start getting some visions together.

This is the type of stuff I wish I got to do more. I've told my dad countless times I'd love to help with the decor teams for hotel openings, but it isn't my place as his daughter to help with business. It's only my job to attend parties and make the family look good.

But I'm excited about doing this.

It's a good thing that Archer insisted I share his room with him from now on because the one I used to sleep in is covered with different hues of tans and greens, and I'd be annoyed moving it every night.

"Archer said you guys had a smooth flight last night. I'm glad to hear that. We decided to stay here in the Hamptons for a couple more days. And by we, I mean Beck insisted on getting me alone to celebrate us having a baby."

She giggles, and I roll my eyes until the first half of her sentence registers. "Wait, you talked to Archer?"

Margo's quiet on the other end of the call for a moment. She whispers something to someone, making it obvious that Beck has been listening to this entire call. I should've known. They're attached at the hip most days.

"Briefly," Margo begins, her tone suspiciously higher. "He called Beck late last night just to say you guys made it back and to thank us for the weekend. *Super* casual."

I frown because Margo is a terrible liar, and something in her tone tells me she's keeping something from me. I turn around, my lips pursed deep in thought when a figure steps in the doorway of the bedroom.

The scream that leaves my body is loud and completely dramatic, considering it's Archer's chestnut-brown eyes that meet mine. It takes me a second to register it's him. He avoided work all weekend to spend it with me, so I expected him home late tonight, not in the middle of the afternoon.

"Are you okay?" Margo asks, worried.

Archer closes the distance between us, wrapping his arms around my waist. I notice the deep frown on his face immediately.

"Yes." I take a breath. "Speaking of Archer, he just got home, and I wasn't expecting him, so he startled me."

Margo lets out a relieved sigh. "Oh my god, I thought I was going to have to fly there and kick some ass. You scared me, Win!"

"Sorry," I mutter, my eyes roaming over Archer's face to try and figure out what's wrong and why he's here. "I'll call you back later, Mar."

"Love you!" she responds.

I hang up the phone and toss it onto the bed. My shoulders shake with another calming breath as I try to breathe through the rush of adrenaline. "Hi."

His lips twitch, but he doesn't fully smile. "Hey," he responds.

"I wasn't expecting you until dinner. Maybe even after dinner." I lift up on my tiptoes, placing a kiss to his cheek. He closes his eyes the moment my lips hit his skin, like he's savoring the feel of it.

"I need to talk to you." My heart begins to hammer in my chest at the deep intensity of his voice. It's weird how well I know the man in my arms. He doesn't have to really say anything at all for me to know something's wrong.

Apparently, my feelings for him are far deeper than I thought because the thought of something upsetting him makes me upset, too.

"Okay," I whisper, my eyes searching his face for answers.

Suddenly, his lips are pressing to mine, and he's kissing me in a way that terrifies me. He's kissing me in a way that makes it seem like he's losing me, and I have no idea why.

I kiss him back, too lost in my worry to stop anything. I try to put everything into it so he knows that whatever it is, we'll figure it out. He's the first to break the kiss. He pulls away but still keeps his hands around my waist.

"Before we talk, I wanted to take you somewhere."

"Right now?" I look down at my outfit. I hadn't planned on going anywhere today, so I stole some of his clothes because they smelled like him and they're comfortable. The pants are too long and too baggy, but I've rolled them at the waistband to try and make it work. The sweatshirt hides my body entirely, but I've been surrounded by his rich, spicy scent all day, and it's been worth it.

"If you're okay with that." I hate how tight his voice sounds, like it's filled with worry and regret.

"Should I be nervous?" I blurt out as he leads me downstairs. I wish he'd give me some sort of hint of what's on his mind, but he's eerily quiet.

When we were first married, I got used to his silence. I knew it was his thing to be quiet and think thoughtfully about things. But since things changed between us, he's always told me what's going on in his head. He hasn't hidden things from me, but right now, it feels like he's hiding something.

We stop in the entryway. He hands me my shoes, gesturing for me to sit on the bench as he slides each one of my boots on. He looks at me from the ground, the position reminding me of the weekend when he knelt between my legs.

"It isn't you that should be nervous. It's me," he finally answers.

I think his answer makes me feel even worse. "That doesn't make me feel any better."

He looks up, resting his hands on the tops of my thighs. For a moment, we just look at each other. I try to figure out what's going through his mind as his eyes scan my face like he's trying to commit every inch of it to memory.

"Ready?" he finally asks, standing up and reaching out his hand. I take it, letting him lead me to the waiting car.

We're thirty minutes into the silent car ride before I finally break the silence. "Where are we going?"

"Greenwich," he answers, keeping my hand firm in his grip.

"Why are we going to Connecticut?"

"There's somewhere I want to take you."

"And you can't tell me before we get there? We've got to have at least another thirty minutes left."

"It'll probably be more like forty minutes," he says, that ghost of a smile playing on his lips despite the sadness in his eyes.

"That seems like a lot of time to explain to me what's going on."

He brings my hand to his lips and presses a kiss to my knuckles. "I promise I'll explain everything to you. I don't want to hide anything." He actually smiles. "I vowed to earn your trust, and I meant it. There's just somewhere I want to take you first. Does that sound okay?"

I nod because I don't know what else to say. The only thing that keeps me comforted the rest of the drive there is the way he clutches my hand tightly, his thumb brushing over my hand in circles as he looks out the window.

43
Archer

"ARCHER," WINNIE BEGINS, HER VOICE CAUTIOUS AS SHE STARES IN front of her. "Why did you bring me to this massive house?"

I look down at my phone, sending a text message to the real estate agent, letting her know we have arrived. Marcie responds immediately, telling me that she's unlocked everything through the security system and to let her know when we leave so she can lock it back up.

"Because I wanted you to see the house," I answer, holding the double doors open so she can walk in.

"Why does it matter if I see this house or not?" Her eyes take in the sprawling foyer. "It feels weird calling it a house. It's a mansion. A castle," she marvels.

I laugh because at over twelve thousand square feet, it is a huge house. But I don't know if I'd go as far as calling it a castle.

"I want you to see this house because I want to buy it for you."

Her shoes squeak against the marble flooring as she spins to look at me. "You what?"

"Technically speaking, I put in an offer on it this morning, but I can back out if you don't like it."

Her head rocks back and forth as she goes from staring at me with wide eyes to looking around the space. She focuses on a table that has brochures and shoe protectors so no one tracks mud into the house. She rips the paper from the table and holds it in the air. "Archer, this house is more than fifty million dollars." By the end of her sentence, her voice has gone up an octave from the shock.

I don't blame her. It's a lot of money for a house, but the property is breathtaking. It has a waterfront view with its own private beach. I can already imagine waking up and walking down the beach in the morning with Winnie and watching her drink her coffee on the porch while the spring breeze kisses her cheeks.

I can picture it so vividly it scares me. I'm imagining a future with her when I have no idea if there's a chance of one together after what I have to say.

"I don't care about the price," I say, my voice controlled.

She rolls her eyes at me like my comment is ridiculous. It might be, but I have more money than I even know what to do with. If I want to buy her a fifty-million-dollar house, then I'm going to do it—as long as that's what she wants, too.

"This seems like a very elaborate gift for your fake wife." Her tone is teasing, but it doesn't quite reach her eyes. She explores the foyer, running her hand along the bannister of the grand staircase as she refuses to look in my direction.

It hurts to hear her diminish what's developed between us like that. "Don't do that," I mutter, my shoulders tense with nerves.

"Don't do what?"

"Say that what's happening between us is fake."

She spins so she faces me directly. She looks so tiny compared to everything in this house. If I wasn't sick with anxiety about telling her my father's plan, I might comment on how absolutely adorable she looks in my clothes that are far too big for her.

"Is it not?" she finally asks, her words coming out shaky.

"If I tell you something, you promise you won't run?"

She lifts her chin. "I've never been much of a runner."

This makes me smile. "You haven't heard what I have to say

yet." I try to keep my voice smooth and not let her in on the fact that my heart races in my chest with nerves. There's a high chance I tell her I love her and that she runs. It's even likely she could decide that my feelings for her are too much and not what she signed up for, and she could ask to leave the marriage altogether.

Even if she doesn't run from me confessing my love, she probably will when she finds out what my family is planning to do to hers.

Winnie watches me closely for a few moments, like she's trying to figure out what I'm going to say before I even say it. Finally, she lets out a long, controlled breath. "What do you have to say, Archer?"

I hold on to the way she says my name. It might be the last time I hear her say it with affection. Soon, she might be cursing my name because of the terrible history between our families—and the fact that mine can't leave the baggage in the past.

"I've fallen in love with you," I say, talking slowly so she doesn't miss what I'm telling her. I stuff my hands in my pockets instead of reaching out to touch her. All I want to do is pull her body into mine and tell her I love her while kissing every inch of her skin, but I want to do this right. I want her to have a clear head so she can really think about what I'm saying.

"What?" she asks through a gasp. Her eyes go wide in disbelief as she shakes her head. "I don't think I heard that right."

"I love you," I repeat, keeping my words clear and concise. "I love you so much that it completely overwhelms me. I don't really understand it, but I know that..." I take a deep breath because my words no longer come out controlled. My voice quakes ever so slightly from the weight of what I'm confessing. "All I know is every time you leave a room, it feels like I can't breathe. And then the moment you return, the air returns to my lungs, and I'm able to breathe again. You've always consumed my mind, but through the course of our time together...you now consume my heart, too."

Her entire body stills, and I stand in place, willing her to give me some kind of indication that she's right there with me. Or at least that me telling her I've fallen for her isn't the worst news she's ever heard.

"I..." she begins, her mouth opening and closing like she doesn't exactly know what she wants to say.

I wave at the air, wanting to get all of my thoughts out before asking her to give me any kind of response. "I know you weren't expecting me to admit that, so you don't have to tell me anything right now." I give her a smirk while rocking back and forth on the balls of my feet. "It's kind of funny. I'm a man who prided himself on keeping every thought and feeling to myself because I liked to hold all the cards. Then I met you. Now, here I am, laying them all out and telling you to take your time with your next move."

"I'm sorry, I just wasn't expecting..." Her words die off as she meets my eyes. She's always worn her emotions all over her face, but for once, I can't tell what she's thinking. Or maybe it's my own self-preservation because whatever is written on her face right now, it doesn't seem like it's happiness.

"I know, baby. Please don't say anything yet. There's still more."

"How is there anything more than that?"

I laugh, looking around the house. "For starters, I want to buy you this house so you can make it your own. Well, more that I hope you'll make it a home—for us. For a future family for us. All weekend, it was obvious how happy you were decorating Beck and Margo's new place. I wanted to give you that. I hired designers for the Manhattan place, not knowing your passion was interior decorating." I hold my arms out wide, doing a circle in the middle of the entryway. "So I found a house with a lot more space for you to have fun with. If you're interested, of course." I hate how timid the last sentence sounds, but I can't change it.

Winnie Bishop makes me nervous in a way no woman has

before. She completely unnerves me, and it's something I've come to accept—even appreciate. She makes me anxious because all I want is to make her happy. I'll weather the feeling of butter-flies in my stomach from anxiousness in my pursuit to give her everything she's ever wanted.

"Archer, you're not buying a house that's fifty million dollars so I have more rooms to decorate."

"That's exactly why I'm buying it," I respond. I risk taking a step closer to her, even though I told myself I'd give her space. When she in return takes a step closer to me, I close the distance between us completely.

Maybe I haven't lost her—yet.

I tuck a strand of her hair behind her ear, using the gesture as an excuse to touch her. "Like I said, I love the idea of you making this a home for us. There's nothing I want more than to live here with you, to see you make it perfect."

She laughs, leaning slightly into my touch. "The place is already stunningly perfect."

"Not yet. Not without your special touch added to it."

She's quiet for a moment, her eyes roaming my face. I relish in the silent moment between us, letting her gather her thoughts from everything I've unloaded on her. I desperately want her to tell me she's fallen for me, too, but I don't want to push it. Her still standing here, letting me touch her, is enough for the time being.

"You've acted differently since you first got home. Like you are scared of losing me. Is it because you're…"

"In love with you?" I finish for her, a smirk playing on my lips.

"Yes." Her cheeks turn their perfect shade of pink as she smiles up at me.

I return her smile, but mine is sad, knowing what I still have to tell her. "I've never told someone I love them, so I've been uncharacteristically anxious about finally saying those three words out loud." I sigh, my breath hitting the side of her cheeks.

"I wish that was the only reason, but there's something else I have to tell you."

Two tiny lines appear between her brows with her frown. "What is it?"

I take a deep breath, knowing that me admitting this next thing to her will change so much. With her, with my dad, with everything. It could start a trajectory that'll forever change my life, but I know I won't regret being honest with her. At the end of the day, everything else means nothing if I lose her trust—or don't earn it.

"My father has already put into place a plan for Moore Hotels to completely overtake Bishop Hotels...and he plans on using me to do it."

44
Winnie

ARCHER WATCHES ME CAREFULLY, HIS SHOULDERS NOT MOVING LIKE he's holding his breath, waiting for my answer. I make him wait as my mind races with what he's just confessed.

I was still reeling from him admitting that he's fallen in love with me when he dropped this bomb of news.

"I don't understand," I finally get out, my voice no more than a whisper.

His fingers dance along my skin as he caresses my cheek. "All I've wanted from the beginning of our marriage was for you to trust me. Now that I'm in love with you, I can't bear the thought of not earning your trust—and keeping it. When my dad called me in this morning and I found board members of Bishop Hotels there…I immediately felt uneasy."

I lean into his touch because the only thing that seems to keep me standing is the feel of his skin against mine. I'm trying to process how he went from him confessing his love to me to him telling me his family is planning to take everything mine has ever worked for.

"Tell me everything," I say, not caring that my voice somewhat breaks at the end.

My dad and I have never had the best relationship. I've often felt like his doll to use whenever he felt it was convenient. I never wanted for anything in life, except for maybe the typical feeling of a family. I had my brother, but we didn't have our parents around often. And even Tyson was busy playing the part in my father's world of the only son, the heir to the empire created by our great-grandfather.

Archer leads me to the grand staircase and pulls us both down to sit. His knees press against mine as he grabs my hand and places it in his lap. "I'm afraid this has been his plan all along. From the moment your dad called asking for help, mine started scheming up ways to get payback on your family for what your great-grandfather did."

I swallow, my eyes closing as I try to keep the tears at bay. "So this is all my fault," I croak, my throat feeling clogged. If I hadn't been so stupid to sleep with Blake, to let him use me like that, my family wouldn't be in this position.

Archer shakes his head, squeezing my hands even tighter. "No, baby. It isn't your fault. Please don't think that."

I meet his eyes, unable to hide the tear that rolls down my cheek. He focuses on it, reaching up to wipe it away. It doesn't matter—another one replaces it as shame ricochets through my body.

"How can I not think that? If I never got involved with Blake, then my dad wouldn't have had to make a deal with his enemy. I wouldn't have put him in that position, and your father wouldn't have had the opportunity to get someone from Moore Hotels on the board." I swallow slowly, not wanting to address the elephant in the room but having to anyway. "He wouldn't have had the chance to put *you* on it."

Archer winces like my words were a punch to his gut. I hate them, but neither of us can hide from the truth.

"I had no idea how resentful my dad still was toward your family. I, of course, knew he loved having your dad come running to him for help, but I didn't ever expect him to do this. For him to tell me to be the one to do it after marrying you."

All I can do is nod. If I talk too much, the tears will just keep coming, and I don't want to cry right now. I want to pull myself together and figure out what to do about what Archer's telling me. "Keep going," I prod, watching him closely.

He runs his fingers over the top of our intertwined hands, as if he has to find a way to touch me to make sure I'm still here. "The entire time, he wanted me on the board so I could make connections. With every meeting there's been, I've been nothing but professional. You have to understand, I never knew taking all of Bishop Hotels was his endgame. I was hopeful that we could finally put the sordid family history behind us and work together to benefit both companies." He sighs, looking up at the elaborate chandelier that hangs above our heads for a moment. "But it was stupid of me to not realize my dad is very intentional with everything he does. Of course, he put me on the board so they could get to know me."

"So his plan was to use you to impress them and then what, have all of them turn on my dad?"

Archer nods, his lips pressing together in a sad, thin line. "Yes. He's convinced them that your dad isn't making good decisions and that if they were to hand over leadership to me, I could take Bishop Hotels to a whole new level."

"Do you believe that?" I ask, nervous for his answer.

He sets his jaw before rubbing the back of his neck. "I think I have a lot to offer Bishop Hotels. But I need you to believe me when I say it was never, ever my intention to take it out from underneath your family. I thought our marriage would be a way for us to finally work together."

It isn't until he places his hand on top of my knee that I realize my knee was bouncing. I give him a sad smile. My dad would probably be so mad at me for this, but I believe Archer.

I don't think he knew what his dad was planning, but he's grown up the same way I have. We've both been raised to follow the directions of our fathers—and the one time I didn't, it completely blew up in my face.

I'm scared to know if Archer will continue to do his father's bidding or if his love for me changes things.

"What do we do now?" I finally get out. I scratch at my thigh, the heaviness of our situation hitting me. I felt too many things at once when Archer told me he loved me. Shock, happiness, fear, so many different emotions hit me with his confession. But it was the moment he admitted what his father was planning and the prospect of maybe losing Archer completely that solidified what I am feeling.

Despite everything, I've fallen in love with Archer. The one man on this planet I was supposed to guard my heart from has completely stolen it, and no part of me wants it back.

Archer raises his eyebrows, a questioning gaze on his face. "You said we. Is there still a we?" He doesn't bother to hide the hopefulness in his tone. It makes me fall in love with him even more.

"I want there to be. I hope there is. But how do we figure this out?"

All he does is stare at me, a wide smile on his face. His eyes completely light up, reminding me of a child on Christmas day. He's silent for so long, just staring at me with that beaming smile, that eventually I speak up again.

"Archer, what are we going to do?"

His hands find either side of my face as he pulls me closer to him. "I'm sorry, I didn't hear a thing you said after telling me that there's still a we."

I laugh, shaking my head at him. "I told you I wasn't going to run."

He rests his forehead against mine. His eyelids flutter shut for a moment as he takes in a deep breath. When he lets it out, his body seems to become less tense. "I know. But you *should* run. My family wants to betray yours, and I know it's hard for you to trust me. This isn't the—"

I cut him off by putting my fingers to his lips. I make sure his chestnut eyes meet mine before I talk again. I keep my voice level and composed, wanting to make sure he hears every single word clearly. "Archer Moore, I trust you with everything I am. I *love* you with everything I am."

His hands tremble against my cheeks. "You love me?" His voice breaks with emotion. "Say it again so I know it's real."

"I trust you. I love you."

"God, all I've ever wanted was to hear you say that." His entire body seems to sag in relief as he pulls me into him, his back hitting the stairs as our lips collide. Our mouths fuse together as we get lost in the kiss. His hands grasp for my clothes, running down my body like he's making sure all of this is real.

Finally, the kiss breaks, and we both sit up, but our hands stay interlocked. My lipstick is smeared around his mouth. I laugh, reaching up to wipe it from his chin.

"How are we going to figure this out?" I ask, continuing to try and wipe the pink lipstick from him.

He lets me, looking at me with so much love in his eyes that it makes me still for a moment. "I have a plan. But I'm going to need your brother for it to work. Do you think he'll listen?"

"I think so. Do you want me to call him and set up a meeting?"

"If you trust him to not go to either of our parents for the time being, then yes."

I nod. "Okay, I'll do that." I'm quiet for a moment, hope blossoming in my chest. I hope Archer does have a plan, one that will work out where his family doesn't betray mine, one that we can figure out together that benefits everyone.

"Before we come up with a master plan to finally put an end to this decades-long feud between our families, should I keep the offer on the house or pull it?"

I push off his body to stand up, beginning to climb the stairs of the house. "I do like the house, but it's a bit of a commute to the city."

I can't wrap my head around that he wants to spend so much money on a house for me—for us. But I can't deny that I can already picture exactly how I'd want to decorate it. I'd like to lighten up some of the colors in here; the dark rugs and artwork aren't doing anything to help the amazing light that filters through the house.

"I want to be away from the city with you. I'll figure work out if you picture us living here."

I smile as we reach the top floor. It's even more gorgeous up here. You can see down the hallway and out a large window where the bay is in view. There's a private beach where I can picture us lying in the sand and talking about life. "I can picture it," I confess, turning on a light to explore one of the rooms.

"Then it's ours. Yours to make it a home however you want."

I spin, walking into his open arms in the middle of a small home library. "You don't want a say in anything?"

He shakes his head. "No. I want anything and everything you want."

"Okay," I whisper. "But I can't focus on that until we get this thing with our families figured out. My dad is misguided a lot of the time, but it's still our family's dream. Tyson has worked his entire life to take over Bishop Hotels, and I think he'd be good at it. I don't want him to lose it, Archer."

He nods, placing a kiss to my cheek. "I'll talk to him, and we'll get it settled."

I nod, placing my head against his chest as I look around the room. It's so perfect that I try not to get too hopeful about making this house a home. We've got a lot to figure out first, but I have faith in him—in us—that we can do it. "It's a little sad, isn't it? Our first memory in this house is one tainted by the mistakes of our relatives."

He smiles, lifting my chin and bringing his lips right against mine. His mouth brushes against mine with his words. "We have the rest of our lives to replace them with all good ones. But first, let's figure out a way to right all the wrongs of the past."

We walk hand in hand out of the house and back to the waiting car. When he first led me up the stairs, I was riddled with anxiety about what he was hiding from me. Now, I'm hopeful for us to figure something out together.

After setting up a meeting with my brother for later tonight, I rest my head against Archer's shoulder as I look out the window. I hadn't realized how nice it seemed to live outside of the city until he showed me the house, until he put the idea in my head. Now I'm excited at the prospect of having our own space away from the hustle and bustle of Manhattan.

The only thing left to figure out is how to mend the bridge between our families and stop this feud altogether so we can start the next chapter of our life.

45
Archer

Winnie's brother, Tyson, watches me carefully. He leans back in the wingback chair, his hands clasped on the armrests as he assesses what I just told him. I've never gotten to know Tyson very well; he always preferred to stay away from the parties just like I did—maybe even more than I did. But if Winnie trusts him to help us with this, then I trust him, too. I just need to know if he trusts me.

Tyson looks over at Winnie. "Do you trust Archer, Winnie? Like really, truly trust him on this? Because last I talked with Dad, this arrangement between you and Archer was simply that —an arrangement."

Winnie nods confidently, looking over at me with a soft smile. "I trust him. It's far more than an arrangement now."

Tyson nods, leaning forward and placing his chin in his hands. He puts his full focus on me again. "What's stopping me from going to my dad right now and telling him of your father's plan? He's a smart man; he'd figure out a way to not get his board to sway on him."

I lift my chin. "Because if you do that, we're going to be forever stuck in this perpetual feud between our families."

"Until you and I take over, of course. We don't have to continue to fight the battle."

I nod. I've thought about Tyson's point a lot since my dad

pulled me into that meeting. I feel like I have a plan that will finally put this decades-long rivalry to rest for good. "You and I both know our fathers are greedy. They thrive on having power. Neither one of us will be handed full control for at least another ten years. If that. Do we really want to keep fighting for that long? Both of our companies were founded on being stronger together. I think we can get there again."

"One could argue that we're greedy for even wanting to go against our fathers. Isn't that a tale as old as time? Son gets jealous enough of his father that he tries to overthrow him?" Tyson shrugs, pretending to pick lint off his sleeve. "It sounds rather cliché to me."

"I wouldn't want this if my father wasn't trying to take my wife's family business." I don't bother to hide the venom in my voice. The last thing I want is for Tyson to think I'm doing this for selfish reasons. I've always been fine being underneath my father, as long as I was still impressing him. What I'm not fine with is holding on to a useless grudge when I feel like we can better both our companies if we just worked together.

"Winnie doesn't have any interest in Bishop Hotels," Tyson argues, glancing over at his sister.

Winnie sits there, her hands folded nicely in her lap. I feel a tinge of sadness that even her brother has never noticed that there's so much more to her than a pretty face at a party. "Winnie has the best eye for design I've seen. She'd be an amazing head of design for new hotels and even updating the designs in old ones."

Winnie's head shoots up, her eyes wide as she looks at me. I stare back, daring her to tell me that she wouldn't love doing that. She'd excel at working closely with the design teams—or even leading them. I'm just disappointed her family has been so obsessed with forcing her to attend parties and be the face of Bishop Hotels instead of realizing she has more to offer.

"Is that true?" Tyson asks, focusing only on his sister.

Winnie straightens her spine and looks her brother in the eye.

"I'd love to have a say in designs. So many of the hotels are... outdated." She blushes a little at the last word. It makes me smile. I don't think she meant it as an insult, but either way, it's the truth.

"So my point stands. I have no interest in stealing my wife's family business—the one she deserves more of a say in, might I add. And I'd happily let my father call the shots if I thought he was making good ones, but he isn't. Instead, he's choosing to hold a grudge that's just harming everyone involved."

"We're talking about swaying two boards here, not just one," Tyson offers.

I've got to give him credit, he seems interested in what I have to say. Maybe this will actually work out. Maybe we won't make the same mistakes as our fathers and their fathers and their fathers before them. If Tyson and I can come to an agreement, we can finally end the feud between the Bishops and the Moores.

"I think we'd both be surprised about how interested our boards would be at the prospect of new leadership." I smirk, leaning back in my own chair as I hold my hands out. "Let's not forget that with my name alone, part of your board is already in my favor."

I decide that I actually like Winnie's brother when he laughs, taking a sip of the bourbon I'd poured him. "Not a bad point."

"I know," I clip out.

"So what exactly is your plan? We'll have to make sure everything is completely solid before the vote. And if that vote goes wrong for us at all..."

"We'll both be disinherited?" I laugh. Winnie has taught me that I'm not as intimidated by my father as I thought I was. In my thirty-five years of life, I've done a great job earning money that's completely my own.

Sure, my father could decide I don't get anything from Moore Hotels if he so chooses, but I doubt he will. My hope is at the end of the day, we can both make our fathers see that the most prosperous way out of this is for Moore Hotels and Bishop Hotels to become one again.

"Don't talk like that," Winnie scolds, sitting up in her chair and reaching to grab my hand. "Tell us what you were thinking for the plan."

I keep a grip on her hand the entire time we go over, what in my opinion, is our best path forward.

46
Winnie

I'M BUSY FUSSING WITH THE BACK OF A DIAMOND EARRING WHEN Archer walks into the primary closet.

"My god, my wife looks breathtaking this evening," he muses, placing his hands on either side of the counter in the middle of the closet.

I laugh, leaning into his kiss as he trails his lips along the back of my neck.

"You say that every evening."

"I mean it every evening," he quips. His hands find my waist as he clings to the smooth fabric of my champagne-colored evening dress. It was one I'd fallen in love with while wedding dress shopping before our wedding.

It was perfect, except it hadn't felt bridal. It didn't stop me from loving it. The moment Archer told me we were attending a fancy event tonight where I needed a nice dress, I went to buy it.

I let out a content sigh as he pushes the hair from my back to continue his trail of kisses. It feels so good I melt against his body. Since our meeting with my brother Monday evening, it seems all we've done is work to create a plan to stop Archer's father from taking Bishop Hotels.

I feel confident in the plan Archer and Tyson have put into place, and tonight is vital in making sure we coyly meet with the two final members we don't have a vote from yet. It seems we already have a majority vote, and shareholders willing to request the vote to begin with, but we agreed our goal was to get a unanimous vote on both ends so there isn't any room for arguments.

"I'm supposed to be getting ready," I whisper as Archer's hand roams down my waist.

"I'd love to help you get unready…"

"We'll be late, and that wouldn't be a very good impression for you to make to people you'd like to lead one day."

"This was supposed to be our date night," he points out, his teeth raking against my throat.

"It still can be. You and Tyson will convince them quickly, and we'll have the rest of the opera to enjoy just you and me and the private box you bought for us."

His breath tickles my skin as he lets out a rush of air with his laugh. "I can't fucking wait," he mutters, placing one final kiss against my cheek before allowing me to finish putting in my earrings.

"How are you feeling?" I ask, turning to face him. He looks handsome in a black tux with a bow tie. It's a classic look, and I'm already looking forward to stripping him of the custom-tailored tux later tonight. I never saw him as the kind of man to wear a bow tie, but he wears it incredibly well.

His eyes travel over my face. Despite how busy we've been trying to discreetly set up meetings with shareholders and making sure we come up with a solid business model for a merger, it's been one of the best weeks of my life.

Being able to be a real married couple with Archer, to hear him whisper I love you every night before bed and countless times during the day, has been better than I ever imagined.

Plus, there's the fact that for the first time in my life, my opinion when it comes to the business with my last name matters. Both Archer and Tyson have listened when I've given suggestions, and I've never felt so valued.

It turns out my years and years of people pleasing and attending parties to show face have paid off. I know everything there is to know about almost every board member on both sides. I've partied with the shareholders and attended their weddings, baby showers, and everything else. I know them all well, and for a lot of them, it's the fact that I approve of Tyson and Archer's plan for both of the hotel franchises that has even gotten us the yeses we need in the first place.

Next week, we'll either be in a position where both Archer and Tyson will be taking over the hotels and merging them back into one, or we'll be dealing with the wrath of our fathers. There's no going back—we've already put the plan into place, and now all we have to do is finish executing it.

A shiver runs down my spine at the thought of how angry my father will be. He may never forgive us, but Tyson and I are doing this for him. If he'd handled himself better over the years and even offered to try and make it up to the Moores, maybe Archer's dad wouldn't have ever tried to sway his board in the first place.

I've already disappointed my father once recently. I'm ready to accept that I'll do it again.

"What's going through that beautiful mind of yours?" Archer asks, fastening his cufflinks.

"Just nerves," I answer honestly. "I can't stop thinking about what will happen next week."

Archer's palms find my cheeks as he pulls my head against his. It's an intimate gesture he does often, one that I cherish every single time he does it. He doesn't kiss me, just lets our foreheads press against each other as we breathe in each other's air. "Whatever happens next week, we have each other. It could go terribly wrong or perfectly right, and I'm ready to accept either outcome because I have you, my love."

My eyelids flutter shut as I soak in his words. I never thought I'd be so blissfully in love with a man like Archer Moore—let alone Archer himself. He's the last person I expected to own my heart, but I gave it to him freely, and I don't regret it in the slightest. I never will.

He's my person, my everything, and his words are just a reminder that it doesn't matter what happens because he's right. We have each other.

Archer delicately lifts my chin as he coaxes me to look at him. I melt at the love and affection in his eyes, in the way they crinkle when he looks at me, and he never wears that hardened face I see him put in place around others. "You've been a marvel this week," he mutters. "Watching you interact with people the way you have, read them the way you do…you just simply amaze me."

"You're the one who's charming," I argue. Our driver will be here any moment, and I still have to pick out heels and a clutch for the night, but I also don't want to break the moment between us.

"I'm confident that this vote will go exactly how we want it, and it's because of you." He brushes the loosely curled strands of my hair behind my ear. "It's ironic—the downfall of your father will be because he didn't see what you were capable of. If he'd let you lead things from the very beginning, like the way it was always meant to be…his board never would have agreed to him being voted out."

"You don't know that."

"Oh, I do, baby." He leans in and kisses me. I should be worried about the dark lipstick I'd carefully applied, but I'm not. Having him ruin my lipstick is one of my favorite pastimes.

"Archer." I moan against his lips as his hands travel through the slit of my dress. "We have to go. Right now."

He groans, his fingertips pressing deeper into my skin. "But what if we didn't have to go?"

"You know we have to go. But there's always time to finish this later."

A shudder runs through my body at the sight of his wolfish grin. "Oh, I plan on it."

Archer backs away before one of us gives in to the tension and makes us late for the opera. Everyone will be there tonight, and it'll be a big appearance for us as a couple but also a covert way for us to speak with the remaining people on our list.

I've been to the opera many times, but never in a private box. When Archer told me that was the date night he'd planned for us, I was ecstatic. He's constantly showing me firsts in a world I thought I knew like the back of my hand. At every turn, he's showing me that he's always capable of making things more extravagant.

He's quiet as I pick out a pair of shoes. I go through four different options before finally choosing the ones I feel look the best.

"Can't wait to see you in nothing but those," he muses, his voice nonchalant like he isn't saying dirty things to me. "Better yet, I can't wait to feel those digging into my back as I fuck you hard and deep tonight."

A flush creeps over my body at the mental picture. I'm already anxious for us to finish the job we have to do tonight so we can return, and he can make good on his promises.

"I'm going to hold you to that, *husband*," I tease, loving that he's so much more than just my husband on paper now.

"Do it, *wife*. I'm always a man of my word, and I plan on doing dirty, filthy things to you later."

He offers his hand, grabbing my clutch so I don't have to carry it. His other hand grabs mine, and he leads me down the stairs and to our night ahead.

47
Archer

"I FEEL LIKE TONIGHT HAS GONE BETTER THAN EXPECTED," WINNIE whispers to me, her arm tucked in mine as we walk through the crowd of people mingling before the performance begins.

I place my hand over hers, leading her away from the last person we needed to talk to tonight. Which is perfect timing because the performance is set to begin in just over ten minutes.

"Tonight has gone perfect," I assure her, giving a smile to one of the shareholders, who's already confirmed he'll support voting out Winnie's father.

Tonight, I let Winnie and Tyson take the lead on talking to the remaining people since they were ones from Bishop Hotels. Just like we expected, everyone is open to the idea of merging the hotels once again. Everyone in this city is money-hungry, and once they understood how much more we could make if we did it together—and how we'd blow all competition out of the water —they were eager for the next steps.

We climb the stairs to our private box arm in arm as we give polite smiles to those that we pass. For the first time, I allow myself a breath of relief. I think we're really going to pull this off. In the back of my mind, I worry about doing this to my dad, but he put me in this position in the first place. His persistent messages asking if I'm ready to pull the rug out from Spencer

Bishop's feet only reassure me that no matter the strain this puts on my already rocky relationship with my dad, it'll be worth it.

And I'm excited for the future of Bishop-Moore Hotels. I'm eager to see what Winnie, Tyson, and I can do now that we've agreed to work together.

Most of all, I'm fucking thrilled to finally have my wife alone for the rest of the night. I paid big money to have the best private suite available for tonight. We're at the very top with a balcony view that's absolutely stunning—but more importantly, away from the rest of the world.

It's time I get my wife all to myself.

I show the attendant our tickets on the top floor. It's got its own private bar and dining area meant for only those who purchased the most expensive tickets the opera has to offer.

"What do you want to drink before it starts?" I ask Winnie, putting my hand on the small of her back as I guide her toward the bar.

"I think I might do an espresso martini tonight. I'm tired but want a little pick-me-up before the show."

I lean in close to her ear to make sure no one hears me. "I offered to give you a pick-me-up before we left the house, and I even offered in the car…"

She shivers, leaning against my chest in an attempt to hide her blush. "Archer, you can't say things like that while we're in public."

We near the bar, but it doesn't stop me from pushing my limits, even if it's just by a little. "I can say whatever I want."

Winnie rolls her eyes but keeps the smile plastered on her face as she looks from me to the bartender. "I'll take an espresso martini, please, extra creamy."

I rub my lips together, trying not to laugh at her using the word "creamy." Underneath the bar top, she steps on my shoe in an attempt to stop me from laughing and causing a scene.

Clearing my throat, I lean over the bar to look at the options.

"A Pappy for me," I say, laying my card on the bar as well as a tip.

As the bartender walks away to prepare our drinks, Winnie turns her body to face me. Her elbow leans against the bar as she gives me a smile. "Emma would be so proud of me for ordering a martini. She's a martini girl, although she much prefers a dirty martini—extra dirty."

My hand runs over my mouth as I shake my head at a memory from the Hamptons. "I remember. She asked the waiter for so many olives at dinner it seemed that her martini was more olive than anything else."

"She's back in New York tomorrow," Winnie says, smiling at the bartender as he hands her the drink she ordered. "Once we get everything settled on Monday, she and I are going to have a day where I don't do any work and we spend lots of money."

"Sounds like a great plan," I confirm. Winnie has put all of her time into helping me and Tyson tie up every loose end; she deserves a day off with her friend.

We easily find our suite. One of the attendants holds the door open as Winnie and I walk in. The attendant smiles warmly at the both of us as she compliments Winnie's dress. "That color is stunning on you," she comments.

"Thank you," Winnie says, looking downward because she hates compliments.

"My name is Sara, and I'll be in charge of taking care of the two of you this evening. Would you like to leave the door open or have it closed?"

"You can leave it open," Winnie says sweetly.

"We'll keep it shut tonight," I offer at the same time.

Winnie and I look at one another as a blush breaks out over Winnie's chest. I look to Sara, giving her a forced smile. "If we need anything, we'll make sure to open it. But this is our first time with these seats; we'd prefer to keep it shut for the best experience."

Sara gives me an understanding smile. She nods. "Of course.

That would be my preference as well. Just know if you need anything from me, all you have to do is open the door, and I'll be right there." She looks at both of our hands. "I see you both have drinks and are set. If you need more later, just let me know."

"We will," Winnie confirms.

"If that's all, I'll leave the two of you to it. The show will begin in about five minutes." She points to a little table nestled between the opera seats. "There's binoculars there for your convenience. Enjoy, and please let me know if you need anything!"

Sara sees herself out, shutting the door just as I asked.

Winnie turns to me, a shy smile on her lips. "Why does it feel so private with the door shut?"

"Because I paid a lot of money for it to be exactly that." I walk to her chair, offering to hold her drink so she can take a seat and get comfortable.

Before sitting down, she walks to the balcony and leans over it. She looks from the left to the right, her eyes wide as she takes in the view. Her red hair falls down her back as she turns to look over her shoulder at me. "Archer, this takes my breath away. The view is...incredible."

I smile, setting both of our drinks on the table. "I agree." My eyes travel up and down her body, taking my time with committing the sight in front of me to memory. The glow of the dim lights illuminates her pale skin. She's applied some kind of lotion that makes her skin glow every time the light hits it. Expertly curled strands of her hair fall down her back, tickling the skin that is exposed due to the low-cut nature of the back of the dress.

She's so beautiful that I'm speechless. I can't believe she's made me into a man deserving of her love, but it's something I vow to myself to never take for granted. When her aquamarine eyes meet mine, my heart leaps in my chest.

"I don't know if I've ever seen you smile so big," Winnie notes, twirling a piece of her hair around her finger. She continues to lean over the balcony and take in the view of the opera house around us.

"I don't know if I've ever been this happy." I hold her eye contact, loving getting a front-row seat of her reaction to my words. Her breaths become heavy, and her cheeks flush.

"That's a bold statement, considering you're about to go against your father and lose the respect you've spent your whole life trying to earn from him."

I rub the back of my neck, marveling how even though I've never told Winnie about how my one goal in life used to be to make my father happy, she still figured me out. She can read me like an open book, and it only makes me love her more.

"That doesn't matter. I've learned there's better—more important—things in life."

She swallows, her eyes casting downward for a moment before she looks back at me. "Like what?"

I close the distance between us, molding my front to her back as I pin her against the railing. She gasps but immediately lets her body melt against mine. "Like you," I say, my lips hovering over the shell of her ear. "You're the only thing that really matters to me, Win."

The lights begin to dim even more, cloaking the audience below us in a sea of black. The only light comes from the stage lights shining on the bright red curtain. It's as if the entire opera house goes still with silence as we wait for the opera to begin.

"Archer," Winnie whispers as my hands roam her waist. I only started to run my hands along her body to feel her close to me, but the way she trembles under my touch gives me ideas of wanting more from her—no matter where we are.

48
Winnie

THE ENTIRE ROOM FEELS ELECTRIFIED AS WE WAIT FOR THE performance to begin. It's like everyone has taken a deep breath in but not let it out yet. The lights have gone all the way down, the only source coming from the lights aimed at the stage.

A shiver runs down my spine as Archer presses his lips to the bare skin of my shoulder.

"We should probably take a seat," I whisper.

"Why? The view from here is *spectacular*." He continues to kiss along my skin, making me break out in goose bumps.

"Because you sit at the opera. They'll take the stage any moment, and I want to enjoy it."

His breath is hot against my skin with his laugh. "Are you telling me you aren't enjoying this?" His tongue peeks out, wetting the skin he presses his lips to. "Or this?" he continues, nipping at the hollow of my throat.

The curtain rises right as the orchestra begins to play a beautiful, dark melody. My pulse spikes with anticipation of the show beginning—but also because of the trail Archer's lips are leaving on my skin.

"It's starting," I breathe, my eyelids fluttering shut when Archer's hand begins to pull at the fabric of my dress. A woman in an intricate dress walks out to the middle of the stage, her eyes traveling over the audience as the music begins to build.

"I know," Archer answers, continuing to lift the skirt of my dress. A chill runs through my body as my leg is exposed.

I try to push off the balcony railing to take a seat, but Archer holds his ground behind me. He stands solid, not letting me move. His arms are on either side of me, caging me in and overwhelming my senses. I turn my neck to try and look at him, but all he does is nod toward the performer onstage, who has begun to sing the most hauntingly beautiful song.

"Focus on the music," Archer commands as his fingertips drift up my leg. His touch is featherlight, somehow making the press of his skin against mine more intense. "While I make this experience even better for you," he finishes.

"We can't..." I begin, my grip tightening on the railing as his fingers drift along my hip.

"We can. We *will*." His tone leaves no room for interruptions. I wouldn't interrupt him anyway because before I can even come up with an argument, his hand drifts low enough for him to discover I'm not wearing any panties.

A low growl comes from his chest as he runs his fingers along my wetness. "Why aren't you wearing any panties?" His tone is angry but also filled with lust.

I rub my lips together as I try to hide my smile. It feels so wrong to be up here looking down on everyone else as Archer circles my clit in a delicate way that has my toes curling in my heels. "I didn't want there to be a line," I manage to get out, grinding my ass against him.

"I don't know if I should thank you or punish you for it." He clears his throat, his words coming out husky.

He begins to slide a finger inside me, making me moan. I'm the one who needs to thank him for getting us a private balcony suite since no one can see exactly where his hand is right now.

"You know this wasn't my plan tonight," Archer begins, sliding another finger inside. "I wanted to take my wife to the opera, sit next to her, and watch her enjoy the performance."

"Sure, it wasn't," I tease, letting my head fall against his shoulder. If anyone looked up, they might just think we're opera enthusiasts wanting to get the best view possible. We look like we're sharing a lover's embrace, but none of them would have any idea that Archer's fingers are moving in and out of me slowly and deliberately.

"It wasn't, baby." He presses kisses to my neck as the instruments in the orchestra slow down their tempo. "But there's just something about seeing you in a dress like this that does something to me every damn time."

His fingers circle my clit in a way that feels so good my knees begin to give out. Luckily, he supports my weight, never faltering in bringing me the most euphoric pleasure. "Archer," I moan, my orgasm building at the same time the singer and the music begin to get louder and more fast-paced.

"You were fucking magnificent tonight. I'm in awe of you and want to reward you by feeling your pussy hug my fingers in pleasure." He kisses my neck, nipping and sucking at the tender skin as my entire body tenses with the oncoming orgasm. "Come for me, my love."

The rough way he tells me to come as if he's just as desperate for it as me sends me over the edge. I yelp, the orgasm ricocheting through my body at the same time the singer opens her mouth and belts out the loudest, most beautiful note as my entire body lights on fire with pleasure.

I don't support any of my weight, fully depending on Archer to keep me upright as I ride the waves of the orgasm. He keeps his fingers inside me the entire time, pushing them in and out to ensure I savor every last second of it.

My shoulders shake as I let out a long breath, my mind coming to terms with the fact I let him finger me in such a public place.

I spin, forgetting all about what's happening on the stage for a moment to look at Archer. He smirks, pulling his fingers from me and letting the skirt of my dress fall to the ground.

Keeping eye contact with me, he brings his fingers to his lips and licks them completely clean of my arousal. My thighs squeeze together at the sight.

"This is already the best opera I've *ever* been to, and the show's barely begun," he quips, a mischievous glint in his eyes.

I playfully shove against his chest while shaking my head. "I can't believe I just let you do that to me in public. That isn't like me." I blush, realizing what we just did. No one can see that low on our balcony, but Sara could've opened the door at any moment.

Archer's quiet for a few seconds, his eyes traveling over mine. The tiniest of creases appears on his forehead, his lips pressing together in a thin line.

My head cocks to the side. "What is it?"

He reaches for my face, letting his thumb drag across my cheekbone. "There's something I want to tell you. One last thing I should confess."

I smile, wondering what more he could possibly have to tell me. "What is it?"

49
Archer

WINNIE WATCHES ME CLOSELY, WAITING FOR ME TO ANSWER HER. I let my fingers wrap around the back of her neck, placing my forehead against hers.

My lips twitch with the beginning of a smile. Pulling away, I keep my fingertips pressed to the base of her neck. "Remember when we were giving Ruby that interview and I brought up the first-time things..." I clear my throat, trying to come up with a way to phrase this. "Well, when I was telling her when things changed for me."

"Yes, of course I remember. You somehow remembered all these small details about what I was wearing that night when I don't even remember seeing you."

I swallow, letting my free hand move over my mouth. "I was there. You know I was there..." I add, my voice breaking a little because I'm suddenly nervous to tell her this.

The opera goes on behind us, now multiple performers on the stage. I don't pay them any attention, too lost in staring into Winnie's eyes while trying to gauge every little reaction from her.

"I gathered since you seemed to remember so much of that night. I just somehow missed you." Her voice is so sweet. She wraps her arms around my back, holding me tight as she stares up at me.

My mind goes back to that night, how absolutely breathtaking she was. I remember exactly where I was when I first saw her walk in. She had a mask on, but it did nothing to hide her beauty. I would've been able to pick her out in a crowd of a thousand masked people.

"No," I begin, taking a deep breath. I've thought about telling her this countless times, but I was too nervous to do so. If she knew how long she's had power over me, I didn't know if that would scare her away. But now, something about the atmosphere tonight made me finally want to come clean.

"Archer..." she begins, her voice lowering as she searches my face for answers.

"It was *me* you kissed that night," I admit, keeping a tight grip on her as I feel the intense need to keep her close. "On that balcony, so similar to this one."

Her chest hitches as her eyes search mine with confusion. "It was you?" she whispers. I'm comforted by the fact her grip on me doesn't falter. She continues to hold me close, even if the look on her face is full of questions.

I nod. "It was never my intention for anything to happen between us that night," I admit, thinking about the hour it took me to work up the confidence to go speak with her. I don't know what came over me that night, but I knew if there was ever a time where I could pretend to be someone else—someone she wasn't meant to hate—it was the night where everyone in the room wore masks and pretended to be anyone but themselves.

"It couldn't have been you." She looks downward for a moment, like she's trying to replay the night in her head. "I would've known if it was you."

I smile, lifting her chin so she looks at me again. "It was me. We both had a few too many drinks. The mask I had on was pretty great at hiding my face."

"We made out. We more than made out—I let you..." Her words trail off, but I know the same memory must be running through her head that's running through mine.

"You let me feel you come around my fingers?" I finish, not bothering to hide my smirk. "Trust me, I remember it well—too well."

"Archer Moore. Why was that not the first thing you told me when we got married?" She smacks my chest, but it doesn't do anything. I let out a sigh of relief at the smile on her face.

"Because I didn't want to admit to you—or myself—how much I'd thought about that night." I look at her mouth, trailing my thumb along her painted bottom lip. "I kept telling myself that the night was fuzzy, that I'd had too much to drink and it could've been anyone and maybe I was just remembering things wrong."

"I thought about that night so much after it happened," she confesses, leaning into my touch.

I laugh. "Same. At times, it was all I could think about. Kissing you—speaking with you that night—made me want things I shouldn't have wanted. The moment my dad asked me to make you my wife, I almost told him no because I knew how hard it would be to be around you every day…to pretend… when you'd already unknowingly captured my attention."

"So *that's* why you were so grumpy during that meeting."

"There were a thousand reasons I was grumpy—one of them being I'm just kind of an asshole—but the main reason was I wanted to be as far away from you as possible." I tuck a piece of hair behind her ear before leaning in and placing a kiss to her forehead. "I had this feeling that if I was around you long enough, you'd change my life. And that's exactly what you did, Win."

She laughs, lifting her chin so her lips line up with my mouth. I gladly trap her lips in mine and savor the feeling of her mouth pressed against mine. From the moment I let my guard down enough to kiss her at that gala, I knew that Winnie Bishop held the power to ruin my life.

I was right about her having the power, but instead of ruining my life, she changed it for the better.

"So you're not mad at me?" I ask, pulling away just enough to take her hand and guide us to our seats. Her cheeks are flushed from the orgasm—or maybe it's the revelation I just told her.

She keeps her fingers wrapped around mine, bringing our joined hands to her lap as she stares down at the stage below us. "No, I'm not mad. I knew it was the best kiss of my life—it makes sense since it was with you."

My spine straightens as I give her a smug smile. "Of course, it was. We're meant to be. If you told me you had a better kiss with someone else, I might just have to kill them."

Winnie's eyes go wide. She looks over at me, her mouth open in disbelief. "Archer," she scolds. "You can't say things like that."

My free hand plays with my bow tie as I try not to react to the thought of her with any other man. It'll never happen again. She's mine for the rest of our days. "Sure, I can," I grumble. "You're mine, Winnie Bishop."

She leans over the armrest between us, a bemused smile playing on her lips. "And you're mine, Archer Moore."

I return the smile, closing the distance so we can kiss once again. "Good," I say as we pull away. My eyes flick to the performers on the stage. "Now, could we pay attention to the show? You're being awfully distracting," I tease.

Her mouth flies open. She shakes her head at me. "Excuse me, I was the one paying close attention to the opening when you snuck your hand into my panties."

I lift an eyebrow. "Technically, you weren't wearing any panties."

She rolls her eyes before focusing back on the stage. "My point still stands. You're the one who started the distraction."

"I can't help it. You're too perfect. I wasn't lying when I said watching you close the deal with the last remaining people tonight had me desperate for you. You're so fucking sexy I can't help myself."

She settles deeper in her seat, trying to hide her satisfied smile. "I really didn't do that much," she whispers.

"Don't discredit yourself like that, baby. You're a force to be reckoned with, and I'm so fucking lucky to stand on the sideline and watch you do it."

Winnie looks at me, her lips slightly parted. Finally, she takes a breath. "I love you."

I pause for a minute, not expecting those words to leave her mouth. It doesn't take me long to gather myself. I lift our joined hands and bring them to my lips. "Not as much as I love you."

She shakes her head but doesn't argue with me. Instead, she points to the stage. "Now, stop talking. I'm trying to watch the show my husband spent a lot of money on."

I laugh, focusing on the same thing as her. "Whatever you say, baby."

50
Winnie

"I'm nervous," I admit, staring at my shoes as the elevator doors close.

Archer grabs my hand, giving it an encouraging squeeze. "Everything is going to go according to plan," he assures me.

"There's too much riding on this for it not to," Tyson comments from the other side of the elevator.

My eyes shoot up to glare at him. "That doesn't help at all."

He lifts his shoulder in a shrug. "Winnie, we've spent countless hours planning this. We've had everyone confirm multiple times that they'll support us. Archer's right—everything will go exactly as we have planned it to."

I let out a loud breath, trying to gather myself. I'd barely slept last night, thinking of what was going to happen today. I'm just ready for all of it to be over. No matter what happens, I won't have to live with the pit of anxiety that's lived in my stomach since the moment Archer told me of his father's plan.

"Do you think Dad will forgive us?" I ask Tyson, my fingers tightening around Archer's hand as the elevator climbs to the floor we need.

Tyson runs his hand through his hair, keeping his eyes locked on mine. "Do you want the easy answer or the real one?"

"Real," I answer immediately, my heart racing because he

doesn't even have to answer for me to know what his answer will be.

"Dad will be very upset at first. He doesn't even know Archer's dad was planning a hostile takeover. That'd set him off alone. To find out that I convinced shareholders to replace him on the board? He'll be pissed. Our only hope is that one day, he'll understand why we did it. He'll see what we can do if Archer and I work together in the future."

I nod, fighting the urge to press the button for another floor to buy us more time.

Archer steps in front of me, blocking Tyson completely from my view. He puts his hands on either side of my face, cupping my cheeks and leaning forward until he's the only thing I can see.

"No matter what happens today, we've still got each other. You got that?"

I nod, taking one final deep breath to completely pull myself together. We've worked tirelessly to make sure this plan will go through. I think part of the reason I'm so nervous is because I know that we have what we need. We have a majority vote of the shareholders and board by a landslide with both Moore and Bishop Hotels.

The part that has me nervous is going against my dad. I've never done it intentionally—even Blake was something I never thought my dad would find out about. Both Tyson and Archer are in the same position I am. We're all going against our fathers in hopes for a better future; it's just really terrifying when you've spent your entire life trying to make someone proud of you to then do something like this.

"My assistant is waiting downstairs for your dad to arrive," Archer explains, stepping out from in front of me so he can speak with both Tyson and me. "I've given him strict orders to let me know the moment Spencer steps into the security line."

"And your father?" Tyson asks, tucking his hands into his

pockets. We're ten floors away from where the meeting will take place.

"He'll be in the conference room in ten minutes. There, he'll find people from both hotels—and our plan will begin."

My fingers pull at the skirt I'd picked out for today. Now that I'm in it, I wish I would've picked a pantsuit or something different, but it's too late. I'd paired the black skirt with a black blazer and a pearl headband, hoping to appear businesslike so I'd be taken seriously.

"I can't believe we're doing this," I mutter, rocking my head back and forth as I catch my reflection in the gold glass elevator doors. This is the first time I've ever visited the Moore Hotels headquarters, and I must admit, it's incredibly nice. All I could think about was how classic and sleek everything looked as we were walking through the security line.

I adjust the strap of my bag on my shoulder. Inside, I've got vision board concepts for future projects—just in case either my dad or Archer's dad surprises us by being on board with the plan. I don't think they will be, but I could still show the board members and shareholders my visions in the meeting if I need to. I like to be prepared, and it felt weird to show up to the meeting empty-handed.

The elevator doors open with a *ding*—making my stomach lurch.

It's really happening. Archer squeezes my hand, softly guiding me out of the elevator.

"Here's to a better future for both our families," he notes.

All I do is nod, my throat too tight with nerves to say anything else.

—

"What is this?" Archer's dad yells, his face turning red with rage. His eyes scan over the biggest table I've ever seen as he tries to meet the eyes of the many people seated around it.

My dad leans forward, glaring at Archer's dad from the opposite side of the room. "You thought you'd get away with taking over Bishop Hotels?"

Archer sits at the head of the table, his arms crossed over his middle like none of this is bothering him at all. That makes one of us. My foot anxiously taps underneath the table, but I try to hide it. There are over thirty people seated in this room, and I don't want any of them to know how nervous I am.

"My father's plan all along was to do a hostile takeover of Bishop Hotels. You fell right into his trap, Spencer," Archer says, keeping his voice completely level. "You really should've had more safeguards in place."

My dad looks over at me with fire in his eyes. "Maybe I would've had time to do that if my daughter hadn't made me react so quickly."

I blink, trying not to show that his words were a blow to my feelings. I swallow past the lump in my throat, taking a page from Archer's book and not showing any kind of reaction to the harsh words.

Archer's fingers tap against the table. I think even the people on the other side of the room are able to hear his loud sigh of disapproval. "Spencer, those safeguards should've been in place the moment you created a dynasty. Don't blame your daughter because you don't know how to efficiently run a company. It's tacky—and doesn't look good to anyone here with us."

It's my dad's turn to get red in the face. He sits back in his chair loudly, crossing his arms over his chest as he stares at the members of his board seated around him. "No one on my team would've voted me out anyway." He looks between Archer and Archer's dad. "It was a stupid idea."

Archer's dad smirks, completely unaware of what Archer will

be dropping on him at any moment. He leans forward, his arm pointing to the members of my dad's board that are sitting around us. "Actually, they all trusted my son—an outsider and your enemy—to run things better than you. I bet that hurts, doesn't it?"

My dad's cheeks puff out as his eyes rip to the people Archer's dad speaks about. All of them stare at the table, completely ignoring his attempts to get their attention.

Archer clears his throat. "Actually, Dad," he says slowly. I focus on him, trying to read his body language to see how he's doing. I never expected him to go against his dad like this—especially for me and my family. If he's nervous about it, he doesn't give any indication. He seems calm and collected as he meets the eyes of those around the table before finishing his conversation.

"I didn't bring everyone in here today just to air out the fact you were planning a hostile takeover of Bishop Hotels. To cut to the chase—I'm proposing a vote today to replace the CEO of not only Bishop Hotels but Moore Hotels as well." Archer does an amazing job at keeping his voice completely level. His shoulders are pushed back like there's not an ounce of nerves running through his body.

The air is silent for a moment as Archer's dad, Timothy, lets his son's words sink in. I know the moment they do for both our fathers because they react at the same time.

Archer's dad pushes his chair back in rage, his face getting more red by the second. Dad slaps the glass table, his eyes focusing on Archer in disbelief.

"Son," Archer's dad speaks, his voice low in warning. "What do you think you're doing?"

Archer looks away from his dad for a moment and focuses on me. He gives me a small smile, one that makes my heart pick up speed because I'm hopelessly in love with him. "I'm doing what's right—for everyone."

51
Archer

"TELL ME WHAT'S HAPPENING HERE," DAD DEMANDS, HIS VOICE SO harsh that spit flies out of his mouth from his tone. "Right now."

I focus on him, feeling the eyes of every single person in this room on me. "The moment you told me you wanted to take Bishop Hotels out from underneath the Bishops, I knew you'd gone too far. You weren't making decisions that were best for Moore Hotels any longer. You were blinded by greed and revenge, and neither one of those are things that have any business in the decision-making of running a company, Dad."

My father shakes his head, staring at no one but me. I can count on my hand the number of times I've disappointed my dad in my life, but nothing compares to the way he looks at me right now. I've let him down in the biggest way—I've betrayed him. And I'm not even sorry for it. He should've seen it coming. "Unlike Spencer, my board would never vote me out. You know that."

I lean back, folding my hands behind my head as I look at the people seated around the table. "You sure about that?" I ask him.

On cue, one of the Moore Hotels shareholders stands up. I've always liked Mario. He's a smart man, and has always agreed with me in meetings where my dad and I disagreed. So that's why I can't help but smirk when Mario clears his throat. "I'd like to motion to vote for an immediate removal of Timothy Moore from his CEO position."

My dad makes a choking sound as multiple shareholders stand up and vote for my father's removal.

"Son..." Dad fumes, his angry eyes meeting mine. "What have you done?"

"Nothing you didn't force me to do," I answer, looking over to Tyson.

Tyson clears his throat, sitting up in his chair and looking at his dad. "You've also lost sight of what's best for Bishop Hotels, Dad. You've been too swept up in keeping up with Moore Hotels instead of focusing on how to make ours better. Because of that..."

His words trail off as one of the men from Spencer's board stands up. "I'd like to propose a vote to remove Spencer Bishop from the CEO position at Bishop Hotels."

The only two people who look shocked are Spencer and my dad. Their eyes meet for one moment, and I wonder if either one of them realizes that none of this would be happening if they weren't holding on to grudges that were decades old.

"You can't do this," Spencer argues, his eyes becoming slits as he stares at his son.

Tyson swallows. He keeps his head high and his shoulders pushed back, but I can see the slight bounce to his knee that shows that no matter what front he's putting on, he's nervous.

If I didn't have Winnie, I'd be right there with him. It's crazy how meeting the love of your life can change everything you thought you were. Never would I have imagined I'd deliberately defy my father and overthrow him, but I meant it when I said he's the one who put me in this position to begin with.

"What's your plan here? Each of you overtakes the companies you were raised to earn just because you managed to talk to some board members? Neither of you are ready for it," Spencer spits. He clutches the edge of the table, his fingers turning white with the intensity of the grip.

I lean even further back, enjoying the show both of these grown men are putting on. It only solidifies that neither one of them is in the right headspace to run a company successfully.

"Tell me, Spencer, did you earn Bishop Hotels? Or was it handed down to you?" I ask, raising my eyebrows as I wait for him to answer.

Someone down the table coughs in an attempt to hide their sudden laugh. Winnie shifts in her seat next to mine. She crosses and then recrosses her legs. I want to reach out and take her hand in mine, but I know right now isn't the time for PDA.

"I earned it." He seethes, an angry shudder running through his body.

I purse my lips, giving him a dismissive shrug. "*Odd*. I swore I remember your father only handing it down to you because he was on his deathbed."

His body jolts, and for a moment, I question if he's going to round the table and hit me with a right hook. I'd love to see him try. It wouldn't fare well for him, I know that for a fact.

My dad breaks the tension—or feeds into it even more depending on how you look at it. "Fine. Put it to a vote. The both of you." He angrily looks at every single one of his board members who hold his fate in their hands. "Just because it's put to a vote doesn't mean either of you have the majority. If the two of you are put in charge, you'll tank both companies within the next year."

"Merging into Bishop-Moore Hotels is the best thing we could do for *both* companies. We'll prosper and dominate the market. It's something you both should've done a long time ago," I counter. "It was with that idea alone that we convinced every person sitting here today to sway."

Winnie's dad stands up, pushing his chair out from behind him as he leans over the table. "Before anyone votes, you should have a clearer picture of who you're voting for." The moment his eyes land on Winnie, my defenses go up.

"You should know why I had to go to the Moores for help to

begin with. They're selling you lies—and they all begin with my daughter."

I sit up, grabbing the armrests of the chair as I watch him cautiously. "Spencer," I warn, trying to prevent him from starting down a road he really shouldn't travel.

"My daughter—who has no business sitting in on a board meeting to begin with."

I slap the table, making everyone jump with the sound. "I'm going to stop you right there. Winnie will be the head of design with the merger. She's incredibly intelligent and talented and deserves a seat at the table just like anyone here."

Spencer smirks at me, and I know that he's about to do something I'll make him regret for the rest of his life. He holds his hands up, turning his body slightly to make eye contact with everyone at the table. "Then you should know your head of design has a recent sex tape—and Archer married her to hide it."

Winnie gasps. "Dad," she croaks, her eyes wide as she stares at her father in horror.

My fingers flex into fists as I imagine what it'd be like to send my fist right into her father's ugly face. Would she hate me for it? I take a deep breath, getting my temper under control before I completely lose it on this man for betraying his daughter.

"How would it look if it came out that the new CEO has a wife with a sex tape? And that he married her just to hide it?" Spencer raises his eyebrows, expecting someone to answer him. When no one does, he continues to dig his own grave. "Imagine how much the stock would plummet if the media got ahold of this? You can't trust him to lead with those skeletons in his closet."

"Dad!" Tyson yells, looking at his father like he doesn't even know who he is. I don't blame him. I knew Spencer wasn't the greatest guy, but I wasn't expecting him to out his daughter like this. It's completely unacceptable.

I'm in the midst of taking a deep breath before I completely end this man once and for all when Winnie stands up.

I stare at her, wondering what she's doing. No matter how badly I want her to look at me so I can meet her eyes and try to get a grip on what's going through her head, she never looks my way. She keeps her eyes pinned on her dad and no one else.

"How could you?" she snaps, more venom in her tone than I've ever heard before. "Your own daughter. Your self-preservation at the expense of your family is horrifying."

Spencer's head rears back at Winnie's words. I stare at her in awe, letting her take full control in embarrassing her father in front of his own board. "I'm just trying to look out for Bishop Hotels. I don't want the name tainted because your sex tape is released."

Winnie's eyes meet mine for a moment. We don't need words at all to have a conversation. I give her a nod, knowing exactly what she's asking of me—knowing that she's trusting me.

"It will never be released," she tells him. "It's been taken care of." I'll have to come clean later on how exactly I handled Blake, but I relish how she doesn't ask any questions about it right now. She trusts me enough that I took care of it that she tells the group of people not to worry about it.

Winnie looks away from her dad as she slowly meets the eyes of those seated around the table. "It's true. A few months ago, a moment that was never supposed to get out was videotaped. I never gave permission or consent for this video to be taken. But it still was. And it's the most embarrassing moment of my life."

She takes a deep breath, keeping her spine straight and her head held high as she continues to look at everyone in the room. I've never been more proud to be her husband than at this moment. She's the strongest person I've ever met, even when she's been completely betrayed by one of the people who is supposed to love and support her no matter what.

"My *entire* life, I've done everything possible to make Bishop Hotels look good. I did as I was told. I attended parties, I did charity events, I sat on charity board after charity board to make sure Bishop Hotels made a positive impact on communities. My entire life has been devoted to my last name and never doing something to tarnish it. Until I was taken advantage of. Even then, I put my feelings aside—even though I'd never been so hurt and betrayed—and I *still* did what was right for Bishop Hotels."

I force myself to look away from her long enough to look at everyone she speaks to. They've all leaned forward, their focus completely on her. I don't blame them in the slightest. She's captivating.

When I look back at Winnie, she's turned her attention to me. "My father is right. I married Archer—my family's enemy—because I knew it was the only way to protect not only myself but my family's reputation. It was just another thing I did to make sure the integrity of the company my great-grandfather started didn't go to waste because of me. Although Archer and I didn't have a conventional start, I still fell madly and deeply in love with him."

She smiles at me, and it takes everything in me to stay seated in my chair. I want to knock it backward and close the distance between us. My hands twitch at my sides, desperate to reach for her and feel her skin against mine, to let her know I'm here for her.

"I believe in the merger between Bishop and Moore Hotels so much that I will step down today. I don't have to be the head of design. I don't need to have anything to do with it if it makes all of you feel better. I believe in Archer, and I believe in Tyson. They will do great things for the hotels. Don't let what's happened to me take away from the visions these two incredibly talented men have."

Her hands slide down the front of her skirt, her first sign that she might be more nervous than she's letting on. She doesn't need to be. She's astonishing. Everyone looks at her with wide eyes, completely impressed with the speech she just gave. I wonder if she knows how much she was meant to run a boardroom.

"It's time for stupid grudges to stop getting in the way of making these companies prosper." Her eyes are cold as they meet her father's once again. "And it's time to remove jealous, angry, small-minded men from positions of power. They're only a hindrance."

Winnie takes a seat, a calculating smile on her face as she looks back at me. She looks sweet as can be, a slight flush to her cheeks after she just completely hammered the final nail in both our fathers' coffins.

52
Winnie

THE ROOM IS SO SILENT I'M NERVOUS THAT THOSE AROUND ME MIGHT hear how strong my heart is beating. It pounds in my chest as adrenaline courses through my veins. I hadn't expected to take my father down like that, but I also never thought he'd bring up the Blake incident to a room of over thirty people.

A lot can happen when you realize the person you grew up respecting isn't who you think they are. It allows you to cut ties, to finally realize that all the time you invested in trying to impress them, in trying to earn their respect, was completely pointless. It's freeing, knowing that my life will no longer be dominated by trying to make a sad, pathetic man proud of me just because he's my father.

Instead, I look at my husband. The person I'm most proud to know—to love. He stares right back at me, his lips parted as his eyes travel over my face. It's amazing how we don't have to say anything to communicate everything.

He blows me the softest of kisses, making my heart race for a completely different reason than it was before. Eventually, he looks away from me and at the anxious board members and shareholders all staring at us.

"If I'm not mistaken, before my father and Spencer made complete fools of themselves, a vote was requested." I'm impressed with how smooth Archer can keep his voice. There's arrogance in his tone, and it's incredibly sexy. I love how much power he wields.

Everyone around the table nods in agreement.

Archer leans back, not giving either of our fathers the respect to meet their eyes. "Perfect. We can start with the Bishop vote and then the Moore one. Before the vote, I'd like to make a few things clear. First and foremost, do not vote yes on removing either of these men unless you're prepared to have Winnie stay on as head of design. I will not run a company if she isn't involved."

"Archer," I argue, not wanting him to sacrifice what we've been planning because of my past mistakes.

He looks at me, fire in his eyes. "It's a nonnegotiable for me," he clips out, not elaborating further.

"Agreed," Tyson speaks up. I look at him, blinking quickly to try and hide the fact my eyes are misting over.

Archer clears his throat, continuing to lay out his plan for the merger if he were to be voted CEO. Immediately after Tyson and Archer being voted in to take over control, they'd initiate the beginning of the merger. Archer would have fifty-one percent decision-making power while Tyson would hold the other forty-nine percent.

Archer tried to reverse it, giving Tyson ultimately more power than him, but Tyson didn't want it. He told me if I trusted Archer, then he did, too. And that he was okay with letting Archer have the final say in things.

Archer wants to immediately announce the merger so it doesn't affect the stock. He wants the world to know that we're a united front so investors don't get spooked and pull their money. It takes five minutes for Archer to lay out his plan perfectly. I listen to him, but mostly, I admire the view of watching him command a room like this. It's evident how members of both boards respect him and are interested in everything he says.

Finally, he stops, casually putting his hands behind his head once again. He leans back with a smile. "Now, let's vote. We'll start with voting Spencer Bishop out as CEO. If a majority vote is decided on, it will go into effect immediately. Spencer"—he stares daggers at my father—"upon removal of your position, you will be hearing from my people later today with a very sizable offer to buy you out. If the board decides you're no longer competent enough to run Bishop Hotels, I'd suggest you take it." Archer swallows, clearing his throat slightly. "I also suggest that you don't make a scene on your way out. My patience only goes so far. And if you insult my wife again, I fear I won't manage to stay professional."

"This is ridiculous," my dad spits. For the first time in my life, I see fear in his eyes. He knows this won't go the way he wants it to, and he's lashing out because of it.

I stare at my dad the entire time his board unanimously decides to vote him out. I spent all of my life being scared of him in a way, and I want to break free of that. There's nothing scary about him. I hope that this teaches him a lesson.

Archer will buy him out for a significant amount of money. He and Mom will be set for the rest of their lives. Maybe he'll finally be a good husband to her and give her the attention she deserves.

Dad stands up, his eyes moving from Tyson to me. "I regret having the both of you." He seethes, his focus staying on me. "Especially *you*. You ruined my life."

I manage a smile. "You did that all on your own."

He angrily puffs out his cheeks, muttering something indistinguishable under his breath before he pushes the door open and leaves. You can hear his cursing all the way down the hall before he finally disappears.

Archer whistles. "Well, now that that's over, let's move on to the next vote."

—

"You're unusually quiet," I comment in the back seat of Archer's town car. His hand rests on my thigh, the same place it's been from the moment we both slid into the car to head home.

Archer looks over at me, his lips pressing together as his eyes roam my face. "I'm just thinking," he answers. He brushes his thumb over the top of my hand.

"Thinking about what?"

"You."

"What about me?"

The corner of his mouth twitches with the hint of a smile. "I'm just utterly in awe of you. Watching you today...I think I fell in love with you all over again."

My lips part at his answer. I shift, nowhere near expecting the answer he gave me. "I could say the same thing. Watching you get a unanimous vote on both sides, seeing how much they trusted you to do big things with the merger. You're a force to be reckoned with, Archer Moore."

Archer shakes his head, bringing our joined hands to his lips. My eyelids flutter shut as he presses a kiss against my thumb. "I don't want to talk about me right now. I want to talk about you. God." He lets out a long breath, looking out at the window for a moment before looking back to me. "It's *you* that's the force to be reckoned with, baby. The way you stood up for yourself to your dad, the way you were brutally and bravely honest with everyone in that room. Or even how you came up with some of the best ideas I've heard for the merger and what to do. I'm just so fucking lucky to exist at the same time as you. To know you. To get to love you. To be yours." The last part is said so low I almost don't hear it.

I hurriedly unbuckle my seat belt and close the distance between us. I press my body to his, wrapping my arms around his neck as I fuse our mouths together. His hands find my hips immediately.

"You need your seat belt on," he says against my lips.

I smile, distracting him by kissing him all over again. He lets me, his tongue caressing mine. I'm well aware that our driver can see everything that we're doing, but it just doesn't matter to me right now.

All I can think about is how much I love this man.

"We're almost home," I finally answer, pulling away from him just enough to look into his eyes.

"Something could still happen." He tries to keep his voice firm, but it doesn't work. I know he wants the press of our bodies like this just as much as I do.

Our driver clears his throat, flicking on his blinker. "We're pulling up to the curb now."

I laugh, raising my eyebrows with a look that must scream, "I told you so."

Archer sighs, opening the door the moment the car stops. He doesn't even allow time for our driver to help.

"Inside we go," he commands, gently pulling on my arm. I let him guide me out of the car, throwing a smile back at our driver before following him up the stairs.

I smile at all of the decorations running up the stairs. Instead of the pumpkins that were here when I first moved in, there's a lush green garland with twinkling lights twisted around the railing. Battery-operated candles sit on the stairs in the middle of pine wreaths. At first, I thought I'd want more color on the porch instead of going with the white lights, but I fell in love with the way the yellow, flickering lights look against the red brick of our home.

Archer doesn't waste any time opening the front door—and then slamming it shut. The moment it's closed, his body is pressing mine into the wood.

"All I've thought about today is finally getting you alone," he says as he trails kisses along my neck.

"Really?" I tease, arching my neck to give him more room to explore. "You could've fooled me. You were all business throughout that very long meeting."

His fingers tighten around the fabric of my skirt. He slowly lifts it up, bunching it at my hips. "I'm good at pretending. But don't worry, underneath the professional facade, all I could think about was burying my face in your pussy because I was so damn turned on with how you controlled every single person in that room."

I suck in a labored breath as he kisses along my collarbone. "It wasn't anything special."

Quickly, he pulls away and lines his eyes up with mine. I thought I'd see lust in them, but instead, he stares back at me angrily. "Every single thought in your mind, every word out of your mouth, every single thing you do is special. I know that. Everyone there today knows that." He presses a kiss to my forehead, keeping his lips there even through his next words. "And you should know that, too, baby."

My eyelids flutter shut, and I don't know how long the two of us stay there, his lips pressed to my forehead and my back pressed to our front door. It could be a minute we stay there, it could be ten, I truly don't know. It doesn't matter.

For the first time in my life, I know what it feels like to be in love and to be supported. And it's the best feeling in the world.

53
Winnie

THE SOUND OF MY PHONE VIBRATING WAKES ME UP. I BOLT UP OFF the bed, wondering if I'd somehow overslept.

Looking at the alarm clock on the nightstand, I find that I still have ten minutes before my alarm is set to go off. I look over to Archer's side of the bed, finding it empty.

Before I can wonder where he is, I swipe to answer the Face-Time between my best friends. I try to stifle a yawn while Margo's, Emma's, and Pippa's faces pop up on the screen.

"Happy first day!" they all cheer at the same time, their faces eager even though it's early in the morning.

I smile, shaking my head at the three of them. "I've technically been working for weeks. This is just my first day in the office."

"It's still something to celebrate!" Margo responds, her skin glowing even through the phone screen.

"Now, get up and show us what you're going to wear," Emma demands. She sits at her counter, propping her phone on something as she shovels colorful cereal into her mouth.

"Emma, you could ask her nicely," Pippa scolds, a wide smile on her face. Pippa effortlessly joined our friend group like she's always been a part of it.

"*Please* show us what you're wearing to your first day of

being a bad bitch boss," Emma corrects through a mouthful of the cereal.

I roll my eyes, stretching my legs for a moment before moving. For a second, I look over at the empty spot in the bed. Archer must have gone for an early morning run or something. It isn't like him to leave without waking me up to say goodbye, but maybe he wanted me to get some extra sleep before the big day.

"Emma, technically, I'm not the boss. I'm just running the design team."

"So basically...you're the boss?" Pippa laughs, whispering something to someone out of view on the screen. It's clear she's at the bakery she owns by her background. It's pink everything, the name of her coffee shop and bakery glowing from a neon sign behind her.

"You're a boss-ass bitch," Emma quips. "Own it, Winnie Boo Boo."

I slide on the pair of slippers I keep by the bed and head toward the closet Archer and I share. "I can't with you guys. It's really not a big deal, but I'll show you my outfit anyway."

"It's a big deal," Margo argues. "It's about time for you to put more of your design knowledge to use. Although, I did love having you all to myself there for a bit for help with the Hamptons house."

"I'll help you anytime you want," I respond, pulling the pantsuit I'd picked out for the day from a clothing rack. Setting the phone on the counter in the middle of the closet, I hold the outfit up to my body and back up a few feet so they can see the entire thing.

"Okay, that's hot!" Emma cheers, giving the outfit a dramatic clap.

"You have to wear it," Pippa comments.

"Perfection," Margo says, giving her stamp of approval.

"It's not too...*much*?" I ask, looking at myself on the screen. I'm far more used to wearing blazers and skirts, but I wanted to do something different for my first day in the office. Although I still can't wrap my head around the fact I'll be in charge of design for countless hotels, it's now in my job description. I want to show up and make an impression this morning.

"No, it isn't at—oh, hi, Archer!"

I turn to see what Emma's talking about, finding Archer standing behind me, already dressed for the day. He smirks at me, leaning over my shoulder to talk to everyone on the group call. "Good morning, everyone. If you don't mind, I'm going to steal my wife from you now."

I exchange goodbyes with my friends and hang up, excitedly turning to Archer and wrapping my arms around his middle. "I was wondering where you were this morning. I didn't expect to wake up alone."

Archer's strong fingers wrap around my chin and tilt my head up. "I wanted to let you sleep a little longer. Plus, I knew if you were awake that you'd come downstairs and ruin my surprise."

"Surprise?"

He smiles, leaning down until our mouths are inches apart. "I wanted to celebrate your first day with you before going into the office. Get dressed and come downstairs."

My eyebrows pull in. "It's just the first day. You didn't have to do anything."

"What have I told you about me *having* to do anything?" he questions, his thumb running over my cheek. "I didn't have to. I wanted to."

I don't bother to hide my blush as I press my lips to his. We've kissed countless times, and it's still something I could never grow tired of. I love how strong his lips are against mine. He always possessively holds on to me one way or another. Maybe it's by holding my face or gripping the narrow of my waist to keep me pinned to him. It always seems like he can't get enough of me, and I love it because it's how I feel about him.

"I love you," I say, finally breaking the kiss. We're supposed to be at the office in a little over an hour, and I want to make sure we leave early just in case we hit more traffic than normal.

"I love you, too, baby. Meet me downstairs whenever you're ready." He presses one last kiss to my forehead before leaving me in the closet alone.

I'm so excited about whatever surprise he has for me downstairs that I rush a little through getting ready. I probably would have applied my makeup with a little more caution, but I couldn't wait to get downstairs. Instead of curling my hair like I'd planned, I'd slicked it back in a sleek bun.

Taking a deep breath, I do a circle in front of the bathroom mirror, deciding that everything looks perfect for my first day. I'm suddenly nervous, which is kind of funny because I've already been working closely with everyone, even if today is my first official day. The merger was announced right before Christmas, so we had some off time because of the holidays, but I still wanted to make sure I introduced myself to everyone I'd be in charge of. I'd stop by the office while Archer was working or pop into meetings, but now today is my first day with the title.

I'm excited—and nervous—and all the different feelings. I run my hands along the front of my pants, smoothing out wrinkles that aren't even there to give myself something to do.

Deciding it's time I find out what Archer's surprise for me is, I head downstairs. The moment I hit the hallway, I hear Taylor Swift coming from the speakers in the kitchen. I smile, loving that my husband is such a Swiftie. The moment I step off the stairs, I come to a stop.

My jaw drops as my eyes scan our kitchen. He's got it completely decorated with balloons and streamers. A homemade banner is hung up by large pieces of tape along the kitchen windows. It reads "Happy First Day!" in big bold letters.

I let out a small sob, tears forming in my eyes as I focus my attention on Archer. He's got a silly party hat on, his arms full of a large heart-shaped cake. "Happy first day, baby!" he muses, the most perfect smile on his lips.

"Archer," I breathe, unable to do anything but shake my head in disbelief. I truly hadn't meant to make today that big of a deal, even if it's the most excited I've been in a long time. I hadn't realized how bored I was with my life—with the parties and events—until Archer encouraged me to pursue my love for design.

"It's a little cheesy, isn't it?" he asks, giving me a small shrug as if he doesn't care how cheesy it is.

"It's very cheesy." I laugh, walking deeper into the kitchen to get a better look at his decorations. "But it's incredibly thoughtful. Probably the nicest thing anyone's ever done for me." I wipe at my cheek, trying to stop the happy tears that fall from my eyes.

Archer sets the cake down, closing the distance between us and pulling me into his chest. "Don't cry, baby. I just wanted you to feel special this morning."

I tuck my head into his chest, even though I'm scared I might be getting makeup on his expensive suit. It doesn't matter—I'm just so happy that I can't help but let the tears fall. "It's because I feel so special that I'm crying," I answer, my voice muffled against his chest.

I sniffle, letting him tip my chin up so he can meet my eyes. "So you like the surprise? Camden and Beck gave me so much shit for it being cheesy, but I told them to fuck off. I just wanted you to know how proud I am of you this morning."

"I love you," I whisper, my throat clogged with emotion.

"I love you, too, Win." His eyes go wide for a moment. He pulls away, grabbing the cake and holding it between us. "Pippa might kill me if I forget to give this to you because she had it overnighted, but this is from her." He smiles, his eyes running over the same words as mine.

It's a heart-shaped cake with fancy decorations all over it, the exquisite icing details a stark contrast to the words she's carefully iced over the top.

Archer laughs. "Should I have 'Head Bitch In Charge' put on your plaque instead of your name?"

I shake my head, laughing at how Pippa could've chosen anything to put on the cake, and she picked that. "Definitely not. I do need a picture with the cake, though, because you know…" I look at him with a playful smile. "I'm the head bitch in charge."

Archer sets the cake down before pulling me against him. "Damn right you are. It's so fucking sexy." His hands roam down my back until he playfully squeezes my ass.

I shake my head, swatting at his chest. "Don't get any ideas. Today is all about work. No sex until we're home tonight."

He groans, dramatically jutting out his bottom lip in a pout I've never seen him do before. "But HR would absolutely love it if we broke in your new, fancy office."

"Not happening. Today is all about work." I raise to my tiptoes, having to do it even though I'm wearing a pair of heels. I line my mouth up with his ear. "Although, I do think you'll love what I have underneath my clothes. It's a new set and very see-through."

A growl comes from low in his chest. "You expect me to sit through all the meetings we have today knowing that?"

I kiss along his neck, trying not to get any lipstick on his collar. "I do. I believe in you."

I stop teasing him in fear that if I do it for too long, I might let him undress me right here in the kitchen. Instead, I grab both sides of his face and force him to look at me. "Thank you," I whisper, emotion bubbling in my chest.

"For what?"

"For the job. For this." I point to his decorations. "For everything."

"Don't thank me for the job. It was you who sold everyone; I had nothing to do with it. But I will accept the gratitude for the decorations. There are five banners in the trash because my handwriting looked so terrible you could barely read it."

I let my thumb trail over his bottom lip, completely transfixed that I get to call this man mine. "Are we ready to go to work?" I ask.

"Yes and no."

I smile. "C'mon, husband. We've got an empire to run."

"And I'm so fucking grateful I get to do it with you, my love," he answers.

Our foreheads press together, and for a moment, we stand there in silence as we breathe in each other's air. It doesn't seem like that long ago when I was terrified to marry the man in front of me. Now, I never want to imagine my life without him in it.

"I'm proud of us," I mutter, thinking of how hard we fought for each other. Our families being rivals should've driven us apart, but with each day we had together, we grew closer. When the world wanted us to end, we found a way to make it better —together.

And I'm so freaking thankful that I'll spend the rest of my life loving this man. Not everything in the world we were raised in is pretty, no matter how much people try to pretend it is. In fact, underneath every shiny detail are broken people. But we took something broken and made it into a pretty beautiful thing.

"I'm proud of us, too, baby," Archer answers, his voice hoarse with emotion.

We walk hand in hand to the waiting driver, ready to start our first day running Bishop-Moore Hotels together—the way it was always meant to be.

As I slide into the back seat of the car, I'm reminded of my nanny, who once told me about premonitions. She told me to always trust my gut, and right now, my gut tells me that today is only the beginning of a happy, beautiful life. And so much of that is because of the man holding my hand firmly in his grasp— my husband.

My forever.

EPILOGUE
Archer
4 Months Later

"Archer Moore, quit trying to peek," Winnie commands, her fingers squeezing tightly around mine as she leads me forward.

I groan, letting my free hand drop to my side before I try to inch the piece of fabric she's tied around my eyes up again. "Baby, you know I'm not very patient. Why are you making me wait?"

"Just keep walking." Her little giggle just about does me in. She continues to pull on our linked hands, leading me down the front path to our new home.

She's spent countless hours over the last three months getting the house in Greenwich ready for us to move into. We've kept the house in Manhattan in case we want to stay in the city, but I'm excited to move somewhere a little less crowded. And I'm even more thrilled about seeing what she did with the place. It only took a month of us going back and forth for me to convince her that I truly wanted whatever she wanted for the house. She could reimagine the house into whatever her heart desired and I'd love it because every idea and design came from her beautiful mind.

I'm mostly excited to hopefully begin to take it easy with her. Maybe being away from the noise of the city will allow us to spend more time together. It's been four busy months of making sure the merger between Bishop and Moore Hotels went smoothly. I sold the penthouse next to the Moore headquarters after we bought a new office building with triple the amount of space we used to have. One thing Tyson, Winnie and I were on the same page about was making sure we upgraded to one space that would fit all of our employees. We wanted everyone to be in the same building to be able to collaborate and feel the true strength within the merger.

"Step," Winnie instructs, pausing for a moment and keeping a tight grip on my hand as she waits for me to climb the steps to the large double doors of the house.

"I really don't think blindfolding me is necessary," I tell her, unable to hide the smile forming on my lips. I love how passionate she's been about making the house perfect before we moved in. It's absolutely adorable how insistent she was on surprising me this evening.

"It's your fault," she notes, dropping my hand for a moment. I'm about to complain about her doing it until I hear her pull the doors open.

"And how is it *my* fault?"

"You insisted on not being a part of the planning process. You left me to my own devices while doing the interior decorating. I had to see it all the way through and keep it a secret until the very last second."

A small laugh erupts from deep in my chest. I'm so fucking in love with this woman. She could keep me blindfolded all night if it made her happy, if I got to keep hearing the giddiness in her voice like I am right now.

"I hate it when you're right," I admonish, my words not sounding strong in the slightest.

She sighs. "No, you don't."

My lips quirk. "No, I don't. You're so fucking sexy when you're right."

Her breath tickles my cheek before she plants a kiss against my lips. I grab on to her hips, knowing her body by memory even with my eyes covered. "God, that was a good answer," she whispers against my lips. I don't have to see her to know she probably has the most stunning and wistful smile on her lips. We're together almost every minute of every day, and her smile still completely takes my breath away.

"Are you going to reward me by letting me see what you've done with the house, then?" I ask, my voice rough.

She laughs, her breath caressing my cheeks again. "*Maybe*. Now I'm nervous you're going to hate everything."

My jaw clenches as my fingertips dig into the small of her back. "I'll love every single well-thought-out detail of this house —all because it came from *you*."

"You're quite the charmer tonight," Winnie remarks, teasing my bottom lip between her teeth.

"I'm a charmer *every* night," I correct, pulling her completely flush against me.

Her hands find my shoulders, steadying herself as her body shakes with a laugh. "Are you ready to see everything?"

I nod, eager to see what she's done. I don't know how she managed to find the time to remodel and decorate the house while also taking charge as head of design at Bishop-Moore Hotels. She's incredible, and there isn't a day I don't wake up entirely grateful that she's mine and that she's accepted me as hers.

"It'll just be one minute," she whispers before pressing her lips to my neck. I groan, anxious to see what she decided to do with the house we'll raise a family in.

"You tease," I growl, my grip on her hips tightening as she kisses the skin above my shirt collar.

"I kind of like having you blindfolded," she notes, her fingers expertly undoing the top button of my shirt.

"I'd much prefer to see everything," I quip, relishing in the feeling of her lips pressing against my skin.

My cock gets harder and harder the further she unbuttons my shirt. "What are you doing?" I ask gruffly.

"Having my way with you while you're blindfolded."

"You're teasing me, baby," I croak.

"It doesn't have to be teasing." She bites my neck, making my cock get even harder. I fucking love it when she gets possessive.

"As much as I love the thought of you having your way with me, I want to see the house, baby. I want to see the proof of all your hard work."

She lets out the cutest little huff, one that finally has me braving pulling off the blindfold just so I can see her beautiful face. It doesn't disappoint. I smile at the way her bottom lip juts out in a dramatic pout.

"You weren't supposed to take that off," she scolds.

My thumb traces over her bottom lip. "I've told you I'm not a patient man." I avoid looking behind her and ruining the surprise, but it's hard not to. From the brief glimpse I got out of the corner of my eye of the foyer, she's changed much more than I thought.

Winnie smiles up at me, her eyelids fluttering shut for a moment as I cup both of her cheeks. "Well," she begins, "what do you think?" She takes a step back, holding her arms out wide as my eyes rake over the foyer.

"Winnie," I breathe, at a complete loss for words because the space is completely different than when we first bought the house—and it's absolutely incredible.

"Maybe elaborate a little more, Archer," she says, her voice tight. "Does that mean you like it?"

My hand swipes over my face as I take everything in. The space is so open you can see all the way to the back of the house where double doors open out to our back patio and eventually the water. My gaze sweeps over the walls. They're a lighter color than when I bought the house. The cream color helps to lighten up the space. She's made the area feel welcoming but also elegant. It doesn't have the coastal vibes of some of the other houses I've visited in Greenwich. It feels very her—and I've never loved a house more.

"Archer," Winnie continues, her voice pleading. "Do you hate it?"

My eyes meet hers. I feel terrible that for a few seconds, I can't form words. I'm just overcome with an overwhelming amount of love for my wife. "Not at all," I finally get out. I smile, already envisioning us filling this house with as many kids as she wants. "I've never been more in love with a house than I am right now."

Her cheeks turn pink as a beaming smile overtakes her face. "Really?" Her chest barely moves, as if she's anxiously holding her breath.

I let out a content sigh, taking a step deeper into the foyer. My hand runs along the bannister of the grand staircase. She's replaced the carpet on the stairs, using a pattern that catches the eye and puts a personal touch on the large stairs.

"You're quiet. That makes me nervous," Winnie says from behind me. She wraps her arms around my middle, placing her cheek to my back as she allows me to look around.

"I'm sorry, baby. I'm not trying to be quiet," I try to reassure her. "It's just so beautiful—so perfect—there aren't enough words to describe how excited I am to finally move in. To start this next chapter of our lives together."

"Yeah?" she asks cautiously, tightening her arms around me.

"It's better than I could've ever imagined. God, Winnie. You're so talented, you know that?"

She laughs, her breath breaking through the thin fabric of my dress shirt. "All I did was make minor renovations and decorate the house."

I turn to face her, grabbing her chin and forcing her to look at me. "You made it the perfect home for us. The place we'll host our friends countless times over the years. The place we'll bring a baby or two home to. One we'll grow in. You made it absolutely perfect."

"What if I want five kids?" she teases.

I smile, letting my hands travel down her back until I'm cupping her ass and lifting her feet off the floor. She yelps, wrapping her arms around my neck.

"I'll take as many babies as you'll give me," I answer, getting harder by the second thinking about getting her pregnant. I love the thought of us bringing life into this world. I hope we have five little girls that all look like her.

"Five sounds fun," she jokes, her thighs tightening around my middle.

"Let's start practicing right now." I walk us over to a long dining room table that's got to fit at least eighteen people.

"No!" she scolds, rocking her hips against me despite her protest. "What about the tour of the house?"

I set her down on the edge, carefully running my hand along the wood to try and move the fancy dishes she's laid out. I move a little too quickly, accidentally knocking a bowl to the ground with a loud crash.

"*Archer*! Those were expensive," she says, fisting the fabric of my shirt and bringing my body against hers.

"I'll buy new ones."

"They were specially made. Our custom monogram is on them."

I shrug, pushing her hair off her shoulders so I can kiss her neck. "We'll have new ones made. We've got the rest of our lives to discuss every detail and thought you put into the house. But after getting a first look at what you've done and imagining you stepping through the front door with a rounded belly pregnant with our child...well it's made me desperate for you."

She smiles, her face getting flushed with want. It's always when her cheeks and chest get red that I know she's just as needy for me as I am her. "We do have a lot of time to look at the rest of the house. A quick pause wouldn't hurt anything."

Leaning down, I press my lips to hers. She's ready for me immediately, her mouth opening and her tongue meeting mine.

She lets out a soft little moan when my hand snakes underneath the short tennis skirt she put on this morning. It's been teasing me all damn day—even though I had a taste of pushing inside her this morning before we ever even left the bed for the day.

I slip my fingers underneath the fabric of her panties, feeling her already wet and ready for me. Before I push a finger inside her, I break the kiss and look into her eyes. "I love you, with everything that I am and everything I'll ever be. I can't wait for a lifetime of memories in this house with you."

She smiles. "I love you. You're my everything, Archer Moore. I'm happy you love the house. I did it all for you."

"For us," I correct, leaning in to press a chaste kiss to her lips.

"For us," she repeats.

For a moment, we just stare into each other's eyes. It's one of those moments I know will be burned into my mind for the rest of my life. One where I'm completely overwhelmed by my love for this woman. I'm the last person she probably expected to choose to spend the rest of her life with, but I'll thank whatever higher power there may be that despite all odds, we found our way to one another.

She's my entire world, and I'll spend every single one of my days making sure she knows how remarkable of a woman she is. She truly is my everything, the love of my life—something I never even believed in until her.

"I love you," I repeat, feeling the need to say it again.

"I love you too," she whispers, her hips bucking slightly when my fingertip glides over her silk panties.

"Now lean back, baby. It's time I reward my wife for all the hard work she put into our home..."

Then, I spend an ample amount of time making one of our very first memories in this house right on top of the dining room table she had custom-made. It was the perfect first use of the table if you were to ask me.

After we accidentally break multiple dishes from the table after breaking it in, I fall in love all over again with my wife as she takes me through every room of the house. She's breathed life into the perfect home for us, and I can't wait for all the memories we will make here.

Forever has never seemed so perfect.

THE END

WANT MORE BLACK TIE BILLIONAIRES?

It's the end for Winnie and Archer...but the start of something new for Emma and her sports guy in Bright Lights and Summer Nights.

PREORDER HERE: https://bit.ly/BLASN

To read the extended epilogue for Winnie and Archer, make sure to subscribe to Kat's newsletter. You can find it on authorkatsingleton.com

ACKNOWLEDGMENTS

This book was simultaneously the hardest and easiest book I've ever written, and I'm so grateful for the people who kept me going every step of the way while I was writing Archer and Winnie's story. I'll never be able to put into words how much I appreciate their constant love and support, but I'm going to try my best.

First, to *you*, the reader. I wish I could eloquently put into words how much I appreciate you, but every single thing I've typed doesn't even begin to share how much I love and appreciate you. If it weren't for the readers asking (begging really) for Black Ties to become a series, I don't know if I ever would've felt such inspiration to write Winnie and Archer's story. But these characters easily became my favorite ones I've written, and it's all because of your eagerness for their love story. It is you who is the lifeblood of this community. It is you that shows me endless support. You're the reason I get to wake up every single day and work my dream job, and for that, I'm so freaking grateful. Thank you for choosing my words to read. Thank you for supporting me. You've given me the greatest gift by choosing *my* book to read. I love you so much.

To my husband, AKA Kat Singleton's husband (iykyk), A-A-ron. I'm so incredibly grateful for everything you do to keep all things Kat Singleton afloat. I love you.

Selene, thank you for keeping organized and running all things Kat Singleton. Your help allows me to do what I love— bringing new books to readers. I'm so grateful you chose me to work with. Thank you for keeping me organized! I know I don't ever make it easy!

Ashlee, thank you for putting up with me when I come to you with a vision for the cover and then change my mind about it. This cover is everything I wanted it to be brought to life. I'm in awe of your talent and creativity and am so grateful to call you a friend. I love you!

To my soul sisters who spend every day writing with me, encouraging me and cheering me on. I love you three with my entire heart.

To Salma and Sandra. Thank you for breathing life into this book and helping me polish Winnie and Archer's story. Your feedback is so important to me and I'm so grateful to work with the both of you. Thank you for helping making *Pretty Rings and Broken Things* ready to be released to readers.

To my alphas. You ladies were the first people to read this book and you got it in its most raw and real form and you loved it anyway. Thank you for helping make this book what it is. Thank you for believing in me and encouraging me when writing felt hard and I wanted to scrap the entire story. I'm so fortunate to have you ladies in my life. Please never leave me. I love you.

To my betas. Thank you for all of your vital feedback that made this book what it is. I wouldn't be able to do this without you and I appreciate your help in making *Pretty Rings and Broken Things* as perfect as possible. I love you forever.

To the content creators and people in this community that share my books. I'm so eternally grateful for you. I've connected with so many amazing people since I started this author adventure and it means the world to me to have all of you to connect with. I'm appreciative of the fact that you take the time to talk about my stories on your platform. I notice every single one of your posts, videos, pictures, etc. It means the world to me that you share about my characters and stories. You make this community such a special place. Thank you for everything you do.

To Valentine and everyone with VPR. Thank you for everything you do to keep me in check. It's not a secret that I'm a constant hot mess, and all of you are the reason I'm able to function. Thank you for making all things Kat Singleton run smoothly and amazing. I'm so thankful to call VPR home and for your help in getting *Pretty Rings and Broken Things* out to the world.

I have the privilege of having a growing group of people I can run to on Facebook for anything—Kat Singleton's Sweethearts. The members there are always there for me, and I'm so fortunate to have them in my corner. I owe all of them so much gratitude for being there on the hard days and on the good days. Sweethearts, y'all are my people.

Keep reading for the first chapter of Beck and Margo's story in
Black Ties and White Lies…

MARGO - 1

"Margo, Margo, Margo."

A familiar voice startles me from my computer screen. Spinning in my office chair I find my best friend, Emma, hunched over the wall of my cubicle. Her painted red lips form a teasing grin.

Pulling the pen I was chewing on out of my mouth, I narrow my eyes at her suspiciously. "What?"

She licks her teeth, flicking the head of the Nash Pierce bobblehead she bought me ages ago. "Who did you piss off this time?"

My stomach drops, and I don't even know what she's talking about. "Are you still drunk?" I accuse, thinking about the wine we consumed last night. We downed two bottles of cheap pinot grigio with our roommate and best friend, Winnie. Split between the three of us, there's no way she's still tipsy, but it's the best I could come up with.

She scoffs, her face scrunching in annoyance. "Obviously not. I was refilling my coffee in the lounge when *Darla* had asked if I'd seen you."

I stifle an eye roll. Darla knew I'd be at one of two places. I'm always either at my desk or huddled in front of the coffee maker trying to get the nectar of the gods to keep me awake.

Darla knew *exactly* where to find me.

She just didn't want to.

You accidentally put water in the coffee bean receptacle instead of the carafe and suddenly the office receptionist hates you. It's not like I meant to break it. It's not my fault it wasn't made clear on the machine what went where. I was just *trying* to help.

"I haven't heard from her," I comment, my eyes flicking to Darla's desk. She's not there, but her phone lights up with an incoming call. Darla rarely leaves her desk. It isn't a good sign that she's nowhere in sight. The sky could be falling, and I'm not sure Darla would leave her perch.

Emma rounds the wall of my cubicle, planting her ass on my desk like she's done a million times before, even though I've asked her not to just as many times.

"I'm working." Reaching out, I smack her black stiletto, forcing her foot off the armrest of my chair.

She laughs, playfully digging her heel into my thigh. "Well, Darla, that *amazing woman*, told me the boss wants to see you."

"I thought Marty was out for meetings all day today?"

Emma bites her lip, shaking her head at me. "No, like the *boss*, boss. The head honcho. Bossman. I think it's somebody new."

She opens her mouth to say something else, but I cut her off. "That can't be right."

"Margo!" Darla barks from the doors of our conference room. I almost jump out of my chair from the shrill tone of her voice.

Emma's eyes are wide as saucers as she looks from Darla back to me. "Seriously, Mar, what did you do?"

I slide my feet into my discarded heels underneath my desk. Standing up, I wipe my hands down the front of my skirt. I hate that my palms are already clammy from nerves. "I didn't do anything," I hiss, apparently forgetting how to walk in heels as I almost face-plant before I'm even out of the security of my cubicle.

She annoyingly clicks her tongue, giving me a look that tells me she doesn't believe me. "Obviously, I knew we had people higher up than Marty, they're just never *here*. I wonder what could be so *serious…*"

"You aren't helping."

There's no time for me to go back and forth with my best friend since college any longer. Darla has her arms crossed over her chest in a way that tells me if I don't haul ass across this office and meet her at the door in the next thirty seconds, she's going to make me regret it.

I come to a stop in front of the five-foot woman who scares me way more than I'd care to admit. She frowns, her jowls pronounced as she glares at me.

Despite the dirty look, I smile sweetly at her, knowing my mama told me to always kill them with kindness. "Good morning, Darla," I say, my voice sickeningly sweet.

Her frown lines get deeper. "I don't even want to know what you did to warrant his visit today," she clips.

Your guess is as good as mine, Darla.

"Who?" I try to look into the conference room behind her, but the door is shut.

Weird. That door is never closed.

"Why don't you find out for yourself?" Grabbing the handle, she opens the door. Her body partially blocks the doorway, making me squeeze past her to be able to get in.

Whoever this *he* is, doesn't grant me the luxury of showing me his face. He stands in front of the floor-to-ceiling windows, his hands in the pockets of the perfectly tailored suit that molds to his body effortlessly. I haven't even seen the guy's face but everything about him screams wealth. Even having only seen him from behind, I can tell that he exudes confidence. It's in his stance—the way he carries his shoulders, his feet slightly apart as he stares out the window. Everything about his posture screams *business*. I'm just terrified why *his* business is *my* business.

When they said boss, they really meant it. *Oh boy.*

What have I done?

Even the sound of the door shutting behind me doesn't elicit movement from him. It gives me time to look him up and down from the back. If I wasn't already terrified that I was in trouble for something I don't even remember doing, I'd take a moment to appreciate the view.

I mean *damn*. I didn't know that suit pants could fit an ass so perfectly.

I risk another step into the conference room. Looking around, I confirm it's just me and the mystery man with a nice ass in the empty space.

Shaking my head, I attempt to stop thinking of the way he fills the navy suit out flawlessly. From what I've been told, he's my boss. The thoughts running through my head are *anything* but work appropriate.

"Uh, hello?" I ask cautiously. My feet awkwardly stop on the other side of the large table from him. I don't know what to do. If I'm about to be fired, do I sit down first or just keep standing and get it over with?

I wonder if they'll give me a box to put my stuff in.

His back stiffens. Slowly, he turns around.

When I finally catch a glimpse of his face, I almost keel over in shock.

Because the man standing in front of me—my apparent boss —is also my ex-boyfriend's *very* attractive older brother.

ABOUT THE AUTHOR

Kat Singleton is an Amazon top 5 bestselling author best known for writing *Black Ties and White Lies*. She specializes in writing elite banter and angst mixed with a heavy dose of spice. Kat strives to write an authentically raw love story for her characters and feels that no book is complete without some emotional turmoil before a happily ever after.

She lives in Kansas with her husband, her two kids, and her two doodles. In her spare time, you can find her surviving off iced coffee and sneaking in a few pages of her current read.

ALSO BY KAT SINGLETON

BLACK TIE BILLIONAIRES:

Black Ties and White Lies: https://amzn.to/40POdqu

Pretty Rings and Broken Things: https://amzn.to/3Ponrlc

Bright Lights and Summer Nights (Releasing 6.20): https://amzn.to/48d9Kgg

SUTTEN MOUNTAIN SERIES

Rewrite Our Story: https://amzn.to/3KNni8W

Tempt Our Fate: https://amzn.to/3W0K2XW

Chase Our Forever: https://amzn.to/3PIj85V

THE MIXTAPE SERIES

Founded on Goodbye

https://amzn.to/3nkbovl

Founded on Temptation

https://amzn.to/3HpSudl

Founded on Deception

https://amzn.to/3nbppvs

Founded on Rejection

https://amzn.to/44cYVKz

THE AFTERSHOCK SERIES

The Consequence of Loving Me

https://amzn.to/44d4jgK

The Road to Finding Us

https://amzn.to/44eIs8E

LINKS

PLAYLIST:
https://geni.us/PRABTplaylist

PINTEREST:
https://geni.us/PRABTpinterest

Made in the USA
Middletown, DE
19 February 2024

50025162R00215